Bali is about to erupt.

In parallel time, I am caught up in my own struggle to survive at sea aboard *Steel Tiger*, lashed by a typhoon a thousand miles north by northeast of Bali.

What I have no way of knowing is that my little storm in the Halmahera Sea is chopped liver compared to the tempest waiting for me in Bali, an island I had not planned to sail to—at least not this year....

BRONZE BELL

BELL

Stirling Silliphant

BALLANTINE BOOKS • NEW YORK

Library of Congress Catalog Card Number: 85-90640

ISBN 0-345-31745-9

Manufactured in the United States of America

First Edition: July 1985

Pour Tiana—celle qui danse dans mon coeur.

BRONZE BELL

Stirling Silliphant

BALLANTINE BOOKS • NEW YORK

Library of Congress Catalog Card Number: 85-90640

ISBN 0-345-31745-9

Manufactured in the United States of America

First Edition: July 1985

Pour Tiana—celle qui danse dans mon coeur.

CHAPTER

1

At dawn of the day following the new moon, the first day of Saka *New Year*, a time the Balinese call Nyepi ("to be quiet"), only a scattering of determined votaries cross forests and rice paddies to come to Pura Besakih, since all roads are forbidden to transit during Nyepi.

Pura Besakih, Mother Temple of Bali, the island's holiest sanctuary, rises on terraces cut into the southwest slopes of Gunung Agung, the Great Mountain, a volcanic peak soaring ten thousand feet into perpetual cloud.

Twelve women, two children, three old men, enter Pura Besakih through hazy shafts of first light. They kneel to lay offerings at the feet of stone chairs reserved for the trinity of gods, Shiva, Vishnu, and Brahma, and to speak prayers for spirits dwelling in the clouds above the mountain.

As they spread aromatic gifts along the east wall of the Triple Lotus Shrine, a white-robed pemangku, a temple keeper, ladles out holy water to each of the seventeen pilgrims.

During this ceremony men wearing demon masks enter from the adjoining courtyard and fire automatic weapons at the priest and the worshippers.

To make certain there are no survivors, the gunmen pass among the fallen and direct bursts point-blank into each head. Some of the bullets, ricocheting, strike the Great Bronze Bell of Agung, which hangs in the tower of the Triple Lotus.

Strangely, the bell does not resonate. Instead, it gives off only a faint murmur, as though a spirit imprisoned within the bronze is whispering in some ancient, perfumed language.

Then, using a flatbed truck and a mobile crane, the men with the demon masks remove the Great Bronze Bell from its compound and bear it away.

Shortly afterward, the pedanda, Pura Besakih's highest of high priests, entering the shrine of Triple Lotus, discovers the carnage. He has been on an upper terrace in a temple dedicated to the Lord of the Left Mountain, meditating so deeply that his ears have heard nothing of the gunfire. Yet somehow he bears a memory sense of the lamenting of the bell.

At once he sends word to the authorities. They remove all eighteen bodies and dispose of them secretly, without notifying the families of the victims.

To the Balinese, death is a rite of passage; proper prayers and ceremonies give the immortal soul of the deceased an opportunity to resume its eternal journey, to be reborn in still-another living shape. Thus, this secret end for eighteen souls is an unpardonable blasphemy, denying them the chance to close the cycles of their lives. If the families learn of it, vengeful mobs will storm police stations and military barracks from Gilimanuk at the western tip of Bali to Amet on the eastern coast.

At the massacre site, a special detachment of soldiers—under the personal command of Col. Guntur Katrini, head of COIN-OPS (Counter Insurgency Operations for the Indonesian Army)— collect all the spent 7.62mm NATO shells ejected from what the authorities conclude are Fabrique Nationale FAL assault rifles. After plaster casts are taken of the tire tracks left by the over-burdened flatbed truck and its crane, fresh earth is scattered over the area, then swept clean.

All the forensic evidence is removed, cataloged, and placed in a secret depository outside Denpasar, the main city of Bali. There it is guarded twenty-four hours a day by paracommandos ordered to kill any unauthorized person approaching.

Accordingly, the incident receives no media coverage either in Denpasar or in Jakarta, the capital of Indonesia, located at the far western end of Java, Bali's neighboring island.

BRONZE BELL

Even questioning rumors of what might have occurred that dawn at Pura Besakih are suppressed by the vigilant COIN-OPS authorities.

The Triple Lotus shrine is closed to all worshippers until further notice. No hint of the disappearance of the bronze bell can be allowed to spread through Bali and then, like the plague, to leap-frog among the thirteen thousand other islands of the Indonesian archipelago.

A few of the more contemporary-minded Balinese, were they to know, might agree that such stringent official actions are precautions well taken. In a matter of days Bali is to play host to an important group of visitors from SPACTTA, the South Pacific and Asian Conference of Travel and Tourist Agencies. The convention is to be staged at a new hotel complex only recently completed at a cost of multimillions of rupiahs in the new tourist area along the beaches at Nusa Dua. Nothing must be permitted to excite or alarm such important guests or in any way weaken their conviction that of all islands in the world Bali is the most intriguing. These delegates are the Pied Pipers who can bring more tourists to Bali—hopefully a better sort than the rawboned, beer-guzzling Australian surfers now teeming at Kuta Beach. Everyone agrees, despite the potential dangers of a major tourist influx to Bali's culture, that this is the only way to ensure the island's economic survival.

Yet the overwhelming majority of Balinese, given the least hint of the inconceivable events at Pura Besakih, would be driven to appease the ancestors with widespread, even indiscriminate, human sacrifice. There would be no other imaginable way to purge the evil and to restore harmony to the land and sky.

The authorities are left with only one option if they are to forestall such a nightmare—to find the Great Bell of Mount Agung and restore it to its holy and symbolic place in the Triple Lotus shrine as swiftly as possible.

Yet after seven grueling days and nights of low-intensity search and discreet interrogation, all the efforts of Colonel Katrini and his men have proved fruitless.

In spite of every precaution, dark rumors are beginning to circulate; unanswerable questions are being asked more insistently.

Bali is about to erupt.

* * *

STIRLING SILLIPHANT

In parallel time, I am caught up in my own struggle to survive at sea aboard Steel Tiger, *lashed by a typhoon a thousand miles north by northeast of Bali.*

What I have no way of knowing is that my little storm in the Halmahera Sea is duck soup compared to the tempest waiting for me in Bali, an island I had not planned to sail to. At least not this year.

═══CHAPTER═══

2

Do I actually see a plane floundering toward me above this torn and dolloping sea?

I squint up through lashes flayed by sea-foam and watch her buffet closer to my forward masthead. Through the spindrift her red-and-white insignia becomes fleetingly visible.

She's Indonesia Air Force, a Hercules, Lockheed-Georgia's dependable workhorse, probably out of a base in Irian Jaya.

The ravening wind degrades the sonics of her engines so that she flutters over me in pallid silence, wings trembling like some lost Garuda about to plummet into the mystic Halmahera Sea.

But she passes, muted, into the storm.

It seems forever since this mid-August day began.

Soon after dawn I'd observed sun dogs, those fragmentary rainbows that often presage scabby weather. I'd felt *Steel Tiger*'s deck heave up, the sea in fair warning tugging at the rudder and strumming through the hull.

I'd dogged the storm shutters onto the cabin ports, stowed everything below, rigged stainless-steel safety lines from stem to stern, secured all deck gear, closed all seacocks, bunged the exhaust pipe, crisscrossed the cockpit with rope, cooked up stew and heated soup for my thermos bottles, and finally taken an

5

updated Sat-Nav fix on my present position—one degree north of the Equator, twelve miles northeast of Waigeo Island.

It's not the way I prefer to start a day, with barometric pressure at 984 millibars and the center of a depression skanking toward me.

I'd laid an escape course at right angles to the storm's anticipated track, planning to make northing into the Pacific, well away from the island clutter of the Ring of Fire—the central Moluccas, an area the Indonesians call Maluka Tengah, the Spice Islands Columbus sought in vain on the wrong side of the planet. My intended landfall had been Ambon, one of the central islands in the group, but when your barometer can muster up a pressure of only twenty-nine inches, you'd better loop away from the gale's direct onslaught, especially when it's slamming straight at you from your intended landfall.

All morning I'd run off close hauled, under storm jib and trysail, trying to make good my reach into the calmer quadrant of the storm, but the rousing wind began to scant with such force I could no longer lie the course. I'd had to douse both sails and go to scudding bare poled before the storm.

Now lightning whips the sky. Dark flachettes of rain drive against my oilskins, sting my neck, flood my seaboots.

Strapped in at the helm, the companionway boarded up, I skitter *Steel Tiger* down the slopes of successive graybeards at such awesome speed I have to bite my tongue to stop muttering about my choice of life-style.

Ordinarily at sea an event as unique as the sudden appearance of a giant aircraft nudging your mast will engage either your indignation or your speculation for hours after. But the intensity of white-knuckling *Steel Tiger* down blustery slopes, any one of which can overwhelm me, causes me to dismiss the spectral overflight and to concentrate instead on trying to keep the boat on her feet.

Hour after hour now, unable to leave the helm for even a second, already having had to empty my bladder twice into my rain gear, I've had to stay put at the wheel and drive the boat fast enough to elude the monstrous seas crashing behind me, but not so fast I might surf down into a yawning pit and pitchpole or be turned head to wind and slammed onto my beam ends.

I bless my talented father for his design of *Steel Tiger*. With its cutaway forefoot it's much less susceptible to broaching than boats with a deep forefoot. Such burdened boats tend to dig into the back of the wave ahead of them when running before a heavy sea. This moves the center of lateral resistance forward far enough to lead to the loss of directional control of the rudder, and that in turn to the boat being knocked down.

Over the yowling of the wind and the incessant rattling of the washboards in the companionway, I hear the sudden chatter of my radio from the sealed-up salon below.

"STEEL TIGER, STEEL TIGER, STEEL TIGER. THIS IS INDONESIAN AIR FORCE WUN FOWER NINER TREE. WUN FOWER NINER TREE. WUN FOWER NINER TREE. ACKNOWLEDGE, PLEASE. OVER."

Acknowledge?

Hey, clowns, come on!

How do you expect me to unhitch, abandon the helm, open the washboards, go below and shoot the shit with you while *Steel Tiger* is hotdogging in front of a Force 10?

Once more the Hercules bursts free of the clouds and pulses above me, even lower this time than on her first pass.

Its crew appears to be struggling to open the cargo hatch.

Persistently, they circle above me, dissolving in and out of the driving squall like fragmented images in a David Bowie video.

"STEEL TIGER," they call again and once more run their ID by for me, the voice of the radioman coming through more Oxonian than Indonesian.

"ACKNOWLEDGE, PLEASE. OVER."

They've managed to open their cargo hatch.

On their next pass above me, I can make out just inside the open hatchway the blurred figures of wind-fluttering crewmen.

I wave them off.

The poor bastards wave back.

"HOW DO YOU READ?" the Oxonian voice keeps asking over the radio.

I shouldn't be reading him at all. I'd left my UHF transmitter dialed to 243-Emergency. You can count on one hand the number of private yachts that supplement their regular VHF equipment with ultrahigh frequency. I pack mine aboard for occasional conversations with some of the pilots I've come to know who jockey commercial jets across the Pacific—I down on the water, counting a hundred and fifty nautical miles a triumphant day of passage making, they up at the pinpoint of a contrail with dinner that night waiting either in San Francisco or in Hong Kong.

How would the radioman in the Hercules know *Steel Tiger* has UHF capability unless the people aboard the aircraft know one helluva lot more about me than I do about them?

I focus the binos on their hatchway.

A figure appears from inside the Hercules, one of those freeze-frame strangers you know instinctively is about to invade your life. He's wearing a blazing orange jumpsuit, orange crash helmet, swim fins, and a chest-pack chute.

I fast-forward the probable scenario.

He intends to jump.

He's a dead man.

I reject all responsibility.

How can I snatch him from these seas? Unless . . .

Unless he can time his point of entry into the back of whatever wave is directly ahead of me at the moment he impacts.

Steel Tiger has been plunging down the tumbling fronts of the waves at twelve knots, shuddering in the troughs for a second or two while I harden up for the mountain ahead, then climbing for thirty seconds to the new summit before skidding on down again.

This gives the chutist no more than a thirty-second time frame to jump and to be fished out while I'm on the uptick. No way can I grab him while the boat is slanting downhill faster than hull speed.

Assuming this crazy man jumps, assuming the gale doesn't whip him off to Mindanao, he'll need at least thirty seconds simply to make the drop from five hundred feet, then another ten seconds to release the capewells of his chute and to disengage himself from its shrouds. That is a forty-second time package from cargo door to pickup point. But I'll be gone in thirty seconds, up and over the top and down again, leaving him one valley behind!

The conscious part of my mind makes fleeting note of the irony of dying because of being ten seconds short, then just as instantly rejects such specious sentiment.

Each of my buddies who'd been turned back into potassium and oxides had died exclusively from being in the wrong place at the wrong split second of time.

My gut core keeps feeling I can somehow stretch this time frame. Possibly, if I widen my reach up the hump of the wave into which he jumps, I might pick up six, seven seconds, be able to buttonhook him. If I do manage the delay and can reach him, I'll have to snare him on the first and only pass.

There's no way in God's green ocean I can turn the boat around and go back.

Once more the Hercules glides above *Steel Tiger*, this time passing from stern to bow, locked directly on my course.

The aircraft lowers to what appears to be an unconscionable two hundred and fifty feet above the crest of the wave dead ahead.

Unhesitating, as though on a summer day from a practice tower at Benning, the orange-suited figure exits grandly, tossing me one of those noblesse oblige salutes as he vaults out.

I would prefer not to give such silliness my blessing. But like it or not, he's mine now, or he's fish food.

CHAPTER

3

A month ago—when I released my spring line and took *Steel Tiger* back to sea from her temporary slip at the Club Nautique de Calédonie in Nouméa, tacked her out through the Baie de Pêcheurs, and slipped past the dip of Îlot Brun where I lost sight of Inspector Bazin's lone figure on the dock—I felt the resurgence of personal freedom borne on the wind through Passe de Dumbéa.

I was trying to shuck the confusion left over from the spill of events in New Caledonia. I had to let go of the quicksand hours, the recall of lives squandered, of whisperings and drumbeats, of betrayals and riddles hidden behind faces, all the painful images of retrocognition.

So I sailed *Steel Tiger* out into the Coral Sea. There I knew I could exist mercifully out of junk-box range, out of the reach of headlines and other claw marks of insanity, out where there was a paucity of data—except for what related directly to life and death, such data as wind force, wind direction, weather fronts, and the calligraphy of clouds.

It wasn't as much the hope of healing that drove me back to sea again as it was pure flight from the toxic desperation of those ashore.

It had become more and more apparent to me that a crisis of

who's going to dominate whom had seized not only the people of New Caledonia but most of the people of all the world. I was sailing out of the clutches of this compulsion, away from this deadly preoccupation with control, getting out before I ended up letting other people define my premises—as I had let them do in Vietnam—before I let them con me into believing that only they, not I, could influence my future.

Once I'd found the waypoint I'd marked weeks before on my chart of the Coral Sea, I felt released, secure, safe even from the megadeath sheathed in thousands of silos around the world.

I brought *Steel Tiger* to the precise position where Lady *Lex* went down with two hundred and sixteen young Americans in twenty-four hundred fathoms of amethystine water in the late spring of 1942. I bagged my sails and let down both bow and stern hooks so I'd drift in the gentle southeast trades above the probable spot into which my grandfather, then only thirty-five, splashed his flaming Wildcat, his Japanese victor circling above him. I have no way of knowing if my grandfather's enemy survived the war, but I do know that what happened that day prevented my grandfather from watching his own son, my father, grow to manhood and bring me into being.

I hovered over his watery grave for three days and nights, closing the circle of years between us, lying on deck, head over the side, eyes peering down, letting only my subconscious do the work, paying attention only to what I was feeling, not what I was thinking. And after a time I began to *feel* him down there. I replayed his descent, his eyes staring back up as the surface darkened over him, the weight of the engine carrying him down, still strapped into the cockpit, down, down, until the pressure became so overwhelming that he and the Wildcat began to break up. Yet I could track his skull somehow making the descent intact, coming to rest on the bottom, where in time silt or grass would cover it or possibly some sea creature make good use of it as shelter, darting in and out of my grandfather's eye sockets.

I would have liked my grandfather had I been able to know him when he was still thirty-five. Whether I would have liked him as much when he was sixty I have no idea.

Now I was able to tell him so.

The services concluded, a part of me consigned to this place forever, I hauled up anchors, raised sails, and pointed toward New Guinea.

In this part of the world, low barometric pressure prevails on the Asian landmass in July and August, causing an indraft of air from the western Pacific and producing an airstream that thrums the East Indies from southeast to northwest, absolutely ideal for the course I enjoyed all the way up from the Coral Sea, passing up through the Trobriand and Louisiade island groups and between New Britain and the eastern end of New Guinea.

Off to port I'd watched successive knife-sharp ridges fall astern, candescent mountains climbing to heights of three miles, and broad upland valleys vanishing into inland mist as though reaching back into prehistory.

Sixteen hundred miles out of Nouméa, I'd found the loom of the lights of Lae where the chart said they should be, at 6 degrees, 44 minutes south, 146 degrees, 59 minutes east.

A day and a half later, timed to a satin sunset, I'd steered hard by the seaside town of Madang, simply to alleviate my growing sense of isolation after thirty days at sea and hours of relentless soul-searching. I'd observed the black sand beaches, the land-locked little harbor with its one slipway run by the Rabaul Stevedore and Steamship Company. On the hill above the market where dark, somber-faced women sit patiently all Saturday with their baskets of shells for sale, I could see the old German cemetery with its tombstones still bullet chipped from the fire of retreating Japanese invaders, and ringing the grave sites giant casuarina trees and squadrons of wheeling fruit bats. I'd tuned in Radio Madang at 860 kHz, listened to the weather forecast in English, Pidgin, Hiri Motu, and Kuanua. But in none of the four languages did anyone predict the Willie Willie that's now blowing me out into the Pacific.

For a full second I watch the slipstream of the Hercules yank the orange-suited jumper back and down, forcing the static line to pull his chute from his pack. When I see that his canopy is fully deployed, I lock the wheel on my down-wave run, unhitch my harness, rehitch myself to the portside safety cable, then break out a length of line with a big bowline already tied at one end. I secure the other end through the toe rail, then lead it back through a sheave block and take a few wraps around my portside aft power winch.

I time the chutist's fall on my Memosail wristwatch.

Seventeen seconds! Then the jump *was* from two hundred and

fifty feet. By cutting the drop in half, he's given me the extra seconds I need to bear on him.

I watch him pop the capewells on his chute and release the sinking canopy. He slips out of his harness as easily as if he were practicing in an air force swimming pool; then, using his fins, he swims nonchalantly up the sheer wall of the mountain of water ahead of me as I climb *Steel Tiger* toward him and make ready with the line.

I have to save him now, if for no other reason than to determine to my own satisfaction whether he's totally crazed, devoid of the instinct of self-preservation, or actually as good as he's just demonstrated.

As I labor upward toward him, he tugs off his crash helmet and heaves it onto *Steel Tiger*'s foredeck.

Even through the spume blowing off the surface I recognize that brown, deceptive face with its cookie-jar grin.

He looks even younger than he did the last time I saw him, more than ten years ago, in Saigon, when I was attached to DAO and he was one of the thousand officers sent in from the four countries selected to form the International Commission of Control and Supervision—Canada, Poland, Hungary, and Indonesia.

Guntur Katrini.

I suddenly recall that he'd told me one night while we watched the light show on the perimeters of Saigon that Guntur meant thunder in Indonesian.

Or was it in Balinese?

"Good afternoon, Captain Locke," he shouts up at me as I draw abeam and heave him the lifeline.

He snares the loop and slips lithely into the bowline, tightening it before the forward thrust of the boat tightens it for him.

I now remember that his moves were always state-of-the-art.

I start to crank him in, the electric Barient spooning him up as though he were a minnow.

"Had a buddy," I shout at him as I kill the power in the winch and let him plane alongside *Steel Tiger* like a gaffed sailfish. "He was crewing on *Windward Passage* one Trans-Pac, working the foredeck when *Passage* was battling *Black Fin* for first position. He missed his footing and went over, but as he fell, he managed to catch a sheet and hold on. The other guys in the crew lined up along the toe rail and watched him skimming alongside. Then they yelled, 'Hey, man, let go the goddamned sheet, will you? You're slowing us down.'"

The man in the water smiles up at me benignly. "Most amusing," he says. "Permission to come aboard, please."

I fish him in, sloshing him into the cockpit before I lose the boat.

"Why didn't you answer your radio?" he demands.

I can't hear him through the screeching of the wind. Seeing my trouble, he shouts the words at me.

"I said—why didn't you answer your radio?"

I shout back at him.

"Why'd you jump from two-fifty? You took your training where we all did. You know jump doctrine says you don't go out below five hundred!"

He has trouble hearing me against the storm. I beckon him closer. He slides closer to the wheel until we are virtually lip to ear, and I repeat the question.

"We were operating on a short fuse," he says.

"True."

"So I simply narrowed the gap. Impressed?"

"Stunned! How in hell'd you manage?"

"A new chute. An American product—Koenig and Associates Aero Systems. Are you familiar with it?"

"I've been away from the States."

"So I hear. It's a breakthrough design. With this chute, jumpers can be inserted well below enemy radar capability."

I grasp his arm, one of those cornball, macho gladiator grips some of us used to lay on each other in Vietnam when we didn't feel like articulating the words "Thanks, buddy" to some unknown troopie who'd just saved our rumps.

Guntur and I hold to each other now, fusing our memories, lighting up some of the darker recesses of the past, until *Steel Tiger* slides over the crest and I have to pull my arm free to start roller-coastering again.

"You did have some logical reason for jumping, didn't you?" I ask. "Other than testing this new chute?"

"We tried to reach you on your SSB," he says. "But you failed to respond. One of our patrol planes spotted you northwest of Biak, so I flew out to talk to you on your UHF."

"How'd you know I had UHF?"

"I spoke to a gentleman in New Caledonia who gave me a rundown on your inventory."

"Bazin?" I ask.

"Correct. Inspector Bazin in Nouméa. Out here in the China Lake, John, you'll find it's a constricted world. If Kim Il Sung sneezes in Pyonggang, we run it through our computers in Jakarta. When you didn't respond on your UHF, it became apparent the only way you and I could have this conversation was for me to jump."

"It's got to be one nifty conversation."

"It is."

The Hercules is back again. The colonel waves to it. The crew waves back. The hatch slides closed. The plane banks into obsidian clouds.

We both rest our voices for a while. This shouting back and forth, losing parts of sentences to the wind, is taking its toll on our vocal cords. But I can see Guntur hasn't even started. He hunches even closer, cups his hands, and shouts into my ear again.

"What's your next island?"

"Ambon," I shout back into his ear.

"Why Ambon?"

"This time of year the hills are covered with rhododendron."

"They'll still be there next month."

"Then there's the annual commemoration festival—September seventeenth, right? I hear that's a real blast."

"I'll have you back well before then."

"And I've never tasted the Ambon banana—the *pisang raja*. They're in season now."

"They taste little different than any other banana."

"But where else in the world," I ask him, "are women forbidden to eat them? There's something legendary here—Eve and the apple in Eden—that beckons to the Margaret Mead in me, okay?"

"I believe the explanation is purely psychosexual," he replies. "We're dealing here with a primitive people. And a tribal belief that if a married woman nibbles on the *pisang raja*, she'll leave her husband. Why not?"

His smile is slyer than usual, if that's possible. "After all, John, these bananas are anywhere from eighteen to thirty inches long. Even you American jocks might feel some apprehension about letting your women compare your *phalli* to anything as magnificently turgid as the *pisang raja*—so fruity, so succulent. What

15

woman who has put her lips to it can be expected afterward to address herself with any sense of pleasure to her husband's wizened little tube?"

"Ambon sounds more and more like my kind of place."

I listen for his shouted answer, but suddenly I realize he's simply talking forcefully, no longer shouting. I've been so absorbed in our interchange I've failed to feel the wind slackening. I hear him say, "Rhododendra, a festival, and bananas! Is this the John Locke I knew?"

I see by the wind-speed indicator that we're down to a true wind speed of only thirty-five knots. My ears begin to readjust to more reasonable sound levels.

"The real reason I have to go to Ambon is to find a *Conus gloriamaris*," I tell him, managing to reach his ears with only a moderate shout.

"Now *that* I understand!" he concedes. "But how do you propose to find one?"

"Just keep diving till I do. Ambon's got the only water in the world where they live."

"We'll *give* you one."

"Not like finding it yourself."

"You won't! They've all been fished out, what few ever existed. But the finest of all, without question, is in the Marine Museum in Jakarta. The Glory of the Sea—the most precious shell known to man. *Yours*, John. Worth at least twenty-five thousand dollars."

"In return for what?"

"Coming back with me. Forgetting about Ambon—at least for a while."

"Back? To where?"

"To Bali."

"What's the job?"

He smiles so broadly the rain trails off in two cascades to either side of his grin.

I remember that smile. He was smiling it the afternoon he triggered a twenty-round clip from his Beretta SMG into the spines of four ARVN troopers we found gang-raping a village girl outside Duc Hao, west of Saigon.

Not that I blamed him. I'd started to jump in to pull them off the child and place them under arrest, but this slight-figured Indonesian captain moved faster than I could, directing his fire so precisely that he closed the case permanently. He'd reported that the incident was merely one more of the thousands of violations of the ceasefire, that the four ARVN troopers had been ambushed by some ambitious Victor Charles trying to stake out a little more territory in the south. And of course I backed him up, and that was that, nothing that cost anybody any sleep.

"Finding a bell," he says. "A bronze bell. The largest in the world."

"No problem," I tell him. "Last I heard it was still in Moscow. Inside the Kremlin walls. I doubt that anyone's got the balls to try and remove it."

"I'm aware of the Great Bell of Moscow," he says. "But that is *not* the largest bell in the world, despite what the books say."

"You're saying *your* bell is bigger than theirs?"

He nods.

"Then why isn't it in Guiness?"

"We are not a competitive people."

"Come on, Guntur. You can't *hide* things like that. It's got nothing to do with Balinese attitudes. If you people had the world's biggest bronze bell, some Dutchman would have documented it a century or more ago, and it would be in the record books to this day."

"I'm not here to debate what only a few of us know—and deliberately choose to keep to ourselves. I'm here to ask you to find it for us."

"It's *missing*?"

"Stolen."

"Something that weighs more than half a million pounds—and that's what it would have to weigh if it's bigger than the Russian bell—stolen? From Bali?"

"Yes, on all counts."

"But how? Wall-to-wall people. Narrow roads. An island with no decent deepwater harbors. Whoever took it sure as hell didn't *fly* it out. It's got to be somewhere in Bali. Just keep looking. It'll turn up sooner or later."

"There is a time factor," he says. "A critical time factor . . . For the world's finest specimen of a *Conus gloriamaris*, plus the lasting gratitude of the Indonesian armed forces—not an inconsiderable marker considering we are the ruling hierarchy in the world's fifth most populous nation—you will advise us what we must do to find the assassins who carried it off."

I study his features. So much in contrast to the intensity of his

17

words. He must be pushing forty, this Col. Guntur Katrini, for I recall his telling me he'd been eighteen that night in 1965 when his father was hacked to death by young Communist women rioters at the airfield at Lubang Buaja and thrown into a well with other assassinated generals. Yet his face is still as smooth as old bronze, his eyes layered and deep, a face as composed as a tenth-century bust of the Buddha.

He is a delicately boned man, a Hindu of the warrior caste, a deceptive man in the same way a bust of the Buddha is deceptive. The half-closed eyes convey a sense of tranquillity, yet there is fire deep within the bronze.

The storm is definitely passing, the wind moderating. I can even hear myself talk now.

"Suppose I say no?" I ask.

"That never occurred to me."

"Well, you'd better turn it over in your head, because I'm still on R and R from the shitstorm in New Caledonia. I'm switched off—all systems down."

"In all the Pacific," he says, "there is no single man more qualified to do what must be done—and done at once. To come in and banjo a cadre of terrorists."

"Nice stroking, Guntur. My ego is purring. But the lizard in me says it might help if you could give me a reason why all your military apparatus can't do the job better and faster."

"Because we have to maintain an extremely low profile. The least hint of martial law, of curfews, of citizens being pulled out of their homes at night, would precipitate riots. And riots are counterproductive on an island that needs tourists and hard currency to survive."

"You can do better." I prompt him. "Come on, Guntur. Tell me if I say no there'll be global repercussions. Tell me dominoes will tumble from Tokyo to Rangoon. Let me hear it!"

"You joke at a perilous time, old friend. But then, possibly you're right. To us, what are a few thousand more dead? What difference does it make if our rivers are once again choked with corpses?"

"Now you're cooking!"

"If it ends with only a few thousand slaughtered," he says, "the government will consider we've been lucky."

"But you do have a problem of overpopulation," I say. "This could be a plus."

"It's the aftermath of the bloodbath that concerns us," he continues. "The fact that it may take a decade, even longer, for tourists to forget the massacres and return to our beautiful island. In that decade, who knows? Bali itself may die."

"If the Dutch couldn't finish it off, why should your own people, over a missing bell?" I ask somewhat harshly, for Guntur's doomsday prophecy is beginning to exceed the limits of clean horseplay.

"Still," he persists, "I've admired and respected you too long, John, to impose our problems on you. That is, if you are truly not up to the challenge, if that is your final decision, so be it. I'll accept that—and try my best to understand."

"You don't understand shit!" I say, for now I remember how slippery Guntur has always been, pretending to be sidestepping when he's really shoving it to you. In Vietnam I found him frequently causing me to do things I hadn't planned on doing, things I later regretted. He's a born manipulator, a real slyboots. He'd have to be, to skip from captain to chicken colonel in ten peacetime years in a country as highly orchestrated as Indonesia.

"Look," I tell him, "I'm trying to construct some kind of definition of myself that's not so goddamned fragile. One evening six weeks ago I had to terminate seven indigs. From the roof of the post office in Nouméa I blew them away while their backs were turned to me. True, at the time they were attempting to dispose of friends of mine, and I had to stop them at all costs, but the incident started me wondering all over again if there's not a saner way to relate to one's enemies other than by splashing them. Of all people, Guntur, you, with your ethnic and religious antecedents, should feel that maybe—just maybe, okay?—your boy Gandhi had something going that's a lot more positive than sheer firepower."

"Perhaps you never heard what Ho Chi Minh said about our great pacifist Gandhi," the colonel asks.

"No, I haven't."

"He said that if Gandhi had been born in one of the French colonies rather than in India, he would have entered heaven much sooner. It may be cynical to believe that truth speaks only from the barrel of a gun, but it's sodding bullshit to think that truth can stare down the barrel and prevail. *Tanks* took Saigon, John, not an aroused and liberated citizenry!"

"No way I can quarrel with that."

"It's one thing to steal a society's most sacred religious symbol," the colonel adds gravely, "but quite another—in the process—to shoot down women, children, old men, and a helpless priest—then to pass among the fallen and blow their heads open like melons to make sure there are no witnesses to the desecration of our holiest temple. Do you expect people who plan such assaults to merit being reasoned with? Or ought they simply be exterminated like the vermin they are?"

He gazes at me from what appear to be eyes so gentle they'd never trouble the sleep of children. *That's* what it is about Guntur Katrini, I remember now, the startling unconnectedness between his facial expression, his perma-plaqued, jim-dandy smile, and his merciless behavior.

"Not good enough! All you're offering me is the same old stuff—fight or flight. There've got to be other choices!"

"Tell me what they are, John," he asks, much too indulgently for my present mood.

"How do I know?" I yell at him. "But I don't intend to live the rest of my life out here in the Pacific as though I'm locked into a video game—moving from one board of difficulty to the next, taking on every new monster that pops up. Okay? Clear?"

He stares at me without perceptible movement other than the least contraction of his shoulders, as though the cold point of a dagger is being pressed against his cervical vertebrae.

"Look, Guntur, here's what we've got. On my side we're dealing with a guy—*me*—whose days bubble with nightmares. At night I cut to the chase: I'm either running or paralyzed with fear. On your side we're dealing with the simple event that some unknowns took your pet bell. In the process they blew up innocent people. Now you come way out here to impress the hell out of me with that grandstand jump from two hundred and fifty feet and try to tell me I'm the only thing that can keep Bali from coming apart. You're not going to convince me to sign up just to eliminate a few of your local vermin. You understand what I'm trying to say? I can't work up any honest indignation over that. Can I make it any clearer?"

"Then what *will* get you to come back to Bali with me?" he asks.

"Hell, Guntur, I don't know. Maybe time—more time."

"I don't have that. But we do have money. What about money? Not just the seashell, but money."

"No, the shell is more important to me than money."

"But still not enough?"

"It's not even a question of 'enough.'"

"How about 'please'?"

"You're getting warmer."

"Pretty please?"

"Now you're getting ridiculous."

"I remember you saying something to me in Vietnam. About the exhilaration of being on point during patrol. About the high level of consciousness you experienced during those moments of walking the tightrope between life and death. Suppose I tell you that if you come to Bali your chances of being killed are very high? You will definitely experience an extremely high level of consciousness! I guarantee it!"

"Why would anyone want to kill me? Let me run that through again. Why would anyone on Bali want to kill me?"

"I haven't begun to tell you all the ramifications. The night before I flew to Irian Jaya to come look for you, I was ambushed en route to the airport."

"By amateurs, obviously. How can you assume the ambush was related to the theft of the bell? Or to me?"

"I don't know, obviously. But I *must* assume there's a connection. Possibly they felt I was getting close. Or possibly it was an effort to stop me from getting closer—by bringing you into the investigation."

"Did you identify any of the people who ambushed you?"

"Postmortem only. No papers. But we did capture one. He's Vietnamese."

"You make that sound significant."

"It might be."

"Well, what's he told you?"

"He refuses to speak. Even a single word."

"Guntur, with your expertise? Don't tell me all your cattle prods are out on loan."

"Frankly, I've been holding back—until you talk to him. Who knows the Vietnamese mind better than you?"

"Any Vietnamese," I say. "Pick one."

"From papers we found on him, he would appear to be a major in the NVA."

"A North Vietnamese major with a death squad in Bali? Why?"

"Would you care to ask him?"

I let the wind carry that one off.

"Were the ones you killed also Vietnamese?"

"Burmese."

"There are Burmese and there are Burmese."

"We believe these were Kachins. At least our ethnic experts agreed they were not lowland Burmans. Definitely mountain indigs. And please don't ask me why three Kachins would be part of a death squad operating in Bali. We don't know."

"Guntur," I tell him, "you are beginning to fascinate me. The thing that keeps hooking me into cases like this isn't just the fees. It's my curiosity—and my anger—about all these implacable forces and factions that go around chasing each other back and forth in our world. I see them all as an intricate network of fuse cords, all leading to the biggest goddamned blowoff since something or other made all the dinosaurs drop dead. Unless we watch it, we're next!"

"In other words," he says, "it's acceptable to snip off fuse cords but not to exterminate vermin."

I can hear myself laughing, which means the wind is truly softening and that he's got me to swallow the bait.

"All right," I concede. "If I survive this one, help me later to be able to recall how you gaffed me—three Burmese killers and an NVA major all trying to knock off an Indonesian colonel on the way to enlist an American sailor of fortune. It's enough to make any red-blooded asshole jump right back into the Cuisinart. Providing you fatten the fee."

"Name it."

"That new Koenig parachute?"

"It's yours."

"Plus some additional ordnance."

"From what the inspector in Nouméa told me, you're already overequipped."

"Never."

"Let me count the ways. Your Browning pistol, the HK-91, the Hi-Standard .22 with silencer, plus the AK-47 and the French Fusil MAS bull-pup you acquired in New Caledonia. Right?"

"Bazin forgot to mention the UZI SMG he gave me as a going-away present, along with two twenty-five-round mags."

"What other armament could you possibly need?"

"A Bellini 12-gauge autoloading shotgun, their Model 121-M-1," I tell him, "and a dozen boxes of double-ought buckshot."

"Why that particular weapon?"

"Anyone crazy enough to steal a sacred bell in Bali and then to try to ambush a honcho like you is thickheaded enough to need a high-cyclic rate of persuasion. If I'm going back onto the killing ground, my instincts tell me this job is going to call for speedy sight alignment and target acquisition. The Bellini is the perfect tool—a real alley sweeper."

"But you'll have the full firepower of our most elite military units backing you at all times—our Red Berets."

"I don't operate at my max in unit strength, Guntur. You know that. I cover my own ass. You want me, we do it my way. That includes one new Bellini autoloader. You can have one flown in from Rome overnight."

He's smiling indulgently.

"So set 'em up, Joe!" he says.

Another thing I remember now about Guntur—this marvelous incongruity—his dropping show-biz idiom into an otherwise upper-school syntax at the most unexpected of moments.

I scan the sky on our stern quarter.

Toward the Ceram Sea rainbows shimmer like pastel wickets on a heaving lawn.

Bali lies to the southwest through those archways, but fourteen degrees of latitude to the west and nine degrees of longitude to the south—hardly an overnight sail.

I tell Guntur so.

If the situation in Bali is as unstable as he represents, can he spare the time?

He reaches inside his jumpsuit and produces a nautical chart folded into a sealed oilskin pouch.

"I took the liberty of bringing with me the latest Indonesian chart of the waters around Manokwari on Irian Jaya," he tells me. "It's dead ahead, but well in the lee of the storm once we round the point—not more than two hours from our present position. A jet waits for us there. As you can see, John, we don't piss about."

"I'm not leaving *Steel Tiger* in a backwater port like Manokwari!" I tell him. "No way!"

"I have a trained naval crew—six men, all superb sailors—standing by to bring her to you in Bali once the storm has abated. They know these waters better than you ever will."

It's been a while since I've heard anyone drop the word "abated" into a casual conversation. Guntur's choice of words is particularly elegant for a fighting man—out of deference, I remember, to his bloodline, which dates back to the time of Tulsi Das, the supreme poet of Hindu literature, who lived and wrote while Shakespeare was staging plays.

No question, they've sent their best man.

He's reminded me of what I learned in Vietnam but somehow keep trying to forget: that choosing to live close to death is not something you do for an obsessive ideal, not for fatherland, not to the beat of marching bands or to the wind flutter of guidons, but because in a universe of collective struggle for survival, it is truly the natural state for any form of life, sentient or otherwise— the only way to bring yourself into harmony with the choking obscenities around you.

They understand this in Bali.

And presto, all my uncertainties pass with the storm.

I'm back on point again.

CHAPTER

4

Secured by bow, stern, and spring lines, *Steel Tiger* snugs alongside a wharf in Manokwari, the colonel waiting with visible impatience in an army jeep, engine ticking.

Aboard, I run through in a matter of minutes what should be a one-month indoctrination course for the six Indonesian sailors Guntur has assigned to bring the ketch across the Banda and Flores seas to me in Bali.

I'm not as worried about their navigation as I am about their hands-on operation of a yacht as state-of-the-art as *Steel Tiger*. In this part of the world, navigating is less a matter of finding your landfall than of avoiding it. Assuming no storms at sea, essentially all you have to worry about are the currents, the overfalls, and the myriad unlit reefs. But *Steel Tiger* is a complex and sophisticated boat. I am concerned that in the care of seat-of-the-pants seamen she might frustrate and baffle them, to her own harm. But five minutes into the indoctrination I begin to feel foolish for underestimating this eager crew. The young lieutenant in charge is a graduate electronics engineer and a confirmed computer hacker. He promises that during their passage he will, with my consent, adjust my Sat-Nav, which he discovers is on the verge of a glitch.

We run through my checklist, from bow to stern, and in the

process exchange marine nomenclature—English into Balinese. Hull, I learn, is *badan*. Bow is *bungut*. Anchor is *mangga*. Jib is *cocor*. Hoist the *mangga* and let fly the *cocor*. I promise myself to lay that one on the next smartass Australian mate who comes day sailing with me.

Two of the sailors are Balinese and Hindu; the others all from Java, Muslims. At first the two Balinese alarm me, since as a society the Balinese fear the water. They look inland, to the mountains, for all that is good and luminous, turning their backs to the sea and the imagined demons lurking beneath its surface. But these two Balinese, I learn from the Javanese lieutenant, have since childhood built and sailed the sturdy *prahu pangkur*, double outriggers with three lanteen sails, and they've virtually lived their lives on the waters between Surabaya and Kalimantan.

Finally I show everybody my cross-referenced stowage notebook, the key to where all supplies, equipment, and spare parts are kept; then, in closing, I demonstrate how to clear the plumbing if the electric john should back up. As the seven of us huddle around the head, I consider how far humanity has progressed in creature comforts since the time of Columbus when seamen had to hang over the aft rail to ease themselves, sea gulls circling in squawking witness, then had to wipe themselves with tarred rope-ends.

Feeling *Steel Tiger* is in competent and caring hands, I give her a loving last survey below, my private world of teak, ash, and butternut, then climb topside, followed by the five squids and the lieutenant. I return their salutes as they line up formally along the toe rail in their uniforms. "Peace on your way," the lieutenant calls after me. I hurry toward Guntur, tense as a commodities trader. He waits in the backseat of a jeep, his right leg jouncing nervously up and down on the ball of his foot. A uniformed driver sits rigidly behind the wheel, no-nonsense eyes to the front, and a scarred-faced commando type with a red beret cocked over his shaved head rides shotgun next to the driver, an SMG braced on the top of his thigh.

In a matter of minutes Guntur and I are airborne and well above the weather front, which could have buried me in the Halmahera Sea. I watch the last of it go tumbling eastward. To the west, islands rise by the score, jutting up in an endless row like crenellations in a crumbling Punjab battlement. I doubt any man ever lived who could recite from memory the names of all of Indonesia's thousands of islands in the vast archipelago that shags along the Equator in a crescent reaching farther than the distance from Los Angeles to Boston.

"How do you feel?" Guntur asks after minutes of silence.

"I feel stoked," I reply. "I shed all my fat down there during the last seven hours. The minute I set foot on solid ground, I'm going to rack out. Does your timetable allow for any sack time?"

"Why else would I have asked how you feel? When we get in, where would you like to stay?"

"I have a buddy I can crash with. He's been after me for years to come and visit. He's married to a Balinese girl. They live in Ubud."

"That would be Tip Bradley?"

"Right. Tip was my One-One for a while when I was attached to SOG."

"Did you know his batiks are becoming world famous?"

Yes, I know about Tip's batiks. He used to put his weapon down whenever he could in Vietnam and bring out his sketchpad. I never knew another artist who could capture the inner look of combat the way Tip could. Now he's designing and making batik for tourists. He writes to me about the success of his designs. What they actually are, he writes, is the flip side of his nightmares but disguised as traditional Balinese symbolism, the sunken eyes of the dead rendered as full moons, the bomb craters as the mouths of children wide with laughter, the sparks from a burning hootch as fighting cocks. He works these into batik patterns, rendering the terrors of his memories subliminally. It seems to give him a quiet satisfaction. It indicates that some of us at least have found a way to turn a buck from post-Vietnam syndrome.

"Or I could check into a hotel. It's been a long time since I've had room service."

"Too difficult to provide you with the kind of security you're going to need. But I do know the ideal place for you to stay. With a Balinese family. In the village of Batubulan, just outside Denpasar, not too far from my headquarters. The head of the family is my younger brother. He will give you your own house within the compound, and I shall assign a squad of my best men to set up perimeter patrol. Between them and the dogs on constant duty, you can at least sleep soundly at night, certain that nobody will cut your throat. And by living with my brother's family, you will learn our customs that much faster. This will help you with the investigation, I'm sure."

"Sounds fine," I agree. "Especially the part about my throat. Let's do it."

The sun has already sunk below the volcanoes of Lombok, Bali's eastern neighbor. Lombok Strait is the theoretical dividing line between Asia and Australasia, if we're to believe Alfred Wallace, a contemporary of Charles Darwin's, who theorized that Bali was not only the last outpost of Hinduism in a Muslim world but was also the southeastern extremity of Asia itself.

Now I can see Cape Ibus, Bali's easternmost point. Around it the water appears glassy, blotted here and there by home-going *gujungs*, but we're still too high to make out the fishermen aboard them. It's the old Caribbean effect, where the clear air can mislead you into underestimating distances, fatal when you're in line-of-sight combat.

I gaze off at Mount Agung. It never fails to awe me, the few times I've come to Bali, its pure cone piercing the sky like a syringe.

The last time I was here was—when?

Come on, Locke, you know *exactly* when!

July to November 1975.

Only a few weeks after your last day and night in Saigon.

After you elected to stay in Asia awhile.

First it was Bangkok. You were waiting to hear if there was any news, anything at all about Doan Thi.

How stupid of you to think any word would come out that soon—if ever!

She'd kissed you good-bye and gone bicycling out to welcome your enemy.

Oh, yes! Do I remember that final day in Saigon!

On our short-wave set we picked up Radio Hanoi that last afternoon, and I heard again the foreboding little poem I'd heard so often before:

> *Yankee, I swear to you*
> *With words sharp as knives,*
> *Here in Vietnam it is either you or me,*
> *And I am already here,*
> *So you must go.*

BRONZE BELL

And go we did. At DOA, General Smith and the last of our staff except for me flew out that night at 2000 hours in two CH-53s. Thirty minutes later our marine landing force was dusted up.

I stayed behind with the demolition teams. As we worked, we heard angry Vietnamese voices breaking in over our radio frequencies and shouting obscenities at us. These voices were not northern. These were the voices of the allies we were leaving behind.

So we wired up the compound and its equipment and a few barrels packed with four million dollars in U.S. currency, and not one of us took so much as a twenty, even as a souvenir.

Just before midnight we blew up the whole enchilada, and shortly after that we heard the incoming NVA tanks. Not until we sensed we were dead center in their cross hairs did we lift off.

I gazed down numbly at Ton Son Nhut, littered with fireballs, and at dark, silent Saigon, where the only woman I have ever loved had spent the previous night in my arms. And now she was gone from my life, how else but forever?

This had not been a war.

It had no beginning, no real ending. All it had ever been since the French landed almost a hundred and fifty years ago was an open-ended contract for death. A first man had been killed, and who and when would be the last?

I knew I wasn't ready to ship home. The Freedom Bird was no answer for me. I couldn't even find my way around in-country unless I was stalking Victor Charles. You can't stalk people in New York and Chicago, and that's all I could do at that time with any sense of commitment. No way was I going back to the States yet.

But I found that Bangkok was not the answer, either, for the city still swarmed with our military, mostly air force types, their main preoccupation multiple orgasm or hanging out over the trees through the wonder of chemistry. I needed to find a place where people believed in something other than indulging their nervous systems or in trying to deaden their fear and pain.

So I came to Bali.

I looked for Guntur, but he'd just flown off to England for advanced commando training with lobos who go in hard and fast, so hard and fast they don't mess about trying to take surrenders—not out of savagery but simply because they can't waste the time

29

of saying please stand over there now and be a good prisoner while we continue to tidy up around here.

I stayed awhile in Bali, in zone GMT minus seven—the same time zone as Hanoi's. I spoke to no one, asked nothing of anyone. I was as shadowy as the puppets of a Javanese shadow play, like them, so pierced with holes that if anyone had held me up to the light in those days, I would have shone like one of those ceiling mirror globes in an Atlantic City ballroom.

Night after night I squatted for hours watching the *dalang* sitting cross-legged in the flare of his oil lamp as he manipulated gods, mortals, demons, and animals, moving their shadows at will across the screen while the Balinese spectators stared in childlike wonder to see their myths played out for the millionth time, as new to them as the first time.

But I watched the *dalang*, not the shadows, because at that time in my life I was seeking the manipulator. I had been one of the manipulated for so long I needed to find my way back.

Bali was too vibrant for me then, too riotous with music and the joy of its people at simply being alive. I was in no mind to accept joyousness as a way of life. I fled from Bali back to America, ready or not.

Now, nine years later, Bali once again glimmers below me.

In the interval, which of us, I wonder, has changed more—if at all?

The jet's tires burn on the runway of the airport at Tuban. We stop five hundred meters away from the terminal and the nearest of the three Garuda Air Lines passenger jets and a Quantas 747 parked closer in.

A circle of armed paras with submachine guns take up positions on our perimeter. Two Ferret Scout cars roll in toward us, bracketing a British Saracen troop carrier.

"I hope that's not our transportation," I say to Guntur.

He smiles at me. "Being a colonel in charge of COIN-OPS means never having to say you're sorry."

"Cute," I say.

"If they tried to kill me when I was leaving, why shouldn't they try when I return?"

"Do you have men on the roof of the terminal?"

"Please, John, don't insult me. Believe me, no gunman can possibly get within a thousand meters of us at the moment."

We climb down toward the waiting transport.

BRONZE BELL

A young Indonesian captain—with red beret, curved mustache and sideburns, mirrored sunglasses reflecting the sunset, and sterile fatigues, sleeves rolled above the elbows, exposing delicately muscled arms—stands rigidly in his jump boots and maintains a doctrinaire Sandhurst salute so rigidly I wonder if Guntur might not have had him carved for the occasion and placed out to welcome us. Guntur flips him a return salute. I'm reassured; the captain's arm is made of flesh, not stone.

"John, my aide-de-damp, Captain Amir Hamzah. Hamzah, John Locke."

The man snaps another perfect highball my way.

"I have been counting the hours, Mr. Locke," he says, his English pure Oxonian. "It is a great honor."

Yet there's something about him in spite of his too-instantaneous hero worship, or possibly because of it. I can feel my cortisol level rising. Maybe it's the mirrored sunglasses. I never went in for all the trappings, not even when I was playing mean cop on the streets of San Francisco. Yet I can sense that this young officer is a fighting soldier, not just a dress extra. There's definitely hard bark on him, and he appears to have a lot of throw weight in reserve and fire in his belly. But I suspect he's got a pissing-match ego and that his welcome-aboard greeting is all cosmetics. He wants Guntur's job so much you can smell it like cordite after a fire fight.

I file him under wait-and-see.

Guntur is beckoning me toward the armored troop carrier.

"Sorry," I say. "I never get into those sardine cans. They draw too much fire. I'll ride in the lead scout car if you don't mind."

"Suit yourself," he says, and ducks into the Saracen, the young captain with him. I step into the back of the first Scout car next to a burly noncom with muscled arms, grenades pinned to his cammies like convention buttons, and a Baretta SMG looped over his shoulder. Clearly he hasn't been expecting any brass to sit in back with him. He jumps to attention as I climb in, spits out a jet of red fluid to one side of me, thoughtfully downwind, puckers out the thick quid of betel, lime, and sirish he's been chewing, and salutes me.

"*Selamat datang, tuan,*" he says.

"*Terima kasih,*" I reply, expending most of my twenty-word vocabulary of Bahasa Indonesian.

"*Sama-sama,*" he says, grinning, exposing perfectly filed teeth.

"But that's it," I say. "*Ma'af*—I'm sorry. I have only a few words in your language. Please sit down."

But he continues standing, his palm grafted to his forehead in salute.

"No English?" I ask.

He smiles at me without comprehension.

A rebuking siren growls from the armored car. The colonel is obviously annoyed by our delay in moving right out.

The driver of our Ferret instantly obeys the siren. He guns the scout car forward, my companion in back thrown down by the sudden lurch of the car.

He is embarrassed, having lost face in front of me, but I pretend I haven't seen the ungraceful pratfall, and he instantly recovers his dignity.

Along the road from Tuban I am bombarded not by hidden snipers or lurking terrorists but by the vertiginous sights, smells, and sounds of Bali. Old women, bare to their bellybuttons, wizened figures with sunken breasts folded on their chests like giant ticks, carry loads on their heads that would stagger me. A line of girls in rainbow silks winds across a newly planted *sawah*, taking care to follow the balks between the flooded mirrors of water covering the rice to approach a distant temple, on their heads palm-leaf baskets tiered with fruits and flowers. Naked boys in a rice paddy form a laughing circle around two copulating buffaloes. A two-story building is under construction, at least fifty men and women swarming over it. They hand up pails of wet cement from a chugging mixer to others above them on scaffolds, a human chain reaching to the form boards on the roof, where the pails are emptied. The empty pails glide down slanting ropes to two women on the ground; just as they reach maximum velocity, the women gracefully swing the ropes up to slow the hurtling pails. A tour bus of elderly Americans is parked in front of a temple, the purple-haired ladies besieged by local women hawking batik. "Whasa your name?" one of the more aggressive Balinese salesladies calls out. "My name Eda. You don't like, you come my shop. Got lots more. You no hafta buy, you don't want buy. You buy, I guarantee." Two American women stand stiff with indignation in front of a sign that reads: DURING MENSTRUATION, WOMEN ARE NOT ALLOWED TO ENTER THE TEMPLE. The viridian fields fuse, terrace after terrace, stepped up along the hillsides toward distant palms. Plastic shopping bags, blue, pink, and white, attached to a network of strings strung above the *sawahs*, flutter in the wind, worrying birds away from the grain. I smell a profusion of odors borne from every direction as we pass along the teeming roadway, the smell of peanut oil, of shrimp paste, of the dead being cremated, of champac blossoms and frangipani—the sharp, almost overpowering, pungent impact of another culture, another society totally— and even the subtle scent of naked brown bodies, sweet and earthy and sensual and beckoning. More sounds than I can possibly identify. Some, of course, are easy—the din of traffic, not as strident as Saigon's, less waspish, more like radiator pipes warming up, but clearly a decibel separation between the thump of poorly maintained cars and exquisitely maintained motorcycles, and the rumble-rattle of *bémos*, miniature buses built for eight, four sitting across from four, swaying as one, but at this hour the *bémos* lean perilously off their shocks from the weight of all the hangers-on. Amid this ceaseless racket, for split seconds between cars, I imagine I can almost sense the rustling of the tjemara trees. But over everything, even above the sound of traffic, I hear again the sweet, crystal sound of the *gamelan*, the chimes and the gongs of orchestras in every village, their metallic melodies unrolling with endless counterpoint and stops and starts.

Finally, I hear a sound that violates my concept of what one should hear in Bali at sunset.

Angry shouts, harsh outcries, a rising uproar of voices.

The noncom next to me chambers a round from the magazine into the SMG and peers ahead professionally as the observer next to our driver speaks into a hand mike. Colonel Katrini's voice barks back through the transmitter.

Ahead, in the next village, a mob blocks the road, their attention directed not toward us but toward two frightened-looking officers on the porch of the police substation now completely hemmed in by the crowd.

The driver pulls the Ferret off the road, permitting the Saracen to speed by, straight toward the massed villagers.

I start to jump out, but the noncom, apologizing in his own language, drops a firmly restraining hand on my forearm. I don't argue.

The Saracen stops just this side of the assemblage. Colonel Katrini climbs out with his captain.

He begins to speak to the people. Almost at once they quiet down to hear what he has to say.

I can't hear it from here, but at least his body language appears persuasive, nothing threatening either in his movements or his posturing, in spite of the alert captain backing him up or the Saracen standing ten yards off with its machine guns trained on the people.

Miraculously, the crowd begins to nod, to murmur their agreement. Then, at the colonel's urging, they begin to dissipate, arguing among themselves, still highly emotional but clearly defused by whatever it was Guntur said to them.

I discover him on one side of the road with a weeping man.

Guntur brings the man into his arms and embraces him comfortingly. After a moment the man kneels in the road, scrawny chickens darting past him, village dogs leaning in warily to sniff at the colonel.

The captain trots back to where I wait.

"It is all right," he says. "At least for now."

"What *was* that?" I ask.

"The man you see with the colonel came to the police to demand why they have not yet located his wife and son. Both vanished early on the morning of *Nyepi*, and no trace of them has been found since. He does not accept the word of the police that sufficient efforts are being made. He and his village were about to burn down the police station, but the colonel has given his word as an officer and a gentleman that he will personally investigate the matter."

The captain catches me evaluating him. How much has the colonel told him?

"I know everything," he says. "Every man and officer in this detail knows. We were all together at Pura Besakih within minutes after the massacre. We are part of the conspiracy of silence—until we find the terrorists and find the Great Bronze Bell. But that poor *Audra*'s wife and child will never be found. How can we tell him that—at least until we deliver up the guilty ones?"

The colonel joins us.

"Now you can understand," he says, making a visible effort to calm himself, "why I jumped into the sea to beg you to come back with me. This is only one of the many in Bali who are demanding to know why family members have vanished without a trace and why the Triple Lotus temple is still closed to worshippers, ever since *Nyepi*. As you can see, the Balinese are not like Americans. If they feel their authorities are deceiving them, they don't simply write letters to the editor. They take direct action. We may seem placid and resigned, and we are, but there is another, darker streak in our natures—the conviction that evil cannot be purged by forgiveness, only by blood."

I nod toward the lone figure of the man still kneeling in the road in front of the police station.

"What happens now?"

"He has promised he will not resort to any more violent action. But he will remain on his knees in front of the station without food until we find his wife and son. Or until he dies."

"If he dies, then what?"

"Then his village will come back to burn down the police station. We shall, of course, have to stop them, and people may be killed. The time frame of our crisis is beginning to take on its own inevitable form. The SPACTTA convention starts twelve days from now."

"He can certainly live that long!" I say.

Guntur elects not to answer.

"It is not only *this* one," the captain volunteers. "Similar incidents are occurring in front of other police stations. It has only begun."

"I'll take you to my brother's house now," Guntur says. "Forgive this delay, but immediate response was required. Besides, how better could I convince you of the urgency of your mission unless I'd staged the incident for you?"

"Did you?" I ask.

His look makes me regret asking. He motions to his men and climbs into the Saracen, which has backed around and eased up to my lead Scout car.

I get back into the Ferret. We rumble off.

My eyelids tremble from exhaustion.

I feel a twinge of guilt for having to surrender to sleep. Then I remember nothing more of the drive to Batubulan, not even the shadow of a dream.

CHAPTER

5

The roosters do not awaken me, although I audit their challenge of the dawn while I still linger in that magical borderland between sleep and waking. Nor do the pigs rouse me, despite their persistent grunting only yards away, where someone is diligently chopping disks of banana stalk for their breakfast. The bleating goats, the quarrelsome dogs, the gardener's stiff broom scraping the gravel pathways clean, the occasional muffled laughter of girls working in a nearby kitchen—none of these makes me relinquish my sleep. After many years in Asia, certain indigenous sounds are so grooved in as nonthreatening that their very presence only lulls me.

But what does filter through these comforting noises and causes me abruptly to up periscope is an unknown scooping of water, a joyous dribbling, accompanied by a cooing more human than birdlike, musical and rhythmic—a resonance so imperceptible, so subtle, that it crashes through the other screening sounds.

I open my eyes.

Ordinarily, first bit of the day is an automatic time check of wristwatch. But this morning I have no motivation for looking. Something has happened to my time need. It has simply vanished with yesterday's sunset over Bali. It seems enough for the moment simply to accept the unarguable reality that daylight has come.

Like a tourist in a glass-bottom boat, I let my eyes follow the lines of the ceiling above me. I am inside the *bale* I remember Guntur bringing me to last night, one of the many houses and pavilions within the family compound. The ceiling is thatched with *lalang* grass strung to the ribs of coconut fronds. On the rafters the carved wooden figure of the Hindu god Vishnu looms above me in protective mode. I am lying between batik sheets on a mattress set upon a carved platform made of teak. A chest of drawers stands against the only wall in the *bale*, the other three sides given over to an ornately carved double door and to verandas to either side with boundaries of shrubbery and flowers. Above my bed, airy mobiles made of rice stalks decorated with red hibiscus twirl from the ceiling.

I sleep naked, so I rise naked, feeling no need to cover myself despite the two open sides of the *bale*. Like time, clothes in Bali are merely a concept, quickly shed. From one of the verandas three steps lead to a dressing room and a tiled area with toilet, washstand, and a tub of fresh water, a flower floating on the surface. I spot the standard Dutch colonial bucket and soap for tidying one's self after bowel movement, but I am less interested in basics than I am in pursuing the liquid sound that awakened me. I find another door at the back of my dressing room. I open it.

Outside, a bathing area is sequestered within a walled garden onto which four doors, of which mine is one, give access. The pool is not much larger than your standard suburban hot tub, and is replenished by water streaming from the lips of a muraled god.

In the pool, waist-deep, her back toward me, a naked girl is washing her long black hair with a series of delicate gestures that seem part of an intricate, almost courtly private dance she is performing to her whispered song—less a song, actually, than a sequence of musical sounds.

She is the color of fresh cinnamon. She is young and strong and beautiful, and everything about her is rounded—her shoulders, the contours of her breasts, only partly visible under her arms as she washes and arranges her hair.

I feel blood rush to my groin. I tremble with needs I haven't indulged in weeks. Suddenly, I am fully erect, painfully erect,

37

without conscious summons, as abruptly, as effortlessly as though I were a divining rod.

And in that second the girl elects to turn my way. I am over-whelmed by embarrassment. On this, my first morning in the home of Guntur's family, I am caught in the act of peeking, if not of presumed rape, from the appearance of my anatomy. I whirl to flee, crash into the doorway, almost breaking myself off at the roots, and stumble blindly back the way I've come. Jesus Christ, Locke! People can't invite you anywhere!

I snatch a towel from the dressing room and run up the steps and back into my *bale*. There's no place to hide in there. I leap back into bed. For the first time in years I'm tempted to pull the covers over my head. Wait until the colonel hears about this! John Locke, the only man in the China Basin who can save Bali, revealed to be an incipient rapist! I start to laugh. I'm still laughing when a woman enters with my breakfast, sliced banana and pa-paya, fried eggs, toast and jam, and fragrant tea. She sets the tray on the chest of drawers, places her palms together in front of her lips, and bows her head slightly.

"Thank you," I say.

I've breakfasted, bathed, dressed, and managed to compose myself as much as possible by the time Colonel Katrini arrives with Captain Hamzah.

"Good morning, John."

"Morning, Guntur."

"Morning, sir," Hamzah says.

"Good morning, captain."

"Did you sleep well?" Guntur asks.

"Like a winner, thank you. I was so zonked I can't remember much about last night. I didn't meet your family, did I?"

"No. They were out for the evening. You'll meet them shortly. By the time they returned, you were asleep. But they assured me the first matter they tended to when they came home was to busy themselves at the house altar and do those reverences to the gods which you, as a white man, do not know how to do. Now the house is guaranteed divine protection. Within these walls you are safe."

"I'm ready to start whenever you are, Guntur. But why don't we have some tea first and discuss a basic plan of operations? I have a way of working that needs to be discussed, okay?"

"Excellent," he agrees. "I have already ordered the tea."

He leads the way through the compound, along a gravel walk past champak blossoms to a structure larger than the other *bales*.

"This is the social pavilion," he explains to me, "what we call *bale tiang sanga*."

We enter a building whose thatched roof is supported by elaborately carved columns. The expansive central room is furnished with bamboo-covered benches. Guntur settles down, cross-legged, on one of them. I follow his example, the captain sitting to one side of us.

The same woman who brought me breakfast appears now with our tea. I detect a change in her manner. She is smiling at me, almost giggling, and when she serves me, her hand brushes my thigh. As she leaves, Guntur looks after her sternly.

"I shall speak to my brother about that one!" he says.

"Please don't," I urge.

"Oh?"

"She did not mean to show disrespect," I say. "On the contrary, she was trying to tell me something else entirely."

"John," he says, a note of rebuke in his voice, "no one is earthier than we Balinese, but I would expect you to set your sights somewhat higher than the first servant woman who smiles at you."

"I shall try to control myself."

But I find that I'm still smiling, much to Guntur's annoyance. He plunges straight into business.

"Captain Hamzah is anxious to propound his theory about the theft of the Bronze Bell."

The captain is indeed brimming with eagerness to talk. He needs little prompting. "What is your theory?" I ask.

"Sir, I believe the theft is only the beginning of a campaign to destabilize our government, to rouse our people to violence, to insurrection, in reaction to a series of sacrilegious acts."

"Why do you believe that?"

"Two weeks before the massacre at Pura Besakih a district administrator in Tabanan was seized by a team of unknown men wearing demon masks. A drumhead trial was held beside the road, in plain view of the villagers. Then the man was executed by gunfire. The terrorists fled in a stolen *bémo*."

"Why didn't you mention this?" I ask Guntur.

"All in proper time," he replies. "I didn't want to overload you. Too much too soon can send you jogging down the wrong trail."

"Please overload me. It's part of my MO."

"Then," the captain continues urgently, having held his breath during the sidebar exchange between Guntur and me, "came the desecration at Besakih—the massacre of the eighteen. And finally the ambush at the airport."

"The empties you picked up from the execution site at Tabanan and those from Besakih—did they match?"

"Yes, sir—7.62mm NATO standard-issue rounds fired from Fabrique Nationale FAL assault rifles."

"Which you acquired from the three Burmese you shot at the airport?"

"Yes, sir. Ballistics made the matchup. The guns that killed the administrator and the pilgrims were intended to kill us."

"Conclusive enough. But hardly grounds for assuming you've got an incipient insurrection on your hands."

.I catch a glint of something in the captain's reaction to my challenge. For a split second I see the creature within.

"Let him finish, John," Guntur urges.

"It's evident to me, sir," the captain says, "that a hard-core cadre of assassins with sophisticated weaponry and substantial financial backing is operating inside Bali. They are following chapter and verse the procedure of the Foco Theory, exactly as the National Liberation Front did in Vietnam: committing a series of acts of terrorism planned to frighten or anger the people in a way that will make them strike back against their most visible targets—Muslims and Christians, the landlords, the army, the police, and ultimately the government in Jakarta."

"What terrorist groups are still operating in Indonesia?" I ask the colonel. "The last I heard, you'd pretty well mopped up the OPM in Irian Jaya."

"One thing we knew from the outset," he says. "We knew they weren't OPM. Nor were they leftovers from our own shattered Communist party. And I was sure they couldn't be Chinese. The Chinese, as you know, reject the Foco Theory. At their guerrilla training center in Nanking they call isolated acts of terrorism 'romantic adventurism.' So our first target was the New Equality Party, a front for Moluccan terrorists—a Trotskyite group, extremely pro-Moscow. But what remnants we could dig out proved to us they were not implicated. That wasted thirty hours. Then we took after the Japanese Red Army, thinking that possibly they might be behind this. It wasn't too long ago the JRA seized the U.S. Embassy in Kuala Lumpur and attacked the Shell refinery in Singapore. But the JRA is reduced to only thirty members, most of them in North Korea. And then the captain had a stroke of genius. Why not, he suggested, play language tapes for the villagers who witnessed the mock trial and determine if anyone could recognize the language spoken?"

"Nice clean idea," I compliment Hamzah.

He grows at least two inches in the sunshine of my approval.

"So we played language tapes," Guntur continues, "and came up with a match."

"Let me guess," I say. "Vietnamese."

"Precisely!" the captain says. "Therefore, sir, my personal theory is that the Vietnamese are exporting revolution to our part of the world, acting as surrogates for the Soviets."

"One Vietnamese leading three Burmese hardly makes a revolution, captain," I say. "What other evidence have you of a Vietnamese involvement?"

"Let *me* talk to that point, John," Guntur says. "Currently, we have a delegation of Vietnamese touring Indonesia—part of a cultural exchange. They're due in Bali tomorrow."

"Sounds like a lessening of tensions between Hanoi and Jakarta," I say. "Cultural exchanges usually don't go hand in hand with covert acts of terrorism."

"The Vietnamese, like the Chinese, Mr. Locke," the captain interjects, "have tortuous minds. It is exactly the kind of Trojan-horse ploy they would plan—an olive branch in one hand, a rifle in the other."

"Well," I say, "of all people I don't wish to sound like an apologist for Hanoi, but the Vietnamese are not adventurist. They've got enough problems at home without trying to take on yours."

"Then what are they doing in Kampuchea?" Guntur asks slyly.

"Come on, Guntur!" I say. "We both know Vietnam dominated that part of the world for centuries before the French grabbed it away from tnem. Even the ancient kings of Siam paid tribute to the Vietnamese emperors. Hanoi is simply reclaiming some of its old turf in order to protect its borders. You've got to give them the same right of historical perspective a lot of other nations are claiming, including your own. If you want to discuss land grabs, let's talk about Timor and New Guinea!"

"This is not the time or the place," Guntur mumbles.

"Yet think, Mr. Locke, how the Soviets would benefit from revolution in Indonesia," the captain persists. "With the bases their navy already enjoys in Vietnam, and with control of certain Indonesian islands that could quickly be developed into airfields, they could cut the world in half at the China Sea."

"All because a bell is missing?" I ask, more archly than usual, for these War College types with their unconvincing rhetoric remind me of outtakes from *Apocalypse Now*. "Look, captain, I'm not saying you don't have some really nasty Apaches operating on this island. But to construct a theory as geopolitical as yours out of the existing facts is too fanciful even for my fevered imagination. Suppose somebody simply wanted your bell, the world's largest, possibly most ancient, bronze bell. To get the Indonesian army to look the other way, to get them thinking in political rather than in simple criminal terms, the thieves stage a mock trial, kill a district administrator, then take a few shots at you and the colonel at the airport. That's all that's actually happened. And from that you cut the world in half!"

You could drill the silence with a Roto-Rooter.

"But I do compliment you," I add.

I see I'm confusing him.

"For positing a ridiculous conclusion, because that's the way I try to solve problems too. But the difference is, once I've reached a ridiculous conclusion, I set about to disprove it, not to affirm it. Thus I keep an open mind."

"I—I don't understand," he says.

"Let me lay it out for once and all—for you, too, Guntur, because you might as well know what you're in for now that you've got me involved. I always start on a case the same way— give myself as much burn-in time as possible."

"Burn-in time?" Guntur asks.

"Seeing, hearing, smelling, feeling, absorbing, storing—piling up a data base, okay?"

"You mean indoctrinating yourself?" the captain asks. "Collecting the facts?"

"No, not what I mean," I correct. "I'm talking about everything *except* the case itself. I'm talking about the atmosphere *around* the case. Once I have that layered in, I begin to use the stored images, playing them back in my mind and inspecting them just as if they were actual pictures. The most important creative thinking takes place in images, not words. By piling all this sensory data around me, I begin to spot certain syndromes, constellations. I get an idea, suspect a possibility. Once I do, I start looking for more data."

"To prove the idea," Guntur offers.

"To disprove it."

"*Dis*prove?" the captain asks.

"Correct." I try to smile sweetly at him. "Let's say I'd come up with your theory—that this is a Vietnamese-inspired destabilization effort centered in Bali. Right?"

"Yes," the captain says. "That's what *I* believe."

"Okay, now. While you're out looking for *proof* of that theory, I'd be trying to find *dis*proof."

"That seems counterproductive," Hamzah says.

"On the contrary. By locking yourself into one theory, you get instant tunnel vision. You may miss the real truth just off to one side. So I use natural reasoning—mostly analogical, that is, noting the likeness between objects and events, then making an inference based on the likenesses. My mother, who's a painter, taught me this from her work. The aggressive use of images, the value of conjectural and probablistic reasoning—what I call the 'lack-of-knowledge inference.' You see, captain, like most people, you use deductive thinking. You start with true statements and then proceed to what other truths can be logically produced from them. I find that too restrictive. I prefer to use inductive thinking—starting with a set of special observations and then by extrapolation or analogy make a series of generalizations based on them, expanding from the known to the unknown, rather than straightlining from one known to another known. It's what the fellas in the new cognitive sciences call 'plausible-inferential thinking based on recognition of similarities.' That kind of thinking requires a large data base, and that's why I need the burn-in period. Any questions?"

I wish I could read the captain's thought bubble, for he sits staring at me obliquely, like a cartoon character frozen in place. I can visualize the thought bubble leading from his head in the cartoon, but I cannot read the words. Possibly because they're in Indonesian.

"So," I say, "I'll begin this process of soaking up the environment as soon as you wish, Guntur. *Now*, if you're ready. Starting at Pura Besakih."

"At Pura Besakih? Why not with the Vietnamese prisoner?" he asks.

"I'll be able to deal with him more effectively after I've seen the place."

"Very well, if that's what you wish."

"Captain," I say to Hamzah, for he's looking somewhat dispirited, "please forgive me if I seem to have been a little rough on your theory. Lord knows, in today's unpredictable world, anything's possible, and you may be right. It's just that my experience with the Vietnamese suggests that your theory is out of character. On the other hand, I've been away from Vietnam for almost ten years, so who knows? By all means you should continue to pursue your theory while I'm going at things from another angle. Incidentally, have you questioned the local Vietnamese population? What has their response been?"

"There aren't that many Vietnamese in Bali," he replies. "What few are here have blended in with our Chinese population. To be honest, sir, we find it virtually impossible to differentiate between them—and the Chinese are totally uncooperative. We're now trying to penetrate their societies with ethnic Chinese agents loyal to us, but so far we've had no luck at all."

"Well, stay with it," I encourage. "We'll see if I manage to get anything from your Vietnamese prisoner. By the way, when you get back to headquarters, would you please see if my shotgun has arrived?"

"Yes, sir. The colonel has already instructed me to look out for it. It should be here by this afternoon."

"And there are some additional items I'll need. Okay, Guntur?"

"What items?"

"A bulletproof vest."

"I brought one for you. It's in the car."

"A one-pound box of granulated sugar, a bottle of potassium chlorate . . ."

The captain produces a small pad and a pen and begins to jot down my needs.

"One dozen igniter leads, a dozen blasting caps, four yards of ballistic-resistant plastic, and two rolls of Velcro tape."

"Ballistic-resistant plastic?" Guntur demands. "Whatever is *that* for?"

"For night work. Against people with imagers and night scopes.

It's just an update of a technique developed two thousand years ago by the Roman legions using mirrors on their shields."

"I'll have to see that in action!"

"You just may," I say.

The captain salutes us both and hurries out.

"Why don't you like him?" Guntur asks.

"Did I say I didn't?"

"It worries me, John. Your reaction to him."

"Why should it?"

"He's the best man I have in COIN-OPS. He's had jungle experience; he's cool under fire; he's ambitious. And he's really quite brilliant. Is it because he's Muslim you don't relate to him?"

"Why should I not relate to a Muslim? Some of my best friends are Muslim."

"Because, my friend, I remember you from Vietnam. You're a confirmed pagan—even more so than some of our animists back in the mountains. You believe in rocks and rivers and clouds."

"Okay, I'll tell what it is about your captain—he's too quick with a smile. And too full of unmeant smiles."

"He's only trying to impress you, to win your approval. You can be quite formidable, John, and he's awed by your combat record."

"You know I'm a marshmallow."

"You're a cobra! But then, so am I. At least we are immune to each other's venom."

His eyes brighten at the sight of something behind me. He rises, speaks in Balinese to someone entering. I, too, rise, face the way Guntur's facing, see a younger replica of Guntur, chubby where Guntur is slender, soft where Guntur is hard, but with eyes more compassionate than his. This must be Guntur's brother, younger not in looks but because Guntur has told me so. With him comes a fine-looking woman, just past thirty, I judge. She's wearing a *kain* of handwoven cotton, her skirt wrapped tightly around her waist, held up by a bright floral sash reaching to her slender ankles. She has the soft but angular face of a high-caste Indian. I have seen paintings of such proud women in the pink palaces of Jaipur.

"My brother and sister-in-law," Guntur announces. "Chairul and Sayu Katrini. John Locke."

Palms against palms, heads bowing gracefully. I return the gesture.

"Peace upon your stay," Chairul says.

"May it be well with you," Sayu says.

"Thank you," I reply.

"Have you everything you need?" Chairul asks.

"More than enough. I hope I won't be a problem."

"Problems are denied entrance to our home," Chairul says, smiling. "We keep our altars constantly supplied with offerings to the gods. In addition, Guntur has posted ten sharpshooters along the walls and in the various trees without telling us why so much security is necessary. We can only assume you must be the most important guest we have ever entertained. Even a prince, our most recent guest until your arrival, had only two bodyguards."

He must have noticed I am no longer in eye contact with him nor hearing a word he's saying.

I feel as though I'm on a spit, being basted over the fire burning my cheeks. I watch the approach of the girl I'd seen naked in the outdoor bath.

She's barefoot, her shapely feet gliding like a dancer's along the floor, a tiny bell on the big toe of her right foot jingling softly as she enters. She's wearing cut-off jeans by Jordache. I notice the brown leather patch on the denim over her firmly rounded backside, and from her shoulders hangs a loose T-shirt mercifully devoid of smartass messages. A moist, heavy lock of hair hangs from below her headband, a sign of her maidenhood.

"This is my niece Dasima," Guntur says. "Dasima, John Locke."

"I have a feeling I've seen Mr. Locke before," she answers. I notice that she's peeling a tangerine and is smiling at me without rancor. Can it be the guest-rapist is to be forgiven?

"He was in Bali eight or nine years ago," Guntur says. "You'd have been nine at the time."

Making her seventeen or eighteen. A signal to the white voyager to look elsewhere. No cross-pollinating here!

"So I don't think it's possible you saw him . . ."

Is Guntur still rattling on?

". . . or that you'd remember if you had."

Thank God he's Hindu, not Muslim. Otherwise, the incident at the bath might have proved terminal. I remind myself to ask him later why he seems so excessively protective of this niece of his.

"Nevertheless," she says firmly, "I feel I know him—in every detail."

She flows to me. We are face-to-face. I feel as though we're center stage with a spotlight on us. Then I can no longer sense the audience. It is only the two of us, eye to eye. Here's that Pacific high again, that ancient calm, the serenity that eludes me, blooming in her eyes.

Gently, Dasima places a segment of the tangerine between my lips. It is the consummate gesture.

"Welcome to Bali, Mr. Locke," she says.

"Thank you," I reply. The tangerine is especially sweet.

"I hope it won't be all work," she says.

"I hope so, too," I say.

Strangely enough, Guntur is smiling.

CHAPTER

6

In deference to my distaste for riding in tanks and personnel carriers, Guntur has two Ferret Scout cars waiting outside the *aling-aling* wall and the gateway to the family compound. The *aling-aling* intrigues me. It's erected two meters inside the gateway, a solid barrier of sandstone as you come inside, forcing you to turn left to enter the walled compound. Guntur explains that it's placed there to block the passage of malevolent spirits. Ideal cover for defensive fire, it strikes me. Fighting house-to-house in Bali could prove costly for invading ground forces.

Pura Besakih, our morning destination, is more than sixty kilometers northeast of Batubulan. I put on the flak jacket Guntur gives me.

Once more I give myself over to the assault of the myriad images around me. They enter you directly in Bali, like actinic rays, the light beams in the ultraviolet part of the spectrum that produces chemical change, as in photography. Simply staring around in Bali begins to imprint images that will stay with you forever. Off on the mountains I see men, small and dark, struggling in the shining mud behind wooden plows drawn by buffalo. I watch a file of village girls striding uphill with queenly grace, on their heads plastic pails filled with shimmering water. The sun plays through the plastic, transmitting the pails into pink and blue and red halos above the girls' heads.

"She has *never* been that forward!" Guntur says, out of nowhere.

"I've been wondering how long it'd be before we had this discussion," I reply.

"What discussion?"

"Your basic 'hands off, Locke' discussion. A reminder that I'm here on lethal business. That every second counts. That even the least distraction from the grim work at hand will bring Indonesia crashing to its knees. That the girl is only seventeen."

"Eighteen in October."

"That I'm thirty-four. That's thirty-four, calendar time. But in hard usage, maybe ninety-four, okay? That I'm still preoccupied with loving a ghost who won't die, so how could I possibly love a living girl? That I'll be gone in two weeks. If I live that long. All true, right?"

He smiles. "How does your 'plausible-inferential thinking' deal with the fact that in spite of all those evidential facts, I still approve of the relationship?"

I glance at him and observe that he's indeed serious.

"You mean, if she lets me hold her hand, you have no objection?"

"I encourage you to try."

"Well, Guntur, this definitely defies all the information I've stored in my data bank about you. I've always considered you rigid and traditional."

"I am indeed."

"Then how would you feel if it went beyond holding hands?"

"I am traditional and rigid only about my religious faith, my loyalty to Indonesia, and my personal principles. But not about the natural feelings of free people, honestly given and taken in open exchange. It would be much better for Dasima to know one night of love with you than a lifetime with someone at a lower level of consciousness than her own. She is a gifted dancer, as you will see—a national asset, in my opinion. But far more than that, she is a very special spirit. That makes her lonely. The young men here, I must confess, are baffled by her. They wait outside my brother's home for her to pass. They suck in their breath, as boys have done for centuries in Bali to court girls. They flare out their nostrils like proud stallions to show their desire for her. But all she does is snort back at them in mockery. She needs to find her match—and soon, John, very soon!"

"Why soon?"

"I am not at liberty to say. But you have my blessing. Let happen what may happen."

"We're both presuming a lot," I say. "She may snort back at me, too."

We enter Klungkung, once the center of power under the Dewa Agung, the last king of Bali. Guntur points out an elaborate stone gateway opening into a flat, barren field.

"All that remains of one of the greatest palaces on the island," he tells me. "Dutch artillery destroyed the palace but somehow spared the gateway. It was here in 1908 that the Dutch overwhelmed the king's forces and Bali fell into their hands. My great-grandfather died here that day. But we were more fortunate than other Asian countries. Our years of servitude were briefer than most. Only a little more than half a century."

We speed on toward Besakih. The scout cars leave the narrow coastal plain and loop upward with the rice terraces of Bukit Jambul to Pesaban at the top of a ridge. From here the view over the valley is one that would keep my mother camping at the side of the road for weeks, trying to capture on canvas the mortised green flakes of the contoured *sawah*s. Surely some giant once stood here and flung emeralds by the billions across the mountainside.

Soon we rumble through Rendang, and from here the road fires straight up the flank of Mount Agung's volcanic cone. Above us the peak vanishes into a crown of cloud, its furrowed ridges arching up in folds of purple lava beyond the reach of my vision.

"Pura Besakih," Guntur announces with evident dramatic enjoyment, despite the gravity of our mission.

He provides me with a waist sash to wear while I'm in the temple, de rigueur for visitors.

Flanked by paras, we make the steep walk from the parking area, teeming with aggressive vendors, to the temple complex crowded with worshippers.

I am stunned by Pura Besakih's towering ascent. It appears to rise out of the slope of the volcano, its tiered *merus* dominating the skyline as majestically as the ten-thousand-foot peak of Mount Agung looming directly behind them, the jet-black *ijuk* fiber on each tower standing in sharp foreground contrast to the mottled purple of the mountain backdrop.

We approach the main central section, the Pura Panataran Agung, six walled courts, each court higher than the last, until we arrive at the Triple Lotus, a wide stone platform into which Guntur leads me, the paratroopers taking up positions outside. Other Red Berets are already on round-the-clock duty, keeping the temple off limits to the Balinese passing just outside.

Inside, from the center of the platform, I stare up into the empty thatchwork of the lofty eight-tiered tower in which the Great Bronze Bell of Agung had hung until one morning nine days ago.

After allowing me a measured interval of response, Guntur painfully leads me along the east wall of the temple and indicates where each of the eighteen victims had fallen. It is as though he still sees them lying there, here the woman from Menanga and her six-year-old daughter, there the old man from Selat, one leg twisted so.

"The wife and child of the man I saw last night, the one kneeling in front of the police station?" I ask. "Where were they killed?"

He shows me. "They fell there, the woman's arms lifted to protect the child."

I can feel his emotion. I know the feeling.

Suddenly I'm back in the City by the Bay, on homicide again, seeing for the thousandth time the first civilian victim I had to deal with, a girl who'd been raped and strangled. The really sloppy aspect of that one was not so much her neck contusions and splattered lips as it was what had once been her eyes. The rapist had seared them out with a car cigar lighter. The combat deaths I saw in Vietnam were more violent, the havoc to the human bodies more extensive, yet somehow they troubled me less than this inert and waxen girl.

Yet in San Francisco, in any American city, a girl with her eyes burned out is more explicable than the machine-gunning of Balinese bringing fruits and flowers to their gods. In San Francisco we are not in harmony with the elements around us. We have forgotten, if in fact we ever knew, how to inhabit a landscape without disturbing it. In Bali the people are in harmony with the land and themselves. In San Francisco our flywheels don't run smoothly. Anything can happen. You can hear the clash of gears in the air, the killers boarding the buses, the stalkers in the shrubbery outside the garages and on the fire escapes. There is no indecency you can conceive of that a police officer won't see, sooner or later, if he stays on the job long enough and out in the streets where it all comes down. It's never acceptable, but we keep acting surprised every time it happens. There it is, there it always is, coming at us on the six o'clock news, the one you thought nobody would ever do. In Bali it is not that dark forces don't also lurk, but the Balinese believes he can not exist among all his demons and dangers unless he constantly propitiates them, lays out offerings for devils and witches and exteriorizes his fears in paintings, sculpture, and dance dramas. Maybe we should dance more in San Francisco or burn more incense.

I ask Guntur to let me wander around the temple for a while and sense what I need to sense, whatever that may be, and I open all the channels, letting it all slow surface until after a while I become both the executed and the executioner, until I can hear the profane gunfire and smell the acrid brass rejects flying hotly from FAL chambers.

Where the Great Bronze Bell has been taken becomes less the question than *why* it has been taken.

Now that they have it, what do they intend to do with it?

What can you possibly do with a bell that justifies the time, trouble, and expense simply of hauling it away, let alone the cost in human life?

There must be a *purpose* involved here. Not money, for where can one exhibit or sell such a bell?

A higher purpose! In the minds of the thieves worth killing for—and therefore worth dying for.

I tell Guntur I am ready now to learn more about the bell itself.

Ready to meet Ida Bagus Dewata, Bali's holiest of high priests, keeper of the bell.

CHAPTER

7

It is as though he appears the instant my mind reaches out for him.

From nowhere he materializes, startling me.

He stands before me in a long white robe, his skin creased by decades of tropical sunlight—ancient, not antiquated, a painting Tintoretto might have done had he known of Bali, classical and eternal.

I am an instant captive of his eyes, twin vortices composed of an infinite number of smaller rotating circles disappearing back into a complex universe of memory.

Guntur, more obeisant than I have ever known him, introduces us.

Dewata raises his dazzling eyes to the tower above our heads where the Great Bronze Bell had hung for centuries.

After a while, he asks me, "What may I tell you?"

"Is the bell truly that immense—large enough to fill that belfry?"

"It is," he replies. "Fifty people have gathered beneath it at one time."

"I wasn't aware the Balinese ever made bells that big," I say.

"We didn't," Guntur says. "The bell is of Burmese origin."

"How'd it get from Burma to Bali?"

Guntur defers to Dewata.

Dewata settles onto the earth at our feet, spreading the fall of his white robe about him. I glance at Guntur. What is the proper thing? Should I, too, sit?

As though reading my mind, Dewata, his eyes fixed on the empty bell tower above us, speaks to me.

"You may sit or stand as you wish. I sit not because I am old but because the Dutch, when they were here, demanded politeness from us. Over many years I have formed the habit of sitting before white men."

Guntur breaks in. "It wasn't politeness they wanted. It was their personal safety. They demanded that all Indonesians sit down before they could speak to a European. It takes a seated man more time to pull out his kris, leap up, and attack his enemy than it takes a standing man to strike out."

"You asked how the bell came from Burma to Bali," Dewata continues, as though he has not heard Guntur's belligerent interjection. "Our people say the bell was an earring of the god who made Gunung Kawi. But that explanation will not satisfy you, will it?"

"I'd prefer something more pragmatic."

"Some say it was a war drum. Surely, I say, so heavy a drum could not have been a war drum. A gift, then? But from whom? To whom? It was ancient even when the great bell of Mandalay was cast three hundred and fifty years ago by order of King Bodoahpra. I have always felt it may have been cast early in the fifteenth century. But when it came to Bali, and how, no man knows. We know only that it has been here for centuries."

"Could the Burmese have come here to take it back?" I ask Guntur. "That at least fits in with those three Kachin hit men."

"Our first assumption. But we have agents in Rangoon and Mandalay, even in Moulmein and Teknaf, who would know if the bell had been returned to Burma. They've picked up nothing. Not even rumors."

"I have heard the Great Bell ring only a few times in my life," Dewata continues, as though addressing the Invisibles around us. "I heard it first more than a hundred years ago when I was still a child during the rice famine in Cirebon. I heard it before the Great Eruption that darkened the sun for months. I heard it when the Japanese invaded this land more than forty years ago. I heard it again in 1965 when the killing frenzy began from island to island and a million souls were driven from their bodies."

"But not when it was taken away last week?" I ask.

"Only the little voice."

"The little voice?"

"Do you know the Mandarin word for 'shoe'?"

"Yes. I speak Vietnamese. Many of their words derive from the Mandarin. 'Shoe' is *hsieh*. Why?"

"There are many legends about our Great Bell. But one I know *is* true—that when the bell is struck it will never give off its true sound. Only prior to a great calamity—or, it is said, to mark the passage of a most unusual human being—will the Great Bell release its powerful tone, and then only of its own volition."

"You're saying it . . . rings itself?"

He ignores the question as not worthy of notice. "Then its true voice can be heard for many kilometers around. Those within range feel it in their blood. The vibrations set their bodies trembling. Once you have heard it, you will carry the sound within you always. But the Great Bell itself decides when it will ring. No man can command it, not even I, its keeper, even after I have read the *maveda*, made my ablutions, and performed innumerable *mudra*s. I have tried, but the only sound I can bring from it—or that anyone else who has ever tried can bring from it—is a low, wailing aftertone—like the crying of an anguished girl calling 'hsieh . . . hsieh.'"

"What is the legend about that?" I ask.

"The story goes that the artisan who cast the bell had made two previous castings. Both these earlier bells were honeycombed, their tones impure. The emperor warned the artisan that if he failed with the third casting, he would be torn apart by elephants. The man had a beautiful young daughter. She consulted an astrologer to see if he might tell her why her father was having such difficulty. The astrologer told her that the next casting would also fail—unless the blood of a maiden were mixed with the other ingredients."

"You can guess the punchline, can't you, John?" Guntur asks.

"*Adiós, muchacha*, right?"

"Right."

Again, the little interplay between Guntur and me passes without notice from the priest.

"At the precise moment when the hiss of molten metal caused

all those observing the third casting to turn away from the heat," Dewata continues, "the girl cried out, 'For my beloved father,' and pitched herself headlong into the seething mold. Vainly, her father reached for her, but managed only to catch one of her shoes, which came off in his hand. The prediction of the astrologer was then confirmed. For when the Great Bell had cooled and hardened, it suddenly sounded without being struck by any man, and the thundering of its tones could be heard from sea to mountain, from one end of the empire to the other. And then, following after it, came the wavering cry of a girl, '*hsieh, hsieh*'—asking for her missing shoe, which she needed in paradise."

I observe that Dewata has placed his hands together, with some of his fingers pointed like tiny steeples, others interlaced in mystic ritual gesture. Yet magically, before my eyes, he seems to change, to shed half a century as his psychic energy is renewed, the hands apparently the conductors of a higher state of consciousness.

Clearly, the interview has come to an end. Guntur touches me on the elbow, nodding for us to leave.

I follow Guntur outside, across the flagstones bordering the temple of the Triple Lotus.

"What exactly is he doing in there?" I ask.

"*Kundalini*—Serpent Fire. The Tantrics believe that there are seventy-two thousand astral nerve tubes connecting every part of the body's psychic energy. The plain physiological fact is that Dewata is capable of controlling the circulation of his blood, his metabolism, his glands, his organs, his limbic system, and, I suspect, even his electrochemical impulses."

I stop, as though the Great Bronze Bell has just struck across the empire, causing me to reverberate, filling me with the centuries, lifting me outward across the skipping stones of time. I look back and behold this priest sitting there, his long white hair tied up in a knot softened by yellow champac blossoms, the broad black *selimpet* lying over his shoulder and twisted around his breast, his white robe in folds on the ground about him. Now, as his hands move into a different posture, he flicks a flower toward the east.

It occurs to me there is a more profound reason for my having come to Bali, a reason hidden until this moment.

Not only to find the Bronze Bell.

But to sit on the earth with this *pedanda* and to try to learn even from his silence the least of what he knows—simply to let his shadow fall on me, if that is all he'll grant me.

Sensing this, being a man of first things first, Guntur touches my arm gently, stealing the gold from my vision, the dream from my mind.

"You and I, John, belong to the Satria, the warrior caste. He is a Brahmana, an Ida Bagus. Our path is different from his."

"Could be we're on the wrong path," I suggest.

"We are given our roles before we are born. Our lives are a stage with only one entrance."

"But with one helluva lot of exits! How old is he?"

"We Balinese have very little idea how old we are. Our calendar is much too complicated. And since this is only one of many lives, why bother to mark each day? So we give up counting. But that famine in Cirebon he spoke about—I believe that happened in 1853 on your calendar."

"My God! He must be a hundred and fifty!"

"You are awed. But who would want to be locked into the same life that long?" Guntur asks.

We descend the steps toward the parking area, our paratrooper escort in a file to either side of us.

I untie my waist sash and hold it out to Guntur.

"Keep it," he says. "You'll be entering many temples before you're through in Bali."

I look back at Pura Besakih rising on the slope behind us, then down the long flights of steps to where we stand.

"All right," I say, bringing myself back to business. "They kill the witnesses. Now—how do they move the bell?"

"They drive a flatbed truck and a mobile crane from the parking area to the temple. The crane hoists the bell onto the truck."

"Where did they get that kind of equipment on Bali?"

"They stole it from Pac-Pet."

"Pac-Pet?"

"Pacific Petroleum, an English oil-exploration company working out of Bali under a production-sharing agreement with Pertamina, our national oil company."

"Did you recover the truck?"

"We did."

"Sans bell, of course?"

"Sans bell."

"Where did they leave the truck and crane?"

"In Denpasar, near the market. We had our best forensic investigators from Jakarta fly in to check the equipment over. What little evidence they collected has proved meaningless. We have it, as well as other physical evidence we took from here, under guard. You are welcome to review it, of course, although it would be a waste of your time."

"I not only want to review all your forensic reports. I want to see, touch, and hang around every piece of physical evidence. It's the way I work, Guntur. It's definitely *not* a waste of time!"

"Whatever you wish."

"Okay, so now the bell is out of the tower, on the flatbed. The assault team is ready to take off. How many men?"

"We have no way of knowing."

"How much brass did you pick up?"

"Only a few pieces. Either they were using brass catchers attached to their weapons, or they went around and meticulously picked up all their empties."

"Footprints? Fingerprints?"

"I'll give all that to you back in Denpasar."

"So now the truck goes—where?"

"The only possible way—back down to the parking area, then out to the road leading to Rendang. There is no other way out. We made casts of the tire tracks the length of the dirt road. We lost the tracks on the paved road to Klungkung."

"How is it that nobody saw them while they were moving the bell with the truck? I spotted dozens of villages and hundreds of roadside stalls on the drive up here. What did these guys do, paint themselves with invisible paint?"

"They moved the bell during *Nyepi*."

"Oh, *Nyepi*. Which is—?"

"Our sacred day of quiet, the first day of the *Saka* New Year. *Nyepi* is an island-wide observance forbidding any movement outside the house. It forbids work or the making of noise. So at the time, the roads from one end of Bali to the other were deserted. No person ventured outside."

"Obviously the people who were killed did."

"They broke religious law. Their punishment was swift and harsh. But they are to be forgiven, since they came to worship. Except for these unfortunate few, everyone else was obediently indoors. Believe me, John, I could have moved a tank corps through Bali and not have been seen."

"What about tourists? They certainly weren't staying in their hotels because it was *Nyepi*. Some of them must have seen the bell being moved."

"This happened at dawn. Few tourists are out that early. Breakfast and bed are too important to them."

"But how can you be sure of that? Some romantics might have been out to catch the sunrise. You should be checking at every hotel, every guest house."

"John, we cannot risk a security leak! If we go around asking if anyone has seen a missing bell, I tremble to think what would be set off. We don't dare. But we do have men posted in every hotel, listening to tourist gossip. Not a whisper yet!"

"All right, then, let's drive out the way you think they might have driven."

"There is only one road out from here to Rendang. At Rendang one can go east to Muncan or west to Bangli or continue south to Klunkung."

"I want to drive *every* road," I tell him, "at the approximate speed they drove."

"Which is?"

"The speed any prudent man would observe if he were trucking a bell weighing two hundred and fifty tons down a mountain road. It's critical, Guntur, that we establish an elapsed time and a distance-traveled factor."

We get back into the scout cars and move down the mountain road toward Rendang at twenty-five kilometers an hour.

I permit myself a moment of romantic fantasy that as we drift along this cold, invisible trail, suddenly the countryside will thunder with the ringing of the Great Bronze Bell, calling to us as we pass, telling us where it has been hidden.

We arrive soon enough in Rendang—with no such luck.

I tell Guntur I feel that east feels warm, not west or south. East toward Muncan.

We head east, feeling our way.

═══CHAPTER═══

8

As we descend toward the coastal plain, I ask the driver to stop at an intersection between Muncan and Selat.

I consult the map, then climb down from the scout car, Guntur getting out and following me. I walk to the fork in the road, look off first to the east, then to the south along the other roadway. Guntur watches with what strikes me as overconfidence in my oracular abilities.

"What do you call witch doctors in Bali?" I ask him.

"*Balians*. Why?"

"We need one. Right about now. We can either continue east, which, it looks like, will take us to a large town..."

"Yes," he agrees. "Amlapura. It is quite populous."

"Not good," I say. "Not if you're hoping to hide a gigantic bell. Or we can loop back to the southwest and come in again at Klungkung."

"Even bigger than Amlapura," he says.

"Exactly," I say. "Two counterproductive options. Assuming the bell came this way at all."

"What is your instinct?" he asks.

"Out to lunch," I have to admit. "The trail is ten days cold, and at this point I'm picking up nothing. How sophisticated is your computer center?"

"Extremely," he says proudly. "We are the first country in Asia to have a satellite in space."

"Where's central control? In Jakarta?"

"Yes. But we have an independent system at my headquarters in Denpasar."

"You can do graphics, introduce your own programming?"

"We can even play war games. And often do," he says, smiling.

"Okay. We may save ourself a lot of time. But I want to see that flatbed truck and crane first."

Sixty-one minutes later we roll into the noisy center of Denpasar, where the city's main artery, Jalan Gejah Mada, is suffering from terminal midday coagulation. Nine years ago these narrow downtown streets were only partially clogged by pony carts. Now they appear totally impassable, jammed with trucks and buses somehow grinding their way ahead inch by inch, like glaciers shaving a trench to the sea.

"It is faster to walk," Guntur advises.

We pile out, ten of us, four Red Berets to each side. They shove people out of our way with the machismo that paratroopers of every nation seem to relish. I am pleased to see, though, that as we approach a group of Balinese boys playing their own form of checkers on the sidewalk with beercaps and stones, the Red Berets lead Guntur and me carefully around the children. We pass video shops and music stores hawking the pirated American rock hits. Their blare is as deafening as the car horns.

In the Denpasar market, we slide on the slippery alleyways, an amalgam of mud and food pulp, past trussed pigs and fresh-killed goats hanging above grills, past turtle steaks and frog legs displayed for sale, through acres of fruits and vegetables heaped in baskets tended by smiling women in costumes as colorful as their edible wares, past younger girls squatting one behind the next, patiently exploring the hair of their friends for lice, while a friend is carding theirs. We descend to a darker world pungent with the scent of mysterious, fresh spices, more spices than I ever dreamed grew on earth, spices assailing the senses until I'm on a spice high by the time we slither through the last narrow aisle and come out into daylight at a lower level.

The flatbed truck and a mobile crane loom dead ahead, nearly blocking the street. Ropes have been strung on stanchions around them, and paratroopers stand guard in a circle around the ropes. Beyond, the people and traffic of Denpasar drift by, paying little attention to guards or equipment, finding no interest in either.

"This is where they were left?" I ask.

"They have not been moved."

"What about your forensic team?"

"They disturbed nothing. Anything they have taken—earth and plant samples and prints—is all at my headquarters, properly labeled."

"When was this equipment found?"

"Oh-eight-thirteen hours," he tells me. "A Muslim police officer, not bound to observe the Hindu holiday, found it here. Since we had already alerted the police to be on the lookout for the kind of equipment required to transport the bell, they were careful to preserve the integrity of the scene until I arrived. But the original call from the officer was logged in at the station at exactly oh-eight-thirteen."

"What is your estimate of the hour the equipment left Besakih with the bell?"

"We know within a minute or two when they left. Ida Bagus Dewata informed me at oh-six-two-nine hours. He had just discovered the bodies in the Triple Lotus—and the fact that the Great Bronze Bell was missing."

"That doesn't pin down when *they* got away, only when he discovered they'd gone."

"We have timed it during a dozen rehearsals," he says. "Once the killing is done, exactly two minutes and twenty seconds are required to move the equipment into place. Five minutes more are required to lift the bell from the tower. Three minutes to secure it on the truck and to cover it with a tarp. Three minutes to return to the parking area and leave along the road to Rendang. We have therefore alloted fifteen minutes to the entire dismantling operation. The victims are known not to have arrived before dawn, since Ida Bagus Dewata himself was in the Temple Lotus at sunrise. On that morning sunrise came at oh-five-four-seven. Putting all these elements together, John, we've set oh-six-ten hours as the assassins' estimated time of departure from Besakih."

"Fair enough," I concede. "So we're dealing here with a time-span of one hundred and eighteen minutes—call it two hours—from the time they left Besakih until they hid the bell somewhere, then abandoned this equipment here, right?"

"Correct."

"All right! That's the skeleton. Now, let's see if your computers can put some flesh on those bones."

Guntur's headquarters, "near" Denpasar, are actually in Tabanan, twenty clicks northwest. But to the Balinese, I am learning, every village in south Bali is "near" Denpasar, from which all roads radiate and return.

The same type of traffic lights I've seen in Denpasar now surface in Tabanan, except that here they are humanized by umbrellas and police officers on duty with supplemental hand paddles.

The army base itself resembles a county fairgrounds behind a vast, arching gateway. Overlooking the entry is one of those inky statues of modern soldiers that Asian governments often erect in tasteless violation of their own culture. I suspect they do this to give the people something to tear down during periods of revolt— better the statues than their builders, apparently.

Guntur has radioed ahead for lunch. We eat on a breezy veranda opening off his office, the parade ground our principle view. It is crisscrossed by units learning how to drill. The shouted orders of the DIs sound as harsh in Indonesian as they do in English.

Our main course is a buttery freshwater fish that Guntur tells me is called *belanek* and is bred in flooded rice fields. It has been boned, mixed with spices and coconut milk, wrapped in its skin, and baked. I chase it with warm Bintang beer served with ice cubes.

"Have you plans for tonight?" Guntur asks.

"I'd like to see Tip Bradley if I can steal some time off. Ubud can't be more than fifteen minutes from here, I understand."

"I'll assign my best sergeant to drive you."

"Okay, thanks."

"But tomorrow night please set aside for the two of us."

"What's on?"

"I am one of the official hosts at ceremonies to welcome the Vietnamese delegation to Bali. And Dasima will be dancing."

"Elephants couldn't tear me away."

Captain Hamzah clicks his heels and salutes from the doorway of Guntur's office. He is holding a shotgun over his left shoulder.

"I just picked it up at the airport, sir," he reports to Guntur.

My Bellini autoloader—Parkerized finish, gleaming walnut stock, buckhorn rear sight!

I am charged with love for Captain Hamzah despite his unmeant little smiles. Anybody who brings me a Bellini is my friend for life.

The colonel returns his salute.

"You may hand the gun over to Captain Locke," he says, as though making it clear that any residual credit for having the weapon flown in overnight from Rome must vest in him, not in his aide-de-camp.

But I'm up from the table and over to Hamzah. He gives me the shotgun. I turn away, check its action, heft and fondle and sight it out over the parade ground.

"I'll want to make a couple of modifications," I tell Guntur, "but I can do them myself—just add a stock and a cheek pad, brighten up the front sight a little. Then we'll take it out on the range and see what kinds of patterns it delivers at what ranges."

"Straight into the hearts of our enemies!" Guntur says. He is not smiling. "Shall we get to work with the computers, John?" he asks. I can see that unlike most Balinese, he is following the time on his wristwatch.

The COIN-OPS computer center in Tabanan is not only state-of-the-art, it has Japanese microchips so ultranew I feel as though I'm being shown the secret innerchambers of our own Silicon Valley. The young men and officers who staff the center in this air-conditioned building on the army base remind me of the Asian-American students I remember from Berkeley who terrorize their less motivated Caucasian fellow students with straight As.

Guntur introduces me to their head programmer, a Javanese army major who is so in love with the equipment, Guntur tells me later, that he virtually lives full time in the center, working late into the night on all kinds of scenarios.

"This one," I tell him, "is going to be so simple you could solve it on an abacus. What we want you to do is to create a series of overlays against the grid of Bali so that we can study every existing road pattern between Besakih and Denpasar, allowing for every conceivable loop and detour connecting them that would permit a caravan of heavy mobile equipment to transit from point A—Besakih—to point C—Denpasar—within a time-period of one hundred and twenty minutes, also allowing for a stopover at point B and traveling at both differing and varying speeds, averaging out for each run-through from twenty-five kilometers an hour, the minimum overall speed, to sixty, the maximum."

"And where is point B?" the major asks.

"Unknown. That's what we need to determine. Point B is our target. I will want patterns showing where point B might be along any given route at whatever the given speed, allowing variants for each pattern of a five-minute stopover."

"By road patterns, sir, are you saying these grids have to conform to the existing road system in Bali?"

"I am."

"What about trails?"

"Let's not rule them out—providing they have the structural strength and the width to accommodate the size of the vehicles involved."

"Captain Hamzah will provide you with that data," Guntur says.

"I'll have it for you within fifteen minutes," Hamzah tells the major.

"In short," I summarize, "we need to know where an object could have been concealed in Bali within a two-hour time frame allowing for transit between Besakih and Denpasar."

"Then it could never have been dropped off in Singaraja on the northern shore or as far as Negara to the west, since even at sixty kilometers an hour no caravan could reach either point from Besakih and return to Denpasar in two hours. Is that the thrust of your problem, sir?"

"That's it, major. Except for something else I just thought of. Can you work up a set of graphics showing me the water depth of any offshore area in South Bali available to the road system? However, the water has to be deep enough so that a metal object weighing five hundred thousand pounds could not be seen from the surface."

Guntur stares at me so intensely I can feel his eyes on my shoulders.

"It's a place to hide it," I say to him, over my shoulder, while I'm still smiling at the major. "Can you factor that in while you're at it?"

"Yes, sir!" he says. He virtually rubs his palms together, salutes us, and hurries off to collect his staff.

"*Now* will you talk to our prisoner?" Guntur asks.

"As soon as I've checked through the forensic evidence."

"That shouldn't take more than thirty minutes," he says. "The ballistics are clear-cut, both as to the weapons used and the ammunition fired. The transport you've seen. Also the site of the crime. Nothing else that might be incriminatory was found—no convenient packet of matches from a nightclub at Kuta Beach, no letter fallen from a jacket pocket—only a few sets of fingerprints left behind with no suspects to link them with—except our prisoner."

"What about shoes, boots?"

"The casts of their footprints indicate standard combat boots, the sizes all small enough to indicate they were worn by Asians. But since Asians comprise the majority of mankind, I was unable to develop any great sense of elation about this conclusion."

It does not take me thirty minutes to check through the evidence bags and the written findings of the Indonesian Intelligence Unit.

It takes only eight minutes.

Nothing there for an inferential thinker except the conclusive evidence that the assassins were either Asian or Caucasians with uniformly small feet.

"Now I am ready to meet your prisoner," I tell Guntur.

═══CHAPTER═══

9

The colonel leads me along a dim and silent corridor of cells, our footfalls muffled by patches of caustic lime sprinkled over the central concrete walkway. My nostrils constrict against the overpowering stink of piss. Phantoms seem to float inside the dark cells, vaporous shapes without faces, yet here and there I can detect the whites of eyes drifting like ectoplasm in the black-velvet parlor of some quack medium.

At the end of the corridor a soldier snaps to attention at our arrival. He is posted in front of a massive door.

Guntur fishes from his tunic pocket what must be the only key to this VIP lockup.

"How long do you think you'll be with him?"

"Ten minutes? Ten hours? As long as it takes."

The colonel unlocks the door. It swings open onto a black, fecal tomb.

"*Ciau*," I say. I enter. The slab is sealed behind me.

From the far corner I get a sense of something human huddling.

I'm not sure the man actually exists, that he's not a trick of the darkness.

I say nothing until my eyes begin to deliver him to me. He fades into my vision as though emerging from a developing solution in a photo darkroom. First, the prominent head, the skin of the forehead pulled drumtight over the sloping frontal bone, the facial vents closed. Now I begin to perceive the huddled articulation of the bones of his extremities.

In Vietnamese I ask him when he last ate.

He does not answer.

I cross to him, kneel on the dank stone beside him. Nowhere do I see a rice bowl, nowhere a cot, even a pallet. Nothing except the floor to sleep on, to defecate and urinate on.

His eyes peer at me without betraying even the edge of his thoughts. He's Vietnamese, all right, probably in his late thirties.

"Is it that you're refusing food or that they haven't given you any?" I ask him in Vietnamese.

Still no answer.

I jump up, cross to the door.

"Open up!"

Faster than I'd have thought possible, Guntur pushes the door open. I suspect he's been standing outside with the key in the lock.

"Yes?" he asks hopefully.

"When was this man fed last?"

"Fed?"

"Yes, goddam it! Fed! Rice, fish, chicken, water, anything you'd give a dog, okay?"

"We've given him nothing since the attack at the airport."

"Guntur, don't make me think I'm with the wrong team! Why haven't you fed him?"

"We told him—no food until he talks. Standard interrogation procedures are much more severe. I was only saving him for you; otherwise . . ."

"Jesus! Didn't you learn *any*thing in Vietnam? You don't get shit by threatening these people! Get some clean water and a bowl of rice or some fucking fish down here inside of the next five minutes or our deal's off!"

Guntur speaks softly in Balinese to the guard. The trooper trots down the corridor, slipping on the lime patches in his haste.

I motion that I want back in. Guntur swings the door. Once more I disappear into the cavern.

The prisoner has not moved. I really can't bear the sight of his pitiful skull. It reminds me of an afternoon in San Francisco on one of my too-frequent duty trips to the coroner's lab when I saw one of the lab men filling a child's skull with dried beans. That one must have seen my look of nausea, because he grinned at me with the obscene little grin these fellas with the rubber aprons carry everywhere, and he said, you're probably wondering what I'm doing and I said, Yeh, it occurred to me it's not an everyday thing a dude sees, even a dumb cop like me, and he said, I'm filling the skull with beans, and I said, I can see that—but why? He'd have been offended if I hadn't asked. Well, he said, warming to it, when I get all the dried beans in here I fill the skull with water, like this, okay? Now, the pressure of the swelling beans will eventually loosen the natural sutures of the skull, so we can separate the occipital bone from the phenoid from the temporal, et cetera, et cetera. Of course, we can only do this with skulls of people up to the age of fifteen. After that, sutures almost disappear, due to synostosis. As he rattled on, I knew I had reason to celebrate no longer being fifteen.

The soldier enters with a bowl of rice and a gourd filled with water. He sets them on the floor in front of the prisoner. Pieces of something or other decorate the rice, although in the semi-darkness visual identification is iffy.

"Where are the chopsticks?" I call through the open doorway to Guntur.

"No chopsticks!" he says. "He could thrust them into your eyes or your trachea."

"Forgive my carelessness, Guntur," I compliment him. "See what happens when you let your humanity get in the way of kicking the shit out of someone?"

The soldier heaves the door closed behind him.

Again I speak to the prisoner in Vietnamese.

"If you wish to die, don't eat. At least my conscience will be clear. If you wish to live, please accept the food."

"Why should I eat?" he asks. "I will only feel the torture more."

"Ideally," I say, "nobody is going to torture you."

"You? An American? You say that?"

"Americans don't torture people!" I tell him.

"Perhaps not. Americans look the other way when their torture is done for them by others. I have seen it."

"I am not here to fight the war again."

I settle on the floor beside him, my back against the chill rock.

The cave seems to be a natural aperture except where steel and cement have been joined to it around the door. The stone rises precipitously on all sides to a peak, like the inside of a fluted chocolate kiss. Three one-inch holes have been drilled through the rock at the peak. Three shafts of reflected sunlight spear the floor just beyond my feet.

"You speak Vietnamese better than most Vietnamese," he says.

"I had a good teacher."

"Because you speak good Vietnamese, I hope you will not underestimate me and think I will tell you anything."

"I wouldn't expect you to tell me anything simply because I speak your language. That diminishes both of us. But I might expect you to give some serious thought to getting out of this place alive and going home—as a free man."

"I cannot think such thoughts. I am already dead."

"All you have to do to be able to walk out of here," I tell him, "is to give us the name of the people who paid you to kill the colonel. As far as they know, you and the others were all killed in the assault. Give us that name, then give us time to check out the truth of your information, and we will not only release you but put you on a plane to wherever you wish to go—to Hanoi, to Ho Chi Minh City—you name it."

"I will never see my village again," he says.

"That's up to you. Think of yourself stepping off a plane only three days from now at Tan Son Nhut airport."

"Tan Son Nhut," he whispers, as though blowing out a candle.

I can finally see his eyes. They are limpid, even passive. Not the eyes of a terrorist. But what *are* the eyes of a terrorist?

"You're wondering how you can trust us," I continue. "I don't know how to convince you. This time we're all going to have to operate on trust alone—or at least from the position that you have only two possible choices: death, which is what my Indonesian friends are urging—and death, I might add, in a most prolonged and agonizing fashion—or life, which is what *I'm* offering you. You're also wondering why an American is working with counterinsurgency forces of the Indonesian Army. My command of Vietnamese is not good enough for me to make that clear to you. Please simply accept the fact I'm working with them and that at the moment they're giving me a certain freedom to do what I can to help them find the people who paid you.

"Now, if you attacked the colonel out of patriotic motivation, or for some political ideal, I will not expect you to betray that ideal, stupid though I believe it is for a man to die for *any* reason except in the act of defending his own life or the life of those he cares for. But if you attacked the colonel simply for money, or any material payment, then I ask you to consider how much your life is worth—in terms of money. I have only contempt for a man who would die for money. And I feel that you share that same contempt for such meaningless death."

I rise from the floor.

"Give it thought," I say. "It is the single most important decision of your life. It *is* your life. If you decide to trust me, then please eat the rice and drink the water. If you decide not to trust me, then you're right. The faster you starve yourself to death, the swifter your death will be. And the less painful."

I cross through the triple shafts of light and pound on the door.

Guntur opens it, his eyebrows raised expectantly.

I come out past him and slam the door.

Back again on the parade ground, the sun still piercing enough to make me squint even through my Polaroids, I inhale the candied air of Bali and watch a flight of orange cattle egrets scattering overhead.

Beyond, on the parade ground, I can still hear sergeants barking at the recruits wheeling awkwardly in new squads. I feel Guntur's eyes on me, his patience at the straining point.

"Those papers he was carrying are forged," I say. "He's no major in the North Vietnamese Army."

"What?" Guntur exclaims. "Did he confess that?"

"He said nothing," I reply. "But *I'm* telling you. He's a southerner. He tried to speak in the northern dialect, but he kept slipping in and out, especially when I shifted back and forth between the two. When he said 'Tan Son Nhut,' for example, he pronounced 'Nhut' the southern way, *ngac*, not the northern or Tonkinese *nut*. He also said he'd seen Americans with Vietnamese torture teams. That sounds as though he might have been VC—or even ARVN— during Langley's Phoenix operation."

"What does it mean? False papers? Why would anyone want to pass him off as being from the north if he's actually from the south? What does that gain them? And what does it have to do with the bronze bell?"

"I don't know, Guntur. But it sure as hell doesn't help your captain's pet theory—about a Vietnamese-inspired terrorist campaign. Let's add it to the list of unknowns. Do you have a polygraph?"

"A polygraph? Of course! But why do you ask?"

"While he's still got some strength we should give him a test. As soon as we get a list of the places the bell may have been hidden, we can hook him up to the machine and see what kind of emotional response the various locations key in him."

"We have not had the best results with polygraph testing," Guntur says. "We find direct methods more productive. Electric shocks to the genitals are almost one hundred percent effective."

"Not while I'm on the team!"

"You must have a terrible time sorting out what you can and can't do, John Locke. So many moral inhibitions!"

"Not at all! Anything I wouldn't want done to me I don't do to anybody else. Except in self-defense. Then I can blow ass with the best. You'd be amazed how uncomplicated a philosophy that really is, Guntur."

After a moment of watching another flight of birds, Guntur looks back at me.

"Assuming we were to give the prisoner this polygraph test . . . You're aware, of course, that some people can deceive the detector. Particularly those of us who have learned something about controlling our physiological functions with our minds."

"True. So in this case I'd recommend the prisoner be given harmaline or some other effective psychochemical drug to counteract such mind control. You must have contacts with both the KGB and the CIA. Either will happily make available what we need, if only *you* ask."

Guntur awards me his sly grin. "Harmaline is derived from plants we grow on Java. We do not need to look to outside agencies."

"You are truly an emerging nation!" I comment.

Guntur appears pleased by the march of the day's events.

"I don't wish to exhaust you on your very first day," he says. "If you have no objection, I will send you home now with the driver I'm assigning to you. You can then refresh yourself for your evening with your old comrade-in-arms Tip Bradley."

"Oh, my God, I forgot to call!"

"I had the captain tend to it. Tip is delighted. He is expecting you for dinner."

CHAPTER

10

My driver is a Balinese sergeant named Maru. He's a gungi with whom right away I feel tight. I sit next to him up front.

We rumble across a bridge spanning the slim riverbed alongside the main road into the village of Ubud.

Maru points out the Pura Langon, a temple sanctuary facing a reflecting pool spotted with water lilies and the still image of the ornamented gateway to the temple.

We enter a forest of giant banyan trees. The gardens and lawns of the Art Museum are over to that side, Maru informs me, and off there you may see the house of Han Snel, a Dutch painter who has lived and worked in Bali for many years. Ahead now you will see the palace of your friend, the tuan Tip Bradley.

The setting is still ancient Bali, but the signs pointing the way to TIP BRADLEY BATIKS are contemporary American graphics. The one at the last turn of the road is a gigantic flowered neon sign.

Maru stops the jeep in a lot big enough for the four tour buses already there, along with a dozen air-conditioned limousines. The drivers are all squatting together under the largest of the trees, where local Ubud women have set up food stands for tourists come to buy Tip's famous batiks.

"It's liable to be a late night," I tell Maru. "This is an old

73

buddy I haven't seen in years. So you don't have to wait. Just come back around midnight, okay?"

"Thank you, tuan. But my orders are to stand by. In case an extra gun is needed."

"I brought two of my own," I reassure him. "Nobody's going to get to me, Maru, without paying his way."

"I shall wait, sir. It is not only an order. It is an honor."

"Thank you, Maru. In that case, I'll let myself have *two* drinks."

He hands me the gifts I've brought for Tip and his wife and salutes me.

I approach Tip's domain across a walkway so crowded with Japanese tourists setting up their most advantageous camera angles that I have to push my way through, all of us bowing and apologizing to each other until I'm across. The place used to be a rajah's palace, Maru has told me. It stands on an island completely surrounded by a deep moat glutted with lotus blossoms. On the island itself there is nothing that does not appear green—the palms, the breadfruit trees, the glazed-green tiles of the palace itself. All green.

I follow the crowds toward the entrance.

"Freeze!"

Tip's voice.

I lift my hands in mock surrender, the gifts raised high, turn my head to see Tip rushing toward me from a secret footpath bordered by flowers.

He grabs me in a bear-hug.

"Goddam it, Shit Hook!"

He lets me go and we stare at each other with foolish tears in our eyes. He's wearing a batik shirt loose over blue jeans. His hands are streaked with indigo dye, and he smells like hot wax. He's got a crimson hibiscus tucked behind one ear, but he's still the same unbent six feet three he was when he fought alongside me out of Command and Control North. Every time I'd glance over and see him humping through the shrub, my heart would catch, because he never blended with the environment the way the rest of us did. He shone at all times. He always looked as though he'd just stepped straight out of one of those old *Saturday Evening Post* covers—the handsome Protestant white man with cleft chin and noble heart, blue eyes shining with innocent certitude. When he first joined my Black Mambas, despite his impressive list of missions and kills, I despaired for him. No one that fucking magnificent, that tall, could possibly survive the consecutive shit we were into. You needed to be dark as midnight, uglier than a toad, and only six inches tall to come through. Yet Tip never picked up a scratch. I don't think even the leeches came after him. He was Achilles with forty layers of Kevlar over both heels.

"Got yourself quite an operation here," I say.

"Want the tour now or later?"

"Right now."

"Okay. I'll save our living quarters for the finale. We'll start with the retail area."

We enter through the tourist entrance. Twelve clerks are scrambling to serve forty tourists all loading up on batik, either by the yard or already made into a variety of apparel for both men and women.

Behind the cash register a Balinese girl sits on a high stool, watching everything and everybody.

"Sarna," he tells me. "My wife. You'll meet her later. Right now I couldn't get her away from that cash register if we blew the place up. She's the only reason we've got bread in the bank."

He takes me out the back way to the drafting room.

"Heart of the operation," he says, and shows me some of his latest design sketches he's working up.

"How do you like this one?" he asks me.

"Very compelling. But it reminds me of something."

"Yeh? What?"

"Of a man with his guts blown out."

He grins, pleased that I have not lost my perception of such niceties of life. "That's what it is, dad. But everyone around here thinks it's a fucking flower opening at sunrise."

He leads me into the factory where a dozen Balinese artisans are working. He's already drawn this newest design with pencil onto white cloth. Now workers apply wax onto the cloth with cantlings.

"We're sort of unusual here," he explains. "We put the wax on twice for each color rinse—on *both* sides of the cloth. Then..."

He brings me to the rows of huge clay pots, each like a suburban hot tub.

"...we dye the waxed cloth in those."

I watch the streamers of cloth being dipped into the indigo-filled vats.

"Over there we boil the cloth when all the dyeing's finished, to melt the wax out of it. Then we recycle the wax. Neat, huh?"

I grin at him. "You're goddamned right it's neat, Tip. I'm really proud of you!"

He brings me to the living quarters.

No raja ever lived in more splendor.

Tile and bronze and gilt dancing figures and water fountains afloat with lilies.

"Scotch or lavender rice wine?" he asks.

"I can always get scotch. Let's go with the lavender rice wine."

He brings me the drink. I put the gifts down and take the drink. We touch glasses.

"Peace," he toasts.

We drink.

Then, while we wait for Sarna, we let it all flood back. I don't realize until later how he's maneuvered me into doing most of the catch-up talk. He wants to know more about the years 1976 to 1980, when I worked for the San Francisco Police Department. I tell him it served as an effective anodyne for a while. Back in 1977 the use of excessive force was not frowned upon. We were taught that to be a good officer you had to go out into the street and kick ass, so my readjustment from Vietnam to San Francisco wasn't as difficult as I'd feared. My first instructor at the Police Academy wore a T-shirt announcing: WE DON'T HESITATE. WE TERMINATE. He used to tell me, "Locke, you don't look like the asshole the rest of these asshole rookies look like. If you have any time to kill, go back into the holding cells and practice your choke holds on the scumbags in there. You don't strike me as a dude who signed up to do social work, right?" But once I got out of the academy and onto the street, I found it wasn't all sirens and flashing lights the way they show it on TV. It was dull routine. You didn't need a gun. All you needed was an unlimited supply of county-issue yellow legal pads. You'd stand around for hours every day and talk to people, taking down the basics. Just the facts, ma'am. But you never got the facts. I was down in L.A., visiting a buddy who worked homicide in Parker Center, and I saw this sign: WE THE WILLING LED BY THE UNKNOWING ARE DOING THE IMPOSSIBLE FOR THE UNGRATEFUL. WE HAVE DONE SO MUCH FOR SO LONG WITH SO LITTLE WE ARE NOW QUALIFIED TO DO ANYTHING FOR NOTHING. I realized I was looking at my epitaph. Then I got transferred to vice and my kick-off assignment was to work the Tenderloin, concentrating on the Dial-a-Dolly Private Booths where dudes drop a dollar and their pants and try to whack off during the three minutes their dollar buys them talking to a real live nude girl on the other side of the glass who's got the phone in one hand, her clit in the other, while they're in a booth about as big as a portable toilet stinking of dried semen and racing the clock to leave droppings of their own.

"Shit!" Tip says. "Why'd you ever go back to the States?"

"I came to Bali first, you know."

"No, I didn't. When?"

"You weren't here yet. You were still back at art school in the States. I went to Bangkok first, but I knew guys there who had their cocks cut off by Thai girls who got jealous of them. That's when I drifted down here."

"Yeh," Tip agrees. "Never fuck around with a Thai. Not just the chicks; the guys'll cut your dick off just as fast. It's dick-cutting country all right."

"How come *you* decided to come to Bali?" I ask.

"I was finishing art institute in New York, okay? I get in this elevator with a bunch of uptight civs, and I was feeling really high, you know. I'd just finished a painting that was really good. So I'm smiling around in the elevator, and I see that everybody's beginning to panic. I try to make eye contact. Forget it! All these assholes are staring up at the panel with this digital shit ticking off floors like a stopwatch. Nobody's touching each other. You understand, John. The fucking elevator is fucking jammed, but nobody's touching. They're all sort of—of shrunk in, separated. They're dead, I tell myself. These fuckers are dead. For these few seconds, until they get to their floors, this is *dead* time. That starts me thinking about all the rest of the dead time back home—like three hours a night watching TV. Eighty million Americans are being sucked out of their living rooms into glass tubes. They're not *there*. They're in never-never land. Shit, if the Soviets ever wanted the U.S.A. bad enough, all they'd have to do is land during prime time. Anyway, I sold my car, dumped my furniture, and came to Bali. I'd read someplace that everyone here is an artist first and something else second. Everyone I know in Bali is either a dancer, a musician, a sculptor, a painter, or some kind of artisan. Once they've got that going, then they go to work, not the other way around. It's my kind of place, John. And I can't recommend it highly enough for you. Especially in view of what I hear your line of work is."

"What do you hear?"

"That governments and police forces call you in to take on cases they either haven't been able to or can't afford to handle. I hear you're really good at it. So I have to figure that what brings you to Bali is something more than a vacation."

"You figure right. But don't ask me what it is, Tip. This one is really sensitive. Matter of fact, it's so sensitive that if we don't get anywhere with it, things could get hot around here. You might even need some protection if it comes to that."

"That bad?"

"Could be. But don't sweat it. Not yet. I'll let you know in plenty of time."

"Okay, we've skipped all over the map. Now I have to ask you the big one." He pauses. I don't help him. "All right?"

"She's dead, Tip," I say.

This is the first silence between us since Tip shouted, "Freeze!" an hour ago. Only the *tkitjak* lizards can be heard somewhere on the walls or in the eaves, smacking away.

"I was with her the morning of the last day. But she still wouldn't come out with me. Would you believe that the CO of the NVA forces waiting in Loc Ninh for us to leave so they could march in was her old history teacher?"

"General Tran Van Tra?"

"In person. She got on her bike and went out to welcome him. Last I ever saw of her she was heading toward the Newport Bridge."

"Jesus, man!"

"Then nothing for five years. Not a word! I couldn't believe it, because you know I have a lot of connections in high places. There was just no way anyone as well known or as important as Doan Thi—the leading poetess in Vietnam, in Asia for that matter—could simply disappear for five years. Unless she'd been executed and buried secretly. But even that would have come out after five years! Then I got word through the Quakers that she was alive and well—but in a reeducation camp. That's about the time I was getting ready to leave the police force in San Francisco and begin working down in San Diego with my dad, building *Steel Tiger*. I was well into the South Pacific and heading this way when I heard she'd died. But exactly when, and under what circumstances, I still don't know."

"She was one beautiful lady," Tip says. "I was glad I was there when you met her. Just seeing the two of you together was a real high. I guess it's one of the reasons I knew I had to find *my* ideal woman over here, not in an aerobics class in New York City. Hey, man, if I don't clean up for dinner, I'll hear about it later! I need about fifteen minutes. You okay here?"

"Fine."

He leaves, but is back at once.

"Phone call for you. You can pick it up over there."

He disappears again. I take the call.

"Locke here."

"Mr. Locke," a man's voice says. The accent is Asian, but nothing I can isolate as being Chinese, Japanese, or anything regionally identifiable. "There is still time for you to withdraw. We have no wish to harm you. But by agreeing to assist lackeys of a police state you are placing hopes and aspirations we have for our own freedom in jeopardy. If you give us your word that you will not cooperate with Colonel Katrini and his repressive forces or with any other Indonesian government unit, we will spare you and your friends."

"Friends?" I ask.

"Your wartime buddy, Tip Bradley, and his wife, Sarna, and their son, Raku."

"Why involve them?" I ask. "I give you my word Tip knows nothing about what I'm doing in Bali. I have no intention of telling him. Leave him out of this!"

"I'm afraid," the voice says, "we are unable to do that. He is a much easier target than you, Mr. Locke, and far easier than Colonel Katrini or his Captain Hamzah. If we do not have evidence within forty-eight hours that you have withdrawn your services, we shall kill Mr. Bradley and his family."

"How will you know if I've withdrawn?"

"We will know."

The call ends. I hold the phone to my ear for a full minute, not having the least notion of what I must do now.

"Good evening, Mr. Locke."

I look over. Tip's young Balinese wife enters with a five-year-old boy. Sarna is dressed in a trailing sarong with a silk breast band. Her hair is drawn back from her high curving forehead and adorned with flowers.

"Good evening," I say. They come to me, Sarna handing a

blossom to the child, who reaches up toward me. I kneel, and Raku tucks a flower behind my ear with his chubby child's fingers.

"I hope you and my husband have been catching up with old times," Sarna says. "There is no one he can talk to about Vietnam. Sometimes I hear him talking to himself about it. But that is not the same as talking to someone who shares your feelings."

"Not quite," I agree.

But my thoughts are elsewhere. Still with that voice on the phone. With his message.

"Would you please excuse me?" I ask. "I have to speak to my driver. I'll be right back."

"I hope you like Balinese food," she says.

"I do," I tell her.

I try to leave as swiftly as I can without giving the appearance of flight.

Outside, the last of the tourists are packing it in for the day. The clerks in the retail shop and the workers in the batik factory are sweeping up and closing for the night.

The last bus is loading as I run to the parking area. The jeep is there, but no sign of Maru.

A pebble lands at my feet. I whirl.

Maru is partly concealed behind a tree. He lowers his leveled SMG and grins at me.

"Tuan looks for me?"

"Stay where you are," I tell him. "You're a good man, Maru, keeping under cover, not just standing out here on the bull's eye. I want you to get on the radio. Tell Colonel Katrini to come out here as soon as he can with half a dozen men."

"Yes, tuan."

"And don't leave your back uncovered. Somebody just called me on the phone. Threatening to kill my friends. They could already be on site. So be warned."

I run back to Tip's island, wishing he had a drawbridge he could raise and a squadron of ruby-eyed crocs patrolling his lily pond.

CHAPTER

11

The main course at dinner is the Balinese delicacy *lawar* served on banana leaves. Sarna tells me with pride that Tip has personally prepared it in honor of my coming. While the women in Bali prepare the everyday food of the household, the men, she explains, assume charge of dishes for festivals and other special occasions.

Lawar is sea turtle. The meat is chopped and cooked with grated coconut and spices flavored with tamarind leaves. Following the *lawar* comes *saté lilit*, this being a paste of meat, spices, and coconut cream roasted on bamboo sticks over charcoal.

With each successive course, and seeing how Sarna's eyes seldom leave her husband, how she touches him at every opportunity as if to make sure he is not a dream, I feel more and more constrained about how to warn Tip of the peril my coming to visit him has introduced into his idyllic life.

Only when the colonel has arrived, his men been positioned outside, and Guntur has joined us for *ketan* and coffee, do I feel I can no longer postpone telling Tip about the influx of snakes into his Eden. I wait until Sarna has reason to excuse herself and Guntur and I are alone with Tip.

"May I tell him *every*thing?" I ask.

"In this case, by all means," Guntur agrees.

From the massacre at Pura Besakih to Guntur's chuting into the Halmahera Sea to the telephone call of two hours ago, I lay it all on Tip, bringing us to this moment of decision—what are the moves to be now that Tip and his family have unwittingly become part of the kitty?

"Sounds like you're dealing with some pretty seasoned tarantulas," he says when I've finished spelling it out.

"Something got lost in the translation," I correct. "Not just us! You, too, Tip! You and your wife and your son! The sonofabitch on the phone couldn't have been clearer on that point. I told him you weren't involved. He said that didn't matter. What did matter was that you're a softer target than we are. He's right, ol' buddy. And you're in deep shit because you've lost your surveillance awareness. You lack both force structure and design characteristics that ensure you any kind of long shelf life. Can we start from that basic assumption?"

"Know what I used to call the skipper here?" Tip asks the colonel. "'Shit Hook,' I tagged him. That's what the grunts called the army's CH-47 Chinook choppers, because they could lug around some real heavy loads. John was always getting us out of ambushes and leading us safely through undesirable elements and generally saving our pussies to the point where the whole team began calling him 'Shit Hook.' Right, skipper?"

"You've never lived," I tell Guntur, "until you've been called 'Shit Hook' by men who mean it as a compliment. But you changed the subject, Tip. I asked if you agree there's no way you can fight back against these people."

"I agree," he concedes. "Besides, I promised myself I'd never pick up a gun again as long as I live. What am I going to do, Shit Hook, dye them if they move in?"

"The colonel has men outside—positioned far enough out that no gravel belly with an ART-IV mounted on a sniper rifle is going to wax you from four hundred meters. They'll hang right out there, patrolling, until the colonel and I have scoped out the competition and put all the assholes in a box and closed the lid. Meantime, we want you to stay indoors, not put yourself or your family in anybody's lane of fire."

"You still without a religion, John?" Tip asks.

"Not your kind," I say. "But I'm working on something of my own."

"I'm a Lutheran," Tip tells the colonel. "Five hundred years ago Martin Luther nailed his list of ninety-five objections to the Inquisition on a church door in Wittenberg and said, 'Here I stand. I can do no other. So help me God!' I can't say it any better. We'll stay indoors, John. How long do you think it'll take you to stake out their watering hole?"

"It can't be more than ten days from tomorrow—that's when the first delegation of tour agents arrives. Either we'll have it taped before then or there'll be tanks in the streets."

"I hesitate to suggest this, Mr. Bradley," the colonel interposes, "but it might be advisable for you to close down until then. Anyone could come onto the premises, disguised as a tourist shopping for batik, and use either automatic weapons or grenades against you and your family."

"We could use the time to get caught up with back orders," Tip agrees. "We'll simply shut down the retail end of things, give the salesgirls a week off with pay, and keep just the factory going. All these people in the factory have worked for us for six or seven years. I trust them with my son's life. I'll give you their names and photographs. You can have your men clear them through each morning."

"Thank you, Mr. Bradley. I hope this inconvenience will pass quickly."

"How will your wife take it?" I ask.

"She'll complain into my ear all night, every night about the business we're losing, especially since you tell me I can't give her the real story."

"I remind you," the colonel says, "that though she is your wife, first she is a Balinese. The mere knowledge that the Great Bronze Bell of Mount Agung has been stolen will send her into a frenzy unlike anything you could imagine. She will be unable to keep it a secret. She will tell a sister, a brother. And then!" Guntur raises his hands in imitation of a volcano erupting.

"Blame your troubles on the Vietnamese," I say. "Everyone else does. Tell her a Vietnamese group arrives in Bali tomorrow, and since both you and I are at the top of a secret hit list kept by Hanoi because of our wartime Psy-Ops with SOG, you've decided to follow the advice given you tonight by Colonel Katrini, head of COIN-OPS, who has assigned soldiers to protect you until the Vietnamese have gone home. If that crock of shit doesn't snow her, Tip, nothing in the world will!"

* * *

I head home to my *bale* in Batubulan in a Scout Ferret with Guntur.

"I need a car," I tell him. "A car of my own."

"You did not like the jeep and the sergeant I assigned?"

"Sergeant Maru? I couldn't ask for a better man. But I need to move around less conspicuously. Also we're too bunched up. We need to divide forces so we can cover more ground."

"Very well. I'll get you your own jeep."

"No jeep, no driver! Just a car, so I can look more like a civilian and have more loiter time. I'll drive myself."

"What have you against the jeep? They are the backbone of my operation—jeeps and helicopters!"

"Jeeps flip over on high-speed turns. The way things are going, I may be doing a few such. I want something user friendly for the kind of workouts I may have to give it."

"Will a Mercedes do?"

"Rather nicely, thank you. With a few modifications. First, the tires. Only radials. Filled with flat-run foam. In case somebody shoots them out, I can still make a few miles down the road, pick my own stopping point."

"Consider it done."

"I want quartz-iodine lights, not the standard sealed beams."

"What is the advantage?"

"Quartz iodine doubles the scope of your night vision—makes it possible for you to drive faster than the people trying to follow you."

"You shall have quartz iodine."

"And a locking gas cap."

"Balinese do not steal fuel."

"Not worried about the Balinese. I'm worried about some clodo dropping shit into my tank."

"Then how about our also welding a bolt into the tailpipe to prevent someone from stuffing a bomb up there?"

"Guntur, my compliments to the chef. By all means—and a good thick bolt while you're at it. I also want the bumpers reinforced—a two-inch pipe welded to the frame, right out in front of the bumper. Okay. Are you remembering all this, or do you think you ought to be taking notes?"

"I'm remembering it."

"And please have your mechanics put aluminum plates around

the backs of both front seats—at least three-quarters of an inch thick. That should stop anything up to fifty caliber."

"Why don't I simply assign you one of our tanks?"

"I've told you how I feel about tanks! Oh, and please hide a package of razors in the trunk."

"Do you plan to shave there?"

"Also a crowbar."

"A crowbar? Razor blades? Exotic, John, even for you."

"If some bushers should overpower me, what they'd probably do in an area as populated as Bali—to avoid having witnesses able to identify them later—is toss me into the trunk and drive out to some isolated place where they can splash me in private. With the razor blades I can cut my bindings. With the crowbar I can break out of the trunk."

"Shouldn't I put a gun back there, too?"

"The Bellini will be riding shotgun back there," I say. "My little ace in the hole."

The radioman up front in our scout car responds to some sudden electronic sputtering in Indonesian. He takes the message, replies in a clear affirmative, passes a scrawled note back to the colonel.

Katrini appears pleased. "The major and his computers have our roadway grids," he announces. "He wonders if we would like to evaluate them tonight or wait until morning."

"Tonight, of course."

Guntur gives the driver his orders.

The Ferret accelerates, racing through Batubulan and past the family compound where I've stashed my shaving kit and duffel bag—my home away from *Steel Tiger*.

I have a momentary flash of regret that the computer major is so gung ho. The day has taken its toll, and the thought of crawling between my batik sheets with good men awake on the perimeter and Vishnu guarding my ceiling is a seductive one.

The recalled vision of Dasima in the bathing pool rises in front of me like a new billboard going up on Sunset Boulevard. It must be an evocation of the music I hear coming from everywhere between Batubulan and neighboring Tohpati.

The metallic jangling of *gamelans* floats above the hollow throbbing of drums, but I hear more than one orchestra. The sounds emanate from different platforms, some borne thin and distant, others close and furious, but all to different drummers, stopping, starting, creating a rippling perspective, layering the night.

Then again we are in Denpasar, having to slow along its rubbly streets. We pass the Kreneng Bus Terminal, where two police officers in light khaki uniforms with snugged-in Sam Browne belts sit arrogantly in a white Suzuki jeep marked POLISI and stare out with brutal blindness through black glasses at the birdlike blonde Aussie girls boarding a bus for eastern Bali.

We crawl past the open-air night market. The odors of fried rice and noodle soup blend with the acrid bite of Nepalese hash. In back lanes I catch sight of dark, furtive moves—twelve-year-old pushers and pubescent hookers.

"Javanese," Guntur comments, seeing my policeman's eye roving these backwater negotiations.

"Javanese what?" I ask.

"Javanese whores. Balinese girls do not sell their bodies."

"Have you worked these people?" I ask. "I can't believe they were all obediently indoors that morning. One of them must have seen something."

He points to the old women selling clothes and materials. They flail unabashedly into the hundreds of people of all ages and races milling through the market.

"*Ibus*, we call them," Guntur says. "The sellers. They are everywhere in Bali. If anyone would have seen anything, *they* would have. Most of them are paid police informers. I have spoken personally to their leaders. They saw nothing, know nothing we can use."

I listen to their sales pitches in English, French, German, and Japanese. "It's up to you," they cry. "You make offer. It's up to you."

Then, thankfully, we are free of Denpasar again, out of the bottleneck, back into the countryside and speeding toward army headquarters.

In a special screening room of the computer section at COIN-OPS headquarters in Tabanan, Guntur and I are met by Captain Hamzah. With the computer major explaining while we project, we study electronic overlays beamed onto a map of Bali. Each overlay has been given a code number. We ponder forty-seven successive overlays, each pinpointing a location where a truck carrying a heavy metal object could have dropped it off, then completed the transit between Besakih and Denpasar within the allotted one hundred and twenty minutes. Of those forty-seven locations, nineteen are in areas adjacent to the sea. And of these nineteen, only twelve are near deep water, the others opening onto shallow water confined inside the reef.

The longer I watch the overlays being projected over the map of Bali, the more the configuration begins to resemble Snoopy's head, the cocky, slightly uptilted nose the island's long western thrust, the brow at Singaraja, the eye at Lake Buyun, the neck at Benoa. The bell becomes the flea, hiding somewhere along Snoopy's neck in South Bali. But, of course, I keep this similitude to myself. One does not share such frivolity with Indonesian hosts, still smarting from the colonial complex.

I compliment the major on his speedy graphics and ask if he will give us a printout of these locations. Morning is soon enough.

"I'll start with the twelve deep-water locations where it could have been dumped for pick up at a later time," I tell Guntur and Captain Hamzah. "That leaves seven places on the shoreline where it could still be hidden ashore, plus twenty-eight other inland sites. May I suggest we divide the work? Using helicopters for overview and ground teams with metal detectors for on-site search, let's eyeball every square inch of space within these forty-seven specific areas. And let's remember that the more remote the site from human presence, the more likely it would have been chosen as a place to conceal the bell."

"Forgive me, sir," Hamzah says, "but is it not more likely that the thieves have already removed the bell from Bali and that our time and effort might be better directed toward tracking down the terrorists before they strike again?"

"The bell is still in Bali," I say.

"How do we know that?" he asks.

"We don't. But I'm sure that by now Colonel Katrini has had a complete report from all ships in the waters of south Bali on the morning of the incident and has interviewed their crews and checked out their cargoes. And since there are no decent ports in Bali able to accommodate any vessel large enough to transport the bell nor any civilian aircraft capable of taking it by air, and since this *is* an island, I have to assume the bell is either still on Bali or submerged in the waters along its southern shoreline."

The captain glances at Guntur. "Sir, I was not given any assignment to search ships."

Guntur appears surprisingly brusque with this officer he has defended from my denigration. "I turned that over to the navy, captain! Mr. Locke is quite right in his assumptions. I, too, am convinced the bell is still in Bali."

"Allah be thanked!" the captain says fervently.

On the road back to Batubulan near midnight, I can no longer hear the tinkling of the ubiquitous *gamelans*.

Only the distant wailing of a dog.

I observe Guntur muttering to himself.

"Am I missing something?" I ask.

"Miserable *anjings*!" he says. "The cursed dogs of Bali! Mangiest in the world!"

The wailing trails off. Now I can hear nothing from the night except the rustling of palm fronds.

I see that Guntur is praying. "I have asked the gods to punish those who are putting us through this with a lingering and painful death, then to bring them back as street dogs in Denpasar. I can conceive of no worse fate."

Of course, I can, but it is too late an hour for arguments in this arena.

We stop at the gate of the family compound.

A personnel carrier hunkers in the darkness a hundred yards down the road. A Red Beret stands behind a machine gun and watches us through his night scope.

"Your Mercedes will be delivered to you by midmorning," Guntur tells me. "In return I expect you to take my niece with you."

"Why?"

"She can interpret for you—not only the words but the thoughts and the true reactions of those you'll be interrogating. She can also serve as your guide. Otherwise, you'll waste more time fending off street hawkers than you will searching for the bell."

"You forget I'm a class-A primary moving target. What if Dasima gets into the crossfire?"

"No Asian will kill the leading dancer of Indonesia," he says. "Her mere presence with you is more protection than your armored vest and all your guns."

"It's your turf, Guntur, your niece, and your idea! Okay, we'll give it a day or two and see if it flies. Fair enough?"

He's wearing that cookie-jar grin again. What devious scheme of his does this arrangement benefit?

"May your dreams be blessed," he says as I climb down from the Ferret.

"Thank you, Guntur. Good night."

I leave him, enter through the gateway, remembering to take a sharp left to avoid piling into the *aling-aling*, and find my way through the darkness to my *bale*.

I shed the day's sweat and dirt in the bathing pool where only this morning I had marveled at Dasima's beauty. As I wash and sponge myself, I keep hoping one of the four doors leading to the pool will suddenly open and there she'll be, smiling at me, that she'll say nothing, but step down into the water with me. Of course, such fantasies are never realized. Moments later, having saluted Vishnu, I am between batik sheets and buried in sleep.

Sometime later I drift up again and dream of Dasima.

She is dancing. She performs the classical motion I remember from watching Balinese dancers when I was here before. They call it something that sounds like "*gelayak*," the bending movement of a tree bowing under the weight of many flowers.

I open my eyes.

I am not dreaming.

Dasima hovers inside the veranda of my *bale*. She holds a silk robe closed at her breasts. She appears diffused in the darkness, milky looking through the white mosquito netting, as though the moon has set into her body. Yet she smells of dawn.

"The time is propitious," she whispers. "I have consulted all the omens, every calendar, any number of priests, even the *balian*s who know both left-hand magic and right-hand magic. All agree it is my time for *pengipoek*."

She comes to the bed, her movement serene, yet sinuous, the tiny bell on her toe tinkling.

She unties a binding of the net.

"*Pengipoek?*" I ask.

"Lovemaking."

The silk robe slips from her.

She is as naked as I saw her this morning.

Except that now she does not stand in waist-deep water.

CHAPTER

12

Dasima slides through the opening in the net and into my bed, placing herself only inches away, her great velvety eyes wide open to mine.

"Together," she whispers, "we shall turn crystal into gold."

"Dasima, at a moment like this any guy who insists on a few words of discussion before turning crystal into gold would by all criteria be considered the world's number-one nerd. But at the risk of looking an incredible gift horse in the mouth, I do have to ask some basic questions."

"From everything I know of you, I expected you to say that."

"It would have been gutsier to say nothing, simply to go with the flow."

"But not in character!"

"Right! Okay, primary question: what would your parents think of this?"

"I've discussed it with my mother. She's taken my father to stay with her family until tomorrow. She wants us to be able to awaken together as the sun rises and sheds its light on us, then to be able to bathe together in the pool where you first saw me— with no thought of interruption."

"I believe we can dispense with my first question. Now, what about the servants? Gossiping."

"Gossiping?" She laughs. "That's all they've been doing since I told them how I saw you naked at the pool, wanting me. They are filled with envy!"

"All right. Final question."

She places a finger on my lips. "No, I have never yet made love with any man."

"That wasn't the question."

"No, I will not become pregnant."

"Can we be a little more specific about that?"

"You do not have to take precautions. I am protected."

"Something more reliable than a bowl of rice at the foot of the goddess of love?"

She laughs against my neck.

"A Balinese device my mother gave me."

She throws back the batik sheet I'm under and gazes with almost childlike wonder at my tumescence, her interest at the moment more anatomical than erotic.

"It is one thing to see a phallus carved of stone on our statues, another to see one of living flesh. I have wondered how it would feel within me, painful or pleasurable."

"I wouldn't recommend the stone version," I say.

"When I was a little girl, I watched stallions mount our mares. The males appeared to be doing everything, having all the pleasure; the mares simply stood and waited until the stallions had finished. One mare was quietly grazing while a stallion mated with her."

"Very bad for his morale," I say.

"And it was the same with the dogs I watched, with the pigs and the chickens. The bitches and the sows and the hens were all receiving—giving nothing back. I will never be like the mare or the bitch or the sow or the hen. My body and my spirit are too eager. I want to make love with you, John, as though I am both mare *and* stallion!"

"Fair enough," I agree. "But for a little while, until the right moment comes, there's nothing wrong with receiving. Let me show you."

I reach my palm to her cheek. It feels moist against my hand, as though she's rubbed herself with coconut oil, yet she has no scent of oil on her body.

Slowly I bring her lips to mine. It is less a first kiss, less the hungering of lips and tongue, than it is a simple touching, a first contact, a scenting. I rotate my face against hers, our noses ridged together, our cheeks, our foreheads, our ears in exploration.

"May all devils, djinns, lions and every enemy stay far away from my love," she whispers into my ear.

I ease her onto her back and arrange her long raven hair over the pillow to either side of her face. I take her right hand in mine, hold it palm up, and begin to rub it with my thumb in ever-widening circles. Then one by one I massage her fingers, pulling at the caps of her fingertips, finally kissing her palm, then repeating the same massage on her left hand.

She watches me, surprised I have not already seized and possessed her.

I slide down her body to her kneecaps, curve my fingers so they're lightly touching the side of her knee. I listen to her breathing. As she lets out her breath, I start my stroke, moving my thumbs around the bony parts of her knee. I continue the motions as her body begins to come even more alive.

"Where did you learn to do that?" she murmurs.

"In Tinian," I tell her. "From a blind Japanese masseur."

"Imagine how wonderful that feels to a dancer!" she exclaims. "My legs always ache!"

I drum lightly on her kneecap with my fingertips, then go to work on the hollows at the sides, pressing my forefingers into the cleft on the bottom of her knee just above her calf.

She trembles under my touch. My body begins to listen to hers, feeling for her inner rhythms. I do not intend to fail by rushing. Dasima is that rare being with whom you create a circle together, not the kind of girl who isolates you, making you feel even more detached when you're done with each other.

I finish with Dasima's knees. She reaches up her arms to me, but I spread them above her head and roll her onto her stomach.

Lightly, I place both hands, palms down, at the base of her spine, fingers pointing toward her shoulders, and with the sides of my thumbs slowly and progressively outline each side of her vertebral column until I've reached the base of her neck. I soothe the nape at the same instant I move my other hand back to the base of her spine and for a while I continue to alternate hands, running the heel of each successively up her spine. Then I spread my palms over both cheeks of her buttocks and begin to move them in slow circles.

BRONZE BELL

She is moaning and purring as I roll her over face up and massage her inner thighs, barely grazing her genital lips. I work on her toes and the bottoms of her feet. From there I move to her neck, her cheekbones and her temples, then finally to her breasts. They become captives in my hands, but I deliberately avoid touching her upthrust nipples. I move both her breasts in the same direction, using slow, circular motions, then in the opposite direction. She's breathing heavily, continuously reaching out for me, making delightful little sounds.

I drop between her knees, her thighs yawning to encompass me, but instead of entering her, as she expects, I rub my thumbs down both of her hipbones, forming tiny circles as I work toward her groin, caressing the trenches where her legs join her pelvis. Starting at the peak of her vulva I gently massage the folds, turning them outward and skimming my forefinger down her inner lips, barely touching the opening of her vagina.

I bend, press her mons to my face, and with my fingertips grasp and pinch her nipples.

Sobbing with delight, she winds herself around me, clutching my head to her, her hard young body seeking and pliant.

From somewhere in the past I dredge up the words of a long-forgotten poem I'd read somewhere. It idles through my mind again:

> *I kiss her moving mouth,*
> *Her swart, hilarious skin.*
> *She breaks my breath in half.*
> *She frolics like a beast.*
> *And I dance round and round,*
> *A fond and foolish man,*
> *And see and suffer myself*
> *In another being, at last.*

With Dasima I tap a reservoir of primal needs. We fuse as wildly as naked cells.

"Mold me, shape me," she pleads. "Make me into a gate no one after you will ever be able to unlock."

She begins the night as my pupil. By dawn she is my teacher. Her dexterous body summons me up and recycles me until finally I let myself plunge into the abyss of lost identity, escaping from the neutral zone where all tomorrows must be faced alone.

CHAPTER

13

By the time Guntur arrives at the compound, Dasima and I have bathed together in the pool, and she has learned what I have tried to tell her—that humans are not porpoises and that copulation between consenting adults under or in water is not what that famous roll in the surf in *From Here to Eternity* would have you believe. The natural lubrication of the female is sluiced away by water, and things become much too abrasive.

After the water sports, Dasima watches me run through my dutiful morning conditioning. She's especially fascinated by a backbend pushup, one of my mainstays. You lie on your back, then form an arch with your body thrusting upward from the floor, both hands and feet drawn as near to your back as you can possibly get them. This arc stretches and strengthens the back, arms, and legs. I find that for fluidity and combat readiness it is the primary exercise of them all, although I supplement it with splits and stretching.

Dasima bends like bamboo. "Is this right?" she asks. Her arc is one-eighty to my forty-five degrees. She joins me as I stretch, and I quit while I'm ahead and simply watch her. The grace and ease with which she can articulate every joint in her body is awesome.

Just before Guntur arrives, the whole gaggle of kitchen girls troops into my *bale* to serve Dasima and me breakfast in bed. They bombard her with questions in Balinese even as they stare with mischievous eyes at me and sigh with wonder and envy. Or so I would like to think.

Then they are gone, in a laughing flutter.

And Dasima soon after, but not before she has come toe to toe with me, knee to knee, thigh to thigh, our bodies holding, sensing each other exquisitely, our lips close, the tips of our noses touching.

"I am going with you," she says. "To be your eyes and ears."

"I know."

"May all devils, djinns, lions, and every enemy stay far away from my love," she repeats. Then, like a honeybee exhausting the flower, she is gone.

Moments later Guntur appears at the *bale*.

"I brought your Mercedes. With all the modifications completed. Your Bellini is concealed in the trunk, along with the razor blades and the crowbar."

"Be a goddamned shame if they didn't jump me now, wouldn't it?"

"Pac-Pet is demanding we release the truck and crane. Have you any reason to keep their equipment longer?"

"None that I can think of, except—" Something fires an electrode in my head. "Why wasn't there a report in that evidence I went through about the theft from Pac-Pet? I don't remember seeing any witness interview with the guard who discovered the equipment was taken—or any report on the location from which it disappeared."

"That is my fault," Guntur confesses. "It was such a minor detail I suppose I overlooked sending the intelligence team to Pac-Pet to talk to the guard. But in fact I handled that aspect personally. I had a call shortly before dawn the morning of the massacre from Chartwell himself reporting the equipment missing. Matter of fact, he called me at the base and woke me up. Just after oh-five-hundred. He was furious and made certain accusations which I must admit angered me. Since then we have both apologized to each other, although I must say I suspect he's a bloody racist, implying that *all* Indonesians are thieves and that it is a matter of historical record that we Balinese used to plunder all European ships that piled up on our reefs."

"Chartwell? Who is Chartwell?"

"Walton Chartwell. Regional director for Pacific-Petroleum. He's well connected in Jakarta and one of the richest foreigners working in Indonesia. If I did not have better connections than his, I could have put myself in jeopardy shouting back at him as I did."

"Where's Pac-Pet located?"

"Their offices are in Denpasar. Their equipment depot and engineering center is up the coast near Padangbai. Apparently the truck and crane were taken sometime around four that morning during a period when the guards were changing shifts. The five o'clock watchman was the one who called Chartwell. He'd found the truck gate unlocked, and when he investigated, he discovered the missing equipment."

Guntur hands me the printout of the computer locations we'd screened the night before.

"I've got Captain Hamzah and his team already working over the places I've checked in red. Yours I've checked in blue. I'll take the remainder. I've got photo crews out shooting slides of each location. By tomorrow we will be able to screen them for your Vietnamese friend, once we've dosed him with the appropriate truth drugs and hooked him up to a polygraph."

"Is he eating?"

"Like a vulture."

"That's good news. Damn good news, Guntur! We may not have to use the polygraph. He may just volunteer the information we need if I work on him. But don't let anybody fuck this man over! He's our key to this thing. All he has to do is drop some names and we can toss away the rest of the ball of wax. Double the guard on him! And *be nice!*"

"We're due at the reception tonight at twenty-hundred hours," he reminds me. "Please be sure to be back here no later than two hours before then. Dasima is dancing. She requires a great deal of time to prepare."

But I only hear him off the lobe of one ear. Something about the Pac-Pet thing won't go away.

"Did you get an engine-log report?" I ask suddenly.

"An engine-log report? I don't understand."

"For the truck. The engine hours are always logged in big oil operations like these."

"Of course!" he says excitedly. "Why didn't I think to ask?"

BRONZE BELL

"You're a bird colonel, remember? You never have to say you're sorry."

"I shall inquire at once! That will let us pinpoint exactly how far the truck traveled, eliminate all margin of error. Thank you, John! You see, police training does have a value, doesn't it?"

Dasima's arrival spares me from having to comment on the value of my police training. She's wearing basic white: short skirt, gauzy top with spaghetti straps, and a white band across her marvelously curving forehead and tucked under her long black hair. I think to myself that a lot of Balinese boys are going to be flaring their nostrils today to see her tooling around with an *orang barat* in the Mercedes, but those are the breaks, kids.

She kisses her uncle, takes my hand, and leads me out of the compound.

The Mercedes is a full-fledged 350-SEL. It looks new enough to have just come out of the crate.

I take a few minutes to checklist the modifications. Guntur's mechanics have done wonders overnight. In the trunk I find the Bellini strapped in behind a false wall. It is fully loaded. Two boxes of shells are held in place by Velcro. Along with the razor blades and the crowbar. No way am I going to get lucky enough to be tossed into this trunk. Never happens when you're prepared. I learned that at sea. Spot a squall, change sails down, the squall disappears. Spot a squall, stay overcanvased, you'll get blasted nine times running.

I climb behind the wheel, belt up, and start the engine. It purrs like a well-fed tiger. Dasima settles beside me up front, her miniskirt hiking to the top of her glistening thighs. As we pass the Saracen troop carrier parked at the end of the compound wall, I wave to the machine gunner. He salutes me, but I suspect he's looking down at Dasima's thighs.

"May we make one stop in Denpasar?" she asks.

"Whatever," I agree. "Especially since we have to go through Denpasar, anyway, to get to Kuta Beach."

"Why are you going to Kuta Beach?" she asks.

"Surfers."

Her right hand reaches across her and steals to my crotch. Her long nails flick at me. After a moment, I grow in her palm. "It has a separate life from yours, does it not?" she asks.

"I try not to let it out on its own," I say, "but sometimes it slips its leash."

97

"I am still in a trance from last night." She manages a delicious little shiver without actually moving her body. "There are parts of me still moving, even though I command them to stop. Feel."

She brings one of my hands from the wheel and cups it over the mound under her cotton underpants. I can feel the pulsing between her legs. "And my breasts tingle. How can I wait until tonight?"

"We have to help each other," I say. "I promise not to touch you until tonight if you promise not to touch me, okay?"

I remove my hand from her, and laughing, she takes hers from me.

In Denpasar again, locked into a mushroom cloud of diesel fumes, we approach a complex of buildings within walls, the Kokar, Dasima informs me, Bali's leading dance academy. I drive through the gateway into a spacious courtyard faced on three sides by buildings from which the music of a dozen *gamelans* jingles. I park under a flamboyant tree, its trunk painted curiously blue and white.

"Here I studied dance for nine years," Dasima tells me. "Now I teach others. I shan't be long. If you wish to, look around."

She gets out and crosses toward the administration building. I watch her and delight in the lightness of her going. When she's floated away into the building, I get out and walk along the open fronts of the classrooms. Girls are being taught in one section, I observe, boys in another. The dancers wear black leotards, cotton sweatshirts, and sashes ranging from yellow and orange to green and blue. They are following the fixed gestures of their teachers, either to tape machines or to live *gamelan* groups, every movement linked to the rhythm of the music. I watch one class of girls who can be no older than twelve. They appear to be working solely on foot accents. Another group is practicing glances of the eyes, glances that project anger, violent glances sweeping up and down as though piercing some imaginary enemy, dreamy glances, glances that stare off into the distance. I watch nine-year-old boys leaping off the ground as if their feet were on fire. It strikes me that many of the movements I'm seeing I've seen elsewhere in Bali since I arrived. Of course! I've seen these attitudes in the very posturing of the everyday life of the people and in the positions of the stone figures in their temples. These dancers, I see, are being taught not to express *themselves*, as our dancers in the West do, but to function solely as mirrors, to serve as the living transition from stone to flesh and to perpetuate the myths and the traditions of the people.

As I approach the building into which Dasima has gone, I hear raised voices. Not angry voices but definitely argumentative. Guntur has explained to me that the Balinese do not flare up the way we do at life's little annoyances. They don't shout at you to show their anger. They simply stick a kris into you if you push them too hard. But quietly. And stylishly.

I glance through the open veranda toward the voices and discover Dasima in the center of a circle of men and women who appear to be both harassing her and pleading with her. And now I can see the dancer in her, one foot planted in a way that indicates no compromise, the slightly averted head, the violent glance sweeping up and down, one arm stiff at her side in rejection, hand turned up, fingers bent like talons. Then she sweeps out of the midst of the group and strides toward me like an infuriated princess.

The Balinese follow her out, speaking softly, yet insistently. She ignores them, gets into the Mercedes, and slams the door. They continue to implore her from the steps. I slip behind the wheel and start the engine.

"Would it be rude if I just drove away?" I ask.

"The sooner the better!"

I circle the courtyard and ease out into Denpasar's traffic.

I wait for her to discuss the incident or not, as she chooses. After a while, it's apparent she has no intention of clarifying the event. She points ahead.

"Stop over there, please, Tanah."

"Tanah?"

She doesn't answer. I stop the car.

"I have been puzzling all morning what I am to call you," she says. "John is not a suitable name for my lover. I have selected Tanah instead. *Tanah* means 'the earth.' This is what you are to me, my love: earth—everything that feeds and sustains life. Come, I wish to show you something."

I get out, lock the car, and do an eye sweep of the area. Denpasar is hardly a qualified site for a terr ambush. No way to break out of the traffic jam. Possibly Guntur is right. With Dasima I may be safe from attack.

I accept her arm, slipping my hand into the cleft between her arm and her breast. No hand-in-hand stuff with a Balinese girl.

The left hand is considered unclean. This obviously precludes walking hand in hand unless one of the couple walks backward.

We arrive at the intersection of Jalan Thamrin and Jalan Hasanudin.

Here Dasima stops.

"This is Puputan Square."

"Who was Puputan?" I ask.

"It is not a person. It is a way of dying. On this corner," she says, "you see Puri Pemecutan, a palace that is now also a hotel. It stands on the foundations of the original *puri*, which the Dutch destroyed when they marched into Denpasar. Across there is Museum Bali. What is today?"

"Monday."

"Ah, then I can't take you inside. It is closed on Mondays. Later in the week, possibly?"

"Whenever."

She walks us to an enormous statue at the teeming intersection of Jalan Gajah Mada and Jalan Veteran.

"The Lord Teacher, Batara Guru," Dasima says. "He faces all four directions at once."

"I wish I could learn *that* trick!"

"He commemorates the day of the *puputan*."

She watches the gridlock of traffic, the procession of motorbikes, the *bémos*, the tour buses, the private cars with their rattling air conditioners, all struggling to move past us in and out of Denpasar.

"Where are they all going?" she asks.

She expects no answer. I don't have one handy, anyway.

"How simple life was then!" she says.

"Then?"

"A morning in late September, almost eighty years ago. The Dutch had nothing superior to us—certainly not courage—except they did have cannon and rifles, while we had only daggers and spears. I can comprehend that kind of defeat. But now we are invaded by steel and aluminum and plastic in the shape of things we can no longer live without. This time we have been conquered not by force but by our own desires."

Then, as though she were dancing, shifting motion, she changes her body language and manner to that of a tour guide. She points to our left.

"The Dutch troops came marching in from there. Their Sixth

Military Expedition under the command of a general named Van Tonningen—three battalions of infantry, a detachment of cavalry, and two battalions of artillery."

"You talk as though you're a military expert."

"We are of the warrior caste. Except for my father, all of my family have been active warriors. I suppose this is why I feel closer to my uncle Guntur than to my own father. There were walls along this road eighty years ago, leading to the royal palace."

She marches me along the path the Dutch took.

"Listen!" she whispers.

I listen.

"You can hear drums beating within the palace walls. You can see smoke and flame rising from the palace grounds."

Guided by her voice, prompted by the magic of her wide eyes, I do indeed conjure up the sound and the vision.

She stops abruptly, as though being ordered to halt. Must be the dancer in her—every move reflecting a tired trooper, weary of humping, coming to a stop.

"The Dutch take up their positions around the main gate: infantry there . . . there . . . there. Cavalry here . . . and massed into the center, the artillery. Then they see—what an immense surprise!—a procession. Here it comes—out of the main gate of the *puri*. At the head the raja himself. He is dazzling!"

Now she transforms herself into the raja.

"White cremation garments sparkle with his finest jewels, a golden kris is in its ornate scabbard. He rides high above the procession, sitting with his legs crossed on a silken pillow in his state palanquin carried by his followers. And, look, Tanah, following him—the officials of his court and all his armed guards, his priests, his many wives, the temple dancing girls, his children, his retainers—all dressed in white, all armed, all ornamented with jewels, and with flowers in their hair."

She gives me a while to watch this evocation advance toward us.

"As they come closer, you can smell the frangipani in their hair. The Dutch stand with their weapons ready and smell the flowers and are confused. What kind of enemy is this? But the advance stops—just over there—within a hundred feet. The raja steps down from his palanquin and makes a signal. At this sign, a priest plunges a dagger into the raja's breast. The Dutch are aghast. What insanity is this? Then they discover this is merely the beginning. Guards and wives and retainers begin to stab each other. Mothers cut the throats of their children. Some of the Dutch— standing here—begin to weep. Others are sick on the ground. But there is a stray gunshot, and the general orders his men to fire. Rifles and cannon tear the few survivors to pieces. Our family tells that my great-great-grandmother laughed at the Dutch, even as they were shooting at her, and tossed her jewels and gold coins to them in mockery. Fortunately for our family line, one of her children, my great-grandfather, was staying with another branch of the family in a distant village that afternoon. Otherwise, I should not be here with you now, telling you this story. And that, Tanah, is what our word *puputan* means. A way to die. Surrender without defeat."

Her story arouses feelings in me I struggle to keep locked away—my perpetual sorrow for the victims, my rage against the brutalizers. That's another reason I had to cease and desist being a cop. Cops divide the world into two categories—assholes and cops. They may have a point, but I tend to feel there ought to be other categories, as well.

The statue of the Lord Teacher that commemorates the slaughter of the raja's court is far too benign. Memorials, I believe, should be built only to remind us of our savagery. At least at Hiroshima there is a proper memorial. It compels your revulsion. You can see and feel the apocalyptic flash and imagine yourself unjustly trapped in the expanding circle of searing heat.

"I tell you this for a reason," Dasima says. "My dance group has been offered the sponsorship of a wealthy European who has arranged a foreign tour for us. We are to dance in London and Paris and Brussels and Rome. It is a great opportunity to bring our culture to the attention of the Western world. And a chance for us to see what the outside world is like, for our own edification. After Europe, the sponsor is considering sending us to America for a month or two. Our government in Jakarta is urging us to accept the contract. All our musicians, all the other dancers, are eager to go. Yet I have been undecided, wondering whether I should leave Bali or not, even for a while. But after last night, Tanah, I am no longer undecided. I cannot leave you. This is what I told them at the Kokar this morning. This is why they are angry with me."

We return to the Mercedes.

"If my great-great-grandmother laughed at the guns of the Europeans and threw her gold at them even as they killed her, why should I dance for the descendants of such barbarians? Especially when dancing for them would take me away from you, Tanah."

I follow the road signs toward Kuta Beach.

"How does your uncle feel about this?" I ask.

"He has been opposed to my going. As have my parents."

Now I perceive the hidden motive in Guntur's snaking me into the family compound.

He was hoping the chemistry might work, the beautiful son-ofabitch!

I begin laughing aloud. Dasima smiles at me.

"What is it, Tanah?"

"I'm guilty," I tell her.

"Guilty? Of what?"

"Of falling into the greatest of all traps—happiness."

"You make a joke, of course. Why is happiness a trap? Why should it not be the normal condition?"

"No reason at all. Yes, I'm just joking."

"It does not trouble you I have made my decision because my body needs your body?"

"It does not trouble me in the least."

"And you agree I should not go?"

"Definitely! But not because my body needs your body, too. But because, Dasima, you belong to the past. Why should you be sacrificed to the present? They've already got enough of us on their altars!"

Red occluding lights dance in my rear-vision mirror.

The reflection of a POLISI jeep grows larger in the glass.

"Why would they want to stop us?" I ask Dasima. "I'm not speeding."

"Some of our young police officers resent Westerners who are seen openly with local girls. But when they recognize me, they will not trouble us."

"Could also be something else. If they can steal mobile cranes, they can steal police jeeps and a couple of uniforms. Get your head down below the top of your seat."

I slip the Browning free, thumb the safety off, and level the front sight at the inside of the door with one hand while I continue steering with the other. A lot of good men have been shot through car doors. Why should these two be the exceptions?

I slow the Mercedes and let the jeep close in.

Two officers in it. All four hands visible. No guns drawn. Things are looking cooler.

They draw alongside, shout something, and point up ahead.

I look off and discover an army chopper hovering above a ploughed *sawah*, fallow at the moment.

I pull onto the shoulder of the road and brake fifty yards from the hovering chopper. A trooper carrying an SMG jumps out of it. I'm deciding whether or not I should initiate a fire fight when I recognize him as Sergeant Maru, who drove me to Tip's place the night before.

He runs in and salutes me.

"Sir," he says, and I notice he's not even puffing from exertion, "the colonel would appreciate you taking my place in the chopper. It is urgent, he asked me to tell you, that you join him at headquarters at once. My orders are to drive his niece to her home, then bring the car to you at the base."

"Looks as though we won't get to Kuta Beach today," I say to Dasima. "See you at home."

"Peace on your way, my love," she whispers.

We clasp hands a moment, then I tuck the Browning into its holster, safety notched back on, and run across to the waiting chopper. The pilot lowers the skids so I can climb in.

He lifts off, and turns northeast, giving it the max.

Below, the Mercedes and the police jeep fall from sight.

Nine minutes later we set down on the parade grounds at the base in Tabanan.

The OD, a lieutenant, is waiting for me.

He leads me on the run to the prison section.

I descend to where Guntur waits in the cell of the Vietnamese prisoner.

Guntur stands beside the constricted figure of the man.

"He is dead," Guntur says in bafflement.

My thoughts are suddenly all thumbs. I've been letting myself count on this man. Now he's gone and disappointed me. Without him we aren't even in the ball game with the opposition.

"Goddam it, Guntur!" I hear myself shouting. "How the fuck did this happen?"

"I have permitted no one to touch him. He is as he was found," Guntur says, a note of surprise in his usually affirmative voice.

The stink of the cell fills my lungs, choking me.

I squat on the stone floor next to the dead man. He lies on his back, his eyes open to the three sunspots that pock his face from the holes drilled in the ceiling rock. His flesh appears to have drawn even more tightly onto his skull. He is lost to us forever, liberated without our consent, an effrontery Guntur is unable to accept, a deliberate act of Vietnamese treachery.

I stretch my fingers, shutter down both his eyelids. I have still to make my adjustment to lifelessness within the cosmos of the human eye. Nothing is more melancholy than emptiness in what before were tiny suns, self-generating orbs of light and life.

"I have the base surgeon standing by," Guntur says. "He will make the medical examination and perform the autopsy, but I wanted you to see him first."

"Who had access to him?"

"Nobody has been alone with him since you were in here. As you must have noticed when we entered, I have *two* guards on duty. Neither entered his cell."

I glance at the empty rice bowl and the tin of water near the dead man.

"If nobody came in here, how'd he get his food and water?"

"They were put inside—the door unlocked, the bowls placed on the floor just inside. Nothing more. Both sentries swear they did not approach him or even speak to him. They are men who have served with me, men I trust completely."

I pick up the empty rice bowl and bring it to my nostrils. It has a peculiarly offensive smell.

"I know that smell from somewhere," I tell Guntur. *"Where?"*

Fragments now. Information processing. The unwinding spool of memories. Stop frame! Focus in! A kitchen! I'm watching the head of a fish being deftly cut off, the entrails removed. In Tokyo. Three years ago.

"Fuga!" I say abruptly. "The globefish—tetrodon. The man has been poisoned, Guntur. His bowl smells like tetrodonic acid. You can get it easily enough from the testes of any of the globefish common to your waters. You can boil it in food for hours, but the poison still won't break down."

Guntur charges out of the cell.

I hear him ordering one of the two guards to run to the OD and get a detachment of men to place all kitchen personnel under immediate arrest, then to send the doctor down here on the double.

Guntur returns, muttering darkly. "If you're right, this is a monumental cock up! One of our own people."

"One or more!" I correct. "And you can't limit your suspicions to the kitchen staff. Anybody could have laced his rice with fish entrails. You'll have to track the movements of that bowl from the time his rice was put in until it arrived here."

"If it is the poison you think it is, how long does it take to work? What kind of time factor are we dealing with here?"

"He'd have started feeling sick anywhere from three to fifteen minutes after he ate the rice. But death can sometimes take as long as twenty-four hours. When I was with him yesterday, when you had that first bowl of rice sent into him, I would have smelled tetrodon if there'd been any in his food. But I didn't. So you can narrow it down to whatever servings he had after that."

"One last night, one this morning."

"Then those are the two I'd concentrate on."

The doctor appears, black bag in hand, a major, corpulent for a Balinese. As he enters the cell, he sneezes. His eyes look bleary to me, even in the semidarkness. Definitely suffering from a head cold.

He peers at the dead man.

"Who was he?"

"That is not your problem," Guntur says sharply. "I want you to tell us what time this man died and of what cause. Then I want an autopsy performed immediately and the report on my desk no later than seventeen hundred hours!"

"He looks thin enough to have been starved to death."

"This gentleman thinks he was poisoned."

For the first time the doctor looks directly at me.

"Are you a doctor?"

"No."

"American?"

"Yes."

"He's working with me," Guntur says curtly. "Please get on with it! Smell his rice bowl!"

The major picks up the bowl, sniffs at it.

"I smell nothing unusual."

"Doctor, do you have a head cold?" I ask.

"Only my sinus," he says. "I'm allergic to prison cells and the sight of human beings who have been starved like this. Very well, let me examine the man. Is this all the light you have in here, colonel?"

"You may move him above ground if it will help. Any objections, John?"

"Too late for those now. Move him anywhere you want to."

I go back down the corridor and up the long flight of chipped cement stairs into early-afternoon sunlight. A lone *betitja* bird squats on a branch of a tree beyond the prison doorway. The banal symbolism of the free bird and the caged men below nibbles at me for a while. Then the *betija* tilts his head at me. I tilt mine back at him. It is in this position Guntur finds me minutes later.

═CHAPTER═

14

At sunset we leave for Nusa Dua.

Tonight the colonel has changed the makeup of his mobile security force. At the point he's assigned a Saladin armored car, in mid-column three Ferret scout cars carrying Red Berets, the lead car with its driver, himself, me, and Captain Hamzah, a Commando APC packed with additional paras closing ranks astern.

"It will be a long evening," he says, "but I hope a productive one. First a cocktail reception in the Presidential Suite. We have hidden video cameras photographing the Vietnamese reception line so we can later analyze their reactions to various guests. We've invited virtually every important Chinese on the island, especially those we know to have Vietnamese interests and connections. We are also using directional microphones of extreme sensitivity to pick up and record everything said between the Vietnamese and these people. After the reception there will be a dinner in the ballroom. Here, too, we have arranged to photograph and record the delegation. Finally, everyone will move to the theater, where traditional Balinese dances will be staged for our guests, including a performance by Dasima. Here our hidden microphones are especially powerful, since we anticipate that anything the Vietnamese would not have said to each other at the reception or dinner they might be tempted to whisper to each other during the distraction of the dancers and the *gamelan*."

"You impress me, Guntur. I want you to know something."

"Yes?"

"I don't as a rule like—or trust—anyone above the rank of captain. Especially bird colonels. You know what Napoleon said about colonels, don't you?"

"I don't believe I do."

"He said there are no bad regiments, only bad colonels."

"Brilliant," Guntur says, laughing. "I agree with him. Don't you, captain?"

"Yes, sir," Hamzah hastens to concur.

"But in your case, Guntur," I continue, "I suspend my disbelief. You're a bit of bloody all right, old boy."

"Thank you, John."

I let him bask in it for a moment, then ask, "How many delegates are there?"

"Ten. Six men, four women. I have complete dossiers on all ten back at headquarters."

"Why back at headquarters? I would have liked to look through them before I meet the delegates."

"I want to see how keen you are, John," he says, smiling. "After you've met them, tell me your feelings about who and what each of them is. Then I can evaluate your judgment level even more accurately than I'm presently able to."

"That's one of your most endearing qualities, Guntur. With you everything's right out in the open."

Our column turns onto the highway from International Airport to the Nusa Dua resort area, the newest tourist development on Bali.

I'm sorry Captain Hamzah is sitting within earshot. Since Guntur operates out of such closets of duplicity, it would be an ideal time to tell him I know why he brought Dasima and me together. I'll hang him later on that one.

"I suggest," he says, "that you do not let the Vietnamese know you speak their language."

"I wasn't planning to."

"Excellent. In that way, who knows what you might pick up?"

"Incidentally, who am I supposed to be?"

"I was thinking of introducing you as a buyer of batik from Los Angeles."

"I don't know enough about batik to get away with that. Only the little Tip showed me last night."

"Why not a correspondent for the San Francisco *Chronicle*?" Captain Hamzah suggests.

"That's a thought," I agree. "But with the Vietnamese you have to bake the whole cake. The frosting alone won't do."

"I don't follow that, sir."

"The Vietnamese mind takes what you give it and instantly rejects it. Example: a delegate asks me who I am. I tell him I'm from the San Francisco *Chronicle*. Which he disbelieves for starters. Now he asks me—not right away, you understand, but later, when he thinks my guard is down—what story has brought me to Indonesia. If I haven't worked that out, he can watch my mental scramble as I attempt to come up with a convincing answer. If I have worked it out in advance and I can throw it away by saying I'm here investigating the systematic killing of criminals by the Indonesian military, a death-squad law-and-order campaign which started in Java and which is attracting more and more unfavorable attention from the liberal world press, he may back away for a few minutes. Then over coffee he may hit me again, asking how the authorities are responding to such candid investigation from the foreign press when they have such a strict policy with their own press. He will judge me from my answer. Then later he may ask me which of the newspapers in Jakarta I prefer. If I can't answer that professionally, he's got me. He *knows* I'm a spook. But that's just the most elementary, superficial example of the searching nature of the Vietnamese mind."

Guntur appears gloomy. "Do you know anything at all about our newspapers in Jakarta?"

"A little. I know that *Kompas* has the largest circulation, that it's extremely cautious about reporting the news in any way that might offend the government. I know that the armed forces daily is called *AB*, that the semiofficial paper is *Saura Karya*, and that the liveliest paper of the bunch is the evening *Sinar Harapan*."

"Are you aware that *Kompas* was established by Roman Catholics?" Guntur asks.

"You see? That's exactly how the Vietnamese could catch me. By asking if I felt that Catholicism occasionally surfaces in the editorials of *Kompas*. How would I know that unless I'd been prepped?"

"And that *Sinar Harapan* was established by Protestants and still carries articles addressed only to members of that faith—imagine, John, in a nation more than ninety-percent Muslim! Can you now understand a little of the excitement that I, a Balinese Hindu, feel in such an explosive country?"

There is, I must admit, a contagion about Guntur. He is imbued with something we have lost, we Americans, a genuine nationalistic fervor, and he is driven by the need to find a stance between the twentieth century and the ancient cultures layered within his complex society and to evolve as part of an indigenous new culture. It is not an easy matter, but it has its compensating excitement, I must assume.

It occurs to me I have given no personal attention to Guntur's hardworking young aide, Captain Hamzah, for whom I am developing a grudging acceptance. If only he wouldn't wax his mustache!

"Are you married?" I ask him.

"No, sir. I am following the colonel's example. My life is given to the army."

I am stoked by the company of these two dedicated men. And about this hour of day we can all use some stoking. For it's been a downhill plunge ever since the death of the prisoner.

By late afternoon the autopsy had confirmed that he had indeed been poisoned. And by tetrodonic acid obtained from the testes of one of five local species of globefish, probably the stonelike one, a critter the doctor called *ikan buntal batu*. While I sorted out my thoughts about death by *ikan buntal batu*, asking myself how I'd feel about being taken off by anything that esoteric as opposed to a simple round between the eyes, Guntur has gained such respect for my inductive sensing that I'm fearful he's expecting from me a miracle every hour from this point forward.

Interrogation of all suspected personnel had produced zilch. No one was apprehended with the dead fish in his footlocker or still in his knapsack. That trail ended where it began—nowhere.

By seventeen hundred hours another roof fell in on us. Guntur's call to Pac-Pet requesting a copy of their engine logbook for the stolen flatbed truck turned up the startling information that a flash fire only this morning had burned down the shed where the logbooks were kept. Captain Hamzah had been called in from the field and sent up to Padangbai to raise some concentrated hell about so timely and coincidental a fire but had returned convinced

111

the flames were caused by an electrical failure and that no arson was involved.

"They are right on top of us!" Guntur says. "Every bloody move we make, they make a countermove. We're going to have to start taking the initiative. How do you say that, John? We have to kick some ass?"

"That's how we say it, Guntur. Only that's what I feel they want us to do. The more ass we kick, the more we stir up the people. And that's only going to play into their hands. For some reason—don't ask me why—I feel they're letting us make the moves, then topping us so we'll escalate. I feel that's just coverup, that if and when we really do escalate—and the shit hits the fan— that's when they'll make their next big move."

"Which is *what*?" Guntur asks.

"Reclaiming the bell from where it's hidden and hauling it out of Bali."

"Taking it where?"

"That's the biggie! Meantime, it's back to square one. We keep combing those computer locations. I'm starting at Kuta Beach first thing in the morning and working my way east to Ujung. Tonight we devote ourselves to the Vietnamese, see if there's anything to Captain Hamzah's theory."

Hamzah looks pleased.

Our Saladin armored car leads us into the grounds of an impressive hotel on the beach at Nusa Dua.

"The work of an Indonesian architect and a Danish interior decorator," Guntur informs me.

I look off admiringly at two four-story wings sculptured to simulate the terraced paddy fields of Bali. The hotel is set within a tropical garden topped by coconut palms and extends out toward a white sandy beach, now at sunset the color of caramel. The two wings meet in a *wantilan*, an open-air reception area and lobby lounge where water cascades from fountains. The ideal setting for a cadre of remorselessly Marxist North Vietnamese!

I observe Guntur's Red Berets everywhere about the hotel grounds, stationed within twenty feet of each other, an encirclement of protective firepower, yet the flood of guests from the line of arriving cars all appear unaware of the heavy security.

As we're about the enter the *wantilan*, I take Guntur and the captain aside.

"Change of cover story," I announce. "This appears to be an

unusually Continental-looking crowd, mostly European and Asian. I think it would be counterproductive to present me as one of the few Americans—only make me stand out even more."

"But John," Guntur says, "you *are* American! You look American! You even smell American!"

I rebuke him in French, telling him I do not appreciate being told I smell like two hundred and fifty million other people. A statement like that is racist bullshit!

He is surprised. For not only am I speaking French; I *am* French—my body language, my attitude, even my thoughts.

Guntur questions me in French, not very acceptable French, but basic enough to be almost understandable. He asks me where I learned.

I tell him I *am* half-French, that it is my first language, inasmuch as my mother still lives and paints in Paris and kept me with her, joined at the hip, for the first seven years of my life, and that I still divide my spare time equally between my American father in San Diego and my French mother in Paris.

"Present me," I suggest, "as Monsieur Jean Locke of *Avencer*, a Communist daily in Paris."

And so, on a vibrant high to be back again stalking a race of people against whom I miraculously managed to survive, I enter the Presidential Suite at the end of one of the two wings facing the sea. The suite, with its own private swimming pool, is built on two levels, with two bedrooms, a sitting and dining room— and bulletproof glass windows and doors, Guntur whispers. All the rooms are patterned with women dressed formally in the gowns and costumes of at least ten different cultures—Balinese, Javanese, Sumatran, Moluccan, Indian, Thai, Philippine, Chinese, Japanese, and European—a rainbow of women with their husbands, lovers, and escorts. But I focus on a patiently smiling line of ten Vietnamese, the men in Hanoi drab, the women in traditional *ao-dai*s. They stand with beguiling diffidence and shake hands with each guest being introduced to them by an Indonesian deputy minister of education and culture from Jakarta. I can't help wondering if beneath their smiling demeanor these tough Vietnamese are not wondering about the sharp contrast between this thousand-dollar-a-day suite and the bleak austerity of their northern condition, and the irony that the suite is situated in one small island of thirteen thousand belonging to a fellow Asian nation.

I make a sweeping catalog of the ten. One is definitely a military man in the cloak and feathers of a cultural attaché. He is wearing the Vietnamese military haircut, short at the back and sides, the kind of haircut our unfortunate prisoner was not wearing. He strikes me as a trail-hardened fighter who knows how to treat a napalm burn without leaving a mark, with wet sand compresses. Two men next to him, on either side, are straight out of the Dang Lao Dong, the Workers' Party, a direct descendant of the Indo-chinese Communist Party formed in 1930. Two of the women are young, two older, and I sense that the older two are unquestionably members of the central executive committee of the women's union.

"What is your gut feeling about them?" Guntur whispers as we advance like turtles toward our turn at being introduced.

I tell him my thoughts, that half may be truly interested in the cultural aspects of Indonesia but that the other five are on a definite mission, probably to encourage the Indonesian Labor Party to continue to push for aid from Jakarta to Vietnam in the form of grants and credits.

We come closer, and my emotions begin to clash with each other, the love-hate I feel toward these people who taught me life's most bitter lesson, that I am not immortal, that my slaughtered friends were not immortal. Seeing them causes me to recall the first instant I set boots on Vietnamese soil, fresh out of Ranger school and the Defense Language Institute in Monterey, where it was discovered I had a natural aptitude for the language. A group of Vietnamese boys were teaching some grunts how to count in Vietnamese, making our troopers repeat after them until they had by heart the memory of the five words for one, two, three, four, five. Except the true meaning of the words they were teaching the soldiers was Vietnamese not for the numbers one through five but the words for *down with the American imperialists*. And our ig-norant dickheads stood there with raw Oklahoma honesty and ticked off the words proudly. I knew in that first instant we were fucked. But what I didn't know was that despite the horror of the years that followed, I fell in love with the country and its people, even with my enemy, whom I could never learn to hate no matter how hard I tried.

I hear Guntur introducing me to the deputy minister. "Jean Locke, from Paris. He writes for *Avencer*."

I'm then presented to the leader of the delegation, Tran Hoi Ham, the honcho with the military trim. Since a Vietnamese does not appreciate uninvited physical contact, I do not offer my hand.

But he smiles and extends his to me. We clasp hands, and he tells me in French that *Avencer* is one of the world's most intellectual publications and that I must indeed be a formidable talent to be able to write for them.

In French, I tell him I am honored and pleased by his compliment and that possibly someday soon I may come and interview him in Hanoi. I have always yearned to see the Bay of Ha-Long, north of Hanoi in the Gulf of Tonkin, especially the rock formation called the Circle of Surprise. He responds that all things are possible, given time, and I move on to the rest of the delegation. Yet somehow I feel that Tran Hoi Ham, though clearly convinced by my French, has filed me in a special niche in his thoughts.

I sense him watching me during the short time remaining before everyone is led down to the banquet chamber for dinner. I am convinced that it is at his whispered command that the youngest of the Vietnamese women, a girl with large eyes and a thin, cultivated face, searches me out. "Le-Yuan," she says to me in French, smiling apologetically, "is my name again. It is impossible to remember so many names. I was just in Paris. But July is such a desolate month in your city. With everyone away."

"I believe I remember being told you're with *Nan Dan*, the party daily in Hanoi," I say.

"Yes," she says, smiling. "We have much in common. Do you speak any Vietnamese?"

"I wish I did," I say. Then, seeing that she is genuinely shy and is under orders to come back with something, I decide to play the sterotypical Frenchman. "If you have any free time on this trip," I suggest, "possibly you might be able to teach me some basic vocabulary."

She blushes. "Our schedule has been worked out to the second," she says. "Otherwise I should be delighted."

"Such a pity," I say.

All through dinner, our table placed strategically close to the dais at which the Vietnamese delegation sits, I see her glancing at me. Once, when I catch her eye directly, she dares linger a moment, smiling at me, for I see something of my lost love Doan Thi in the eyes of every Vietnamese girl. It has nothing to do with their beauty or lack of beauty or with resemblance. It has only to do with an elemental spark, a centered calm, the eye of the hurricane common to all Vietnamese.

Even the food reminds me of loving Doan Thi against a fated

calendar running out of numbers, clocking our last days together in Saigon.

The star shape of the carambole slices—Doan Thi fed me the first carambole I ever tasted! The red of the pepper on the plate against the porcelain white of soya sprouts! Tea flavored with areca flowers and served in tiny cups! In honor of the Vietnamese, the Indonesian hosts have provided delicacies from Vietnam, served in conjunction with Javanese and Balinese food.

I have to excuse myself.

I walk through the garden toward the beach.

A group of women *ibus* appears from the darkness near the shoreline but are blocked by Red Berets from approaching any closer to me. "Beautiful red shirt," one calls. "Dyed both sides. Finest material. It's up to you." Another woman shouts at me, her teeth gleaming in torchlight. "What are you doing?"

From nowhere I remember a wonderful phrase in Malay I was once taught for occasions when you're asked mindless questions such as "How's it going?" or "What are you doing?"

"Saya makan angin," I call back to her over the heads of the Red Berets. "I'm eating the wind."

The women approve, howling with laughter and flagging their batik shirts for sale at me even more insistently.

No refuge out here, I see.

I return to the banquet room.

A shadow behind a nearby coconut tree causes me to shift gears. I stop and appraise the shadow. Suddenly it detaches itself. It is a man, apparently one of the guests. He hurries off before I can see his face, but his movement, the lines of his figure, and the back of his head cause me to sense he is Chinese. Was he watching me or simply taking a piss? Definitely he wasn't Balinese. Balinese men urinating in public simply squat down with their knees closed to cover themselves and let fly.

Just before I enter the banquet room, I almost collide with a young European woman hurrying outside. I had noticed her earlier, seated on the dais near the Vietnamese delegation, and wondered who she might be, for she looks truly astonishing for Bali. For London, perfect. For Bali, incredible. She's wearing a Zandra Rhodes gown open to her navel. Her hair is tossed and stippled with punky dye, her face daubed with fluorescent paint. Yet despite the camouflage I can see linear perfection in her slender body and gracefully turned ankles. Her lips are too sensuously pouty, but I suspect that might come from too much money, for she reflects high style gone neo-punk, almost a parody of a Fellini character trying to hide her sexuality under street-wise chic, a bimbo smoking with exhausted decadence.

"Don't you like my hair, Mr. Locke?" she asks me in English.

I reply in French, suggesting she must have made a mistake, that I am Jean Locke of the Paris *Avencer*.

"And I'm King Kong's jockstrap!" she says. "Why the deception?"

I stay with the French. I ask her if she would please speak in my language, that I have little English. I tell her that her accent sounds Dutch to me—or German, possibly?

"Dutch," she says, hanging right in there with the English. "Look, I'll make a deal with you. Just talk to me for a minute—as yourself. Then you can go back to being anybody you want to be."

"You've got one minute!" I say in English.

"Much better. Don't you feel more relaxed now?"

"You just blew seven seconds."

"I asked you if you liked my hair," she insists in a hectoring voice.

"May I be blunt?"

"Please!"

"Okay, I'm not really into postpunk coifs. I like a woman's hair to be a little more malleable. I guess it's the spikes that turn me off."

"I find that surprising. I should think that spikes would be your thing."

"Oh? Why?"

"I'm told you're a professional killer."

"Whoever told you that is careless with his nouns."

"Then you aren't a killer?"

"I prefer to think of myself as a survivor. May I ask who spoke so highly of me?"

"You may ask, of course. But I don't intend to tell you."

"Your minute is up! Excuse me!"

I start to enter the ballroom, but I feel her hand grip my arm more needfully than harshly. At least that's the reading I give the finger lock on my forearm.

"Please! Not yet."

"All right. What have you got in mind?"

"What do you think of my makeup?"

I run my eyes down the tribal stripe she's painted along one cheek. I puzzle a moment over her multicolored, patterned forehead.

"I have no trouble with the stripe," I tell her. "I have friends in New Guinea who wear them on both cheeks. But I'm not sure I can relate to your forehead. Are those supposed to be Rorschach blots?"

"You're the first person who ever guessed! What do you do, Mr. Locke, to make you so perceptive? What *is* your work?"

Fuck it, I think. This little fox is on to me, whatever her game is. The Jean Locke number has gone down the tube. Better go with the straight talk here. And assume the Vietnamese will continue to believe I'm French. I doubt there will be any fraternization between this stylish punker and the moralists from Hanoi. If she ever so much as entered their city limits, they'd pack her off frothing and kicking to the nearest reeducation camp.

"I was a cop," I tell her. "A nark."

The information makes her catch her breath. As she does, her breasts pop halfway out of the Zandra Rhodes. One of her nipples, almost virginally pink, remains still exposed when she resumes her breathing.

"Where?" she asks.

"San Francisco."

"How *could* you?"

"Like they say, it's dirty work, but somebody's got to do it."

"But you're not any longer?"

"*Some*body?"

"A nark."

"No, I got out of it. Once I saw the problem wasn't what the doper was taking but what made him a doper in the first place, I figured I was on the Band-Aid end of the business. So I hung it up."

She considers me with so steady and contemplative a gaze that for a moment I suspect I may have underestimated her. She may not be a loony, after all. Or as the Indonesians call them, *kasar* characters, characters who "do not speak their brain."

"I'm usually uncanny at understanding people," she says. "I hate it. I see right through them. But you confuse me. I see sensitivity, almost a delicacy of spirit, and a giving heart. But I also see something else—something dark and dangerous."

"Are you complimenting me or analyzing me?"

"Do you mind?"

"No. I need the help."

"*Are* you dangerous?"

"Well, there are people around who are never going to wear campaign buttons with my name on them."

"I'd like to see you again."

"Do you think the most lasting relationships are those in which the man never even gets to know the name of the woman?"

"I'm sorry," she apologizes. "Juliana Duurstede Chartwell."

"Juliana Duurstede is the Dutch part, right? And Chartwell is your husband's name?"

Not difficult, Locke, not when the lady is wearing a flawless fifteen-karat diamond on her pledge finger.

"You don't fraternize with married women, Mr. Locke?"

"I don't know any."

"It was my husband who suggested I come talk to you."

"Why didn't he come along?"

"I don't know. Usually, there's nothing about him that ever surprises me. But this did. His asking that I have this little tête-à-tête with you. You see, he's maniacally jealous."

"Without reason, of course."

"I could take offense at that."

"But you're not going to."

"Not at all. Because I don't sleep with men. Nor with women for that matter. I don't even sleep with my own husband."

"No comment."

"You can't understand chastity, can you? A man as highly sexed as you!"

"Do I appear highly sexed?"

"Why else would you sail around to all these Pacific islands? A good-looking, virile white man like you, exploiting the tropics, stepping ashore like a conqueror, scattering your trinkets among the native girls. Oh, I'm sure you have a knack for getting on sleeping terms with all the primitive virgins in remote villages!"

"Actually, the more primitive the better. Have you ever tried it while hanging from a tree by a nose ring?"

"I can see the whole dreary scene all over your arrogant face!"

"You may be right," I concede. "But I'm only half-arrogant, since I'm only half-French. My French mother taught me to read not from primers but from the travel books written by a nineteenth-century French novelist, Pierre Loti, a voyager whose life-style was an endless sequence of landing, loving, leaving—and grieving. Do you suppose that might have influenced me?"

"I'm not entirely sure I want to see you again. The longer I talk to you, the more I dislike you. You have a way of speaking that suggests everything you're saying has some deeper meaning. Whatever that meaning may be, I find it disquieting. And annoying! You are not a man who is at peace with himself, Mr. Locke! And more than anything else in the world, that's what I need at this moment in my life. Someone with a calm heart, someone with a tender, loving touch."

"How about a neutered masseur?" I suggest.

"Cruel, too, aren't you?"

"Not needlessly. Good night, Madame Chartwell."

Once more I begin to leave. Then it strikes me there may be a value to this relationship. God knows what, but it simply can't be discarded out of hand. And why do the Chartwells both know so much about me? Why the interest?

"If I've offended you, I'm sorry," I say to her. "But you have a very waspish tongue, and I was simply trying to defend myself."

"My husband will be going away for a day or two. May I see you again? Tomorrow night? Nine o'clock. Anyone can tell you where we live."

"You expect me to come to your house?"

"Just drive by at nine. I'll be waiting in my own car. Follow me."

"I am definitely not what you need, Mrs. Chartwell. We both know what you *do* need, don't we?"

She peers at me from under her eyelids, a half-dazed, half-petulant glance, and in it I recognize that she's beginning to sense I can indeed see the bread-crumb trail of her life leading to this moment. Clearly she is a woman who has run out of bread crumbs.

"Remember?" I say. "I was a nark. I know the signs. What you really need is to get straight. You look to me as though you're coked out of your mind for the ten-thousandth time. I'd make you as a real garbage-can addict—a polysubstance abuser. Ready to swallow anything."

She actually sauces one hip toward me and pouts her lips into my face. "Even you!"

"But you're not ready for detoxification. You haven't hit bottom yet."

This is the killing shot, for she knocks off the sex-kitten bullshit and whispers desperately, "I have! I have! Just tonight! My little girl—I went to kiss her good-night before we came to this party— and she drew away from me! 'You frighten me, Mommie!' she cried, and she drew away from *my* hand! My hand, Mr. Locke! How much harder do I have to hit bottom? The only thing in this disgusting world that has any meaning—any beauty—is my daughter. And I *frighten* her! Oh, my God, what am I going to do?"

"I can't help you. There are people who can. There are some really effective programs around these days with a fairly high rate of cure—experienced street people, therapists, counselors They can help you. I can't. I'm sorry."

"Then why do I have this feeling—I had it from the first second I saw you tonight—that you *can*? That *only* you can! When my husband suggested I get to know you, ordinarily I would have refused. But I wanted to talk to you. I *needed* to!"

"What you're feeling has nothing to do with me. You've just got the coke jitters. Take a downer. You'll steady out soon enough."

"Oh, God, you are cruel, aren't you?"

I smile my box-top smile and move inside the ballroom to rejoin Colonel Katrini and Captain Hamzah. I find them looking anxiously toward me, wondering how I could possibly have been detained so long.

From the doorway behind me I can feel Juliana Chartwell's stare along my spine.

Okay, put me on top of her wimp list. Can't be helped.

Morality, I remind myself, requires a commitment to something outside one's self.

I'm already overcommitted.

Tran Hoi Ham is beckoning to me from the dais.

I'm not sure that of all the many people in this crowded room he wants me. I glance around, and see that no one else is coming forward. I look back at him. He's still beckoning, smiling that half-apologetic Vietnamese smile that is not really a smile at all.

I hurry to the dais.

In French he asks me if I would mind posing for a photograph with Le-Yuan, since she is a fellow journalist. The girl nervously brushes a strand of black hair from her forehead and moves closer to me. Tran Hoi Ham nods to one of the older women in the delegation. She smiles at Le-Yuan and at me and in Vietnamese scolds the girl. "Don't be so stiff," she rebukes Le-Yuan. "He is not going to bite you. And if he did, it might be good for you." Then she photographs us. Tran Hoi Ham asks that one more picture be taken. This, too, is done. I thank Le-Yuan in French, thank the photographer, thank Tran Hoi Ham, and ask him if he has any free time in the two days he and his party will be in Bali if we might have a few minutes together. He politely says their schedule has been prearranged, but if I will call him in the morning, he will see if a few minutes cannot somehow be set aside for me. I have no idea what value a few more minutes with him may have except to convince me even more that the Vietnamese are guiltless in the matter of the Great Bronze Bell. However, he could teach me, if he would, how to sling a sleeping hammock between trees so that at the first sound of an approaching enemy I could release the nylon ropes with one tug and vanish into the night, as our NVA enemies did repeatedly as we tried to close in on them.

As I leave Tran Hoi Ham, I see a man in his dramatic forties near the end of the dais whom I assume must be Walton Chartwell. He has been watching me with amiable fascination, as though he finds me droll and amusing, if not downright comic. He's actually an aristocratic figure with a definite Rudyard Kipling flair about him. He looks to be only about ninety years misplaced in time, given a little more lace at the neck and velvet on the lapels. For a second I even think he might be Michael Caine in a scene from *The Man Who Would Be King*. There is a dash of the old empire about him, even as he sits. He only requires a falcon on his shoulder to be the ultimate English lord.

He smiles at me, and I nod to him.

I step down from the dais and cross toward the table where Guntur grins at me as though congratulating me on having ingratiated myself with the Vietnamese.

A young man steps in front of me. Deliberately. One second he hadn't been there; the next second his eyes are directly in line with mine. He is Chinese. Cold as a Manchurian sunrise. As tall as I and obviously with the same panther moves. I have this flippy thought that I have bumped into a full-length mirror, but instead of confronting my own image, I am confronting the image of this arrogant young Chinese.

I know he is the man who'd been watching me from behind the coconut palm.

He stays in front of me, unmoving, for the precise tick of my remaining patience, and just as I'm about to dedicate myself to putting him out of my way, he slips to one side.

All this happens within the time it might take to snap your fingers.

I settle in beside Guntur at our table and look everywhere for the young Chinese. I see him nowhere.

Guntur is whispering to me in a conspiratorial tone. "Wait until we play back their conversation about asking you up there to be photographed! There *has* to be something in that! Why would they do that? What does it mean? We may have some fascinating answers."

But I am thinking of one thing only now, not listening to Guntur prattle on.

"Have you a list of all the Chinese guests here tonight?" I interrupt.

"Certainly."

"When I point out one of them to you, it's important you identify him. That is, if I see him again."

"Important? Why?"

"He either wants to kiss me or kill me. He was close enough to do either. Or both."

"Show him to me. Point him out."

"I don't see him anywhere now. And I have the strongest feeling I won't—until he chooses to see me again. Can you get me photos to match up with the guest list—just the Chinese?"

"If they're resident in Bali. If they're here on tourist visas, we don't hold their passports and would have no photos of them. But believe me, John, the only Chinese here tonight are those who are residents and who were invited either by us or by the Vietnamese delegation."

"No tourists or influential Chinese who might have flown in just for the occasion?"

"No, sir," Captain Hamzah says. "Right after the incident at Pura Besakih we made a check of all Chinese tourists in Bali at that time. There were not more than two dozen, and we cleared all of them of any involvement within a few hours."

"We've kept that check going on a daily basis," Guntur adds. "The immigration people at the airport call us after every incoming flight if any Chinese land on Bali."

"And likewise any Vietnamese or Burmese," the captain says.

"There is no one floating around this island we're not keyed into," Guntur states with too much assurance to settle my stomach.

For in the eyes of the Chinese stranger I have seen the laser look I know comes into my own eyes as I center my front sight on an enemy's kill point, the look of knowing for certain your shot is first in and terminal.

Whoever he is, he truly believes I'm dead meat.

His dead meat.

CHAPTER

15

Guntur, Captain Hamzah, and I sit directly behind the Vietnamese delegation in the outdoor theater of the Nusa Dua Hotel. To one side, and just forward of us, Juliana Chartwell has joined her husband and is pointedly ignoring me.

As we wait for thirty Balinese musicians to take their places on an unlit platform, Guntur explains to me that what is about to be presented is merely an adaptation of traditional Balinese dancing. I must not expect too much. We are to see only a form called *prembon*, a revue-style presentation devised solely in response to the needs and limited tastes of the tourist market—demonstrating, he insists, that the Balinese are resilient enough not to prevent commercializing the sacred dance forms they perform regularly for their own people in temples or distant villages. What is being staged tonight is designed to be fast-moving and easily understood, since tourists are quickly bored by such subtle and prolonged dance movements as the *kidjang rebut muring*, representing a deer being pestered by biting flies, or the *sayar soyor*, a ballet of trees swaying in the wind.

I watch the musicians revving up. Nobody has charts or lead sheets. They all look bored and slightly stoned. It is because they "have the music in their bellies," Guntur tells me. The instruments

125

appear to be percussive—gongs, drums, cymbals, and xylophones, augmented by bamboo flutes. The drums, Guntur explains, are called *kendang* and are played with the palms of the hands and the fingers. He informs me that the old man about to start playing the "male" drum is the leader of the orchestra. A seven-year-old boy sits between his legs. He's already being conditioned to feel the vibrations through his grandfather's belly.

The music begins without pomp or overture, as though somebody has just pushed a start button, and now I find myself in the immediate presence of the kind of orchestra I've been hearing at night from every village. My cells vibrate to the interplay of myriad sounds, all miraculously blending in harmony, even though they all seem to be chasing each other in and out of a steel beehive.

One of the xylophonists strikes the bronze keys with a mallet in his right hand, then mutes them with his left hand; another plays a different type of xylophone with both hands.

There is a curious cutoff of emotion about the musicians, a personal vacuity, yet the tinkling multiplicity of their sounds is deeply affecting. It permeates the body, not only through the ears but through every pore, immersing me within it. I feel that these thirty men whose faces I cannot see in the darkness are all driving some kind of runaway music machine, yet if the lead drummer should suddenly get up to take the seven-year-old to the potty, the whole sound machine would instantly stop, and when he came back and started drumming again, the machine would instantly speed up once more exactly where it had left off.

Her back to the sea, stepping through a gateway onto the stage where imitation shrines conceal the spotlights, Dasima appears barefoot in a dazzling costume.

She is performing a dance called *Kebyar Bebancihan*. She portrays Candra Kirana, a princess disguised as a young man searching the world for her true love, some cat named Panji. Over the course of the twenty minutes alotted to this tourist version, she visits the court of a foreign kingdom and there performs a dance for the assembled courtiers while she searches the crowd with her eyes for her lover.

The musicians start and stop in abrupt cadences each time Dasima comes to an accented pause, her limber fingers extended, flexing backward in the spidery characteristic Eastern attitude. Her rolling eyeballs and body movements portray an incredible variety of moods as she searches in vain for poor Panji, then suddenly exults to discover him seated in the audience. This is no zig-zag dance routine such as those staged for tourists in Bangkok hotel ballrooms. This is the poetry of a people being whispered by the soft rustling of a girl's body in measured ancient verses.

Her eyes fix on me with such joy, such singularity of focus, I feel as though one of the lighting engineers is bathing me with his spotlight. I sense heads turning to see who the lucky man in the audience might be.

Dasima accepts the tumultuous applause, then vanishes gracefully backstage through the gateway.

Guntur is beaming at me. "Well?" he whispers.

"*Incroyable!*"

"Pure eloquence!" he exults. "A national treasure, no?"

"No doubt about it," I agree. "I could watch her for hours."

"Then you understand why I brought you together?"

"I'm flattered—and deeply appreciative. But I do like to be consulted, not manipulated."

"There was no time!" he insists. "Had I discussed the matter with you, it would have introduced an element of logic, a factor of reality that might have jeopardized the magic. I had to gamble that the chemistry would be there between the two of you. Even one more day of delay might have been too late. Dasima was at the point of accepting, even though her heart wasn't in going. Now she has good reason not to leave Bali. And the whole tour is kaput, since the others will not go without her."

"Why don't you want her to go?"

"I don't want her confused. Beyond Bali lies a world that both saddens and angers me, but I can deal with it, because we have tanks and artillery and jet fighters and young men willing to follow me to the death to preserve our culture. But Dasima has no such armor. Can you imagine the impact upon her of Rome and Paris and London? I haven't permitted her even to go to Jakarta."

"Forgive me, Guntur, but she is not your daughter. Only your niece. Is such avuncular authority common in Bali?"

"My brother is a poet, a metaphysician. He defers to me in all temporal matters."

"What is the sponsor going to think about this?"

"I'm certain we'll be hearing soon enough. From the way he's been watching you all night, it's apparent he's already been informed of Dasima's decision."

"He's here?"

"Walton Chartwell."

Guntur enjoys shooting from the hip.

He watches me for some flicker of reaction, but I'm goddamned if I'm going to reward him every time he springs the trap.

I don't even snap my eyes over to Chartwell, sitting not more than twenty feet away. But what perfect typecasting! Chartwell is the ideal sponsor for a Balinese dance troupe. He has the style, the flamboyance, the ego. And the means.

"Well," I say, "that's one loose end I can tie up. So far the only one."

"What do you mean?"

"When I took my walk outside, Chartwell sent his wife out to buzz me. She claims he's the jealous type. I've been asking myself why a jealous husband would send his wife out on point. Now I can understand."

"He won't make things easy for you."

"Who does?"

"You could have been on Ambon now, nibbling on three-foot-long bananas. Do you wish I had not invaded your life? Is Dasima worth the danger in your being here?"

"You really want blood, don't you, Guntur."

"You are the only one who understands me," he replies with an air of amusement.

"I don't intend to answer you. I can't! The one thing the last ten years have taught me is I don't know shit about what *is* and *isn't* worth dying for!"

"How can you expect to?" he asks. "Unless you first know what's worth living for?"

Of course, it's one of those slick little aphorisms you can pick up once a month from *Reader's Digest*, but the danger in disparaging these handy axioms is that they keep coming back to slam you with their simplistic core of truth.

Dasima appears on stage again, this time performing the Legong Dance, a classical form enacting a story taken from the mythical *Malat*. She is dancing Princess Rangkesari, and another girl is dancing Prince Lasem. Dasima is wrapped in a skirt held in place by a binding of cloth from her waist to just under her arms and tied by a sash of gilt cloth. A collar set with jewels and mirrors reflects the back of her head. The front of her skirt descends in a train that passes backward between her legs. Guntur whispers to me to watch how skillfully she sweeps this heavy train aside with her foot when moving backward or making a turning motion. In this dance the prince has abducted her from her true love, who even now is approaching the palace. She begs Prince Lasem to set her free and thus avoid bloodshed. He refuses and goes out to meet her betrothed and gets himself zapped for his stubbornness.

My eyes drift away from Dasima and fix on Chartwell. I observe him half turned in his chair, glancing back at me. As which character does he see himself, I wonder—the contentious little bastard who abducted the girl or the avenging lover?

I turn back to watch the ending of the dance, but I still sense that I'm being watched. Not by Chartwell. He's busy whispering to Juliana. By the mysterious and obscure Chinese challenger? I can't spot him anywhere. And then I see!

Tran Hoi Ham himself is studying me from behind the partial screening of the other Vietnamese sitting around him.

I am troubled about letting him con me into having those two photographs taken. It makes no sense that he would want them. Why?

I add this enigma to the list. It seems to get longer with every hour I'm on Bali.

I whisper to Guntur, "The minute you've got those video tapes and surveillance tracks ready, contact me no matter where I am tomorrow. I need to listen to every word the Vietnamese said tonight."

We're outside the hotel later, Guntur and I, with Captain Hamzah and our Red Berets, waiting for the scout Ferrets to pick us up, when Walton Chartwell, still looking more like Michael Caine than any stunt double ever could, saunters up.

"Good evening, colonel," he greets Guntur. "Mr. Locke. I feel we already know each other."

"Was it you who told your wife I'm a professional killer?" I ask him in the indirect way I have with people.

"Ah! No dodging about, my darling, is there? Straight to the heart!"

"I asked you a question!"

I don't really know why I'm being so belligerent with the man. He's actually as charming as a poised little finger at teatime in Londontown. Possibly it's because I feel I've been peered at too much tonight by too many strangers and he's the first punching bag to come my way.

"I may have said something of the kind, but if so, it would

have been said with admiration. We're all into some kind of killing or other, aren't we, whether it's beating the other chap out of a contract, enforcing a mortgage, or simply failing in a marriage. At least, from what I hear about you, it's all stand-up. Just you and the chap having a go at you."

"Apology accepted," I say. I extend my hand. He accepts it and holds it firmly, with a steely strength I would never have assumed he had. I find myself opening to him. He has a winning smile. It appears to be natural, not one of those by-the-numbers flashing of teeth.

"Please come to see me when you can," he urges. "As soon as you can. The colonel will tell you where my offices are. I think we have things to discuss. We might be able to help each other."

"You'll be out of town for a day or two, I understand."

"Juliana invited you over?"

"Does it bother you?"

"Does it appear to?"

"When will you return?"

"Day after tomorrow. Please do call. Good night, gentlemen," he says to Guntur and the captain.

He moves off, rejoining the others in his party, but I do not see Juliana with them.

On the drive home to Batubulan, Guntur can no longer suppress what I can feel he's been trying to hold back.

"He will offer you money," he says abruptly.

"For what?"

"To leave Bali. To leave Dasima."

"I'll be leaving in ten or twelve days. Why should he pay me to do what I'm going to do, anyway?"

"Why do you already set your departure time?"

"Because by then we either have to bag the opposition, or Bali will start coming apart. Right?"

"That's right, John."

"We've got only ten more days before the rivers are choked with the bodies of the slaughtered. Or have you forgotten?"

"Hardly."

"Well, just about the time it all starts caving in, if we can't nail it down before then, I'll be sailing off. There isn't the least doubt in your mind about that, is there?"

"I haven't thought that far ahead."

"The hell you haven't! I'm sure you've already drawn up contingency plans for the rioting. But I don't even want to consider the possibility of our failing. I'm talking about another matter entirely. About Chartwell! Suppose he does offer me money to split? Since I'm leaving, anyway, why should it be such a big deal?"

"You'd take his money?"

"Of course not! But that's not the issue. I'm beginning to see you have still other plans in mind for me. Shall I tell you what I think they are?"

"You are not known, John, for your sensory aphasia."

"Sensory aphasia?" I repeat, and can't stop myself from laughing. The sonofabitch! He must have taken a special course in words that start with *a*. He'd stopped me out in the Halmahera Sea with "abate"; now he lays "aphasia" on me!

"Most of the people I hang with would simply have said I have a big mouth," I respond. "But since in your case I'm dealing with an especially erudite colonel, I shall have to say I'm beginning to perceive you may have intentions of luring me to settle down in Bali."

"That never entered my mind!"

"Bullshit!"

"Whatever happens between you and Dasima now that she's decided not to leave with the troupe is no longer my concern. My immediate purpose has been served. And that is the end of the matter as far as I'm concerned."

"But you're hoping?"

"Not really, John. If you were to decide to stay on and if you and Dasima were to make some living arrangement between you, the social complications could be extremely complex. The ethnic, religious, and cultural disparities could prove overwhelming, even to the most rocklike of lovers."

"All right, Guntur. We've kicked it around enough. But we both know what I'm talking about, okay?"

"I ask only this. If you do go see Chartwell and he asks you to release Dasima from your spell—if he asks you to help persuade her to make the tour, whether now or next month or next year, whether you do or don't decide to stay in Bali—what will you say to him?"

"So you know exactly how I feel about it, Guntur, I will tell him to take his goddamned money and go hire a dance troup in Thailand, where the people are already fucked by American and

Japanese money, where hundreds of thousands of Thais have been turned into whores—and to leave this island and these people and this girl alone!"

"Thank you," he says in a tone of such monumental sincerity that I'm tempted to set it alongside the gateway among all the other carved figures.

CHAPTER

16

Dasima comes to me sometime after midnight, notching herself into my arms without words. Our lovemaking is natural, virtually inconspicuous, the more passionate for its ease and silence. She watches me with open eyes as I move about her, her calm, serene face infinitely flexible in its variety of expressions, the oohs and ahs conveyed by her dark eyes alone. I realize how similar she is in bed to what she is on stage. When she dances, she responds to the music as another instrument, not as a performer. Here, joined with me, she is equally possessed by her role, letting it dominate her rather than commanding it, all the images of her existence from birth until this moment fused within her body and modulated into a single flowering.

I begin to understand what Guntur meant when he told me that dancing in Bali is not there to be looked at the way Westerners watch it because it's on the tour, watching it compulsively for deeper meaning to the point of self-exhaustion. The dancing is simply there to be seen and heard like the wind through the forest or water down a stream. Nor is the music to be listened to as music, but simply as a sound in the night. Making love with Dasima is equally elemental. Not since I was with Doan Thi in Vietnam have I felt such primal bonding. There you go, Locke!

You have to analyze it, psychologize it, don't you? *Primal bonding?* Shit, man! Just accept the simple joy! Stop being a spectator! Get into the act!

Later, Dasima spooned in sleep against me, I lie awake, my body run off somewhere with hers but my senses still in high boost.

I play back the floppy disc labeled "bells."

Isn't there some legend about the Jersey bells of the English channel?

I seem to remember my mother taking me one summer while I was still a child to St.-Ouen's Bay while she sketched the fishermen poised attentively at water's edge as they listened for bells upon the wind. Didn't she tell me then that if they heard a warning sound from under the sea, they would not set out? But if everything was quiet, they would go to sea?

I know for a fact there are innumerable accounts of sailors hearing the sound of church bells agitated by the waves over the sunken steeples of Port Royal in the West Indies after that city was submerged in the seventeenth century.

Debussy used this same theme of the sound of buried church bells in his "Disappearing Cathedral." And at Lochen in Holland it is told that two bells were stolen by Satan and hidden in ponds near the town. To this day the local peasants still hear the bells sounding from these ponds at midnight on Christmas.

What about church bells ringing without human assistance? It is recorded, I now remember, that the bells rang of their own volition when Thomas à Becket was murdered. And at Avignon there is a silver bell famous for its power to ring on its own. It is reported that it tolled for twenty-four hours at the death of a pope in distant Rome long before the news reached Avignon.

I listen to this turmoil until dawn. I don't know what, if anything, it means, but I do know that it has an obligatory significance, or I wouldn't be so hyped up. Take the case of the Pacific salmon. Electrodes in its olfactory bulbs fire when its epithelium is exposed to water from its spawning grounds. Then it zeros in toward home port without charts or Sat-Nav. Something is brushing at my epithelium, something about the Great Bronze Bell being buried, but since I'm a salmon without a spawning ground, I have to keep swimming aimlessly.

I determine that I must speak again, as soon as possible, to Ida Bagus Dewata at Pura Besakih.

I awaken Dasima.

"I'm going to Pura Besakih," I tell her. "I didn't want you to wake up and find me missing."

"I'm going with you."

In the semidarkness before dawn we approach the parked Mercedes outside the main gate. I hold one hand high over my head to make certain the colonel's sharpshooters don't mistake me for a terr. As I unlock the car, I observe one of the kitchen girls bringing offerings to the gate and spreading them on the ground. They appear lumpy, unartistic, nothing to compare with the ornate tiers of flowers and foods I have seen arrayed in the temples.

"Those are the *banten rin sor*," Dasima tells me. "To propitiate evil spirits. Every five days we lay them on the road outside the entrance so that the malevolent spirits will accept them and not try to come inside."

"They look like scraps, leftovers," I say.

"What else does evil deserve?" she asks.

At this early hour, when even the water buffalo are still sleeping, I open the Mercedes up and paint us into the parking lot at Pura Besakih before dawn.

Dasima and I ascend the forty-nine steps leading to the split gate opening into the first court of Pura Panataran Agung. We climb another twenty-one steps to the second court, which is guarded by a pair of carved lions. Twenty-four more steps bring us to the third court, from where I can see a row of *merus* built of brick and tiered with lime mortar.

"In those pavilions," Dasima tells me, "repose the souls of the former rajas of Bali. We call that sanctuary Kings' Area."

She leads me to an open-air oratory only now emerging from darkness, a small platform to one side of Kings' Area.

There Dewata sits alone, cross-legged on a mat, his face eastward to the dawn.

His head, body, and legs appear as stonelike as the carved gods we passed in the lower temple courtyards, but his arms and hands move sinuously and from his throat the tones of an incantation issue: "*Om mani padme hum*"—the traditional, "Om, the jewel in the lotus, hum." But Dasima informs me that in Bali this means he's assigning a color to each finger of his hands—*om* is white, *ma* is blue, and *ni* is yellow.

Over his lap he's spread a prayer napkin of red silk ornamented with gold leaves and in one hand he holds a natural vase, a *sesirat*

Dasima calls it, made of leaves from the lontar palm. From this, she explains, he will sprinkle holy water, *toja-tirta*, on the people who will come later this morning with offerings. One of his primary duties as priest is the consecration of water. Now he begins murmuring passages from the Balinese vedas and intermixing them with mantras.

"How long might this take" I ask Dasima.

"Anywhere from half an hour to three hours," she whispers. "We can go somewhere and make love while we wait."

"Very sensible," I comment.

"We are a practical people," she says. "When our men feel strongly about a girl and wish to sleep with her, they say so. Why should only men have this right of honesty? I want you inside me again, filling my body as you fill my thoughts. I wish it not only for the coming night, but for this moment, here, where the gods can envy us; but that would be indiscreet, since we must not let them see how happy we are, or they might punish us. Still, there are places nearby where not even they can peek."

She leads me back the way we came. En route she pauses here and there at the feet of certain deities to raise her hands in the *sembah* of reverence, as though blessing our way to mislead the gods.

When we arrive at the *wantilan* at the end of the road, I start down toward the parking area, where the Mercedes is still the only car. Like most red-white-and-blue-blood Americans, I found my earliest sexual refuge in an automobile, but Dasima catches my hand and leads me in the opposite direction, toward a ravine.

We climb down mossy tiers toward a distant temple, the Kidul, off to the east, but plunge suddenly through the looking glass into a wonderland of grass and trees at the bottom of the ravine.

While I'm evaluating the privacy factor and the likelihood of interruption, Dasima has already blithely removed her *kebaya* and is unwinding her waistband and opening her batik *kain*. Naked and smiling, she hurries to me. Without clothing she is even more beautiful than when she's hidden within their color and texture. In this place she does not look naked. I, with my white skin, do. Or at least imagine that I do. But the blending of our skins, brown with white, into the olive green of the damp moss, soon makes me forget my self-consciousness.

I lie back on the moss and plant her astride and above me. Finding her ready, I enter her. I bend her closer. She folds upon me, her breasts to my lips. Past the blossom in her hair I see the distant peak of Mount Agung looming over us, startlingly clear of its usual cloud cover. I find myself engaged with the erotic imagery of my personal escalation, so pitifully minute in comparison to Mount Agung's awesome erection, but after a moment of Dasima lustfully plunging herself up and down upon me, I am so overwhelmed by waves of feeling that I become molten and fiercely eruptive.

Later, as we climb back toward Dewata's oratory, I marvel at how untouched Dasima appears, how inviolate, except for the private light in her eyes as she peers at me with growing wonder and excitement to be discovering the never-ending surprises within her own body.

Dewata remains as graven as when we left, except that his fingers are now flicking blooms toward the four points of the compass.

"He is finishing," Dasima whispers.

Soon, like rising smoke, the old man comes to us.

Dasima joins her hands to her forehead in obeisance. He returns the reverential gesture.

"I'm sorry to trouble you," I say, "but I have two questions. Would it be proper to ask them now?"

"Tomorrow's business should be done today," he replies, "and the afternoon business in the forenoon, for death will not wait, whether a person has done his business or not."

"Amen!" I agree. "When I was here with the colonel, you said two things that keep bumping around in my head. May I ask what you meant when you said you didn't think the Great Bronze Bell could originally have been a war drum?"

"Because of its size."

"But suppose," I suggest, "it was a war drum not intended to be carried into battle? But a drum to sound the alarm?"

"Yes," he says. "That is a possibility. Is it important?"

"I don't know. Except that at this point everything is. Do you recall using the words 'one of the legends I believe in' when you were saying that there are many legends surrounding the bell?"

"Yes," he says. "Since I believe only in the one legend, that is the one I told you—about the bellmaker's daughter throwing herself into the molten lava."

"Are there others in which you *don't* believe that you might tell me, any which explain the aftertone of 'hsieh' in a different context?"

"There is one other," he says, "about the bell being cast by a great warrior king who conquered most of the lands around him because of the magic sound of the bell. Before every battle he would strike the bell, and it would give off its soft cry of 'hsieh' as a reminder to all the soldiers, a reminder to protect their feet from their enemies. As long as they came on the eve of battle and prayed before the bell, then touched it with proper reverence, they were made invulnerable in battle, except for their feet. If they protected those vulnerable extremities, no enemy could ever vanquish them. For thirty years and three the king and his men defeated all their enemies and grew ever more powerful. Then, one day, on the eve of a great battle that would have given the king all the land from sea to sea, the bell sounded by itself, letting out a great thunder of warning. But the soldiers became so frightened by this sound they had never heard before, they ran barefoot from the palace, to be slaughtered by the waiting enemy. I have never believed this legend and so refrained from mentioning it to you."

"Thank you," I say. "It has roots in common with the Greek legend of Achilles."

A sense of excitement starts to bubble within me, for no reason I can isolate at this moment. Yet the excitement is palpable. I feel it coursing through me as though I'm on the threshold of some significant awareness that will illuminate the *why* of the theft.

"Have you any knowledge of where this mythical kingdom was?" I ask.

"The land we now call Burma," Dewata says.

"The land from which the bell came?"

"If the legends are true."

"Well, thank you. If I have to come back again, I'll hope you'll understand. I still need to learn much before I can ask productive questions."

"If you come again," he says, "you are welcome. And should you return, I would not be offended if you were to bring me a personal offering."

"Please name it."

"An orange Popsicle."

I am his follower forever. The highest priest of Bali, a man Guntur tells me many believe is the reincarnation of a Bodhisattva spirit who has elected to return to mortal form, after he's already achieved enlightenment, so that he can help others, wanting an orange Popsicle! With this single incongruity, the living Buddha makes me his. I will follow Dewata wherever he leads, bearing his Popsicles.

Leaving Besakih, I point us toward the sea and wind down through villages along roads lined with tall bamboo poles from which palm-leaf tassels droop. These are the *pandjors*, Dasima tells me, left over from *Nyepi*.

Out of nowhere she asks me what the Western belief is about the creation of woman.

"God took a rib from Adam, and from it he fashioned Eve," I tell her.

She appears disappointed. "That is all? Only a rib?"

"That's it."

"In our legend," she says, "Twashtri, the Divine Artificer, came to the time when he was to create woman and found that in the making of man he had exhausted all his materials. He had no solid elements left to work from, so he fashioned women out of the odds and ends of creation. He took the rotundity of the moon and the curves of creepers and the clinging of tendrils and the trembling of grass and the slenderness of the reed and the bloom of flowers and the lightness of leaves and the tapering of the elephant's trunk and the glances of deer and the clustering of rows of bees and the joyous gaiety of sunbeams and the weeping of clouds and the fickleness of the winds and the timidity of the hare and the vanity of the peacock and the softness of the parrot's bosom and the hardness of adamant and the sweetness of honey and the cruelty of the tiger and the warm glow of fire, and the coldness of snow and the chattering of jays and the croaking of the *kokila* and the hypocrisy of the crane and the fidelity of the *chakravaka*—and compounding all these together, he made woman and gave her to man."

Beats the hell out of our version, I tell myself, as we enter the buzz-saw tourist ghetto of Kuta Beach. I find myself back among my own in the sleaze zone where few know or care that the *chakravaka* can be faithful and the crane hypocritical.

Kuta Beach is a bamboo town sweaty with Australians, Swiss, French, Germans, and Javanese. Here the dress code is tank tops and dirty, frayed shorts, considered indecent by the *imigrasi* agents in Denpasar. Surfers with furry legs and boards thrusting out of rented jeeps speed off toward the morning's top-to-bottom tubes.

European girls with underarm hair sprouting like artichokes wander from shop to shop. There is a slatternly look about them. I suspect that if you were to hold a Ban-stick up in front of them, they would recoil as painfully from it as a vampire from an upraised cross, but in their defense I must confess that my American father raised me in spiffy sphincter tradition, and I may be too fussy about personal hygiene.

I park in front of the Sunshine Surfboard Shop on Jl. Legian, and leaving Dasima to fend for herself with the cluster of young Balinese surfers hanging around the place, calling me "mate," I go into the shop and buy a dozen expensive bars of imported board wax to use in barter. Sure enough, the Balinese surfers are flaring their nostrils and tugging on their silver neck pendants when I come back out, and Dasima is laughing at them. I may have imagined it, but I think I hear one of the boys muttering, "I'm a Heavy in a Chevvie" as I get into the Mercedes, but it only amuses me as I drive to the sea.

The surf has topped out at six feet. Dasima and I settle on the sand, and I watch the surfers trying to scramble to the reef through the crosscurrents. The smart ones are riding out on *prahus*, the others battling the undertow. I use my binos and track the surfers outside the reef as they catch the combers. Most of the surfers are Aussie, but I spot a number of Balinese boys staying right out there with them, firing through the tubes and shooting back out still proudly on their boards.

Four old women approach us and ask Dasima something.

"Would you like a massage?" Dasima inquires on their behalf.

"You mean they're actually not selling batik shirts?"

"These women have hands as strong as yours, my love," Dasima says. "They will massage your body with coconut oil and *boreh*. You will smell like a flower afterward."

"Right here in the sand?"

"They will spread a towel. You take off your clothes. Except for your shorts. They would not object to your being naked except that the police do not permit it."

I check out the four women. Grandmothers. All grinning at me toothlessly. I pick the one with leathered hands like an eagle's talons and strip down to my Jockey shorts, stretch out on the towel, and let her go to work on me. Dasima is right. This one has hands that could pluck off my scapula.

"Ask her what she was doing the morning of *Nyepi*," I moan to Dasima through my pain.

There's an exchange, then Dasima tells me, "She says she was at home where she belonged. She wants to know why you wish to know."

"Tell her I'm curious about that morning. I'm seeking knowledge of any surfers who may have been out between dawn and eight o'clock. Where might I find this out?"

Again the exchange in Balinese.

"The surfers hang out at Ula Watu's souvenir shop," she says, "where you can buy good *pukkah* necklaces."

"Would you like a good *pukkah* necklace?"

"I might."

Smelling like a flower, slathered with *boreh*—a yellow paste made of flowers, aromatic roots, and cloves—I transfer our base of operations to Ula Watu's shop in the crotch of Kuta's Coney Island.

Dasima and I select the best pukkah necklace in the place. I drape it over her flowered head, arrange it around her lovely slender neck, and observe I am being watched enviously by a Balinese surfer. An oversize T-shirt with cut-off sleeves hangs from his shoulders. It reads SINGAPORE BILLY GRAHAM CRUSADE.

"Hey, Spunky," he calls to me. "How's it going?"

"Just eating the wind," I tell him. "How's your supply of board wax?"

"Shit, man! Low!"

I toss him one of the dozen bars I've bought at the Sunshine Shop. "Yours. For zip."

All his arrogance vanishes. "Thanks, man!"

"It's okay," I say. "I'm in a giving mood this morning."

"You're all right! American, huh?"

"Yep. Your English is really up there. Where'd you learn?"

"Just hanging ten with the Aussies."

"Where's the best place for me to hang out if I want to pick up some pointers about surfing conditions around here?"

"Ayu's Juice Shop, right on the main road. They make great jaffles there."

He waves at us and takes off with the coveted bar of board wax.

Dasima has never before tasted the Australian jaffle, a filled sandwich that gets properly baked before it's served piping hot.

The jaffles and the cold beer have packed Ayu's Juice Shop this midmorning. The Aussie surfers at the surrounding tables leer at me approvingly for having corraled such a stunner as the Balinese bird perched on my arm. It's all open and friendly, and I lean over to the nearest table and ask if anyone's short of board wax, that I just happen to have scored a few extra bars I can donate to the needy. I pass out six more wax cakes to the most indigent, and in return everyone wants to buy Dasima and me beers. After half an hour we're all sitting around swapping surfing stories, and I manage to work in my question about how was it that early morning a couple of weeks back when all the Balinese were at home, the morning of *Nyepi*. But not one of the Aussies at Ayu's Juice Shop has been in Bali more than a week. One of them mentions a *losmén* where a group of surfers he knows are planning on spending their entire thirty-day visa allotment before they go back.

I thank them, and we skid over to a beachfront bungalow.

The surfers I'm hoping to question are already out beyond the reef, but Dasima talks to the owner of the *losmén*. Yes, he acknowledges, his guests will be here for a month and for that reason he has reduced the normal charge to a mere six thousand rupiahs a day. When did they arrive? Only ten days ago. Here it is marked on their statement, as we can see. We thank him and leave, empty-handed. Ten days ago does not go far enough back in time to have put them on the beach after dawn of Nyepi.

"You have chosen a difficult way," Dasima comments as I cruise bumper to bumper in Kuta's late-morning traffic. "Are you assuming the bell may have been brought to this area?"

"I didn't know you knew exactly what I was doing in Bali."

"My uncle told me when he asked me to accompany you. He knows he can trust me not to whisper a word to anyone, not even to my mother and father."

"I have to start where there are surfers and work my way up the coast," I explain to her, "questioning them wherever I can find them. It's unreasonable to assume that not one of them was out that morning or failed to see the bell being moved. If, in fact, it was hidden along the shoreline or in the sea, some surfer, somewhere, must have seen it. But not knowing *what* he was seeing, he has had no reason to talk about it. I've got to find that person!"

"How do you know it was hidden in the sea?"

"I don't. But your uncle and Captain Hamzah are checking out all the inland sites. I'm taking the shoreline. I guess because I'm a water person. No other reason."

Again I park near the beach, and we walk onto the sand, heating up as the morning advances. Beyond in the lagoon, fully clothed women are moving ghostlike through the water, immersed to their waists. They seem to glide through the lagoon, gossamer kitelike cloths held out ceremoniously before them, partly in the water, partly trembling in the wind above the surface.

"They gather baby shrimp," Dasima explains. She points to other women along the shore, each with a pail filled with seawater. "The cloth captures the tiny creatures. Then they're dropped into the pails and flown to Java, where at shrimp farms they grow into huge prawns for the Japanese market."

I am so fascinated watching the water ballet of these graceful fisherwomen I almost fail to see four young Balinese surfers sloshing out of the water a few meters away. Only as they pass us and flare their nostrils at Dasima do they make their imprint on me. Not so much the boys as the board one of them carries. The words CURRUMBIN BEACH CLUB are stenciled on his board. The letters are partly concealed by transparent tape that covers the board near its tip.

I feel hairs rising on the back of my neck.

"Call them over," I urge Dasima.

She calls to them. They swagger over, their lean shoulders glistening in the sunlight from the water still dripping from their black hair.

"Ask him where he got his board."

She asks him.

Suddenly, the boy streaks away, board and all.

I leap up, run after him.

He's fast—seventeen years younger—but I'd chase this particular boy and that particular surfboard across the Sahara if I had to.

I gain on him.

I shout for him to stop.

But he keeps running.

I have to tackle him.

He falls, wriggles out of my arms, scoops up sand to throw in my eyes, but I spin around on my shoulders and side kick his hand. He tries to run off again, but I trip him. As he falls I jump up, overshadowing him.

"Take one more step, I'll cripple you!" I tell him.

He lies on the sand, clutching his board and not moving. Dasima runs in with the other three boys.

They start shouting at me in Balinese.

"Tell them," I say to Dasima, "that I'm taking this young man and this board to army headquarters in Tabanan. If they have any objections, tell them to get in touch with Colonel Katrini."

"What has the boy done?" Dasima asks.

I grab the surfboard from him and rip the tape off, exposing four bullet holes.

"He's done nothing," I tell her, "if he can explain how he got this board—a board that belongs to some Aussie from the Currumbin Surfers Club in Queensland—a board with four bullet holes in it!"

CHAPTER

17

The boy's name is Hatta.

He is seventeen.

Like ninety percent of the Balinese population, he belongs to the fourth, nonaristocratic caste, the Sudras.

He lives on the Legian village side of Kuta. There his family owns a *losmén* that they rent out to tourists. His job is tending the garden and doing the dishes, although there are not too many dishes, he admits, since the free breakfast his parents give their guests at these neighborhood hostels is served on banana leaves that are later fed to the pigs. This gives him time to surf.

All this is translated for me by Dasima as she and I sit off to one side in Guntur's office and listen to his interrogation of the frightened young man in a language Dasima tells me is low Balinese.

Her uncle, she informs me, speaks six languages in addition to English, but this is uncommon for a Balinese of the Satrias, the military class. Bali itself has three languages, high, middle, and low Balinese, the words in each mostly dissimilar. Then there is Kawi, used on ritual occasions in classical writing, an ancient form of Javanese, its words predominantly from Sanskrit and used today only by the priests. But her uncle has so many political

145

dealings with the *pedandas*, he learned Kawi to be sure the priests could never trick him. And finally there is Bahasa Indonesian, the country's official, state language. And of course Malay, the lingua franca of the East Indies.

"It was the morning after *Nyepi*," Hatta tells Guntur. "I was bodysurfing with two of my friends off the reef at Point Sari in Padangbai. There on the reef I discovered the board wedged between two coral heads. There was no sign of its owner. Only my friends and I were in the sea. I recovered the board and took it ashore."

"Were these little holes already in it?" Guntur asks, tapping each puncture in the board.

"Yes, colonel."

"What did you think had caused them?"

"At first I thought they might have made by the teeth of a shark and that the shark had killed the one who owned the board. But when I looked more closely, I saw they could not have been made by a shark."

"Then by what?"

"I could not imagine. But covering them with tape mended the board, and I have been using it ever since."

Guntur permits the boy to leave but keeps the board, promising Hatta he may come for it in three more days if the original owner has not claimed it by then.

"In late-morning traffic, it takes an hour to drive to Pedangbai," Guntur says. "But by chopper we can be there in fifteen minutes!"

Guntur assigns a driver to take Dasima and the Mercedes to her family compound. Before she leaves, Dasima places a flower from her hair behind my ear and touches her nose to mine.

Guntur and I fly in over Padangbai, rotoring down into a scorched town of sleeping dogs and lethargic roosters. Terraced hills march off the bay, completely encircling the town on the land side. Out in the deeper water offshore a white Norwegian luxury liner lies at anchor. Its shore boats are even now streaming tourists over the shallow, pale-green water to waiting tour buses parked at the end of the long rickety quay. At the dock a *kapal laut* is casting off on its shuttle run for Lembar on the neighboring island of Lombok. Another vessel, a car ferry, is getting up power to leave. I read K. M. KUDA PUTIH on her port bow, though the letters are in critical need of a major sanding and paint job.

We dust down at the quay near maritime offices in front of which three jeeps and a knot of police officers, already alerted by radio, wait for us. "All private yachts entering South Bali must clear here at Pedangbai," Guntur tells me. "This is where *Steel Tiger* will be cleared before she is brought to you at Benoa."

"What is her latest position?" I haven't yet gotten *Steel Tiger*'s daily fix report from Guntur.

"Seventy miles northeast of Wetar Island in the Banda Sea," he informs me. That translates to another four or five days before I'll be able to get back aboard her.

We climb out of the chopper. I feel the sweat dribbling down my spine and creeping into the crease between my glutes. The sunshine is blinding.

Guntur introduces me to the police officers, climbs into the lead jeep, motioning for me to sit in back with him. The head of the Pedangbai police occupies the front seat next to the driver. We grind officiously through town. The other two jeeps follow as though linked to us by short lengths of chain.

Minutes later we park in front of a hotel on a hill overlooking a beach. From this elevation I can take in the bay at Pedangbai— the passenger liner lying to the wind in deep water to the east of the bay, the reef structure massing both east and west, and stretching back to the west beyond Point Bungsil, an industrial complex with a fleet of small boats and oil-drilling rigs anchored offshore.

"Pacific Petroleum," Guntur says, following my gaze. "It was from that depot the truck and crane were stolen."

He sweeps me into the hotel with him while I'm still evaluating the fascinating coincidence of Pac-Pet being so close to where a Balinese surfer recovered a shot-up surfboard.

The owner of the hotel is summoned. I evaluate his ethnic mix as Japanese and Sumatran. Guntur excludes the Pedangbai police from the interrogation, choosing instead to defuse the man's fear at having to confront so many uniforms, so many flat bellies, so many unforgiving faces, and such an encirclement of threatening sunglasses.

Guntur removes his own Polaroids, letting the man look into deceptively friendly eyes, and suggests the three of us take a stroll along the hotel grounds above the sea.

For my benefit, Guntur speaks in English to the owner.

"In Queensland, Australia, there is an area called the Gold Coast," he tells the man. "From that area come some of the world's best surfers. And some of them belong to a club known as the Currumbin Surfers Club."

The owner is already appearing more at ease. He keeps bowing slightly with every word Guntur speaks. He has the polished courtesy of a Sony vice-president and is every bit as noncommittal.

"That is the first point I wish you to bear in mind," Guntur continues. "A second point is that we are having problems with young tourists who come to Bali and fail to apply to Immigration to have their visas renewed. As you know, I am sure, failure to leave the country within the thirty days allotted can result in a jail sentence unless the visa has been extended by applying to the proper authority. And any Balinese businessman who fails to report such tourists overstaying their time limits can also be imprisoned."

Guntur stops at the wooden railing around the deck above the vast Indian Ocean, which washes Bali's southern shoreline.

"Do you have both those points fixed firmly in mind?"

The owner bows again.

"Your coming here this morning, colonel, is most timely," he says. "I was about to call the *imigrasi* in Denpasar."

"Ah!" Guntur says. It is not easy to *say* "ah," believe me. Either you have to let it rasp out of your throat or deliberately exhale the sound. Guntur, I suppose because of his dexterity with so many tongue-twisting languages, is able to *say* the word. This is most effective, since it offers the listener an array of meaning from which he can choose. In this instance, the implication is "How fortunate for you, my dear owner." There is an element of congratulation in the word, as well, an assurance that it will not be necessary, after all, to haul the poor bastard away.

"Some two weeks or more ago," the owner says, his heels now lined up and clicking anxiously as he talks, "four of my guests failed to return from their regular morning surfing. At first, I thought nothing of it. It is common for some of our guests from Australia to engage a room here, then to hire a jeep and surf the reefs along other parts of the shoreline, and stay out on the beaches. I assumed this accounted for their failure to return, especially since all their clothes and luggage remained in their rooms. I kept expecting them to return any afternoon. But tomorrow will be the thirtieth day since they checked into the hotel, and according to the regulations they have until then to renew their visas. You see, colonel, I am very aware of the law and of my responsibilities under it, since I was planning to call the *imigrasi* this very afternoon if the four guests did not reappear today."

"You are to be commended," Guntur says, smiling, even bowing a little to the owner. "And now, if it would not be too much trouble, I would like you to take us to their rooms."

Somehow I know, looking through the things they've left behind, these four young Australians will never be seen again. Guntur, too, senses it as we comb through their luggage, obtain their identities and home addresses, see photographs of their girl friends, a wife in the case of one of them. They were all members of the Currumbin Surfers Club.

"Do you or any members of your staff know where they were surfing on the morning of *Nyepi*?" I ask the owner.

"I would assume they went where they'd been going regularly—to the reef off Point Sari."

Where Hatta had recovered one of their boards.

Guntur and I thank the owner. Guntur assures him he has conducted himself in a most exemplary manner, and now he expects him to say nothing, absolutely nothing, to anyone—especially not to the *imigrasi*—about the matter. In this way there will be no further investigation and more importantly no fine. All necessary details, the collection of the personal clothing, the notification of the Australian officials, will be handled directly by the army. Guntur gives the man his official card.

"And what of the unpaid hotel bill?" the owner asks.

"This, too, will be adjusted," Guntur promises. "Meanwhile, absolute secrecy must be observed. You are not to speak to any of your staff or family about this meeting with us. This is a matter in the national interest."

Guntur is elated when, en route to the jeeps waiting out front, we are alone.

"Why else would they have vanished," he asks, "unless they'd been seen by the terrorists and eliminated as witnesses to the hiding of the bell? Their bodies and their boards were all scooped up and taken away, except for the one board, which must have been swept off by a breaking wave—the board with the telltale bullet holes of the fusillade that killed them. I congratulate you, John, on coming up with this. If this is an example of inductive reasoning, I am totally revamping my present method of thinking."

"Let's not fail to give Lady Luck a couple of points, too," I say. "That's all good police work is—putting yourself out where the dice are being tossed and getting lucky."

"Well," he says expansively, "it is now obvious that the Great Bronze Bell lies hidden off the reef at Point Sari."

"There's still one key question to be answered before you jump to that conclusion," I point out. "How did they manage to get the bell from the beach into the water, across the lagoon where they wouldn't have left it because of the shallow water, then out over the reef and into deep water? All they had was a truck and a crane."

Guntur stares at me bleakly.

"You see," I explain, "inductive reasoning works in all directions. If you back into a crazy concept and it looks promising, you have to look for ways to blow it apart before you start patting yourself on the back."

"Nevertheless," Guntur insists, "I am proceeding on the belief that the bell lies at the bottom of the sea off Point Sari. The depth out there runs from two hundred and fifty feet to five hundred. I am immediately ordering surface craft to crisscross every square meter of the harbor area with sonar and bottom-scanning equipment."

"Do you have anything that reliable?"

"I can get a submarine from Surabaja in a matter of hours."

"I have another idea," I suggest. "If anyone has the proper equipment to help us locate the bell, it should be Pac-Pet. Between their aeromagnetic equipment and their seismic reflectors and their geophones, they should be able to pinpoint the bell for us in a matter of hours."

"Splendid!" Guntur exults. "You see the American technical mind at work! Beautiful! I wish I had been born American, not Asian. I often pray that in my next incarnation I can come back as a Balinese with an American mind. I would dominate the world!"

"In the meantime," I say, "if you'll forgive me, the question still remains—how do you move an inert object weighing more than five hundred thousand pounds across a beach in a matter of minutes, through the shallows, and over a reef into deep water? You might want to hold up the search until we can solve that one."

He elects to ignore this.

Flying back to headquarters at Tabanan, I hear him calling through to his radio dispatcher to ask that a conference call be set up for one hour from now with his commanding general in Jakarta.

"I'll bring the navy into this now," he says. "I shall request that all three T-43 ocean minesweepers, two of our Kronstadt patrol craft, and one Type-209 sub be assigned to the mission."

For a moment it strikes me as ironic that the naval inventory Guntur has just ticked off is of Soviet origin, but in the munitions business nothing is to be thought of as ironic. That Communists are selling weapons to an anti-Communist government should be viewed as perfectly normal.

"While you're doing that," I say, "I'm going to take Walton Chartwell up on his invitation. I'm going to ask him for his help—the minute he gets back from wherever it is he was going."

"If you ask him for his help, John, he's going to ask you for yours. And you know what that involves. Dasima!"

"I'll worry about that when it happens."

We hover above the drill field.

Below, lines of recruits are out defying the afternoon sun. From up here they look even more ragged than I recall them being from ground level.

Suddenly our radio operator receives an incoming message.

He turns to the colonel, with me in the back of the chopper, and speaks to Guntur in Indonesian.

Guntur snaps back an immediate order.

The chopper aborts landing, spins around, and climbs for altitude, turning to the northeast.

"What?" I ask Guntur. He's staring at me strangely. Without looking me in the eyes.

"They have just attacked your friend."

"My God! Tip?"

He nods. "Rocket-propelled grenades."

"Is he alive?"

"They don't know yet. At this moment they are still in a fire fight with the terrorists."

I look off toward Ubud.

I feel as though I've just been kicked in the balls.

CHAPTER

18

Even ten clicks out as we power in toward Ubud and the mantling forest of *waringin* trees I can see the pillar of smoke drifting up from the target area.

At the site, Guntur is chattering on the radio with his Red Berets.

He gives the pilot instructions.

"The attackers are dead," he tells me. "The area is secured."

"Goddam it, Guntur! It's Tip I want to know about!"

"We're going right in," he says. We squash down in the empty parking lot. I'm out of the chopper while the skids are still a meter off the ground.

I start on a run across the bridge to Tip's island. A four-foot section has been blasted away. Pieces of the bridge have landed among the lily pads and thrust up like obscene monuments. I jump the space and charge straight into the living area, shouting for Tip.

Sarna appears with her son and raises her palms to me. She shows no evidence of alarm.

"Thank God!" I cry. "At least the two of you are all right! Where is Tip?"

"Putting out the fire," she says. "In the factory."

I run out back.

Six Balinese factory workers are dipping pails into the pond and handing them along a pail brigade to Tip, who throws the water on a corner of the building that is still burning briskly.

For reasons of the past, but making no sense within the present context, I automatically ask Tip, not in English but in Vietnamese, *"Ong manh gioi khong?"* How are you?

Without looking away from the fire he calls back to me, *"Toi manh gioi."* I'm fine.

"What were they using on you?"

"Luu dan," he says. Grenades.

Guntur trots in with half a dozen men. He orders them to take over from Tip and put out the fire.

Tip surrenders the pail.

"Fucking lousy shots," he says, "whoever they are. Incidentally, who are they?"

"Come," Guntur says. "I will show you."

Tip and I follow him out and across the bridge. As we move out of the perimeter into the forest, I hear the *champ-champ-champ* of more choppers bringing in more paras to augment the defensive force.

In a small clearing Guntur leads us to the sprawled bodies of three young men who lie in the ultimate pose I have seen so many times, like deflated rubber effigies still sinking into the earth. So often combat dead remind me of cast-off condoms.

Tip moves around them with a remembered expertise ten years of peace have not yet stripped from his sensorium.

"Who *are* these gooners?"

We don't answer him immediately.

There are—were—three of them.

All three are suited up like some James Bondish paramilitary group—same parachute-type zippered cammie jumpsuits, same boonie caps, same spanking-new jungle boots.

"Burmese!" I say to Guntur.

He nods.

"But not so much Kachin as Shan. You sure the others were Kachin?"

"No," he admits. "They, too, might have been Shan."

"What others?" Tip asks.

"Our bad guys," I tell him.

153

Then something comes right off the ground and drills me straight between the eyes. I stand there transfixed, almost unable to breathe.

"The boonie caps, Guntur! Look at the emblems on their boonie caps!"

Guntur bends to retrieve the cap from the nearest body. He stares without speaking at the symbol pinned to the front of the cap above the visor.

It is a replica of a bell—of a bronze bell.

Guntur's eyes rise to mine and hold. We both feel we're in the presence of something always one step ahead of us that we're running late, terribly late.

Tip is busy looking over the equipment they'd used against him. Their weapons are Soviet RPG-7 antitank rocket launchers with OG-7 high-explosive grenades, with enough unfired grenades left in the crate to have smeared Ubud off the map. Only swift moves on the part of Guntur's Red Berets limited their time on target.

Tip tells me they'd managed to get off only three rounds before it was over.

I lift my chin and let the afternoon wind ruffle my hair. I listen to the foliage around us rustling in the fresh breeze.

"That's where they miscalculated," Tip observes, watching me feel the wind. "The OG-7 is subject to crosswinds. And the optical sighting procedure on these babies is still far from soldier-proofed. The grenade is smaller than the PG-7 we had, John. It tends to veer off target in this kind of wind."

Tip was my tail gunner, bringing up the rear a good ten meters behind our team, his elephant gun primed with a flachette round ready to go at the first sign of contact. I've seen him lay a grenade into a cave at three hundred yards, through an entry so small you'd never guess an enemy sniper could crawl in there.

"They made another mistake," he says. "They were too far out—almost out to their max range, damn near nine hundred meters."

Tip squats next to the unfired grenades in the crate. "OM-4 point-detonating fuse," he comments.

"I'm relieved to see the incident hasn't stressed you too greatly," I say. "You're just too fucking cool, man!"

"How do I explain the attack to my wife?"

"I'm going to leave that up to you, ol' buddy," I say. "If we blame this on the Vietnamese, the people around here are going to start slicing up some harmless Chinese citizens."

"I can always blame it on Darga."

"Who's Darga?"

"The goddess of death," Guntur says.

"We have to improve the quality of the shit we've been putting out for the evil spirits," Tip says. "I'll tell Sarna *that*."

"You mean she'll buy that?"

"A lot easier than if I told her three Burmese indigs tried to light us up with a weapon she doesn't know anybody's ever invented."

"Excellent!" Guntur agrees. He orders the Red Berets to pass the word among the villagers that Darga is demanding a better class of *banten rin sor*.

"Let's stop evading the issue," I say to Guntur. "What do you make of that emblem on their caps? Is that or isn't it a replica of a bronze bell?"

"It is."

I feel a chill dart up my back, one of the better body experiences when I'm hyped like this.

Following an instinct, I drop to my knees alongside one of the dead men and unlace his combat boots. Even his brown socks are new issue, still due for their first wash. I strip the sock from his right foot.

What I knew without looking would be there *is* there—on the back of his right heel. And on the back of his left.

The tattoo of a bell.

Guntur rips off the boots and socks of the other two dead Burmese.

The bell is there, too.

"What does it mean?" Guntur asks.

"They belong to somebody's private army, I'm beginning to think. Those tattoos are supposed to make them invulnerable."

"You're joking, of course."

"Just laughing at myself, Guntur, for daring to let my imagination jerk off."

I tell him and Tip the legend of the Burma war bell—thirty-three years of victory. Then, because the king's troops fled when they heard the bell's thunder and went unshod into battle, they were all slaughtered.

"Could there be some new hotshot warlord in Burma?" I ask

Guntur. "Could these be his men? Did he send them to Bali to bring back the bell as a rallying symbol of the victory he hopes to gain?"

Guntur promises to make immediate contact with every one of his Indonesian agents in Burma. Within the next forty-eight hours, he promises me, we shall know the infrastructure and troop strength of every armed contingent inside Burma.

"I want to see the bodies of the first three Burmese you shot," I say to him. "And that Vietnamese, too. I can't believe nobody noticed tattoos on *their* heels!"

Tip has been watching me, his head tilted like that old dog in the long-ago RCA ads, one ear cocked into the megaphone.

"You okay?" I ask.

"Yeh," he says. "I'm fine. It's you I'm worried about."

"What's to worry?" I ask.

"I thought you learned in 'Nam you can get killed fucking around with guns. When are you going to pack it in, John, come in off the TA?"

"That's pretty stupid, Tip!" I say. I feel myself getting angry. "*You* gave up guns, didn't you? And look what almost happened to you!"

"Nobody's shot at me for ten years, John," he says quietly. "Not until *you* showed up."

I try to glare at him. But he just stands there looking like the all-American Mr. Right.

How the hell can you glare at Mr. Right?

CHAPTER

19

At headquarters Captain Hamzah is virtually toe-dancing with congratulations as we return.

Guntur has radioed in from Ubud to disinter the three Burmese killed at the airport and to lay out our murdered Vietnamese prisoner alongside the others.

By now Hamzah has seen for himself the tattoos on the heels of each man, and the moment we arrive in his improvised morgue at one end of the army infirmary he starts chittering away that if anything proves his theory of a planned insurrection within Bali, these markings indicating a secret society certainly do.

He recommends that the Vietnamese delegation, scheduled to leave by plane this evening, be placed under immediate arrest and that Tran Hoi Ham, known to be a high-ranking officer in the North Vietnamese Army, masquerading on this so-called cultural tour, be put to torture until he confesses.

For a moment I suspect that Guntur may actually slap his fervent aide-de-camp across the face. "We are not at war with Vietnam!" he screams at Hamzah. "Why are you so desperate to impose your personal theory on the rest of us? Did *you* come up with bells tattooed on the heels of these terrorists? No!"

Hamzah falls into the military sanctuary of standing at rigid attention before his infuriated superior.

"I am going to give you one last chance, captain, to prove you are worthy of being my aide! I am putting you in charge of the search operation tomorrow morning at Point Sari. You will act as my liaison during the sweep of those waters. I expect you to be calling me in a matter of hours once the search has begun—to report the bell has been located."

"Yes, sir!" the captain says enthusiastically.

"In the meantime, have you assembled the tapes of the Vietnamese delegation's conversation at last night's reception?"

"Everything is ready for you, sir, in Operations."

The three of us settle back into chairs in a darkened room and begin to watch a playback of three hours of the covert taping of the Vietnamese delegation. We watch ourselves being introduced. We watch a replay of the previous night's entire bash at the Nusa Dua hotel. Was it only last night?

Just before that point in the tape that shows me being approached for the two photographs to be taken of me with Le-Yuan, I pick up a whispering in Vietnamese between Tran Hoi Ham and one of the other Vietnamese men in the delegation.

"Run that sound back!" I tell Hamzah. "And boost the volume, please!"

He reverses, then re-forwards, and now I can hear the conversation more audibly. In Vietnamese Tran Hoi Ham is whispering to the man, "Something about him . . . I've seen him before. Or at least a picture of him. Now I recall. I believe he is an enemy of the state. I must get photographs!"

I ask Hamzah to play it one more time.

Aside from this single reference to me, there is nothing in the whole dreary three-hour playback that in any way indicates the Vietnamese are doing anything in Bali except winding up an economic mission that they had actually concluded in Jakarta with appropriate Indonesian officials. The Bali leg is merely a courtesy, part of the official entertainment.

I am the only factor to emerge from all the taping and eavesdropping. There's not even a single frame of my mysterious Chinese. Obviously, whatever he was doing at the party, meeting the Vietnamese was not a part of his purpose.

"Why would they need a photograph of you?" Guntur asks when we've finished, the lights back on.

"I have no idea."

Guntur turns to Hamzah.

"Are you still of the opinion the Vietnamese are behind our problems?"

"No, sir!" Hamzah replies. "I have permanently discarded that theory! I now share your opinion, sir, that a Burmese secret society is the enemy."

"That is *not* my opinion, captain! That is a flight of fancy from Mr. Locke here. A fragment of his inductive reasoning. Nevertheless, it is a fragment I intend to explore with every facility at my disposal."

I ask Guntur to assign me a driver and a Scout Ferret.

"Where are you going, John?" he asks.

"To deliver orange Popsicles."

Shortly before sunset my army driver brings me to Pura Besakih.

I tell him to wait.

I ascend the steps and search for Dewata.

I come upon him in the second court.

"I could only find six orange," I tell him. "The vendor told me there was a run on orange today. Three tourist buses all arrived at one time in front of his stand. He still had plenty of grape, but I'm not sure you're into grape. I was lucky enough to come up with some dry ice, so they should keep for a while, anyway."

He selects a Popsicle from the box I'm carrying and leaves me to hold the box with the remaining five Popsicles while he savors the first of the half dozen I've brought him.

He looks off contentedly at the sunset and licks the Popsicle as vigorously as any seven-year-old.

"How may I help you?" he asks. "You are in great pain, are you not?"

"Yes," I say. "Usually I don't feel it. I'm like these Popsicles. Frozen. Numb. Except when I'm hunting or being hunted. Then I'm all feeling. Every sense is operating at full capacity. But I didn't come here to discuss the pain. I'd be lost without it, I think. I came to ask about something else. Please help me, if you can."

"I can listen."

"I almost lost a dear friend today," I tell him. "Some people—the same people who took your bell—tried to kill him, to frighten me away. I grieve for my friend, for the uselessness of the act—

since I was not frightened—but mostly I grieve for myself. Am I truly *l'amant fatal* whose love or friendship inevitably brings destruction? Am I condemned to staying away from anyone I love simply because they dare to love me?"

"Why do you grieve for your friend?"

"Why? Because he was almost killed! Brutally and unnecessarily!"

"You should not grieve for what is imperishable. Wise men do not grieve either for the dead or for the living. All of us are immutable beings. No one can bring about our destruction, for we are not slain when our bodies are slain. For the one that is born, death is certain; and certain is birth for the one that has died. For what is eternal and permanent, for what is unavoidable and natural, one should not grieve. The dweller in the body of everyone is eternal and can never be slain. Therefore you should not grieve for any creature, dead or living."

"What if I believe there is only one life?"

"Then you are ignorant. And if you are ignorant, you will cause yourself pain. Do you pray?"

"No."

"Why do you not?"

"Who is there to hear?"

"All the universe. All the imperishable elements everywhere about us."

"Not *my* universe. In my universe, a man is born alone. He lives alone. He dies alone. It's only a life."

"In your universe—who is your god?"

"I am my own god."

"And why have you chosen yourself as god?"

"Because there are no others in whom I can believe more than I believe in myself."

"I perceive your dilemma. If you are your own god, to whom, then, can you pray—except to yourself? And if you cannot respond to your own prayers, then indeed your ears will hear only silence. And you *are* alone. Neither I, nor anyone, least of all yourself, can help you, since none can enter a universe where you are the only inhabitant."

"But that's Catch-22!" I insist. "Whenever I *do* admit another person, either they die—violently, more often than not—or I deliberately push them out of my life to keep them from dying. I

160

keep losing those I love, yet I keep on surviving! And the longer I survive, the more alone I become. How do I break that circle?"

"Only by dying."

"It's not the solution I'm looking for."

"Only by starting your next life."

"I don't believe there's a *next* life."

"Doesn't that seem contrary to all the evidence around you? Is there anything in the architecture of existence that is not constantly being replicated or renewed? Does the rice grow only once in a million years, or do we harvest three crops each year? Why should the human form be limited to only one chance at the wheel of life when everything else around it is so unlimited? Why of all the elements should we be singled out for only one opportunity?"

"I'm talking about a second time around for John Locke. In which I retain my personal identity, my own conscious memories."

"Buy why, if this life is such a burden, would you wish to retain any memory of it? Why not move on to a higher stage and continue to strive until you ultimately gain release from mortal reincarnation?"

"I don't *choose* to die," I say. "I've seen too many good guys taken before they were ready. I feel obligated to *them*. It's not because I'm afraid to die. It's just that the only thing I've learned how to do is stay alive. That's what I'm best at. That's what I do for a living."

"The colonel tells me you travel."

"Yes."

"Have you found a perfect place where everyone lives in harmony—without pain or suffering?"

"Of course not."

"Such a place does not exist on earth, does it?"

"No."

"If it does not exist here, then it must exist elsewhere. Why look for it here?"

"Because there is no elsewhere!"

"Not in *your* awareness," he says. "But a man who is born blind can never see a sunrise, even though he may feel its rising warmth. I cannot see the 'elsewhere' any more than you can, but I can *sense* it. This is why *my* universe is alive with people—with gods I can pray to."

He has finished his Popsicle. For a while he studies the stick as though it might turn into a golden wand. Then he holds out his arms for the box containing the other five Popsicles packed in dry ice.

I give him the box.

"What is your name?" he asks.

"Locke. John Locke."

"It passed through my head without lingering. Now I shall keep it inside. John Locke."

He moves closer.

I have never seen eyes like his.

They are windows into places I have never been.

I have never stood in such proximity to a man who stripped me away from myself simply by looking into me as Dewata does now. Whatever sense of time or place I may have had until this moment vanishes. Merely with his eyes he causes the neural pathways to my brain to empty themselves.

I am instantly decanted.

"You may hear the bell," he says. "Not the little whispering, not the crying of '*hsieh*.' But the tone of its true thunder. I see now that for you this is possible."

"Why should I hear it if no one else can? Not even you, except for a few times in an entire century."

"Because you are alone in your universe and your need to hear something from another universe is very great. And because I see other things in you, rare qualities. And a destiny."

"What destiny?"

Without answering, he leaves.

I am alone in the temple.

The world rushes back into me.

I become aware the sun has almost set, that I am indeed in Bali.

For a while I had been somewhere else in a timeless place.

The driver has a message for me radioed from Guntur at army headquarters.

Walton Chartwell has apparently returned from wherever it was he'd gone and is requesting a meeting with me as soon as possible.

He has left his office and will be in guest bungalow number 3 at the Maya Hotel in the mountains at Puting. Can I come? Guntur's message urges me to go.

The driver speeds me back to the family compound at Batubulan. I pick up the Mercedes without going in to change. Unquestionably, Dasima will be there, and I don't want anything as distracting as she to pull me away from the place Dewata has put me, at least for the moment.

Driving back into the mountains in the ebbing light of day, I keep asking myself how even an inductive intellect can accept unseen, unconfirmed input.

I park the Mercedes in front of the mountainside hotel. Under a banyan tree a young woman wearing a long-sleeved Malay blouse over her skirt is selling the last of the day's jackfruit from a pony cart to a cluster of Javanese tourists.

She watches me get out of the Mercedes.

"Tuan!" she calls, and hacks off a segment from a jackfruit bigger than a porcupine. "Sweet! You taste!"

"*Terima kasih*," I say. "Maybe later. *Bin pidan*, okay?" I wonder if I can ever get a handle on a language so layered you have to choose your words on the basis of your social relationship with the person you're speaking to. In this instance, since I'm a *tuan* in a Mercedes and she's a vendor with a pony cart, I must speak to her in *Ia* Balinese, the low language. *Bin pidan* means later, I think, or is it *pungkur*? No, damn it, *pungkur* I'd use if she were selling jackfruit from the trunk of a Mercedes.

I must have said it properly, for she grins at me, exposing a gold tooth, and calls *"Santi!"* after me—"peace" in *Ida* Balinese, the high language.

I pass bamboo wind chimes cooing like pigeons overhead. I ignore the curio shop and tearoom to my right, the untenanted small lobby to my left with its weathered WE ACCEPT VISA HERE decal, and advance along a gravel path to a wide decking suspended over the precipitous ridge on which the hotel is built. A sign points the way to the guest bungalows. I hurry along a wooden walkway in need of repair and pass the closed doors of bungalows from which languages beyond my identifying echo softly. I come to the last bungalow—the largest, from the look of it, with a commanding view of Bali, rice paddies rippling off to the darkning sea in descending plateaus.

The curtains in number 3 are drawn. No sound from inside. Properly conspiratorial, I decide, looking around before I make the commitment to approach the door. Only one way out, along the pathway I've come. To the front and side the drop-off down the jungle slope is sheer, to the back high rocks into which the bungalow is anchored.

I knock on the door.

It opens while my hand is still extended.

But it is not Walton Chartwell waiting to admit me.

It is his wife, Juliana.

This afternoon her hair is less *outré* than I remember it from the night before. No stippling with punky dye this time. It's feathered on top, the rest sleek Jackie-O. And no graffiti is painted on her forehead.

*Some*thing different about her.

The pistol in her hand, possibly?

It's pointed at me.

"Please come in, Mr. Locke."

"Are you in some danger?" I ask, nodding at the weapon.

"We both are!" she says. "Come in."

I enter.

She backs away from me into the room.

"Close the door. Chain it."

I close the door. I chain it.

I look around. It's your basic tourist room, more spartan than most. No TV. But you can't have everything. Not when you've got wind chimes outside.

If Walton Chartwell's anywhere on the premises, he's either in the bathroom or under the bed. From where I'm standing, I'd guess neither.

"No, my husband isn't here," Juliana says. "I lied to the colonel. He isn't here; he isn't going to be here! Just you, Mr. Locke, and I! Only the two of us."

"And the little gun?" I smile.

"Oh, yes!" she agrees. "Definitely the little gun!"

CHAPTER

20

The handgun she's pointing my way is a Walther PPK, a compact 6.35mm pistol. Her hand doesn't quite obscure the Nazi swastika under the eagle's talon embossed into the butt just below the barrel, yet her grip is steady and unwavering. I have absolutely no doubt she is capable of discharging the full clip into me if I give her the least encouragement.

"Been a while since I've seen that kind of gun," I comment, trying to lighten up the confrontation.

"Then you are aware of its effectiveness?" she asks tautly, definitely not lightened.

"I've never fired one, but they were standard issue for SS officers in World War II. And those fellas set high standards when it came to their sidearms."

"My father took it from a Waffen SS Haupsturm führer he killed when he was serving with the Dutch Resistance in Europe."

"Did he teach you how to fire it?"

"Oh, yes!" she says. "He did indeed—for good reason. I was born in Bali. I grew up where their young men often ran amok. My father taught me how to stop them in their tracks. No native boy ever touched me!"

"Sounds like a warm, loving childhood," I comment.

"Take off your jacket!" she orders.

I take it off, folding it neatly over the back of the nearest chair.

"Unbuckle your holster. If you make any move toward your gun, I'll kill you."

Her eyes are fixed on me, blue as Dutch platters, deeply reflective. I can almost see my image reflected in her pupils. I'm looking paler than usual, I must confess.

I unbuckle the holster and slip it off. I toss it and the Browning onto the chair holding my jacket.

"Where is your .22?" she asks.

"What kind of gentleman comes to meet a lady with *two* guns?"

"You didn't come here to meet me. You came expecting to meet my husband. I'm told you never go out without the .22."

"Always on alternate Thursdays."

"Don't play with *me*! Drop your pants!"

"You *are* serious?"

"Desperately so!"

"In that event . . ."

I unbuckle my belt, unzip my trousers, and let them slide to my knees, where they bunch up. I have this sudden perception of myself as the representative asshole of the Western world. Veteran of a score of fire fights with the earth's most relentless jungle fighters, the NVA, done in by a blond strudel from the Netherlands. It would be hysterical if only it were happening to somebody else.

"Kick them off!" she demands.

I can see she's starting to fray. I obey, thus revealing the .22 snugged into a holster attached to my lower left leg.

"Shall I unstrap it?" I ask.

"I would if I were you. But *very* carefully!"

Very carefully I unstrap it and toss it over next to the Browning on the chair.

She circles me, the little PPK fixed to my center line without a degree of deviation, just locked right in there on target. It could be worse, I suppose. Her hand could be shaking. And I can see she's got the safety off.

"Get on the bed, Mr. Locke!"

"If this is an indecent proposal," I say, still trying to keep things frosty, "you didn't really have to go to all this trouble. You are an extremely sexy fox. A simple smile would have made me your slave."

"Don't be patronizing!" she says. "I get enough of that sardonic bullshit from my husband."

I decide I'd better get over to the bed.

"How shall I do this?" I ask her. "Would you like me on my stomach or on my back?"

"Face down!" she orders.

I stretch out, face down.

She scoops up my Browning and the Colt, crosses the room to a cabinet, opens a drawer, puts the hardware in, closes and locks the drawer. Obviously, she's been planning her moves. I do not see what she does with the key.

She comes closer to the bed but maintains a carefully measured distance. She settles into a chair, sitting in it with the back of the chair toward me and in front of her, her skirt hiked up, exposing gartered thighs. I have this wild flash of Marlene Dietrich in *Blue Angel*. Juliana's thighs, bone white against the inky black of her stockings and her lace garters, are joltingly erotic, reminding me that despite my preference for Asian women one can't entirely write off the white female of the species.

"This is not a sexual encounter, Mr. Locke," she says. "I did not get you up here for anything so meaningless. Don't think you can romance your way out of this!"

"It never occurred to me," I say. "I recall you telling me you don't indulge. Not even with your husband. So why *did* you get me up here?"

"You're going to help me kick drugs."

In spite of the PPK I rear up in bed.

She jumps back onto her feet, knocking the chair toward me and instantly dropping into a Weaver stance, the firing position the FBI teaches. Daddy never taught her this posture, believe me. This kind of gun-fighting expertise came well after his day.

"I'm not making any moves to get the gun away from you," I assure her. "What you just saw was simply a spontaneous reaction to something I thought I heard you say."

"I'll say it again. I said you're going to help me kick drugs."

"How?"

"I'm going cold turkey. I've already gone twenty-four hours past my usual fix."

"You don't know what you're getting yourself into!" I tell her.

"But *you* do! You were in narcotics. You've been around addicts. You must know how to help them!"

"All we did was scoop them off the streets or use them a tipsters to get us to the dealers."

"Still, you have some experience."

"Enough to tell you not to try cold turkey. That's a shitstorm of pain to put yourself through without some alternative drug—methadone, or better yet, some of the newer stuff."

"I am prepared to suffer whatever I must suffer. No pain ca be worse than the anguish I feel about my daughter."

"Even if you do kick it, that's only a first step. Getting detoxe is just a start. From there, you have to work back to what mad you an abuser in the first place. That can take forever. But unti you get back on some kind of high ground, you have to be rein forced every minute by people who have been there."

"Listen to me!" she cries. "This is my make-or-break night You told me I wouldn't be ready till I'd hit bottom. Can't you se that I have? Do I have to crawl at your feet? Are you so insensitiv you can't *see* my pain?"

I look at her really for the first time. An incredibly comple: woman, blond and patrician despite her forays into stylish punk My mother would paint her, I know, in layers of dissolution, lik a crumbling sandbank along the Seine, slipping away section b: section.

I suddenly recall what Jeff Carson, a part-time police psy chologist in San Francisco and professor at Berkeley, once sai to me about moments like this with dopers—when the patient i the most disturbed, he's also the most accessible. It remains fo the therapist to find his way through the terror to whatever re maining segment of selfhood the patient has left and then take hi stand beside it. If he is able to do this, the therapeutic proces can begin.

Forget it, Locke! The conscious, reasoning wisp of brain matte I still have left is talking as loudly as it can. You're not a therapist Juliana Chartwell is a dingbat. You have responsibilities waitin down the mountain. The clock is ticking.

On the other hand, a louder voice is saying, You've been tryin to find a way to establish a more extensive data base on Pacifi Petroleum and Walton Chartwell. Maybe in the course of playin along with Madame something may surface.

Why not go for it?

Then I hear Juliana's voice again, breaking in over my inne duet.

"I can't stand the look in my daughter's eyes when she sees me!" Juliana cries out. "Oh, God! I want her back in my arms! Not hiding from me!"

"All right," I concede. "If you can make the commitment, so can I."

"You mean that?"

"Yes."

She rights the chair she's knocked over, settles into it again, the PPK not quite as zeroed in as before.

"I want you to know something," she says. "If this is a trick, if you manage to overpower me, I'll kill myself. When you're gone, I'll kill myself. Not that you'll lose any sleep over so inconsequential an event, but I want you to know that's what I'll do."

"Keep the gun pointing at me if it helps you," I say, "but I'd be more relaxed if you'd at least put the safety back on. You don't need the gun anymore. I'm on your side."

"I'd like to believe you," she says.

At least she thumbs the safety back into its notch.

"You'd better start to make yourself comfortable," I advise her. "It's going to be a long night. Kick off your shoes, get rid of your garter belt, take off your stockings, shuck your dress, get down to basics—bra and panties. Better even no bra, because your flesh is going to start crawling, and it won't want anything touching it."

"I don't wear a bra," she says.

"Well, strip down. Because it's going to get sloppy."

"What do you mean?"

"Going cold turkey is not the way they show it in the flicks. The real scam is there's absolutely no high drama involved. It's just dreary; that's what it is. What happens is that every nerve in your body starts sending feeding signals. Like ten thousand hungry wolves. I can try to help you by closing off some of the pain gates, maybe mislead your nervous system a little bit here and there, but you're going to hear loud and clear from parts of yourself you didn't know you had. And your body temp is going to fluctuate wildly. One minute you'll be bathed in sweat, the next your teeth'll be rattling. You'll wrap yourself in a blanket for a while, then you'll throw the blanket away. And in between you'll be vomiting. It's an up-and-down carousel of agony, all right, but it can be done. There's no walking on the ceiling the way they show it in the movies, no climbing the walls or jumping out of ten-story windows. It's just a lot of lying there being sick and shaking and shuddering and vomiting. We'll need blankets and a bucket. Maybe the best thing we can do right now is to take this mattress off the bed and put it on the floor in the center of the room. That's going to be your circus ring."

She's beginning to be frightened. "For how long?" she asks.

"Until you break through it—or until you ask me to put a bullet through your head."

"You're exaggerating! Trying to talk me out of it!"

"If you really want to get straight, Juliana, take the next jet out of here, sign yourself into a clinic."

"You call me Juliana?"

"'Madame Chartwell' doesn't travel too well under the circumstances. So what's it going to be? You'd better be damn sure, because once you're into this, if that's what you really want, I'm going to take you all the way."

"Thank God you said that! I need that kind of strength! I want you to *make* me do it no matter how much I beg you to let me stop."

"Then put the gun away! We have to trust each other."

Once more she leaves the chair, returns to the dresser, unlocks the drawer where she's put my Browning and Colt, places her PPK beside them, closes the drawer and locks it, and drops the key into an ashtray.

I get off the bed, strip the blankets and the sheets, and wrestle the mattress onto the floor in the center of the room.

Juliana undresses without any false modesty, like a girl in a women's locker room hurrying out of her street clothes to rush to a dance class.

She comes over to the mattress and smiles at me anxiously. Except for her panties, she is naked. Her hips are narrow, her stomach as sleek and as muscled as a long-distance runner's, her breasts as firm and virginal as a young girl's. She holds a photograph out to me. It's a picture of her daughter. The child is lovely, with a delicate porcelain face, perfect lips curling up at the corners.

"If I become unmanageable," Juliana says, "show me this picture of Julia. I'm doing this for her, you know."

"Bullshit!" I say. "She's not in trouble. You are! Don't you have a robe?"

"I didn't bring anything with me when I booked the room."

"Except your gun."

"Well, I don't even have that now. Look at me! Standing virtually naked in front of a stranger. Stripped of everything."

"That's a good analogy," I say. "Keep thinking that! Take off the panties if you really want to carry the analogy to its ultimate. *Be* naked! That's where you're starting from."

Without self-consciousness, trusting me completely now, she steps out of her panties and sees me looking at her mons.

"Yes," she says. "I'm a true blonde."

"Forgive me for looking," I say, "but I've been so long in Asia I've forgotten that all women aren't dusky at the top of the stairs."

"What makes you so anthropological?" she asks. "Don't I attract you? Even a little?"

"You've made it clear you don't indulge," I say.

"I hate intercourse." She shudders.

"But you do have a daughter."

"That was the only time I ever let him near me. I took LRH for a week so I could stand letting him enter me. And then only long enough to be sure he'd given me my daughter."

I realize the lady is heavily into all kinds of exotic shit when she mentions LRH. Here's one of the most potent of the mood drugs, an aphrodisiac that stimulates the brain's sex centers, a drug not too widely known in the States but available in the Netherlands.

"I do like oral sex," she said, "if I care for the person. But not intercourse. One is beautiful, the other vile."

She shudders again, but this time I sense the chill along her spine comes from the ice cubes in her neurotransmitters, not from the thought of sexual intercourse.

I drape a blanket around her.

"Settle down," I tell her. "What was that famous line in *All about Eve*? 'Fasten your seat belt, honey. It's going to be a bumpy night!'"

She crosses her arms over the wrapped blanket and shrinks within it, like a snail caught out by a boy with a shaker of salt.

"Where do you score your dope?" I ask, less for the information than simply to keep her from concentrating on her misery.

"That's never a problem when you're rich," she says.

Again she's trembling with the chills.

"True," I agree. "Affluence and oblivion—the Great American Dream. How'd you catch it way over here?"

"We Europeans had that dream long before you Americans. Have you never heard of my family?"

"Sorry."

"The Duurstede coffee plantations once covered most of Java," she says. "I am the sole heiress."

"Strange," I say. "I had the impression it was your husband who had all the money."

"My husband?" She laughs. "He was a third-rate gambler on second-rate passenger ships. Everything he has today I bought him."

The trembling has stopped. I observe the first rivulet of sweat trickling from her hairline. She lets the blanket slip from her shoulders.

"Feeling the way you feel about sex, why'd you bother getting married?"

"I wanted a blond, blue-eyed little girl. Walton is blond. He has blue eyes. He comes from a good family in Devon. Impoverished, but still good stock. I chose him the way I used to choose my racehorses. To give me a child and accept my conditions for marriage."

"Separate bedrooms, of course."

"Certainly. And for him never to be so indiscreet with other women that I'd be embarrassed."

"And in return what does he get—aside from the right to spend your money?"

"Social position. Executive power. The freedom to travel. And to indulge his fantasies."

"Does Duurstede Coffee own Pac-Pet?"

"I have a considerable block of their stock, yes."

"So you put Chartwell into his present position?"

"Of course."

"Did you start doing drugs before or after your marriage?"

"Don't you know anything?" she asks with sudden harshness. "I've used drugs for years. How else can anybody stand it in this part of the world? This is poppyland, Mr. Locke! People here have been chasing the dragon and going up for centuries! What else could I do, having to spend as much time out here every year as I have to spend?"

"Don't lay it on the people here!" I correct her. "Opium was never here till the Europeans brought it from India less than four hundred years ago. It was Alexander the Great and his armies who brought it to India in the first place—three hundred years before Christ. The opium poppy is native to the Med—I've seen ivory nepenthe pipes from Cyprus more than three thousand years old."

"Why are you so protective about Asia and Asians?" she shouts at me. "Because you're sleeping with that little Balinese dancer? Is that why?"

"I meant to tell you, Juliana, that one of the side effects of trying to kick dope without other drugs to bring you out is that you become very abusive toward the person taking you through it. But it's okay. I can handle it."

"Well, you *are*, aren't you?"

"Are what?"

"Sleeping with her."

"You don't really expect me to discuss that with you, do you?"

"Well, it's driving my husband insane."

"How did he get involved in my personal life?"

"He knows all about it."

"Fascinating. This place is more wired for sound than I suspected."

"You know, he wants her."

"Chartwell? Your husband—*wants* Dasima?"

"He was sponsoring a European tour for the Balinese dance troupe she's in. Everything was arranged—the government approval, the musicians, the director, all the other dancers—until you came along and she decided not to go. My poor dear husband is beside himself. He was banking on buying her furs and jewels and making her his mistress. I can just see him walking into a London club with his little Balinese princess on his arm!"

"Very illuminating," I say.

"Do you love her?"

"I'm in love with someone I cannot have," I say.

"Well, good! Why shouldn't you feel pain like the rest of us?"

"If it makes you feel any better, I have my quota, okay? The woman I loved died in Vietnam."

"She had no business being there in the first place!"

"She was Vietnamese."

"Oh, no wonder you loved her! *Anything* that's Asian. Come over here! When I finish with you, you won't ever want to look at another Asian girl!"

"What have you got against Asian girls?"

"Those glamorized photographs of those Singapore stewardesses, smiling those obsequious little China Doll smiles, with the light filtering in through the windows of the plane as though they're in a cathedral or something! Christ, it's revolting! Are you coming over here, or do I have to crawl over to you?"

"I guess you didn't see the sign on the door—'Patients don't make it with the doctor.'"

"I suck any cock I want to suck!" she screams. She skitters on her knees toward me like a vampire off target.

I slap her hard across the face.

She falls back, lays her hand to her face, stares at me.

"Why do you hate me so much?" she whimpers.

"I don't hate you. Tonight—but just for tonight—I love you."

"What?"

"For what you're going through. For trying to get straight. I wish every poor bastard in the world whose brains are scrambled by pharmaceuticals would have the will to get on his knees and make his stand. I hate waste. I've seen too goddamn much of it. In case you've been wondering why I'm going through this with you, it's not that I really had to. I'm wearing a bulletproof vest. I could have disarmed you."

"Then—why—are you?"

"Some instinct or other. Guilt. Obligation. I don't really know. But I'll tell you something. I'm into it now. I'm a stubborn bastard. I tend to hang in. We'll whip the sonofabitch of a dragon, okay?"

She reaches out a hand to me. I take it.

"How'd I ever get so lucky?" she asks. "I don't deserve it."

Suddenly she's trembling again. I cover her with the blanket. She falls onto the mattress, shaking and shrinking into herself.

I find a bucket in the bathroom. One thing about Bali. No shortage of buckets.

I bring it to her in time. She retches into it as I clasp her head in both my hands, but nothing much comes up from her stomach.

"I haven't eaten since yesterday," she says. "I've read that you vomit a lot."

She lies back on the mattress, shaking slightly, her eyes pleading until I come closer, squatting on the mattress beside her like a Saigon fish vendor, knees up to either side of me as my torso rests on the mattress, arms crossed over my knees.

"You even sit like an Asian!" she cries. "You're the most baffling man I've ever known. One minute I admire you—I even want your sex inside my mouth—then you infuriate me, sitting like that, like all those hippies who came over here to glorify the mystic Asian. The Asians laugh at them! All these white people who come over here and sentimentalize, write books about their culture, their art, their dances, as though everything we have in Europe is decadent and superficial—it sends me into a fury! You should have seen this island before we came!"

"We being the Dutch?" I ask.

"Naturally. Of all the European colonizers we were the most humane, the most enlightened. This country was a jungle teeming with assassins and opium dealers. They burned widows. They kept slaves. They fought interminable tribal wars. Little girls were turned over to the rajas for sexual pleasure and to dance in their crumbling temples. The place was just one gigantic whorehouse. We built roads and bridges and managed to knock some law and order into their savage heads! John, may I please have a drink of water? Let it run. I want cold water, please. Really cold!"

I go to the bathroom, but once through the door, I turn back to watch her do what I've known she's been planning to do for the last few minutes.

She pulls a self-contained packet from her purse hidden under the bed. She takes out a small pearl of gooey substance the size of a pea, places it on a folded piece of tinfoil, and snaps on her cigarette lighter, holding the flame under the foil, and prepares to snort the hot sweet smoke.

I kick the whole bundle out of her hand. She leaps at me, trying to claw my face, but I grasp her wrists. She tries to knee me, but I lift her off the floor, turning her so that her kicks can flail only to the side.

Then I carry her, kicking and screaming, back to the mattress, push her down onto her back, and lie on top of her, my entire weight on her, crushing her until she can hardly breathe. Then I roll off her.

She's staring at me strangely.

"Why did you do that?" she asks.

"Damned if I know," I say. "Just trying to flatten you out, I guess."

"No," she says. "You wanted to fuck me!"

"For a Dutch heiress you talk more like a Vegas hooker!"

"You think 'fuck' is an American word?"

She crawls toward me and suddenly fastens her lips to mine, her tongue darting into my mouth. I neither resist nor respond to her invasion. Finally, she draws back, a strand of the spit from her lips a momentary link between us. She smiles at me seductively.

"You actually turned me on when you were on top of me. What's happening to me? I hate to have any man on top of me."

"You're moving through the whole spectrum, Juliana. Most of what's in your mind is illusion. The reality is that your body'll do anything, say anything, to trick you—or me—into giving it what it wants. What it wants isn't a man. Dope is what it wants. Get the dumb bastard going, the little voice is whispering to you. Then maybe you can sneak a fix. How many other stashes have you got squirreled away around here?"

"You think I'm going to tell you?" she sneers.

"That stuff I kicked out of your hand smelled like high-quality stuff," I say.

"It is. I mean, it was. You know what Picasso called the smell of opium?"

"Sorry to say, I don't."

"He called it the least stupid smell in the world."

"Where do you get your supply?" I ask, something firing in the back of my brain, something irrelevant hammering for a connection.

"From Chien Hsiu," she says, starting to sweat again. She pulls herself into a ball, grits her teeth until her forehead is pocked with wet globules. "John!" she whimpers. "It hurts!"

I give her my hand, and she clutches it fiercely.

"Your stomach?"

"Oh, God, yes, like a thousand periods all in one!"

"Would you rather be a man than a woman?" I ask.

"I'd rather be a woman with a prick!" she moans.

"You know what Freud would say to that?" I say.

"Sometimes I feel like a castrated man," she says. "I think it's dreadful to be deprived of a penis. It's the source and symbol of power all over the world."

She lets out a long breath. The worst of this spasm appears to have passed. "Did you know that the morning prayers of Judaism celebrate the natural inferiority of women? 'Blessed art Thou, O Lord, our God, King of the Universe, who has not made me a woman.'"

While she broods about the indignity of the ancient prayer, I wait. There's something sending me a message. That Chinese name!

"Did I understand you to say you get your dope from Chien Hsiu?"

"What are you going to do? Send for your badge? Arrest him?"

"I don't even know him. Who is Chien Hsiu?"

"My husband's bodyguard. Didn't you meet him at the party?"

"I met someone. Could have been him. We didn't have much to say to each other. Why does your husband need a bodyguard?"

"Well, actually, he's more my bodyguard than Walton's. You see, I put a provision in our marriage agreement. If anything happens to me, if I die, Walton is cut off without a penny. Do you know that Chinese bastard wants me? He actually wants to be my lover."

"How do you know?"

"A woman knows. He's always hinting I don't have to pay him—with money, that is. He says he can guarantee me an unlimited supply of the highest-quality dope in the world—if only we get to know each other better."

"He mustn't want his job with your husband too badly, to play that game."

"It's a strange relationship," she says. "For a while I thought they might be lovers. No such luck. Oh, God!"

She moans louder than before and curls like a wood shaving. I apply finger pressure to the two lymphatic drainage points just below her shoulders, then into the liver-alarm point below her lowest rib on the right side, then finally I press in the two relaxing points on either side of her skull.

"I guess when you had your daughter, you and your husband didn't go in for Lemaze," I say.

"I told you I wouldn't let him near me!"

"The point is they teach you how to concentrate on a focal point and how to breathe in a way that helps you handle the pain. I've used it myself the two times I got hit. It works."

"Whatever you say, doctor," she moans.

She's a quick study. The pant breathing and the finger pressure appear to help her. We come through this series of spasms better than we had through the previous attack. She lies back in my arms, sweat running down between her breasts.

"Your clothes hurt my skin," she whimpers. "Especially that bulletproof vest. Please take them off."

I take off everything except my jockey shorts.

"It would really take my mind off my troubles if you'd let me fellate you," she says. "I love the feeling of my tongue on the skin under the tip of a man's penis."

"It would also take *my* mind off your troubles," I say. "And one of us has to drive. I'll make a deal with you. If you come through this with a straight A, we'll pick a neutral spot and you may have your way with me, okay?"

In spite of her pain, she manages a laugh. "How decent of you!"

She's bathed in sweat.

"Could I get some fresh air, please?" she begs.

"What have you got hidden outside?"

"I just have to breathe, damn you! Come out with me, if you don't trust me!"

We go outside onto the deck, cantilevered over the mountainside.

Juliana gulps at the air currents curling over the summit and down into the dark canyon below us.

Descending ponds of rice paddies glint with star glow. Beyond them, to the southwest, I can make out the light grid of Denpasar. But for the first time since I've arrived in Bali I cannot hear the drums and cymbals of the *gamelan*. Up here in this isolated mountain retreat outside the village of Putung, I hear instead the chiming of wind instruments, *sunari*, tall bamboo poles erected to ensnare the wind, a low boom moaning through the poles into which large holes have been cut, a high crying escaping from those poles having thin slots, the two tones harmonizing in a haunting rise and fall as the wind pipes up or softens.

Juliana comes into my arms simply to be held. We stand unmoving for a long while in the darkness and listen to the wind chimes, the booms and the cries rising and falling in ever-changing medleys. They are more magical than mournful.

"Am I going to come through this?" she asks.

"We both are," I tell her.

I'm thinking of the hours ahead, of her profane outbursts, her panics, her confusions, her hallucinations, the tremor in her hands, her wrenching body turning itself inside out while she struggles to return to the world from which drugs have isolated her.

BRONZE BELL

Although my mind ricochets fiercely with things that need to be checked at once, things she's told me, leading down urgent new avenues, I know I will not leave her now, not until she herself throws the door open and looks tomorrow straight in the face.

CHAPTER

21

"Walton Chartwell! Can you hear us?"

The resonance of the bull-horn disrupts my theta waves and ends a dream of delicious little sausages and good Vouvray.

I know that voice. Even with the distortion through the walls. Captain Hamzah.

My eyes still blur from the abrupt transition from darkness to the sudden blaze of searchlights in the windows of Guest Bungalow number 3.

I can scarcely focus on the luminous dial of my wristwatch. For better or worse, I conclude that the time is on the ebb side of midnight.

Juliana lies winched on the mattress. She whimpers in her sleep like a hungry child.

Hamzah's voice reverberates once again.

"Chartwell! This is a special unit of the Indonesian Army! We request you show yourself immediately!"

I pull on my trousers, take the key from the ashtray, unlock the drawer, and retrieve my Browning, in the unlikely event that the long emotional evening has so attenuated my memory of Hamzah's voice that someone other than he might actually be waiting outside.

I flatten myself to one side of the door.

"That you, captain?" I shout through it.

"Mr. Locke! Are you all right?"

"I'm coming out. Order everybody to take their fingers off their triggers."

"Yes, sir."

I give them thirty seconds relaxing time. Then I open the door and step out with my Browning in my pocket, one hand still gripping it, the other, palm up, to block some of the glare of the floodlights with which Hamzah has flooded the bungalow.

"Can we please kill some of that?" I ask.

As the lights get switched off, I see Hamzah's face as a pulsing corona, but as he moves closer, I am able to distinguish more detail. Even a genuine concern.

"My colonel felt that one hour with Mr. Chartwell should certainly have concluded whatever it was he called about. We were expecting you back in Batubulan no later than twenty hundred hours. When you failed to return, we called the hotel. They reported your Mercedes still parked out front. We checked again at twenty-two hundred hours, and the colonel decided we should investigate."

By now my eyes can make out the figures of a half-dozen Red Berets placed strategically around the area, one of them perched on top of the bungalow with his SMG. I release my grip on the Browning.

"Thoughtless of me not to have called in," I say. "But there's no phone in the room, and I've been too occupied to go to the lobby."

Hamzah glances past me through the black doorway.

"Chartwell isn't in there," I tell him. "Never was. It's his wife. She was using his name to get me up here."

"Madame Chartwell? *She* is in there?"

"Sleeping."

His face changes. "I understand, sir."

"No, you don't. But it doesn't matter. Advise the colonel I am in no danger and thank him for worrying about me. Tell him I shall see him at his headquarters sometime tomorrow, probably by early afternoon."

"Yes, sir."

"And would you ask him to make an airlines booking for Mrs.

Chartwell and her daughter, to Jakarta, Hong Kong, and San Francisco? The first flight available."

"Which class?"

"First. Put her in No Smoking."

"Shall we also book hotel accommodations in San Francisco?"

"No. She won't be staying at a hotel."

"I'm sorry if I've interrupted anything, sir."

"No apologies necessary, captain. Thank you for the backup."

He salutes me. I wave acknowledgment, return to the room, locking the door after me. The footfalls of the para on the roof and the clatter of combat boots along the boardwalk diminish. Once more the only sound in my world is the silent howling of the sleeping Juliana.

Why am I doing this for a stranger?

Guntur will certainly ask. Easy to answer him: To get more information about Chartwell. But then why should we need more information about Chartwell? Not so easy to answer myself. Yet critical that I do.

The dominant need of my life at this period is to grapple with where I've been and to question my premises as I go along. Otherwise I'll end up a scorpion, chasing my own stinger until I manage to catch it, then sting myself to death.

Certainly I've already learned what little I need to put into the data bank about Walton Chartwell. Why, then, do I still sit here doggedly, yearning for the dawn, watching Juliana's twists and turns as though they were my own, catching her bile in a bucket, wiping the sweat from her body, warming her when she shivers?

She must remind me of someone. Oh, sweet Jesus, yes! I *know*! Helen Petrucelli! Up on Russian Hill in San Francisco. White female, age twenty-six, mother of a five-year-old boy, wife of a twenty-nine-year-old fireman. When I was working Homicide.

One afternoon, as she did every afternoon that last year of her life, Helen Petrucelli was driving to the day-care center to pick up her boy. On the way she saw a man molesting a little girl. She pulled in to the nearest service station and called the police. In less than four minutes a patrol car skidded up and busted the molester flagrante delicto. Turned out he was a schoolteacher. Helen Petrucelli ended up as the key witness against him. He lost his job, lost his California teaching credentials, and got packed off to a facility near Chino for psychiatric observation. When they finally released him, he was a free man, but barred from ever teaching again. He wrote to the president of the United States, the governor of California, the mayor of San Francisco, assorted congressmen and newspaper editors, insisting he'd been framed. Somewhere along the way his mind had snapped. He was able to build a really nifty infernal device with nitro and pack it inside a supersize box of detergent. He planted it on Helen Petrucelli's porch as a manufactuer's sample. Sure enough, the housewife in her didn't question it for a second. She picked up the box, and it went off, the soap igniting in her face. She died screaming after four agonizing hours in the hospital, despite all the morphine they could shoot into her. Still screaming, right to the end.

I was assigned to the case. I settled in at a waterfront bar in Sausalito where the suspect was known to hang out. I passed myself off as a deckhand waiting around for an open berth on any sailing boat bound for Bora-Bora, and it got to where the suspect and I were buying each other beers and talking about what a super quarterback Joe Montana is, in or out of the pocket. We all knew for a fact this dude at the bar had killed Helen Petrucelli, and in time he came to know that we knew and used to taunt me with it, because like most people who are supposed to be crazy, he was only a little crazy, maybe ten percent crazy, but ninety percent of him smarter than the rest of us, for he never gave me anything we could use against him in court. I sat there in that bar for four weeks letting him whip me around and jerk me off until I finally asked my section chief to take me off before I pulled my .38 and blew the bastard off his bar stool. What really bothered me was not the fact I'd have done it, but that I would have *enjoyed* doing it.

Juliana, somehow, has tapped into my sense of failure on the Helen Petrucelli case. No physical resemblance. Just zap, out of the atmosphere like an FM station you don't want riding in over the one you're listening to.

I watch the morning daub her face. She looks like stomped shit, but she's beautiful to me, because she's taken step one. She manages a passable smile.

"Are we doing it?" she asks.

"We're doing it," I say.

"I'd like to go home now."

"Okay. I'll drive you."

"I brought my own car."

"Send someone back for it. You can't drive right now."

She's so weak I have to help her dress.

I give her back her PPK, strap my Colt .22 where it belongs, check us out, and drive her down the mountain past Balinese girls at roadside holding long thin poles up in the air.

"You see what I mean about this place!" Juliana says. "Those stupid girls with those stupid sticks!"

"What are they doing?"

"Fishing for dragonflies!"

I laugh.

"Really!" she says. "They tie a line to the end of a bamboo pole and at the end of the line put some gooey, sticky stuff they fling around in the air until the dragonfly gets caught on it. Then they pull off its wings, fry the thing in coconut oil, and eat it."

"Very enterprising," I say.

"Disgusting!"

The Chartwell home is a walled estate near Denpasar.

I stop the Mercedes in front of an ornate carved door at the top of a broad marble steps.

"I won't come in," I say.

I find her hand in mine. Those Dutch-blue eyes are all shimmery with moisture.

"I will never forget you, John Locke."

"As they say—likewise, Juliana Chartwell."

"I promise you. My daughter and I will be on the plane."

"I'll be there to fasten your seat belt."

She leans over, starts to kiss me, but pulls back.

"My breath must be awful!"

She gets out of the car, closes the door, looks back at me.

"You sure they'll accept me?"

"This doctor who runs the clinic, David Smith, is a very special man. He started the Haight-Ashbury Free Medical Clinic almost twenty years ago when the only other place for addicts was jail. In the early days the whole damned medical establishment came down on him and branded him an outlaw for treating drug abusers in a nonpunitive way. I can't think of a better man or better place. He'll accept you. And, Juliana . . ."

"Yes?"

"If that pusher of yours tries to hustle you out of this, just remember last night. You want to spend another ripper like that one?"

"It was the best night of my life!" she says. "But I promise!"

I drive to Batubulan. I need to clean my body. I smell of sweat and puke and despair and hope.

Dasima, as I knew she would, joins me in the bathing pool five minutes after I've slipped into it.

She says nothing, simply unwraps her skirt, enters the pool without causing a ripple, and sinks below the surface, her long black hair floating like a spreading ink blot on water. I feel her lips close over me, then her tongue circling. Not wishing her to drown, since she gives me no evidence that her assertiveness is in any way going to be diminished by a lack of oxygen, I hunch back up the steps until I am sitting above water, she emerging from the depths in perfect harmony with my upward movement and never having missed a heartbeat. She purges me of memory, and when my eyeballs seem to pinwheel at the instant of her taking me, I begin to realize that sailing away from Bali, letting go of Dasima, may not be as easy as I've been telling myself it's going to be.

"Don't you say good morning?" I ask.

"Can you pronounce this word?" she asks, *"Ambarchusi?"*

"Ambarchusi," I repeat. "What does it mean?"

"It comes from the Hindi. It means 'mango-fruit sucking.' I do not want my love to think my skill comes from previous practice. But since childhood I have loved mangoes. It is surprising how much practice a young girl can get with such natural things."

"I have just gained a new respect for the mango," I say. "Incidentally, what do young boys practice on?"

"The word from Hindu for that is *kompalachati*. The licking of the lotus stamen."

"You came to my *bale* last night, didn't you?"

"Why would I not?"

"And I wasn't there."

She says nothing.

"You're wondering where I was."

"Have I asked? Did I when I came into the water beside you?"

"Would you like to know?"

"If you would like to tell me."

"I spent the night with Juliana Chartwell."

"I know," she says.

"Your uncle told you, of course."

"He tells me everything."

"Do you wonder if we made love, Juliana and I?"

"Does she make you feel what I make you feel?"

"So that's what this was? A contest!"

"Can she do mouth congress as well as I can?"

I reach for the girl and pull her in next to me.

"Juliana and I did not make love, Dasima. I was trying to help her give up opium. Do you understand? Like a doctor. A psychologist. A Good Samaritan. Or a simple fool—who knows?"

"I am glad, Tanah. But I was not jealous. Because if you truly need another woman, the fault lies in me, not in your need."

God, how they'd sacrifice Dasima back home for shouldering the cross of man's perfidy. Guntur is so right, so very right, to keep her safely in the game preserve of Bali. She is a rare vintage wine that simply will not travel into today's Western societies.

By midafternoon I join Guntur in his office at COIN-OPS headquarters.

"We have advised Madame Chartwell of her flight plans," he says crisply before I've even come through his doorway. "She informs me you'll be accompanying her to the airport so you should plan your time accordingly."

"Very decent of you, Guntur. And thank you, too, for sending Captain Hamzah to check on my safety last night."

"I felt it necessary to tell my niece about last night's incident."

"She and I have already settled the matter."

His brusqueness falls away. He's smiling at me again.

"Then there *are* no repercussions?"

"None."

"She *is* a bloody attractive woman, Chartwell's wife, despite her serpent hair and painted face. I do not blame you for possessing her when the chance was offered. I see it, John, as an effort on your part to break the spell Dasima has cast over you."

"The last time I remember you saying that, you had it the other way around. You said it was I who had cast the spell, not Dasima."

"That is because of the difference in the natures of men and women. Men start from a sexual basis, then fall in love. Women fall in love, then move to the sexual basis."

"Thank you for clearing that up, Guntur. How is the operation coming along at Point Sari?"

"I have instructed Hamzah to report to me every half hour. His last call, only ten minutes ago, was like the earlier calls—no luck yet."

"You won't find it out there," I tell him.

"How can you say that? It was your idea!"

"Must I remind you I said to hold off the search until we understood how the bell could have been carried out through the reef? Let's assume, for the moment, it wasn't."

"But the board with the bullet holes! The missing Australian surfers!"

"Suppose they saw the caper coming down and then were shot as witnesses. Then suppose the assassins left that location and hid the bell inland because they were too spooked to proceed with their original plan, fearful that other surfers might show up?"

He stares at me as dragonflies must when little Balinese girls zap them with sticky stuff on bamboo lines, pull off their wings, and deep-fry them.

"Another example of inductive reasoning?" he asks.

"Afraid so, Guntur."

A noncom appears in the doorway, saluting for recognition.

Guntur acknowledges the man. They speak in Indonesian, Guntur snapping a quick glance at me in the middle of their conversation. The noncom leaves.

"There is a girl at the main sentry gate on the road outside. Insisting that she speak to you."

"What girl?"

"She identifies herself only as Thanh Hoa."

"Vietnamese!"

"Yes."

"Why would she ask for me?"

"You don't know her?"

"No. I mean, Thanh Hoa is not such an uncommon name for a Vietnamese women, but—I can't remember any particular Thanh Hoa."

"I have asked the sergeant to check our listing of all Vietnamese currently in Bali. We shall have an ID in a moment, since there aren't that many here."

"What exactly did she tell the sentries?"

"That her name is Thanh Hoa, that it is urgent she speak with the American John Locke."

"How did she know I was here—with you?"

"I will expect you to ask her."

The sergeant returns with a list of names.

He speaks to Guntur again in Indonesian. Guntur listens a moment, nods, waves him out.

"She is not one of the Vietnamese who live here," he says. "But we have her name on this other list. The daily arrivals— from the Immigration people at the airport. She flew in early this morning from Jakarta. She states on her entry form that she's staying with a Chinese family in Bedugul near Lake Bratan."

Suddenly I'm standing on the yellow-brick road, Oz in sight.

"Guntur, you know what this could mean?"

"Tell me."

"The fact she came here, asking for me! It could be the first break I've had in finding out what happened to Doan Thi. Why else would a Vietnamese come looking for me?"

"There could be some connection with those photographs of you the Vietnamese delegation made the other evening. The timing seems particularly curious, John. For nine years you haven't been able to learn what really happened to Doan Thi. What makes you think this girl brings you such news? Isn't it more likely her being here is related to the other night?"

"One way to find out!"

I jump into the Mercedes and drive to the sentry gate.

I catch sight of a girl waiting at one side of the gate, traffic on the highway swirling dust around her.

She stares at me with gunsight concentration.

She is Vietnamese.

In her mid-twenties.

As though still uncertain, she approaches tentatively.

I watch her step toward me and I marvel at her grace, her delicate beauty, her fine-drawn waist loosely cinctured by a belt of seashells jangling as she comes.

Straight black hair mantles her shoulders, and I remember the stream of Doan Thi's hair billowing behind her as she tooled her motorbike along Saigon's choked avenues.

Closer now, this girl halts abruptly, as though teetering on the edge of an abyss she intends to invite me into.

I hear the sudden intake of breath and see the rush of discovery in her eyes.

"Thank God I've found you!" she whispers.

"Who are you?"

I scarcely recognize my voice. Must be the pain filter.

"Thanh Hoa," she says. "Doan Thi's sister. Sister fourth."

CHAPTER

22

At first sight of Thanh Hoa I take out my Polaroid glasses, loop them over my ears, get out of the Mercedes, and peer at the girl. An instinctive reaction, learned in the South Pacific.

One of the dreads of yachties in tropical waters is the unexpected appearance of vigias dead ahead. Vigias are those terrifying reefs sprinkled elusively here and there throughout what are supposed to be deep seas to remind the blue-water sailor he's not immortal, shoals that have never been properly charted, only rumored or reported by earlier navigators as possibly having been seen, perhaps existing at one time or another within an inexact patch of sea. And frequently these vigias are spoked by motus, broad fingers of sands extending like tentacles from the sprouting coral heads.

If anything can make the bowels unsteady, it's a night passage in foul weather across a track of deep, current-swept ocean from which suddenly, unaccountably, there rises the din of surf and the white suck of rollers where no land or rock is supposed to be.

In daylight when this happens you fast draw your Polaroids, reduce the rays slamming off the sea's surface into your eyes, you can try to sort out the cloud patterns on the water from the ganglia of coral exploding toward your keel.

BRONZE BELL

At the first sight of Thanh Hoa I'd gone for the Polaroids.

Out of what uncharted sea had she surfaced, lacking visible connections, as surprising as a vigia?

"Doan Thi never spoke of a sister fourth," I say. "Only of a sister three."

"Doan Thi never spoke of many things," the girl replies. "Except for her writings, her life was an overlay of secrets. You, for example."

"Doan Thi and I—a secret? Hardly."

"*You* spoke of the relationship, certainly. An American soldier with our country's leading literary figure. Why wouldn't you brag? But my sister spoke of you only to us, her family—never to outsiders."

She extends a crumpled piece of rice paper.

I elect to ignore it while I challenge her in Vietnamese.

"*Vach lá tìm sâu*," I say directly.

It is a phrase I recall Doan Thi sometimes using when she sought to pry beneath suspect words. Essentially it means you're damned well going to part the leaves and look for worms before you buy the cabbage.

"*Môt mãt mười ngờ*," the girl replies with less diffidence than I expect.

This one translates, "One loses something, and ten are suspected of stealing it."

"What pet name did Doan Thi give me?" I ask her, confident this will blow her out of the water.

Who could know this?

But without hesitation this girl from nowhere tells me, "*Ông gan cóc*."

As she says it, I am again hearing Doan Thi saying these same words, ardently whispering, "Mister Toad Livered."

The first time she called me this was during that hopefully reliable moment of truth, the initial postcoital utterance between new lovers. She exhaled "*ông gan cóc*" into my ear with such febrile gratitude that I, of course, assumed her phrase was ringing tribute to the steamy concupiscence of my youth. Later, when I had the literal translation, I felt deeply censured, until I came to understand that she'd awarded me the phrase as my nom de guerre and that in Vietnamese folklore the toad symbolizes boldness, even foolhardiness. Then I came to perceive Doan Thi's pet name for me as not only enchanting but as surgically precise in delineating my personal role in the shitstorm morass of Indochina. What other man along love's long, bumpy course has ever been called Mister Toad Livered by the woman he adores?

I decide to accept the paper Thanh Hoa has been thrusting at me so insistently.

The handwriting is unmistakably Doan Thi's, though more wavering than I remember her bold brushstrokes.

"Beloved, this morning the curtains steal across the sill—reaching south. Shall I ever again see you? Touch you?"

"The last words she ever wrote," Thanh Hoa says. "When they found her, this note was still in her hand."

Chemical messengers rocket down my neuron tracks, slam into my overly impacted hypothalamus. Comes the surge of cortisol, the dependable squirt of epinephrine. *Skål*, baby! One more for the road!

"When did she write this?"

"Two years ago last March. The twenty-first of March—sometime before noon. Didn't you know she was dead?"

"Only a word here, a word there—enough to know. But until now I didn't know *when*. I only heard she caught pneumonia and probably died in some reeducation camp."

"At Gia RA Z30," Thanh Hoa says.

"Jesus!" I cry. "Why *that* camp? Why the hell were they trying to reeducate *her*? She loved the peasants more than any Hanoi Marxist ever could!"

But I am only rambling on, scarcely hearing what's babbling out of my mouth. All I can deal with is the intolerable void. How could that day two years ago last March have come and gone without my being given the chance to freeze-frame it, to smash the clocks and isolate that terrible moment, and to floodlight my personal memory of the most devastating day of my life—the day my future died?

"What did you mean—Thank God you found me?" I ask harshly. "Why were you looking for me? And in Bali? I had no plans to come here. No plans at all!"

"I wasn't looking for you," she says. "I was simply here—and you appeared—and I saw you."

"Why in Bali?" I ask. "They're not too partial to their Chinese minorities, let alone to Vietnamese."

"I'm trying to get to America."

Tears hover in her eyes.

This appears to be my week for helpless damsels. Maybe I should load this one onto the plane with Juliana Chartwell and make a package deal.

"I just arrived this morning," she says. "I have a visa good for thirty days. I won't tell you what I have had to do to get this far—I'm too ashamed. But I am told that I have a better chance to be noticed here by either an American or Australian young man than I would have in Thailand or Singapore. In thirty days someone may find me pleasing enough to take me out of Asia."

"Go down to Kuta Beach," I tell her. "One of those randy mates will pack you home in no time."

"But now I've found *you*! On my first day! Just by sheer accident. I needed to do some shopping. I came back to Denpasar and saw you driving by."

"And just like that you recognized me?"

"I've seen so many pictures of you."

"Any taken recently?"

"Doan Thi took all the ones I saw. You look younger now than you did then."

"Okay, so you saw me in Denpasar. And followed me?"

"In a taxi. I'm afraid I used up more money than I meant to. But it was worth it. Here you are. And here I am."

Little Girl Blue! Standing here at the gate to army headquarters, looking at me with wondrous naïveté as trucks roll in and out and soldiers stare nakedly at her. Suddenly I don't care if she's Ho Chi Minh's grandniece come to slip a grenade into my pocket. The years rush over my head. I'm powerless to deny her.

I reach for her and let myself be deceived that Doan Thi herself is once more warm against me, nothing changed, the years bridged. I let myself pretend for a moment that this girl's beating heart is Doan Thi's, that the scent of this one's hair is the remembered clove scent of Doan Thi's hair.

"How can I be sure you are who you say you are?" I demand after a few seconds of letting myself be deceived.

She brings her palms to my chest. "Why should I deceive you?"

"Why should you be the exception?"

"Doan Thi told me you were the most disillusioned person for his age she had ever known."

"Why not? I was in Vietnam—the ultimate disillusionment."

"But in ten years surely you've changed."

"Why should I if the world hasn't?"

"I'm not interested in the world's problems, only in my own. How can I convince you I'm sister fourth?"

"Why does it matter?"

"It matters greatly. You can help me get to America."

"Why should I help you?"

"You loved my sister once."

"I'm sorry, Thanh Hoa. I simply don't buy it. God knows I'd love to!"

She lays one of those little Indochinese smiles on me that can mean everything or nothing.

"Then I shall have to convince you, shan't I?" she says. "I'm staying with a Chinese family in the mountains. There I have many things from home. I can show you letters, even more of these..."

From her shoulder bag she brings a photograph and gives it to me.

I'm looking at the photograph of a boy. An Amerasian boy. With incredible haunted eyes. Doan Thi's eyes that on some midnights still burn from various of my ceilings. My features, same high, curving forehead, same cheekbones. I could be looking at a snapshot of myself when I was six, with Doan Thi's eyes superimposed over mine.

"She named him Le Hoang Hai," she says.

I repeat the name as though mumbling in my sleep, "Le Hoang Hai. When was he born?"

"January fourteen, 1976."

Then he had to have been conceived during that last month in 1975, in April, before Doan Thi cycled out to meet the conquerors and I fled with the vanquished, leaving the best of myself in-country. Throughout our love affair I'd always minded ship in the birth-control department. But one night early in those last weeks Doan Thi rose from bed while I was shucking on a condom and reached down, easing off the sheath.

"I want our child," she said.

"No way! Not unless you agree to come back to the States with me!"

"We shall make a child who is pure love," she said. "Half you, half me, yet better than each. Living in a better time."

She had her way, of course, and all through that last month I spent myself incessantly within her, flooding her obsessively, as though trying to dam up within her enough of me to protect her when I'd gone.

"Where is he now?" I ask Thanh Hoa.

"In Hanoi."

"Who has him?"

"The father is the third-ranking member of the Politburo."

"What have they told him about his natural parents?"

"He has been told only who his mother was. But of his father, nothing."

"I find it hard to believe," I say, "that he's getting such special treatment."

"I've learned," Thanh Hoa says, "that Hanoi is preparing a worldwide media campaign to promote Doan Thi as the leading poetess in the history of Vietnam. She is to be immortalized as the peoples' heroine. How could they permit the only son of so important a literary figure to root about in the streets like a starving hog, even if he is half-American? They *have* to isolate him from the others."

"How do I get proof?"

"At the place I am staying I have many other mementoes I brought with me to keep in the United States. I brought a birth certificate, in case I ever found you in America. And photographs of him as an infant with Doan Thi. Poems she wrote to him as he grew. You are mentioned in many of them. Look at his face, Ông Locke! What more proof do you need?"

"I have to get him out of Vietnam!" I hear myself saying.

"Oh, how they'd welcome you trying! They'd prefer you dead! To them you are the one taint, the single embarrassment in my sister's otherwise blameless and virtuous life. That she loved you, that she dared to bear a half-American son, this is not easy for them in Hanoi."

"Okay, I want to see those photos! His birth certificate! The poems!"

"I also brought one of Doan Thi's diaries out with me. I know you will find it especially revealing of her feelings toward you."

"When can I see all this?"

"Whenever you wish. I will give you the address. This is a very fine Chinese family. They are artists. They work in a beautiful town in the mountains near a lake."

"I know," I tell her. "In Bedugul near Lake Bratan on the road to the north coast."

"How did you know?" She seems startled.

"I even know what flight you came in on this morning."

"Then all the more reason you should believe what I tell you."

Now that's a classic example of turning a negative into a positive, I tell myself.

"This is going to sound somewhat ridiculous," I say, "but I'm going to ask you to get into the car because we're going up to Bedugul. But before you get into the car, I'm going to have to search your bag, and then—you've seen American movies where the cops pat people down?—then I'm going to have to make sure you're not carrying a gun."

She hands me her handbag. A brush, a comb, a worn wallet, some papers. No weapon. I run my hands over her body. She feels more resilient, stronger than she appears.

"Okay," I say, "you can get into the car, up front with me."

"Do you always do this with girls?" she asks. "Is this the way you get to feel their bodies?"

"Doesn't the diary bring that out?" I ask. "That the only reason your sister fell in love with me was because I am a sex maniac in constant overdrive?"

"I wonder if I will ever learn American humor?"

"I'm not sure mine is American," I say. "But my ego couldn't take two ladies in a row making an asshole of me. Now *asshole* is an American word!"

She slips into the front seat. I buckle up and circle us north toward Bedugul, some forty kilometers away.

I find the girl glancing at me from time to time with what I assume to be shy but provocative looks. Yet there are hidden dissonances here, layers of counterpoint that continue to nag at me. Shyness does not match up with the rest of her persona. It is almost as though she's following a playbook. Okay, now, when you get into the car with the subject, give him maidenly-shy-look number three.

I decide to test her on the black keys, now that it's evident she's mastered the whites.

"Do you like Doan Thi's poetry?" I ask.

"Who cannot?"

"How much of it do you know?"

"Every word."

"I used to wonder," I say idly, "whether she wrote for herself or for the peasants."

"She wrote for the oppressed," Thanh Hoa replies. "For the peasants, for women, especially for women, the most oppressed of the oppressed in Vietnam. How would you have liked to grow up in a country where your own father wept at your birth because he wanted a son, not a daughter, where the Mandarins taught schoolchildren that 'one testicle is worth a thousand girls'?"

"Speaking as a testicle?" I ask.

She looks at me reprovingly and sees that I'm smiling for the first time since she popped out of nowhere and into my day. She smiles, too.

"Maybe you believe me a little?" she asks.

"A little," I concede. "But tell me more."

"More? Of what?"

"What Doan Thi felt about the status of women in Vietnam."

"Are you sure you wish to get me started on *that*?"

"Why not? It's thirty minutes to Bedugul."

"Thirty minutes? I would need *years*! Well, in times not too long ago, unfaithful wives were trampled to death by elephants. Our emperors learned that from the Chinese. Then came the French, smiling piously behind their Catholic crosses. They were more merciless than the Mongols. They brought us the blessings of feudal patriarchy. Not only did they do nothing to alleviate the misery of being a female in Vietnam; they even called our grandmothers 'con di.' Certainly, when you learned our language, you learned that word early on?"

I nod. "Whore" is a serviceable word for any soldier.

"And 'bazu.' You know that word, too?"

"Monkey."

"Yes, they called our women monkeys. Then why did they throw them to the ground and rape them? Does a good Christian rape monkeys?"

Since I have known a Christian jock here and there who'd rape a knotty-pine wall, I remain in the listening mode.

"As a child," the girl says, "Doan Thi saw women beaten at the Central Market because they failed to respond quickly enough when told by their masters to move on. But why should we have expected the French to treat us with respect? They did not give their own women the right to vote until 1945. Why should *we* have expected any special favors? These were the things my sister wrote about. Her verses are full of the cries of the peasants, the despair of those about to be executed. This is truly remarkable, for until she came along, virtually every major Vietnamese poet before her had been reluctant to reveal even the least hint of feeling or emotion in his work. Such expression was judged a literary flaw. Elder sister repudiated all that.''

"Did she ever talk to you about other poets she admired?"

Here I'm setting a trap, for Doan Thi was ever reluctant to discuss the poets who'd preceded her over a period of two thousand years. She felt that most of them had copped out to the tyrannies of their times and gone along with the literary strictures of their Mandarin upbringing. Only one earlier poet did she admire, and I'm one of the few people who knows which one.

"Nguyen Du," I hear Thanh Hoa saying. "She greatly admired his work. She even told me that she'd taken his folk meters and updated them to this century, especially his double-seven, six meter. Of all poetic patterns in our language, this particular one gave her the most freedom to create the actual rhythms of human feeling."

Most impressive, I tell myself. If anything, too impressive. The girl comes off overtrained and overqualified.

"Did she ever talk to you about Hanoi getting on her case because some of her work could be taken as anti-Communist?"

"Many times. This was probably the most troublesome thing in her life—aside from you. But she insisted she was writing nothing she would not have written had she remained in the hamlet of her birth. In Vietnam we say, 'The rights of the emperor end at the gate of the village.' All our hamlets ring with antiestablishment diatribe. It is the nature of our people to resent and to resist outside authority. Why could your leaders not have understood that?"

"Don't get *me* started," I say.

"Doan Thi took both governments to task, north and south, equally. She was constantly reminding Hanoi that even the socialist system can breed hypocrisy and opportunism. She was aware that strong-willed writers had been suppressed throughout the history of the party, just as they are oppressed by fascist and military dictatorships. There were times, I'm sure, that Hanoi judged her an apostate. But now that she's dead, she'd been politically exonerated."

"And soon to be exploited!" I add. "The songbird of the Third World! Marvelous what the revisionists can do!"

"I prefer to think she is to be immortalized."

"You may or may not be sister fourth," I say, "but you know your subject."

"You don't *want* to believe me, do you?" she asks. "A miracle has happened—our coming together—but you don't want to give it its chance. Are you afraid to open yourself up again?"

"How can you ask that," I ask, "of a man who exhibits all the marks of hard use?" But it doesn't come out the way I'd meant it to. Instead of sardonic, I hear defensive along its edges.

"Are you afraid you might begin to feel toward me something of what you once felt for my sister?"

"*Still* feel!" I remind her.

"Do I remind you of her? Even a little?"

Oh, no! I'm not falling for that one!

"Is that why you're being so doubting—to keep what's dead forever dead?"

It can't possibly be *my* hands on the wheel, steering the Mercedes onto the shoulder of the road, *my* foot on the brake, stopping us, *my* fingers snapping off the ignition.

Without looking, I am aware of a rice farmer passing by, silent on calloused feet, over his shoulder a bell-shaped basket from which a fighting cock glares out at me with glassy, hostile eyes. Beyond, two naked boys scab for eels in the umber waters of a rice paddy. The afternoon is fragrant with *tjempaka* blossoms, even though the car windows are closed and the air conditioning consumes any incoming scent. This same all-seeing bursting clarity drives me across the seat toward the girl, even though I continue to doubt her. I know that I want her regardless of doubts, regardless of whether it's wanting her for herself or wanting her for reminding me of Doan Thi. Forgive me, Doan Thi. Forgive me, Dasima. Forgive me, forgive me.

She doesn't move. She appears to be waiting, eyes widening, lips parting slightly. I see Doan Thi's smile on Thanh Hoa's face, that ancient, enigmatic Asian sexuality flashing for a trillionth of a second in acknowledgment and acceptance of a white alien lover.

I place my lips lightly against hers. I inhale her breath. Then I hear what might be a muffled sob as she cups both her hands over the back of my head and pulls my lips abrasively against hers.

Incredible what cartwheels through your mind at these moments of first fusion. Self-deception, usually, but in this instance it's as though I'm suddenly privy to a digital readout of this girl's genetic tape. She's a no-nonsense animal, all right, one of your orgasm-demanding types. She begins to light me up.

But with an abruptness that can only be premeditated, she releases me and removes her lips a measured inch from mine.

"One way to deal with fear," she whispers, "is to confront it. You've confronted it. Are you still afraid?"

"Sister fourth," I tell her, "you've just gone platinum!"

CHAPTER

23

As we approach Bedugul, the formal walled villages of South
Bali with their contiguous family compounds give way to individual houses, isolated here and there within the mountain mist.

I drive along the southern shoreline of Lake Bratan. To the east
the thickly forested slopes of Mount Catur plunge directly into the
lake. To the west I can see three separate peaks, one of them,
Mount Batukau, rising more than seven thousand feet.

Thanh Hoa points toward a trail zigzagging into the mist to the
west.

"The family lives up there," she says.

"I'd hate to do their shopping," I comment.

I turn up the trail. It's little more than rutted tracks.

"They say it reminds them of their province in China."

"Their TV reception must suck. How can they exist?"

She slips closer to me. "I think I begin to understand your
sense of humor, just a little. You say things in a mocking way to
cover up the fact that you are unhappy. Not only with yourself—
but with the world as it is."

Maybe she *is* sister fourth. She has Doan Thi's hands-on perception of gut truth.

"Have you read her diaries?" I ask.

"Every entry. Time and again."

"I wonder if she wrote anything the morning after our first night together."

"Didn't she write a poem about that and give it to you?"

"I don't mean the poems. I mean what she wrote to herself in the diary. The poem she wrote for me."

"She wrote forty-three poems for you, didn't she?"

"How do you know the precise number?"

"She mentions in her diary, when she wrote you the poem she left behind in Saigon—her last poem, her good-bye—that it was the forty-third."

"Yeh," I say. "That forty-third was the rough one. Every time I read it, I want to shoot myself."

"Do you read it often?"

"I don't have to. I can recite it backward and forward and sideways."

"Do you keep the poems with you?"

"No. In San Francisco. In a safety-deposit box."

"When you bring me to San Francisco, may I read them please?"

I take my eyes off the twisting, climbing trail only long enough to look at her.

"What makes you believe I'm taking you to San Francisco?"

"I have thought of no other man than you, Ông gan cóc, for many years. I have never lost faith in the belief that I would someday find you. It was written that this day come."

I'm beginning to believe her, beginning to perceive she is Doan Thi's immortality—and my own future—that through her I might possibly bring Doan Thi back, and bring myself back, too.

"Do you know the city of Hué?" I ask her.

"I have never been in the Imperial City," she says.

"We made love for the first time, Doan Thi and I, in Hué. In the afternoon. We could hear girls singing a rice-planting song, 'Vui vui len, vui len,' as we touched each other for the first time. 'Happy, happy grow,' Doan Thi taught me the words meant. It was auspicious, she said, that we began together at the same hour as the rice planting. That was the first poem she wrote me. 'Happy grow.' The next morning we walked together up the Perfume River . . . We stopped at Linh Mu pagoda."

"Someday you will take me there?" Thanh Hoa asks.

"Someday!" I promise. "You and I and my son!"

The trail becomes even more precipitous as it scratches up

through the mountain mist, but all at once we come onto a plateau that merges with low-lying layers of compressed clouds and mist.

I follow the road through a pass between boulders bigger than the Mercedes. Ahead I see a lone compound. A pickup truck is parked out front. A rooster leaps, startled, from the flatbed as I slide in and stop where Thanh Hoa indicates I should park. For a moment the rooster appears about to dispute our arrival, then scampers away.

Thanh Hoa slips out of the Mercedes with a spectral smile.

"Let me tell them we have arrived. They were not sure I'd be coming back this soon."

I get out, flexing strained shoulder muscles, and rub my eyes. It is not a drive I would care to make too often.

But then how often are you told you have a son you never knew about?

I become aware after some seconds that I'm hearing no sound of welcome from inside the compound.

Pure silence buffets out at me through the gateway in the front wall of the compound.

I lock the Mercedes, pocket the key.

I approach the gateway.

The house hides within mud walls.

To one side of the gateway a dead cock is pinned, the family's mural against illness in the house. I find it strange that a Chinese family would sacrifice in the Balinese way. Possibly the servants have pinned the bird up there. Its extended wings are secured to the plaster, its tail drooping in a cascade of black and green wafting slightly in the mountain air. Red hibiscus peeks from above the inside of the walls, yet something about it appears unnatural, as though it, too, like the cock, has been pinned up there.

I glance back at a scrawny dog suddenly nosing along the waterless ditch. Why does he seem so unacquainted with this particular patch of earth? Even a mud-marked pig that appears from nowhere seems to be a transient.

I look about more heedfully. Through the gateway I smell the musty scent of the rooms in the house beyond the wall. Where is the odor of frying coconut oil that should be assailing my nostrils? Where the briny smell of *sra*, the fermented shrimp paste so indigenous to Bali? I conclude that the house is deserted. Nobody's lived here for months. The livestock's been inserted as stage dressing. What kind of dog-and-pony show is Thanh Hoa running for my benefit up here in the mountains? Why?

I slide the Browning out, release the safety, edge to the gateway, and peer into the shadowy enclosure. A main house, shutters closed. A sleeping house to its left. Kitchen, bathhouse, and garage to the right. To the northeast the house temple is untended. No offerings for the gods, none for the demons, either, no ritualistic cakes, no flower arrangements.

And no sign of Thanh Hoa.

It's all too Gothic.

"Thanh Hoa!"

No answer.

I glance up at the inside of the courtyard walls. Hibiscus definitely pinned up there. Weird. Enough to jangle a man's central nervous system. But coded for resistance, I ease into the main house, the Browning leading the way.

Thanh Hoa sits with what strikes me as ludicrous solemnity at the center of a long table, the only furniture in the otherwise bare room, a huge candle sputtering in its holder and causing her exquisite young face to float in and out of darkness.

Three Vietnames officers sit at each side of her. All six men are in NVA uniform. The one to her immediate right is a colonel. Even seated, he gives off puffs of freewheeling arrogance.

"You are Captain John Locke?" he asks.

I align the Browning with the button of his tunic closest to his aorta. This is simply a theatrical gesture, for I've already decided to shoot first the younger man to Thanh Hoa's immediate left if this turns into a gunfight. He looks like the type who'd steal your grandmother's pepper grinder. His nastiness is even more open-and-shut because he's clutching a TT-33 Tokarev pistol, resting it on his right thigh under the table. Keeping my back away from the doorway, I ease two steps to one side. Now, if he tries to grease me, he'll have to bring the gun out from under the table; otherwise, his lane of fire will be through his colonel's ribcage. I concentrate my attention on the men's feet rather than on their eyes. If you deal in such niceties, you'll learn that feet can give more early warning than eyes. It's drawing to an inside straight to try and trigger off a magazineful with the good results you're hoping for unless you can get those feet planted properly first. Time for me to clear the board, if it comes to that.

"Somebody said something one time about a situation like this,"

I comment to Thanh Hoa. "It could have been a John Lennon lyric, now that I think back. You might like to put it into your memoirs. Life, he said, is what happens to you while you're busy making other plans. For what it's worth, I'd like you to know that you were becoming a definite part of my plans. What I didn't know was that I was already part of yours."

"This is Colonel Tran Hoi Duc," the girl announces.

He's somewhat older than I. He's tall for a Vietnamese. He gives off a low, intense, almost but not quite unobtrusive hum, like a fluorescent light in a loose fitting. He feels dangerous. On the left side of his head, just above the ear, his hair grows wild as crabgrass out of bullet-ploughed scar tissue. This is a man accustomed to end games.

"I'll ask you one more time," he says. "Are you Captain John Locke, formerly attached to OPS-35 SOG?"

"I'm talking to the lady!" I tell him.

I catch a chill from Thanh Hoa's eyes, a look of unappeasable hostility.

"So the prince turns into a toad," I say. "Too bad. You really had me sold. How did you learn so much about Doan Thi?"

"I am the curator of the museum we are assembling for her in Hanoi," the girl replies. "I know more about her than she herself ever did."

"Tell me one other thing before this escalates. Does Le Hoang Hai really exist? And if he does—*is* he my son?"

"Answer the colonel's question!" she demands.

It's all too bizarre. I'm amused and apprehensive at the same time, amused by the mock seriousness of the seven people confronting me as though they're a drumhead court, apprehensive because I'm beginning to wonder if Captain Hamzah's theory about a Vietnamese-inspired-and-led insurrection in Bali might not have some legs, after all. Or is this confrontation between me and these NVA regulars a side issue, something entirely apart, some beast from my past come now to stalk me and linked up with those photos of me made by the Vietnamese cultural delegation?

"Yes, colonel," I say. "I served in Vietnam as an infantry captain. And my name is John Locke."

Thanh Hoa holds out a crumpled paper.

"Please examine it," the colonel requests.

With my free hand, but keeping the Day-Glo front sight of the Browning centered on the colonel's chest, I take the paper. I see a sketch tinctured with what appears to be fading red watercolor, a childish sketch, obviously drawn by someone very young. It's of an American officer in cammies. His cheeks are sunken, giving him a terrifying postholocaust aura, his eyes laser red. Impressionistic as the drawing is, I recognize the subject.

Me. Myself. Circa 1970. Somewhere in Quang Tri.

"Who drew this?" I ask.

"I did," Thanh Hoa replies. "I was ten years old when you and your men came to our village. Only three of us survived."

"Only three?" I ask, my voice as sunken as her rendition of my cheeks. "I've always wondered."

"I used the blood from my wounds to draw your face so I could never forget it."

What a piece of work this Vietnamese girl is! Hating me all these years, finally finding me, letting me touch her, kiss her, only in order to bring me to judgment now. Such stunning self-sacrifice!

"You blame me?" I ask. "But why not? How could you possibly blame your own people?"

For I know instantly what has driven her to this. Like all the other incidents of those years of insanity, it remains on the front burners of my own memory.

"Captain Locke," the colonel says, "I am with National Security. After Doan Thi's death we began to collect all remaining scraps of her writings..."

His voice drones on, but I am remembering Thanh Hoa's village, shimmering in heat. The fronds of the palms hung limpid above the huts as I led my Black Mamba team in.

Most grunts entered villages warily, crouching forward with hunched shoulders, their weapons extended, as though their Mattels could keep the war at barrel length away, that far, at least.

My Mambas always advanced with the swagger of classic samurai, walking firmly, knowing that each of us was good enough and fast enough that if some bad guy were to leap out at us from behind cover, firing, we had infinite time within the split-thousandths of a second to blow him away.

I eyeballed the village from one end to the other and six times through the middle, observing the squatting women outside their huts, holding to their muted children, all staring at us with their lustrous eyes. I decided we were in Indian country. For one thing, there were no men to be seen. For another, I spotted a defused bomb not quite concealed under a pile of brush. Only trained cadres were capable of defusing a magnetic bomb. The clincher was my sighting a girl throwing away an empty bottle and too casually leaning a broom against the side of a hut.

I signaled my men to freeze in place, some thirty feet separating each of us.

I called the girl to me.

She obeyed and came to stand defiantly before me. She was almost seventeen. Back in the States she could have been a cheerleader.

In Vietnamese, which surprised her, I ordered her to walk ten paces directly ahead of me and to lead the team along the hard-packed dirt track separating the rows of huts.

Halfway into the village she broke to one side and started to run.

Before she took three steps I killed her with the Swedish grease gun I carried back then.

I ordered my One-One forward. I pointed at the ground precisely at the point where the girl had wheeled off to the flank.

Two paces farther than she'd been willing to continue we found the cluster of mines she'd buried just before our arrival.

The empty bottle I'd seen her drop was what she'd used to roll the earth after she'd planted the mines. She'd used the broom to rearrange the ground to give it the natural-looking finishing touch. It never occurred to her that any stupid American soldier could possibly connect an empty bottle and a worn straw broom with death waiting underfoot.

We rounded up every woman and child in the village and I ordered the Mamba team to tie them securely, not only by their hands and feet but to secure them to stakes so that nobody could skip out of town until we were long gone.

One of my men was new to the team. He took exception to my order. He was still in shock that I'd laid a three-round burst up the spine of a fleeing seventeen-year-old girl.

"Why do we have to do this?" he demanded. "Why do we have to tie up these women and children like goddamned animals?"

"If we don't," I told him, "we'll be crow meat by morning. The men of this village are VC. Right now they're out there in the boonies waiting for us. As long as they believe we're still in here, they'll stay out. So we're going to fool 'em. We're going to get a couple of good hours ahead of them so we can set up a counterambush before they can hit us."

Among the prisoners were three nursing mothers. None of my Americans would obey my orders to tie them up along with the others. The argument went—how the hell could they manage to feed their infants if we tied them up? I pointed out that the worst that could happen was their babies wouldn't have milk for two fucking hours. And anyway, in wartime, mothers in combat zones don't give much milk. But my men wouldn't touch the job. I had to get the Vietnamese Special Forces on the team to do the tying. They understood the need.

I remember one little girl of ten. She stared at me more intensely than any of the others. She was an impressive child. Could this have been the girl who's now the young woman sitting across from me in judgment, the one who calls herself Thanh Hoa, fifteen years after that day?

We moved out of the village, leaving the women and children tied behind us so that no one could zip out and warn their men we'd left and point the direction of our leaving.

We were less than an hour out when I heard the first mortar round. Looking back through the binos, I could see their first round was well outside the village. Then came an interval of possibly five minutes before the barrage began, a full-scale bombardment of 81-mike-mike, directly into the village. It kept up, remorseless crump after crump, for a full thirty minutes while the new man vomited his C-rats. Even he, despite his combat inexperience, sensed what was happening. The VC, believing we were camping overnight in their village, were obliterating it—and theoretically us along with it—with their mortars. They were proceeding on the certain belief that their own wives and mothers and sisters would have fled instantly at the first warning mortar round and that we, reacting, would have been so concerned about taking cover that we wouldn't have stopped the villagers from fleeing to safety. That's why there'd been that five-minute interval between the first incoming and the onset of the full-scale barrage, a signal to the women, a chance for them to clear out with the children.

I had no way of knowing what casualties came of this except to assume they were extensive. For weeks afterward, I slept fitfully, wondering if there were any other way I might have extracted my unit on that particular mission, given the orders we were under not to break radio silence for seventy-two hours. I still don't know the answer. I suspect I'd do the same thing again, for a lot of cats were getting eaten as rabbits during those years.

"Only three of you survived?" I ask Tranh Hoa.

"Only three." She is having trouble holding back her tears.

"You were the child who kept staring at me?"

She nods. The motion breaks the tears loose.

"Who was the girl I shot?"

"My sister," she says. "My *real* sister."

It's one of those battered moments.

"I'm sorry," I say. "She'd have brought your men straight in on top of us. How long have you been looking for me?"

"Ever since that day."

"Why didn't you just pull out a pistol and shoot me at the gate when I came out to meet you?"

"I wanted to," she says, "but I had other orders."

The colonel clears his throat.

"In assembling the many things Doan Thi wrote," he says, "it became known to us that she wrote a number of verses of a most intimate and romantic nature and entrusted those writings to you, captain. We have flown from Hanoi to ask you to turn these over to us."

"This is why you didn't kill me on sight?" I ask Thanh Hoa. "You had to get the poems first."

"Yes," she whispered.

"How did you gentlemen get into the country?" I ask the colonel. "Immigration shows only Tranh Hoa arriving this morning. Have you been here a while?"

"That's immaterial, captain. Our interest is solely the recovery of the poems Doan Thi wrote to you. You can understand the need for us to review these works to make sure there is nothing contained in them which might compromise the legend of her devout socialism."

"I never thought I'd be willing to part with them. But if you give me my son, I will give you the poems. That is, if I truly do have a son in Hanoi and if that, too, isn't part of this whole sting."

"If you care for the memory of this Vietnamese woman you claim to have loved, captain, you will do this willingly," the colonel says. "For her sake. And for the country she loved. You will do this without trying to bargain with us."

"Do I have a son by her?" I cry.

"Yes."

"Then deliver him to me in Bangkok and I'll deliver the poems to you."

"We cannot make that trade," the colonel says.

"Then we have a problem," I say. I begin an almost imperceptible five seconds of inhaling through my nostrils. I lock my teeth, tighten my gut, slowly let my breath escape. I feel control flowing back all through me as I turn the problem over to my subconscious and its survival tapes. I separate my conscious thoughts from any attachment to the world, letting go of all my dreams, freeing myself from the obligations of any conceivable future until I reach the state in which nothing exists for me except these seven targets.

"I remind you, colonel," I hear myself saying, "that gunfights are funny things. By the time a man realizes he's into one, it's all over."

"The men with me," the colonel says, after an appropriate moment of reflection, "are skilled fighters. They, along with me, were specially selected for this mission in the event you refused our request. Have you any doubt we can kill you where you stand?"

"No doubt at all," I acknowledge, my left hand coming up now to steady my right, which keeps the Browning ticking in concert with the colonel's pulse. From my present stance to full combat crouch will take less than a hundredth of a second. "And have you any doubt that I will kill you, too?"

"I give you more credit than that," he says. "You may even kill four of us before you die."

"I think I can do better," I say. "But such a pointless game! Why should any of us have to die for the sake of a few hundred words written to me years ago by a woman who's now dead? Especially since those words were written to me alone. I promise you, colonel, I have no intention of ever letting anyone else share them. I promise you that I have no intention of coming forward later on and trying to compromise Hanoi's program for presenting Doan Thi as a poetess for socialism. I'm no longer an enemy of your armed forces. If anything, I'm downright sentimental over the Vietnamese—I've got a lot of guilt working against me and in your favor. I remind you—the war's over. If *I* can try to forget it, so can you! So let me back off, leave here—and let's all try to live another day. Who knows? Tomorrow might be a lot better than today. Can we cut that deal?"

"Captain Locke," the man says with singular lack of humor, "We charge you with crimes against our population. You subjected our compatriots to terror and to massacre. Now you must bear the consequence of your actions. What we do we do in the name of the People's Republic so that those who died will not have died in vain."

What party hack wrote *his* speech? He ticks it off without humanity as he stares straight into the muzzle of my Browning without flinching, and I see in him all the world's blind politicians who openly court death, all its knee-jerk government leaders orchestrating madness in the name of national policy. For a split second I get this spacy flash of me standing on a pile of all the world's flags, all the banners representing contending societies in varying degrees of fury and alarm, me standing there on this summit of flags, my pants down around my knees as I squat and defecate on all their defiant colors and mystic emblems with shit so scalding it sets them on fire, and poof!—up they go in flames, leaving me on a tranquil landscape of endless horizons where there are no longer national boundaries or border guards or customs officials or presidents or chiefs of staff or premiers or prime ministers or bureaucrats. Or people who do their bidding, as I once did.

I even start to smile a little at the whimsy of the concept, at my own stupidity for daydreaming in what may be the final seconds of my existence, when I tune back into the Colonel's voice.

"Rather than condemn most of us to certain death, we propose another solution. Each of us here has lost friends or relatives to you or to the men you commanded. But revenge is not an acceptable tenet of the People's Republic. We prefer reeducation."

"I've heard about your reeducation," I say. "It sucks!"

I'm starting to come unhinged. The bastard is making me revert, lockstepping me back into what I was in Vietnam, jamming me into a sequence of act and response, of tit for tat. I find myself *wanting* the gunfight to start. I hear myself whispering, "Make your move!"

But the colonel talks on. "We've been given this mission as a training exercise—an opportunity to test our skills against an adversary worthy of us. To make the exercise valid, we need to arm you with the weapons you were accustomed to as an American soldier. The Captain Locke who was assigned to SOG was armed with a Swedish submachine gun, a Colt Standard .22 with silencer, and an M-79. Is that not correct, captain?"

"You're forgetting the piano wire and the Randall fighting knife," I add.

"He's carrying the knife in the glove compartment of the Mercedes," Thanh Hoa tells the captain. I wasn't aware she'd opened the glove compartment.

"So—we will place in the yard outside those particular weapons—excepting the knife, which you have, and the piano wire, which you'll have to do without. I'm sure you can find adequate substitutes for a garroting wire if you put your mind to it. We will leave you seven grenades for the M-79—one for each of us. And seven magazines for the submachine gun and seven for the Colt. Then we shall leave you here and wait for you in the forest. It is for you to find us—or for us to find you."

If I didn't know better, I might laugh out loud. The notion that a quasi-official death squad would go to all this trouble to set up a personal war game on an island outside of Hanoi's sphere of influence seems at first blush beyond credibility. But in today's leapfrog world—where Japanese terrorists are trained in South Yemen to exterminate people at an airport in Zurich, where Libya has hit teams in London and Paris, and where anybody who's lost a country feels both exhilarated and exonerated to pull on a ski mask and shoot up a busload of innocents—the colonel's proposal strikes me as solid and well conceived.

"Unless," the colonel adds, "you change your mind and give us what we came for. In that case, we will accept your word that you will deliver the missing poems to us within a reasonable period of time—since I understand you keep them in San Francisco. If you will promise us to do that, we will leave as quietly as we came."

"No poems," I say. "Not without my son in return."

"This hearing is concluded," the colonel said. "We are about to rise, captain. As we do, you will observe that some of us are holding drawn firearms. We will, however, not fire at you within this room, providing you do not fire at us first. We will leave the agreed-upon weapons and ammunition outside. I regret that we will have to render your car inoperable."

"It's not my car," I say. "It's a loaner from the Indonesian Army. They are apt to take a very dim view of your rendering their vehicle inoperable. As a matter of fact, they might even delay your exit from their country."

"We intend to leave the way we came," the colonel says, "without their knowledge or consent. After we've dealt with you. Goodbye, Captain Locke. We shall meet you later—down the road, or in the surrounding forest."

I keep the Browning tracking the colonel as he and his men and Tranh Hoa rise from the table and begin to file out. Four of the men are gripping machine pistols. I'd spotted only two with weapons under the table. Four! Clearly, I wouldn't have made it out the door.

As Thanh Hoa passes, I say, "If Doan Thi had a sister fourth, she'd have been proud it was you."

I see no flicker of acknowledgment on her face as she leaves, not even hostility. Nothing there. Nothing at all.

After they've gone, even the sound of them gone, I stand alone in the room, the Browning heavy in my hand. I am as empty as the room, as deserted. Something animative has left with the girl. What it is, of course, is illusionary, the pretense I allowed myself for a while, that in the living flesh and enveloping warmth of an imaginary sister fourth, I had given life once again to the love Doan Thi and I had.

Now even that ghost is gone.

It occurs to me I should have taken my pain pills this morning. If I'd had any to take.

═CHAPTER═

24

WHAM! WHAM! WHAM!

The hard stutter of a Kalashinkov outside the *bale* scatters tiny fruit bats from the eaves and impels me to hit the deck and to roll onto my back, my feet directed toward the sound of the gunfire. I draw my knees to my chest to provide a shield of tissue in case something comes my way. Better to take incoming on the backs of your thighs and into your glutes than get your head or cardiovascular cavity drilled.

I remain on the floor in this humiliating half-curled, butt-forward posture, offering only a waterbug profile, but my gun arm extended toward the doorway, until the reverberations have stopped.

I hear an engine start. Then the sound of truck tires flinging pebbles as the wheels burn rubber.

The quiet settles in even though my ears still ring from the slamming of the assault rifle.

I roll over, slide along the floor to the doorway, and peer out from floor level.

The courtyard looks unpopulated.

Through the gateway I can see the forward third of the parked Mercedes. The hood has sprung open from the force of the fusillade. It reminds me of a giant nesting chick, beak agape as it waits for Mama Bird's worm. The front tire looks like a half-eaten biscuit of Shredded Wheat. Well, there goes my ride home.

My options are limited—stay here, doing nothing until dark, then try to slip through whatever fireline they're setting out for me or prepare right now to take it to them. I decide to tear the roof off the suckers.

For that I need more information.

I discover a vent higher up along the roof line. I climb up onto bamboo roof poles thatched with *lalang* grass and secured by cords of sugar palm.

Once up, I perch on a rafter that commands an overview of the compound. I can see below me what appears to be that beautifully designed Karl Gustaf Model 45 SMG, the Swedish K. It's been placed like an offering on a palm frond on the ground with seven magazines next to it. Then the M-79, which looks new enough to have come straight from the packing crate. With seven grenades. I'll have to check those out very carefully. During the war in Vietnam one of our dirty tricks was to infiltrate enemy ammo depots and pry open their mortar boxes and plant defective rounds so that combat teams would be killed by the charge exploding in their mortar. Then we'd pass the word through Psy-Ops to the VC that defective factory work in China and Russia was killing them, causing them to wonder each time they got ready to drop a shell into the tube whether it had their name on it or ours. Turnabout is fair play, some idiot once said, so I have to assume that this gungi colonel and his team have booby-trapped the ordnance they've left me. I finally spot the promised Colt .22 lying behind the tubular M-79.

For at least thirty minutes I lie without moving, sensing and imprinting, until I'm tuned into everything within the immediate area. I smell the metallic pismire of ants nearby. I listen to the fruit bats settling back into the eaves. All the outside sounds and smells and sights settle back into a congruity as though making peace with each other. I know then for sure that all seven members of the opposition team have left. I envision them waiting far down the mountain in terrain they will certainly have mapped and scouted before now. I form an image of two of them contriving man traps for me.

I climb down from the rafter and peel out the front door to the weapons they've left behind. The wind, sluicing down from the peaks, has notched up another five knots or so since I drove in here a little more than an hour ago.

I spend minutes staring at the armament placed on the palm fronds, fifteen minutes, not touching, simply looking, trying to make my eyes function as X rays.

Finally I pick up the K-gun. I field-strip it cautiously, one part at a time, holding my breath as I rotate the catch lever, then twist the barrel jacket and pull forward to remove the barrel from the receiver. I am still in possession of all my fingers. I disassemble the piece, then put it back together. One by one I examine each round in each of the seven magazines, thirty-six rounds to each clip. Now comes the M-79, a simple task, then the grenades. Somewhat trickier. Finally, the little Colt.

Clearly, I am dealing with honorable warriors. They have left me killing instruments in first-rate condition. I feel admiration for them, the admiration I always felt when I fought them in Vietnam. Small men, slight in build, almost delicate, they were able to exist for days with little food, able to march for miles without complaint. Their ancestors had fought one war with the Chinese invaders that lasted nearly a thousand years and had finally driven their enemy back over his own borders to the north. They'd fought the French for one hundred years and had humiliated them with defeat. They had made life in Indochina hazardous for the Japanese occupation forces in World War II. And God knows they inflicted immense physical and emotional trauma upon us, too, no matter how much firepower we laid upon them or despite the fact that in virtually every toe-to-toe battle we sent them reeling. Somehow, they kept coming back and back, and when we pulled out, they flowed in. No wonder these six men and one girl consider me a dead man already. To them I am a barbarian, an inferior. Of course, this is the flaw in their perception. Underestimating me. Playing games with me. They assume that all Americans are impatient. That I am incapable of lying stone-still for as long as they. Or of moving as swiftly and as silently without complaint.

They've made another critical mistake. They've failed to shoot open the trunk of the Mercedes to see what else I might be carrying other than the Randall fighting knife Thanh Hoa had seen in the glove compartment.

I unlock the trunk and bring out the suitcase of special gear I'd been given by Colonel Katrini. And my new Bellini shotgun, together with a box of double-ought buckshot. After World War

BRONZE BELL

Il the British brought the shotgun to its highest glory in the no-quarter jungle fighting in Malaya. And in Vietnam, toward the end of my combat tours, I carried a sawed-off Browning in terrain where your chances of survival were enhanced when you could respond to the enemy with the kind of massive pattern the auto-loading shotgun provides.

I carry the suitcase, the Bellini, and everything else back onto the *bale* and begin to prepare myself for a contest with the descendants of men who have been at war for two thousand years.

I spread it all out on the long table where my jury had sat, look it over for a while, and decide I could use some additional combat inventory.

I go out to the courtyard to begin a search of the other buildings. The wind gusts have grown steadier. Now they veer southwest, heralding a front of cold, slashing air. I watch the higher clouds claw right to left. In the Southern Hemisphere this frequently signals that the weather change will be for the worse. For me, at this point in time, worst is best. I've already asked Sky-Six to drive lightning across the sky, rattle the mountains with thunder, dump seas of water into the forest. Amidst such heavenly pyro-technics a lone man, knowing what he's up to, can go for climb-out, even if the odds are against him

Outside the cooking area I uncover a moldy pile of half-rotted burlap sacking. I shake out what I need, making sure to discourage any resident spiders or scorpions. I once lost a good man west of Kontum to a scorpion that crawled up under his chicken plate. I seem to remember reading somewhere that the Indonesian scorpion is relatively harmless, its sting no worse than that of a bee, but it might have been some other island's scorpion I read about. You can't remember everything.

Near the sacks I find a compost heap of tin cans, some of them not yet rusted through. I select the six best. In the same area I root out several empty Coke bottles.

But the big discovery of the afternoon is a magnificent piece of iron pipe, almost three feet long, one end capped with a threaded nipple.

Elsewhere, before I've finished, I find lengths of wire, rope, tattered rags. I even find a shovel. With it I dig up small rocks from the compound and fill one of the cans.

I take all this inventory into the *bale* and place it alongside the weapons, the bullets, and the grenades.

I go back outside to the Mercedes. The engine block and the radiator have been sledged into a ruptured mass of metal, but for my purpose the damage is irrelevant. What I'm after—the battery—remains blessedly intact. I unlink the terminals, loosen the clamps, remove the unit from its bracket, and carefully drain the battery acid into one of the cans.

I fill six Coke bottles each three-fourths full of gasoline from the car's tank. For a moment I question why they failed to shoot into the tank; then it occurs to me they didn't want to risk creating a fire or explosion, which might attract unwanted company if there were army patrols in the area.

The first rain of late afternoon begins to dribble down. I place an empty can under one of the eaves and leave it there.

I bring the battery acid and the bottled gasoline into the *bale*. I start a fire in one of the larger tin cans, and over the flames I suspend the can containing the battery acid.

I boil off the water until acrid white fumes begin to cloud up and I'm satisfied that most of what now remains in the boiling can is pure sulfuric acid.

I remove the can from the fire to let the acid cool.

From the suitcase I take out two items I carry against the time I might need them. One is a small packet of granulated sugar. The other is a vial containing crystals of potassium chlorate.

I step outside and retrieve the can of rainwater.

I heat it over the fire, and when the water begins to bubble, I sift in the granulated sugar. When I have a thorough solution of sugar water and have cooled it, I add the potassium chlorate crystals. I then pour the combined liquid into a bottle, which I seal carefully.

Now, using the small funnel I bring from the bag, I slowly add the sulfuric acid to each bottle of gasoline, sliding the acid into the gasoline with tender care. I fill each bottle to within an inch of its top, then cork each with wooden plugs I carve from the table with the Randall fighting knife.

I take these bottles out into the rain to let it flush them clear of any spilled gasoline or acid.

That done, I bring them back inside and wrap each with rags, then secure the rags with wire to make sure this flammable outer wadding will remain securely attached even if thrown through heavy bush. Then I tie each bottle into its own individual cradle of rope, allowing an extra two feet of length at the neck for slinging.

Now to the pipe. I take from the suitcase an igniter and propellant, standard items wherever I go. I wrap them into a pouch I make from rags, then secure the pouch at the mouth with wire. I roll this touchy little packet gently enough until I can snake it into the pipe, the igniter leads remaining extended all the way out. I tamp it all firmly down until the pouch rests against the cap at the end of the pipe. Now I empty the cans of stones into the pipe. I pack a final wadding of burlap in against the stones to hold them in place.

It's hardly your standard 60-mike-mike mortar round, but it can be unpleasant if you're foolish enough to walk into it.

I tape the bores of all the guns to keep out dirt and debris, then once more check the ammo, this time for chamber fit, discarding some rounds, keeping only the perfectos. I won't be able to afford any ammo glitches once the stonking starts.

Okay, Locke, what else before you go out into Marlboro country? You've got yours. What about theirs? How are the countermeasures? I'll assume, I reply to my inner voice, they're equipped with the latest technology. Lets' give them night scopes, thermal imagers, and laser sights, okay? Okay, but night scopes aren't that effective in dense environments. And anyway, *you've* got a pair of passive night goggles. Assume they have night-scoped, silenced weapons. Bad news, right? Right, but only if I'm down range and they can see me. They have to see me to hit me, wouldn't you agree? How about the thermal imagers?

I take from the suitcase a roll of plastic and bundle it around my torso, securing it finally with Velcro. How about this, I ask my inner voice? With this on I can advance straight into thermal-image scoping and all the enemy will see will be reflections of foliage surrounding me. The voice asks no more questions.

I load everything into the bag except for the shotgun. I step outside into the dying day with its boisterous wind. I muddy my hands and face, saddle up, and move out with all my tools.

I use the last light of day to photograph in my mind the route I will take to reach the sea. I calculate the precise spot on the distant coastline below which is my objective. If I can reach that point, I will come in where I can get a message through to Colonel Katrini at headquarters. My problem is simple. I am at point A. Down there in the distance lies point B. In between I have to deal with seven intransigent people who refuse to let me forget a war I can't seem to forget either.

They certainly have enough respect for me to know I won't come strolling dumb and happy down the road I came up.

I'm almost tempted to try it, just walk out brazenly, the direct, easy way.

But there are, after all, seven of them—manpower to spare.

In sorting out my possible thought processes, they must certainly have speculated that I might do something that outrageous—just saunter out down the road. What they've probably done, simply to cover the contingency, is to spot their least valuable player, Thanh Hoa, three-quarters of the way down, positioned her somewhere on a high bank of the road at one of the many hairpin turns, given her a radio to keep them in touch and a sniper's rifle to pick me off if I opted for the tricky, easy way out.

If not by the road, then what other path do they believe I'll elect?

I observe two ridgelines and one animal trail, all starting near my present high position, all within a quarter of a mile, all leading separately down into the valley.

They may have concluded I might use one of those three routes and have set two men on each.

What other alternatives have I?

Off to the southeast I discover a steep fall of boulders and below them a cliff plunging straight down for two hundred feet to the sloping forest below.

They'd never expect me to go down that way.

No sane person would try.

I wait until darkness, then I start picking my way among the boulders, working slowly toward the cliff.

The membrane of the sky appears to rupture above me, torrents of water beating down as I descend, making the rocks slippery and slowing my progress. Whenever lightning whitens the sky, I cling like a bug to rock, then scurry another few feet downward as the night blackens again. The reassuring drumming of thunder and the pounding rain muffle the clatter of my equipment. At least up here I don't have to worry too much about noise discipline.

It's almost twenty hundred hours when I arrive at the top of the cliff. Like most cliffs, it doesn't look quite as formidable when you're close to it as it does from a distance. I observe cracks and ledges most of the way down. I may not have to rappel, after all

I take my climbing rope and hardware from the bag, make a self-releasing loop, and lower the bag and its contents some thirty feet to a wide ledge. I retrieve the rope and lower the Bellini; then, using both hands and feet, I climb down. I repeat this process three times until I've succeeded in descending to the crest of a straight drop-off. These last fifty feet are so sheer I can almost picture the glacier that shaved them clean.

I check the time. Almost twenty-two hundred hours.

I unzip myself from the plastic body shield, let it float down to the foot of the cliff. Then the final lowering of the heavy bag of ordnance and equipment.

I prepare for rapelling, inspecting the rope for any cuts or fraying it might have picked up over the past two hours of heavy duty. I tuck my shirt and jacket in tightly so that I won't burn hide if the rope should slip up underneath on my way down. Then I hitch up the Swiss Seat, threading the rope through the snap link from left to right so that the rope will be passing around the right side of my body. I make a loop with the rope in front of the snap link and take only two turns around the link. The more turns around the snap link, the slower the descent. With thermal imagers out there searching me out, the faster I can get down the better.

I turn my face to the lashing sky, open my mouth, let the downpour cool me and slake my thirst. Then I step back and out into space, rapelling down, forcing myself to bite my tongue so that I don't shout with joy at the sheer physical exhilaration of the spider drop through space.

I bottom out next to the plastic shield, unhitch myself and rewrap myself in Saran, pick up the Bellini and the bag, and ease down the slope toward the trees. There the brush is intermittent. I dart between bushes at every thunder clap, stop behind shelter whenever lightning emblazons the sky.

In another fifteen minutes I've gained the sheltering forest.

I estimate the most proximate enemy is some half mile to my west, off to the nearest side of the ridgeline where it flattens toward the coastal plain. I imagine him huddled there in the rain, eyes focusing upward, scanning me through all his optical devices, constantly sweeping the trees for any sign of me, using his peripheral vision, for at night the rods, not the cones, take over in the retina, so that you get a better sighting with continuous scanning rather than with straight-ahead vision.

I circle outward, but closing toward the west until I've passed a click behind and beyond where I imagine my nearest enemy is waiting. I continue on until I'm at a midpoint between the two ridgelines and the animal trail.

This will be the killing field. I'd eyeballed it from the mountain peak, and now there it is, a small clearing in the midst of giant *upas* trees rising over one hundred feet, their trunks four feet in diameter. The trees are gnarled with huge buttresses that swell like cancers up the trunk; then the trunks rise clean and bare for sixty feet. I find it ironic that I should have selected this grove of *upas* as the site for what could be my last stand. The milky sap of this tree is used as a highly toxic coating on arrows and the darts of blowpipes all through Malaysia and Borneo.

As I begin to sort out the scene, I observe a loris hunched lugubriously on a nearby bush. He sits with his paws in front of his face as if he's blocking out some terrifying spectacle. These little creatures, a lethargic species of lemur, are said by the locals to be so unhappy because, with their large, staring eyes, they see ghosts everywhere about them. How prophetic, I think, as I set to work organizing the core of the ambush and work my way outward to the perimeters.

When everything is in place, I watch for the rain to become somewhat less intense and the worst of the wind to chase itself eastward.

The time is only five minutes short of twenty-four hundred hours, the witching moment of midnight. The loris is no longer anywhere to be seen. Too many ghosts in the area, no doubt.

Standing in dead center of the ambush area I wait until both hour and minute hands point straight up to twelve.

BLOOK!

I pop the first grenade of my allotment of seven from the M-79 toward the base of the nearest ridgeline.

The sound violates the forest silence.

History supports the axiom that it's easier to attack than to defend.

History, kiddo, be with me tonight.

═══CHAPTER═══

25

I'm well beyond range. The burst from my chunker falls far short of where I imagine the nearest enemy to be, but it won't take them long to calculate my position. I'm certain they're equipped with the same little radar device I have that can locate the direction of incoming fire to within thirty degrees, silenced or otherwise.

To assist them in their calculations, I fire off another round.

They know the maximum range of the M-79 is less than a fifth of a mile, so they'll also know by now I've got to be somewhere within a thirty-degree wedge of a four-hundred-yard circle from the impact points of my two grenades, a position I've done everything within my power at this moment to implant in their thinking.

The moment after I've launched the second grenade, I run out of the center of the ambush area to take up a position a hundred yards to one side. There are earthrises here for shelter, and the ground elevation is slightly higher than the ambush zone itself.

Within ten seconds after I've settled down, their first round from a piss tube crumps into the ambush circle, not more than thirty yards from where I'd been standing when I fired the two grenades. From the hole it churns up, it's pure 81 mike-mike.

My admiration for my enemy zooms ten points.

In the darkness and against this storm, without an aiming stake, to have dropped their first round that close and that immediately indicates that Hanoi has indeed sent its varsity into Bali for this minor event. A good mortar team can deliver anything from fifteen to twenty-five rounds per minute out to a maximum range of three thousand meters. In the next sixty seconds, this team gets off twenty-six rounds in a combing semicircle.

I'm fearful that under so intense a barrage they may have disrupted my arrangements at the ambush center, particularly my emplaced K-gun, but there's no way I can risk dashing back to check things out. It's standard NVA tactics to lay down a heavy mortar barrage, then follow it up instantly with an infantry probe.

Through the night goggles, ghostly in outline, I spot two of them advancing in a self-assured crouch with their slick new AK-47s, slanting in toward where they believe me to be, some fifty yards between them, both men well off to my side but clearly within range.

I wait until both are close to the other perimeter of the still-smoking ambush area, then I pull the trip wire I've led out to me to make the K-gun fire sequential bursts.

I've braced the little gun in a fortified position, and now, firing it by wire, I see them take the bait.

Convinced I'm trapped inside the area they've bracketed with their mortar fire, one of them uses a radio to contact his colonel. I can't hear what he's saying, but I guess he's telling his One-Zero he won't be needing any backup. They've got the dumb Americano flanked and bracketed. They'll handle the job by themselves, thank you, just the two of them, and not even work up a sweat. It reminds me of a line Clint Eastwood's flinty inspector Callahan uses in the *Dirty Harry* movies as he wastes some asshole who's trying to take him out, "A man's got to know his limitations." Obviously, these two don't, so I wait while they come in to sit on my front porch.

The first one snakes his way into a shallow gulley I knew damn well some ground pounder would find utterly irresistible. No infantryman in the world could have foregone the pleasure of slithering up this natural trench. Halfway toward where he thinks I've put up shop, he sets off the trip wire, firing the pipe mortar. I hear the explosion but no answering scream. I feel a momentary twinge of disappointment; then it strikes me. How could he scream if his head has been torn off by the blasting stone? Still, one has to be sure.

I saturate the cloth enveloping one of my bottles with the sugar water and potassium crystals, whip it around by its sling, and heave it out toward the trench where I'd set the pipe mortar. The bottle hits, the potassium igniting with the acid in the bottle to detonate the gasoline. A fireball surges up at the edge of the ambush site, and I see the broken hulk of the dead man exactly where it should be. I pick up a bonus in the split second the flames rear against the carbon sky. I catch the silhouette of the second man. He's not more than fifty yards away, in startled profile as he sees me, too.

One basic tenet of bush work I always drilled into my men is to have your weapon pointed in the direction you're looking. If you don't, the split second it takes to swing it onto target may cost you your life.

I pump three rounds of double-ought Magnum at him as he turns to shoot at me. The Bellini holds its pattern out to seventy-five yards. The target merges into the landscape.

I run, low and fast, to what's still over there to be found. Luckily, his radio has survived the storm of pellets. I thumb on the transmitter.

I speak in Vietnamese to the man with the crabgrass patch on the side of his head, genuinely admiring him, wanting him to come through this night as much as I'd like to.

"Give me my son," I say, "and I'll withdraw. Why should you die for a bunch of sonnets?"

"How little you know us, captain," he replies through the radio. I am impressed by his restraint, annoyed by his ethnocentrism. At least there's none of that fuck-you bravado an American commander would have thundered back, given similar provocation.

I estimate that I have five minutes, no more, before it's ended, my way or theirs.

I start a series of peripheral eye sweeps through the night goggles, while my mind, separate from my body, runs a thought by Montaigne through for the hell of it, something about the fact that to get used to the idea of death, there's nothing like coming close to it. I wonder what kind of a grunt Montaigne would have made. You *never* get used to it. You only get deader and deader in your guts—that's all coming close to it ever does for you: numb you, force your body to produce its own pain-killer, that morphinelike analgesic called endorphin, which raises your threshold of pain and lets you walk around with your head under your arm for a few ticks of the clock without a headache. Bullshit, M. Montaigne!

I detect apparitions approaching across the night, four men and the girl, fanning out around the core that is drawing them to their deaths.

Once more I activate the Swedish SMG by remote control.

All five of the apparitions begin firing at its muzzle flashes.

I employ my five remaining grenades, blasting them from the M-79 as fast as I can, encircling the colonel.

Tran Hoi Duc no longer exists except as scattered fragments around the base of an *upas* tree.

I follow up the M-79 barrage with my remaining bottles of fire and exploding gasoline, heaving all five of them off in less than three seconds, lighting up the ambush site in miasmal reds and blacks, and in the glare I rip off the remaining four rounds in the Bellini, killing the two men nearest me. But one manages to stagger back onto his feet and swing his AK-47 toward me. I use the silenced Colt .22, employing what we used to call in-country the zipper technique. You start firing at the target's waist and zipper all ten rounds in a rising string directly up the centerline of the body. This imparts a lethal shock to the nervous system that is one hundred percent terminal.

I'm down to the Browning now. Plus my own .22 in the ankle holster. I lie motionless, letting the seconds tick like termites.

Something.

I lower my ear to the earth, listen.

Someone is crawling over broken rock. At least seventy meters out. Crawling toward me.

I peer out through the night goggles, the Browning ready.

Thanh Hoa. She has no weapon in her hands. Her fingers dig into the ground to crab herself forward. Her face is gray with blood.

That leaves only one man unaccounted for.

I rise, keeping crouched, and trot away from her in a wide circle, then come in from behind.

But the sixth man is also dead. What I had presumed was burning brush is the sixth guerrilla, his clothes still smoldering with the flames of one of the burst Coke bottles.

I trot through the shattered site to make sure.

Only Colonel Duc is impossible to verify, but I find enough of him here and there to make the body count complete.

The Swedish K-gun has been blown to pieces, as well. They'd charged in to get me, and they got it at least.

I return to where Thanh Hoa still worms aimlessly.

She hears me coming.

She rolls over and stares up at me from the mud.

There is no hatred in her eyes now. The shock of combat purges the mind of such pointless emotion. It forces one to deal with the verities.

"Kill me," she begs.

I kneel beside her to determine how much if any life is left to her. The wound channel is in her neck. Clearly there's been cavitation—probably from a grenade fragment. I'm astonished she hasn't died instantly. I focus the flash of my hand torch on the wound and discover that the fragment has torn through the neck without hitting spine, carotid artery, or trachea. It's one of those miracle penetrations. It looks horrible, but as neck wounds go, this one is a blue-ribbon winner.

Her lips form unspoken words in Vietnamese, *"Tôi móun chét."*

"I want to die."

"Why should I do you the favor?" I ask.

I apply pressure next to her wound, just to one side of the trachea, still letting her breathe but slowing the bleeding. I rip off the burlap sleeves of my improvised cammies and lay the folded cloth above the wound, then I wrap her neck.

I lift her. She is light as a child.

I carry her toward the ridgelines in search of their pickup truck.

I find it concealed in scrub next to their emplaced mortar and a depot of still-unfired shells.

I place her on the flatbed of the truck, first making sure there are no weapons remaining in the back. I tie her firmly, not so much to restrain her as to keep her from rolling off, for we have a long, rough way to go down the mountain.

I hot-wire the ignition, the engine turning at once. I climb up behind the wheel and bump back through the trees to where I've left my combat gear and all the rest of it.

I note as I drive that only twenty-two minutes have elapsed since I fired the opening round from the M-79 at midnight.

For some reason I remember an American kid at some airport or other in the States when I came back from Vietnam. I was still in uniform, still unaware they weren't about to give us any parades. I had all my campaign ribbons on and some of the tougher stuff to come by. The kid pointed at my ribbons and asked his mother what I'd spilled on my jacket.

I recover from the combat zone those things I still need and wish to take back with me.

I turn the truck around and drive with Thanh Hoa down the mountain.

The hammering rain has striated the unpaved trail into two parallel grooves of mud. Here and there collapsing banks of wet earth flow across the trail like lava. Everywhere about me on the slopes the *dap-dap* trees sway under the lashing of the rain, their gray-green foliage blending with their beady flowers into huge wet palettes. Only the traction of the truck's four-wheel drive gets me out and back onto the paved highway north of Denpasar and the modern hospital facilities Thanh Hoa needs.

Before dawn I'm speeding into Denpasar, past boys already herding flocks of ducks to the rice fields just outside the town, driving them like sheep with long bamboo poles topped with feathers fluttering in the wind.

I skid to a stop at RSAD, the army hospital on Panglima Sudirman. Frangipani blossoms cluster to either side of the entrance. They haven't yet decided whether or not to open up for this new day. Light still filters fitfully out of the east, as though being pestled sparingly by the sun from a bowl of cracked sky.

I happen to be fond of frangipani blossoms.

I pick one of the partially opened flowers and place it carefully in the pocket of my jacket.

Thanh Hoa's pupils contract as I climb onto the flatbed and lean close to assess the beat of her pulse. Her color is better than I had expected. Glorious bamboo women!

I untie the rope with which I'd secured her. I lift her off the sodden burlap, which has soaked up the storm as I raced us to Denpasar. The bleeding in the neck has not resumed. Looking good. Gently I scoop her up, slide down off the flatbed, and carry her into the emergency ward.

The duty nurse is young and efficient. She took her training and learned English, she tells me, in Jakarta. She calls the intern, then begins to prep Thanh Hoa. She finds it inconceivable that a girl so beautiful has suffered so hideous a wound.

"From what?" she asks me. "A tiger, possibly?"

"A grenade," I tell her.

"A grenade?" she says, as though the very word is foreign to her lips. I suspect she's never used the word in all of her twenty-two years of living.

During the bloodletting that followed the aborted Communist takeover of Indonesia in 1965, when the rivers were clogged with the bodies of the slaughtered, she would have been only two years old. Even if some shadow of those days and nights of terror were still grooved into her subconscious, her memories would be a nightmare of flashing knives, not of grenades. The Balinese are not grenade people like others of us.

"Yes," I say. "A grenade—not much larger than a mangosteen. Like a small fruit blossoming open. But its skin and its seeds are of steel."

I nod down at Thanh Hoa.

"It does *that* to a person."

"What could possibly have brought her into contact with so inhuman a device?"

"What indeed?" I agree.

"Is she Balinese? Or from Java?"

"Neither. Vietnamese."

This seems to explain everything to her. She asks me no more questions.

The doctor is equally efficient.

By oh-eight-hundred hours Thanh Hao has had transfusions of whole blood, including a pint of mine, a tetanus shot, and antibiotics. Her wound is closed and dressed.

For the rest of her life she will carry a scar from her collarbone to her chin. It will prevent her from wearing off-the-shoulder ball-gowns, but such are not in vogue in Hanoi. She will still be able to laugh and cry, love, bear children, and dream.

I walk along with the gurney as they wheel her to a room. Her eyes cling to me. I tell myself, because now and then I like to pretend there are such things as happy endings, that her eyes have become deep pools of gratitude, that she no longer hates Americans, particularly this American.

I'm straddling the years again, back in Vietnam with Doan Thi, this time walking through a hospital at Danang.

She's come to recite poetry to ARVN wounded. The soldiers are wedged in, two to a pallet on straw mattresses, one with his head at his bedmate's feet, like the Jack of Spades. Wives, mothers, sisters, cousins, grandmothers, and children throng between the beds. Vendors snake through the crush of bodies and cry their wares.

With Doan Thi I push through the last of the families between us and the ward we are to visit. An old woman turns her back to me, whispers something in Vietnamese. The turning away is not abrupt, not intended to convey any meaning whatsoever, yet it is the most dramatic rejection I have ever been given. She doesn't know I understand her language. I hear her whisper to the maimed soldier sharing the bed she's visiting, "An American! Ah, I am afraid even to look at one!"

Doan Thi grips my hand and resolutely leads me into the ward where the soldiers and their families await her.

A young soldier is entertaining the others with his guitar.

When he sees me enter, he stops. Two hundred eyes lock onto me.

I say to him in Vietnamese, "Go on, please. Continue to play."

He answers me in English. "I have finished, captain."

I say to him, again in Vietnamese, "Excuse me, please, for questioning you, but I know that song. It is a beautiful song. But if I recall correctly, it has five verses. Am I mistaken, but had you only just begun the second verse?"

Vietnamese is a language designed to leave avenues open, not to back people into corners or to confront them.

Two hundred eyes exchange unspoken testimony and reach a unamimous verdict. In my favor.

The young soldier resumes his playing.

I move next to him and begin to sing the song in Vietnamese, picking up where he had left off. By the third verse every soldier and all the family members in the room are singing along with me.

Yet even as they sing, they stare at me in wonder, as though they cannot dare let themselves believe this is really happening, that there has come among them an American of a kind they had never met before.

Realizing this brings me close to tears. I have trouble with my voice.

But Doan Thi continues to hold my hand. She, too, is singing. And exhibiting her tears proudly for everyone to see.

That look I saw then in the eyes of the soldiers and their families in the hospital at Danang I see now in Thanh Hoa's eyes.

Bewilderment? That's what it must be. Yeah, must be. Bewilderment.

Who and what are these rangy Americans with the big noses who come halfway around the world smelling of meat and peanut butter, men who fight like tigers yet weep like women when they see a hungry child?

I have asked the hospital people to assign Thanh Hoa a private room. I cannot stomach the thought of a soldier with a neck wound having to share a ward with women suffering normal, peacetime afflictions. I have told the doctor to call the accounting office and tell them I will be along in a few minutes with the appropriate rupiah count, together with the name of a good, dependable local reference, a Colonel Katrini, a soldier himself, an authority figure who believes that life is a stage with only one entrance but many exits. He would certainly understand and approve of the need to guarantee this particular girl a private room. I call him in his quarters at the base, tell him where I am, and ask him to come for me.

So we are alone now, Thanh Hoa and I.

I fill her bedpan with water from the washbasin. I place the pan on the small table next to her pillow. I float the frangipani blossom in the water, stem down, petals up. I cover the bedpan with a towel, closing the flower in.

Thanh Hoa's eyes watch me. I tap my wristwatch, indicating we must wait a minute or two to let the magic work.

"They think you should be able to leave in a few days," I tell her. "I may still be in Bali, or I may not. But if I'm not and you need anything—money, a ticket home—there is one man who will know about you and who will help you. I'll arrange everything with him. Colonel Katrini. But if when you come out you still have this obsession about killing me, okay if I make a suggestion? Get yourself a high-powered sniper's rifle with a reasonably good scope. Pick an elevated spot five hundred yards out with a clear lane of fire and the sun at your back and wait for your best shot. Because with me you'll only get one. We're all walking targets these days, but some of us are tougher to punch out than others. You're not good enough yet, Thanh Hoa, to take me inside three hundred yards. So next time, if you insist there be a next time, give yourself more distance, okay?"

I unwrap the bedpan. The scent of the blossoms, trapped in

that compressed pocket, now billows out like sweet smoke. I move the pan close to the girl's nostrils. I watch her inhale the perfume.

I set the pan down, close to her.

"Doan Thi used to do that for me," I tell her. "Just before we'd fall asleep. If you see my son, tell him that, please. He should know such things about his mother. Not just about her socialist poetry."

I go to the door, but I have trouble leaving.

I look back at her and notch into my memory the dark, still depth of her eyes in which I can read nothing. I shall not forget this wretched little hospital room with its cracked plaster wall, its stained ceiling, its biting chemical smells, scarcely softened by the frangipani, and the girl lying there, watching our lives ricochet away from each other, the girl I had hoped might finally bring Doan Thi back to me. I wish I could hate her for betraying that impossible wish, but I can only acknowledge my own betrayal of myself for ignoring my initial perception of her as an impostor, for suppressing my disbelief that she was Doan Thi's sister fourth. I wanted her to play 'Misty' for me while I battened on fantasies. Even now, I want her to be something she isn't.

Time to let go.

"*Adieu*, Thanh Hoa. *Chào cô*."

I get myself out to the hospital corridor and close the door between us.

How simple if merely saying good-bye, just closing a door, could suture the cherished wounds of the past.

To the cadence of present time, I step into the Denpasar morning.

Guntur and a detachment of Red Berets are waiting.

CHAPTER

26

"**D**o me a favor," I say as Guntur, with concern in his nimble eyes, watches me hump sagging out of the hospital. "Don't give me any more messages! That first call, supposedly from Chartwell, cost me sleepless night number one. Yesterday's message about Thanh Hoa waiting at the gate cost me sleepless night number two. Two nights in a row with people pointing guns my way has debilitated me. I'm at an extremely low level of response capability, at my most vulnerable, all systems glitched."

"As soon as you're debriefed," he says, "you should get some sleep."

"Right! But not at your brother's compound!"

"I can phone Dasima to let you sleep. She was frantic all night when you didn't return."

"What I'd really like to do, Guntur, is to go back to your headquarters—we can get caught up en route—and once I'm there just sack out in the barracks until midafternoon. I sleep better round dirty socks and soldier's sweat."

I have to pump myself up even to climb into the Ferret scout car. I collapse in back and peer out bleary-eyed at Denpasar traffic.

Out of respect for my lethargy, Sergeant Maru at the wheel either tailgates the *bémos* stacked in front of us nor tries to carve

233

two lanes out of one. He delivers a nice steady ride the twenty kilometers to Tabanan, time enough for me to tell Guntur all about my little adventure, omitting nothing, not even my thoughts, from my meeting Thanh Hoa at the main gate until a few moments ago, when in response to my call Guntur came to meet me at the hospital.

"Sorry about your Mercedes," I conclude. "I never got to use the razor blades, but the Bellini was most comforting. I warned them you'd take a dim view of their trashing the engine."

"We have executed people for less!" he mutters.

"But they left behind their assault rifles, their night scopes, their imagers, one perfectly decent mortar, two crates of shells and increments. It's still up there, mostly intact, on the plateau near Mount Batukau. All that ordnance is worth a helluva lot more than the Mercedes, so on balance you're looking at a net gain for COIN-OPS. There's also their pickup truck I left parked right over there. It's probably stolen. You'll find a brand-new M-79 up front and a Colt .22. Since I've already got my own .22, the extra one is all yours. I'd like to keep the M-79."

"It's yours. Give me the location. I'll send a unit to salvage the material and collect the dead."

"I'll show you the coordinates on a map."

"There is no Chinese family in Bedugul. The girl made that up to deceive immigration. When you didn't come back, I sent Captain Hamzah searching for you. Poor sod is spending most of his time lately out looking for you."

"How's he doing off Point Sari? Finding the bell?"

"I'm calling that operation off at fifteen hundred hours today. We've traced and retraced every square meter out there with the world's most sophisticated bottom-sensing equipment and we have found nothing. You were right, John. I should have waited. I have ordered a resumption of the inland search patterns. The bell must be somewhere ashore, since that same nagging problem remains unsolved—how *could* they have got it across the reefs anywhere from Pasat down west to Ujung in the east, using only the flatbed truck and the crane?"

"Right now other things are nagging at me. How did those six Vietnamese I tangled with last night get into Bali without anybody knowing they were here?"

"You know better than I how easy it is to insert covert unit into a country. They could have been air dropped by some low flying plane skimming in under our radar. They could have been put ashore by boat on the north coast before dawn yesterday. There is no way we can patrol the hundreds of thousands of miles of shoreline in all the islands of Indonesia. Put it this way. They came in the same way the terrorists who took the Bronze Bell came in."

"Somehow I don't think so."

"Why not?"

"I don't know. For reasons I can't even begin to understand, what happened to me last night has crystalized certain speculations. Example, my scramble last night and what happened at Pura Besakih on the morning of *Nyepi* are totally unrelated. Don't ask me how or why I know that, but I do. This thing last night—you were right—sprang directly off my being photographed at the hotel by the Vietnamese delegation. They rushed those photos to Hanoi, where the people who tend to such matters identified me as someone they've been looking for. They flew a team in and came after me. It's that simple. But these other people—the ones who did the Besakih job—I think they could be in Bali legally. Not just floating around the countryside. I think they're based somewere—legitimately, with cover identities. You understand what I'm trying to say?"

"Yes and no."

"Okay, let's take a wild guess. That many people, to get lost in the crowd, would almost necessarily have to be employed by a major corporation. Let's take Pac-Pet as an example, since it was their equipment which was stolen for the heist."

"Are you saying Pac-Pet is behind what happened?"

"Not saying that at all. I'm simply saying that Pac-Pet hires hundreds of workers of all nationalities, right?"

"Correct. But they are all processed individually and must all have work permits."

"I realize that. But the fact is that in amongst that kind of diverse cover you could easily introduce fifteen or twenty Burmese insurgents, right?"

"I can have that checked within a matter of hours."

"Then I'd check it if I were you. And not just Pac-Pet. Every foreign company operating in Bali with more than twenty employees. Especially check out the hotel corporations. They could be using Burmese busboys who are really terrs at off hours. Any company that has a large number of employees can manage to juggle the papers and sneak ten or fifteen bad apples in with the others, either intentionally or unintentionally."

"What would any company, including Pac-Pet, which is making millions from their oil contract, want with our Bronze Bell? I simply can't see, John, where this kind of wild surmise will take us, especially since we are running out of time. I have not troubled you with the details of the growing anger among the relatives of the deceased, but things are reaching the boiling point, believe me!"

"Look, Guntur, I'm just bouncing shit off the wall, okay? Seeing what might stick. But you want something more specific? All right! This has been gnawing at me ever since Juliana Chartwell told me she has a Chinese bodyguard named Chien Hsiu. When I was in your office yesterday, I checked the master list of all the Chinese residents in Bali. No Chien Hsiu. I checked the list of Chinese tourists. No Chien Hsiu. I checked the list of those Chinese with work visas. I couldn't find his name there, either. I figured, okay, maybe I don't know how he spells it, and I simply can't spot it on the lists, so I let it go when you told me Thanh Hoa was waiting at the gate. But now I'd like you to make a definite check on this dude with Immigration. What working papers does he have? Who pays him? Chartwell, Juliana, or Pac-Pet? And while I'm tossing darts at the wind—grit your teeth, Guntur—here comes the granddaddy. I replayed my initial bad reaction to your good Captain Hamzah. You remember, at first sight I decided not to become the president of his local fan club. He hasn't worn well with me, even though he's been spending a lot of time lately trying to save my ass from grimly dedicated ladies. I don't know why I still don't trust him. That's not like me. But if you ask yourself who, of everyone we know, could have poisoned our Vietnamese prisoner, who knows every move we're making, who knew about my visit to Tip Bradley, Captain Hamzah is right up there at the top of the list—unless I start developing doubts about you, Guntur."

In spite of himself, Guntur actually laughs. I've seen his smiles but seldom this kind of spontaneous laughter.

"Don't overreact," I caution. "Or I'll move you to the top of my list."

"John Locke," he says, "you are priceless! I never want you to leave me. Every minute with you is not only dynamic but unpredictable! With your consent, I will not waste what little time remains to us by investigating myself, although if we don't make some progress within the next forty-eight hours, I will happily turn over to you my complete personal file, correspondence, diary, bank statements and whatever else you may need. But Hamzah! Why Captain Hamzah as an object of your suspicion? Dislike is one thing. Suspicion in a matter this grave is quite another."

"Why *not* Hamzah?" I ask. "If I were back in San Francisco and I felt this way about a fellow officer, I'd damn well have Internal Affairs run a check on him—his personal habits, his debts, his friends, his enemies, his secret ambitions—work up a personality profile on the man. How the hell do I know *why* Hamzah? I just think at this eleventh hour we'd better start suspecting anybody and everybody and see what shakes out."

"But I know every detail of this man's service record, of his private life. He is especially colorless in his existence off duty. On duty he is a dedicated and exemplary officer. There is nothing, believe me, John, nothing about him which could validate your suspicions!"

"Well," I say, "it's like the minister's daughter. Kid gets straight A's, sings in the choir till she's eighteen, then runs off with Clyde and ends up robbing the First National Bank in Omaha. I guess it's because now I *know*—in my guts, in my marrow—that my Vietnamese enemies were not involved in any way with the killings at Besakih or in taking the bell. Hamzah's insistence on that theory comes off to me as a scam to send us running in the wrong direction. For example, did *you* personally find the papers on that Vietnamese when you captured him at the airport, the papers identifying him as an NVA officer? Or did one of your men? Or did Captain Hamzah?"

Guntur stares at me without answering.

"So it *was* Hamzah?" I insist.

"It was he who captured the man, yes. But he risked his life to do it."

"You *think* he risked his life. It could have all been staged."

"I don't understand."

"Neither do I. I'm just winging it now. But the captured Vietnamese could have been a pawn. You'd be surprised what some of those poor bastards will do to save their families. They'd sell their balls if it meant they could get their wives and children out of Vietnam. I'm saying somebody could have made a deal with this man and Hamzah could have gone charging in bravely, knowing he wouldn't be shot. Why was just this one lone Vietnamese taken prisoner? Why not one of the Burmese? See what I mean?"

Guntur's face takes on an inner illumination, as though I've hit a switch that trips on all his lighting systems.

"Very well, John. I'll see what I can come up with. Now, what do you want me to do about this Vietnamese girl in the hospital?"

"Nothing."

"She has broken our laws."

"How?"

"Conspiracy to murder."

"Who knows that except you and me? And I'm filing no complaint."

"You expect me simply to ignore it?"

"I do. Just as I ignored your killing those four Vietnamese soldiers."

"They were rapists! They deserved to die!"

"Guntur, to Thanh Hao I am a murderer! In front of her I executed her sister. I caused the death of every woman and child in her village except for her and two others. What makes her sense of retribution different from yours?"

"If that is how you feel, John, let us consider the matter closed. She may stay in Bali until her visa expires—or she may leave. I shall not intrude."

"I told her if anything happens to me, you'll help her."

"*Help* her!"

"Yes, Guntur, as though you were helping me."

"I understand. At least she did bring you news that you have a son. If I have to deal with her, I shall bear that in mind."

"Thank you."

We're passing through the main gate into Guntur's headquarters when he tells me, more or less in passing, that *Steel Tiger* has only an hour ago entered the shallow waters of the bay at Benoa and is now anchored off the channel. The navy crew is cleaning her up after the long voyage and putting her back into fully found condition.

"Forgive me, Guntur," I say, "but if you don't mind, I'll take a rain check on that barracks nap. I'd rather sleep aboard *Steel Tiger*. We'll drop you off, and Sergeant Maru can run me over to Benoa. I'll just caulk off for three or four hours while you get all our loose ends together. Then I have to say good-bye to Juliana at the airport."

We drop him in front of his building.

Minutes later we're zipping out the long causeway toward the anchorage in the bay.

For the first time I can remember, I ignore *Steel Tiger*, deliberately looking past her, snug on her bow hook some three hundred yards east of the wharf, to another vessel squatting in the water not too far from her.

It is an LST—landing ship tank—one of the vintage warriors of amphibious combat in the Pacific during World War II.

Wondering, I stare out at her as the sergeant wheels the Ferret around and brakes on the wharf.

I pull the Ferret's binos from their case and focus on the ship.

Pac-Pet owns her, I am able to read off her broad steel transom.

Sergeant Maru patches me through to Guntur via the Jeep's radio.

"They moved the bell off the beach with an LST!" I tell him, expecting hosannas to resound.

Instead, I hear Guntur's cool response.

"That's a Pac-Pet work ship."

"I know. I can read. But you see how it's coming together? Pac-Pet again!"

"John, I know all about that LST. Don't you imagine I checked it out, along with every other vessel around here that morning? For your information, there is only one channel through the reef where that surfer's board was found. At maximum flood tide the depth is four and a half feet. That LST draws six and a half feet even when it's trimmed for its shallowest draft. How could a ship more than three hundred feet long that requires six and a half feet of water to stay off the bottom get through a reef entrance two feet shallower? It would have run aground and never got to the beach!"

He sounds so elated to be one-upping me that you'd almost think he was delighted the LST couldn't have been involved in moving the bell from the truck on the beach to deep water.

"Are you sitting down, Guntur?" I ask.

"No," he tells me. "I'm pacing up and down. How can I sit when we're running out of time?"

"Well, have you ever heard of a navy technique called 'splashing ship'?"

"I am a paratrooper, John. You are the sailor."

"If you have to clear a bar or an impediment that lies in water shallower than your draft, it is possible, given enough engine power and speed and assuming you've got a damned good man at the helm, to 'splash ship' by driving at flank speed toward the shallow area and at the precise right moment throwing everything into reverse, creating your own wave and riding over the bar on the wave, which lifts the ship above its normal draft. All good river pilots on the Ohio and Mississippi rivers can splash ship in their sleep, and I have to believe that there are helmsmen in these waters who could teach them a trick or two."

The silence at the other end of the line is deeply rewarding.

"Are you there, Guntur?"

"Then the bell *is* somewhere in the sea!" I hear him say, as though he is talking to himself.

"It could even be aboard the LST," I suggest.

"No!" he says. "That I know—it's not!"

"How do you know?"

"I personally went aboard every vessel in the waters of south Bali the day of *Nyepi* and the day after. There was nothing aboard that LST except the normal equipment one would expect. And if you know the LST configuration, John, you would know there is nowhere aboard you can conceal a bell as huge as our Great Bronze Bell. No, they've dropped the bell somewhere in deeper water. I shall lead a detachment to Chartwell's office immediately and place him under arrest until we can determine exactly who was in charge of that vessel on that morning and what its subsequent movements were, despite what the ship's log may state to exonerate it. We will take the entire crew into custody and begin to interrogate them *my* way!"

"All most constructive," I agree, "but give me my shot at Chartwell first. I can set him up for you and maybe save us a lot of time. His weak point is Juliana. And Dasima. He has to come through me to get to either of them. That gives me a unique stranglehold on the sonofabitch. Let me squeeze him a little; then you come bursting in."

I check the time. Ten-thirty.

"Give me till twelve hundred hours," I tell Guntur. "Then come with the cavalry."

"What about your nap?" he asks.

"What nap?"

I hang up.

Energized, everything pumping at max, I run to the Ferret.

"Back to Denpasar, sergeant!" I say to Maru. "They're right when they say all roads in Bali lead to Denpasar."

I even forget to look back out at my love, *Steel Tiger*, triumphantly home from the sea.

CHAPTER

27

This time Maru slams us through Denpasar traffic aggressively, running the Ferret up on sidewalks to get around blocklong jam-ups. Denpasar, it strikes me, must be one of the many hells the Balinese believe in. But strident as it is, it is pastoral compared to choked-up Jakarta or Bangkok, and at least there are no clubs advertising the Pussy Smoke Cigarette Show. Not yet, anyway.

Pacific Petroleum's heartland is a former Dutch government estate set within a walled enclosure off Jl. Ratna. An elderly Balinese man is spending the morning shining the brass corporate wall plate as Maru wheels in and lays a cloud of dust all over the front of the building.

I jump down from the Ferret and back into an earlier century of Dutch colonialism. I expect to see pith helmets everywhere.

"When Colonel Katrini gets here," I tell Maru, "please ask him to come directly to the office of Walton Chartwell. Before then, if you should hear gunfire, you might wish to bring your Beretta along and join the party."

I study the colonial building. It is as though the Dutch plucked it out of the earth near The Hague and transported it in one piece to Denpasar. Only the tulips are missing, but then it is July.

I can feel eyes on me. Chartwell's, unquestionably, from the corner office on the floor above me, its windows cooled by the lofting greenery of a banyan tree.

Without asking questions, I pass Go and skip directly to Boardwalk.

Chartwell's secretary is surprisingly aged for a fella who aspires to seventeen-year-old Balinese dancing girls. She's impeccably English, but someone should tweeze the hairs from the end of her aristocratic nose. As I come closer, I smell lavender soap.

"Is Mr. Chartwell expecting you?"

"I'm here at his specific invitation. We left the time open. Sort of catch-as-catch-can."

"Well, at the moment he is on an overseas call. May I fix you a cup of tea?"

"Providing it's strong, thank you."

She does make a dynamite cup of tea. I'm halfway through it when Chartwell himself bursts from his office to welcome me.

"Forgive me, darling," he bubbles. I am reminded of a British commando friend of mine who fought in the Falklands. He loves to call his close male friends "cunt" as a term of endearment. Okay, so I'll be "darling." "What I find so devastating," Chartwell says, "is that here we are using satellites to bounce our voices back and forth from island to island, yet at the same moment we're using such high technology, we're discussing Precambrian time."

"It *is* wrenching," I concede, "when you think about it."

"We've just made an incredible oil strike between the Sunda and Sahul shelves. Oh, please come in. I don't know why I'm standing out here chattering away. And bring your tea. Would you like another cup?"

"If you don't mind. I've had a couple of sleepless nights, and your lady brews a real wake-up elixir."

When the secretary smiles, which she does at the unexpected compliment, the hairs on the end of her nose appear to waggle. I find myself puzzled by my overinvolvement in such minutiae at a moment when I'm about to bait the one man who may hold the key to all our problems in Bali.

As I enter Chartwell's office, I observe that he's wearing Foxcroft sneakers, those lovely little Belgian slippers, the finest and most comfortable handsewn shoes in the world. I keep three pairs aboard *Steel Tiger* for the times I'm not humping through jungle or forest. Chartwell's sneakers come in burnt orange. He sees me studying them.

"You know the Foxcroft sneaker?" he asks as he closes the door after us.

"Yes," I say. "I've been to their factory."

"Near Bruges," he says brightly.

"Actually in a town called Izegem," I point out.

"Precisely," he smiles, pleased with me. For a moment I think he may be going to propose to me. "Please sit wherever you wish." His secretary enters with my second cup of tea. I thank her and settle down; Chartwell and I are alone at last. I sip my tea and sweep the office with my eyes. Chartwell's desk sits catercorner to the door in a commanding position. Over the central window of the room red flowers hang. Fishbowls alive with darting shapes are everywhere about the office. Wind chimes dangle in the open windows. Gold bells and clocks have been placed precisely.

"Congratulations," I say.

"Thank you. You are quite exceptional—to notice."

For it is apparent to anyone who knows about feng shui that Chartwell has relied heavily upon a Chinese feng shui expert to arrange his office surroundings. Someone has created for Chartwell an environment in which he can work at his fullest potential. The fish are there to absorb accidents and misfortune—they must be replaced instantly when they belly up. The clocks reflect away ill fortune. The wind chimes and mirrors attract energy, beckoning all good things to enter.

Foxcroft sneakers and feng shui and a wife like Juliana. I decide Walton is no ordinary petroleum executive. Nowhere on any of his office wall space can a blowup photo of an oil rig be seen. There are no sketches of late Miocene reefs or of stratigraphic traps of shale, no gummy crude-oil samples in glass jars. I find myself regretting the possibility that this man may be my deadliest enemy. I would have preferred him as my friend.

"We have some problems," he says, smiling. "Don't we?"

"It would appear so."

"You won't mind if I tick mine off first?"

"Please."

"Sleeping with another chap's wife is one thing, John. May I call you John? I feel you are uncomfortable when I call you darling."

"John is fine."

"But rearranging her life-style—and therefore the life-style of her husband—is quite another matter. Wouldn't you agree?"

"In general, yes. In this particular case, no."

"But why not?"

"I didn't go looking for her. She called me and misrepresented the cirumstances. I was invited to come and meet you."

"But when you saw the deception, why did you stay?"

"She needed someone. I happened to be there."

"*Needed* someone? She has *me*."

"Obviously you're not giving her what she needs."

"Which is?"

"To help her stop using drugs."

"And you believe *you* can stop her?"

"I took the first step with her. We'll know more when she flies out. And more next week when she settles in at the clinic. And more next month. She's got a hard way to go. And since you brought it up, darling, why did you let her get to this stage without trying to help her? Especially since you're out of the will if she dies?"

"She told you that?"

"A lot more."

"Then you can understand why I can't possibly permit her to fly out of my life. Suppose she had a traffic accident in San Francisco? A runaway cablecar? Who knows what might happen to poor Juliana in a city as violent as the city you come from, John?"

"You have a dossier on me or something?"

"Quite."

"You know, darling," I tell him, "I've been giving some real serious thought to having a detailed biography prepared, along with a list of my hobbies and food preferences, getting it printed and bound, then distributed throughout the Pacific Rim. Do you think that's a good idea? Or do you think all the Apaches already have their copies?"

He finds me amusing, I see. He comes around, laughing, to perch himself on the corner of his desk and to dangle his burnt-orange Foxcrofts back and forth toward me.

"Juliana will not be leaving," he announces. "I've canceled her flight plans."

"She's *your* wife."

"Quite. So much for that. Now, what are we going to do about my little dance troupe?"

"What little dance troupe?"

"Oh, come, come, John! You know exactly what I'm talking about! *Dasima!*"

"What about Dasima?"

"Release her. Please."

"Why?"

"She's far too magical to turn fat in the stomach and broad across the hips. Far too beautiful to wear Balinese clothes. Far too talented to dance for insensitive tourists. Give her a chance to open up to the marvelous potential within her."

"Are you a fella who likes to joust with words? Or do you prefer bottom lines?"

"In this case, I think we'd better go to the bottom line."

"Then let me put it this way," I say, sipping the last of my tea. "If you don't put Dasima out of your mind, out of your thoughts, *forever*—you understand, darling, *forfuckingever*!—if you don't do that, if, after I've left, I ever hear you're back on the subject, I will step up within six feet of you and put three bullets between your eyes. I will make a special trip back to accommodate you in this matter. And if I have to fly too far to get back here, then I'll put *four* bullets between your eyes. Shall I say it again?"

His smile remains on his face, but it appears to be graven there now, locked into the muscles.

"Are you some imperial executioner who can ignore the law and threaten the common man with divine punishment? I could bring criminal charges against you right now for that kind of threatening talk. But I intend to ignore what you just said and continue to try to reason with you."

"Before you try to take me out of my Lord High Executioner mode, let me ask you a simple question. Are you going to reach for your phone right now and call the harbor master at Benoa and have him tell the captain of your Pac-Pet LST that I expect him here in this office no later than twelve hundred hours today, along with his ship's log, his executive officer, his second mate, and his engineer?"

"Oh, come now, John. We're running a full-time operation here with the encouragement and the full cooperation of the government. I can't take personnel off stream simply at the snap of your fingers. What do you wish to speak to these people about?"

"I want to see how good they are at splashing ship."

"What on earth is splashing ship?"

"The way you got the bell off the beach and out beyond the reef."

"Bell?"

"The Great Bronze Bell of Agung. Nobody but Pac-Pet has the capability of removing it. And you're in charge of Pac-Pet, aren't you?"

"Certainly."

"Then *you* took it."

"What in God's name would I want with a bell?"

"You intend to take it to Burma."

He laughs. "No wonder you seduced poor Juliana. You're even more insane than she. Why would I take a bell to Burma?"

"That's what I intend to have you tell me. I have a theory that's been growing legs for the last day or so, but I'd much rather have a nice, simple accounting from you. Frankly"—I feel the first wave of total exhaustion breaking over me, draining me away as it rips back out to sea—"I'm exhausted. Physically, mentally, emotionally. I'm losing my patience. When I lose my patience, I lose my veneer of civilization. When I lose that, I revert to the most elemental kind of behavior, the sort of behavior that was frowned on even in Precambrian time. Am I getting through to you, Chartwell?"

For some reason his smile seems to have spread. I see him now through a window smeared with peanut butter. Why does he rock back and forth, laughing, in and out of focus? I have the vague feeling I'm sitting in a movie theater watching a 3-D movie without the special glasses.

Shit! The tea! That nice little old lady with the lavender soap smell and the hairs on her nose has doped me. But good! I push my hand toward the Browning in my shoulder holster, but my hand won't obey the neural order to goddamn reach the gun and blow that grinning hyena behind the peanut butter out through the back of the house.

"The active principle of what we've given you, Mr. Locke, is antiarin. It's a glycocide akin to strophanthin. It's available locally from the fresh sap of the *upas* tree. I believe what you are experiencing is a series of clonic spasms of your musculature, paralysis, and partial systolic arrest of the ventricles of the heart. But it was a carefully measured dose we gave you, not enough to kill you, simply enough to render you—shall we say, one of the living dead?"

So I'm a zombie, I think. And they killed that Vietnamese prisoner of ours. At least my brain cells don't seem to be paralyzed. I am less alarmed by my situation than I am harshly judgmental of my stupidity. Ever since I've arrived in Bali, I've stepped into one baited trap after another—starting with Guntur, who rolled the dice with Dasima and me, then into the trap with Juliana, then into Thanh Hoa's clutches, now this slick sonofabitch! It has not been a glorious week in the vigilance department. Some major redesign will have to be factored into my future, if I have one.

Now another face smears my vision. This one is so close I feel his breath on my numbed cheeks. I know that face. Those eyes. Of course! My Chinese challenger! Chien Hsiu!

"A pity," he says. I recognize the voice, too. He was the caller that first night I had dinner at Tip's. He was the one who demanded I cease and desist or else they'd come after Tip. "I had hoped I would have the chance to kill you with my hands."

I hear another voice coming from behind the peanut-buttered window. Isn't that Chartwell back there? Yes, it's Chartwell speaking, I'm sure. I think I'm sure. He's speaking to this Chinese lantern blazing yellow and orange in front of me, a lantern with garlic breath.

"He thinks we took the bell."

Laughter. Have you ever heard Chinese laughter coming from a garlic lantern?

"He thinks we're taking it to Burma."

Wind chimes, gongs, and bells and *gamelans* seem to be mixed in with the laughter, but it could be that the glycocides are working on my brain cells now.

"Yes, Mr. Locke," Peanut Butter says. "We *are* taking it to Burma. To a warrior priest—to a waiting army of invincible zealots who will rise up in the mountains and sweep down upon the Burmans and drive them into the sea. There will be a new land, an independent nation dominated by Sellamathu, the Leader, a nation of the pure, protected by the Great Bronze Bell. Only Sellamathu will be *my* warrior priest. *I* will be the true king!"

I knew it! From the first minute I saw him! Nobody can look that much like Michael Caine and not be tempted to carve out a mountain kingdom in the Golden Triangle. It is an obsessive throwback dream for certain types of Englishmen who suckled on Kipling.

"—with the purest heroin in the world at my disposal. And

then our armies will drive out the other warlords. We shall control it all—all of it—worth billions!"

Is that Michael Caine still talking?

I am lying within a sacrificial basin at the top of a flight of stairs that descend into a valley. High priests stand above me, obsidian stone knives in their hands. They bless me. But before they cut my heart out, I feel myself being lifted. I am in someone's arms. Chien Hsiu's arms. Must be. He's taking me someplace. My head goes slack. I can see only the hardwood floor of Chartwell's office and his burnt-orange Belgian sneakers moving along disembodied.

I smell lavender soap. Chien Hsiu must be carrying me out past the kindly secretary who makes the best cup of glycocide a man could ever hope to enjoy. I'll send her tweezers from wherever they're taking me.

Maru will come any minute now. Any second. He will wheel around the corner, crouching, his beautifully machined Beretta spitting punishment at these peanut-butter-and-lantern people. Then Guntur will be here, and I shall be taken back to the compound and put to sleep, and before morning Dasima will come to me, and I will again be merged with her in a world no one else can enter, not even Doan Thi.

I think I smell fresh air. We are outside now.

But not out front, not where Maru waits.

We are out back, and they are putting me into something. A van?

I see only darkness, even though my eyes are wide open.

I feel movement. I know they are taking me away to kill me.

I miss the Mercedes.

And the Bellini. And the crowbar and the razor blades.

But even if I had them laid out next to me, I would be powerless to use them now.

CHAPTER

28

My visual disorientation has passed during this first hour with Chartwell and Chien Hsiu. I am able to see clearly again and to hear with primal clarity. But I am still numb and incapable of physical movement. The drug has bound me with invisible tendrils. I'm as trussed as the pigs I've seen in the market at Denpasar.

From the van they carry me on a litter into a chopper. Apparently Chartwell can fly; only he and I and Chien Hsiu are in the machine as we lift off and fly away from Denpasar. I know I'm not flying the machine. And Hsiu isn't, since he rides turned around in his seat and staring down at me with a look that would take the crease out of a man's trousers. So it has to be Chartwell.

I am devoid of a sense of time or place, but as we lower again, I can see the slope of a rugged mountain and tiers of thatched roofs rising along the slope. We fly over a village with stone walls and a main street that looks more like a riverbed than a street.

A thought comes. Could this be Sambiran?

I had walked through these mountains on my last trip to Bali, up a precipitous trail from Kembangsari, and had come upon an area outside of Sambiran where the dead are laid out on bamboo platforms and left to be devoured by birds of prey. In the days of the Living Buddha the Zoroastrian exposure of corpses to vultures

250

was the usual mode of disposing of the dead. Only persons of distinction were burned, after death, on a pyre and their ashes buried under a *stupa*. I had not known, until I stumbled upon this bleak field of devoured corpses outside Sambiran, that the Zoroastrian code was still observed by some Balinese.

Outside the chopper I see a flight of vultures.

Or do I imagine?

We rotor down and land. Neither Chartwell nor Chien Hsiu moves until the blades have stopped their whirling. In the silence that follows I hear the harsh and throaty cawing of birds, large birds from the sound of them.

I am being lifted out of the chopper on the litter and carried by Chartwell and Chien Hsiu across a field toward a bamboo tower.

My eyes, staring straight up at the sky, see circling shadows.

The two men bear me to the tower, then up crude stairs to the summit, a broad, open platform some thirty feet above the surrounding field.

They lift me off the litter and place me on a grill covering a raised coffinlike rectangle.

Chartwell kneels, his face close to mine. I see it clearly now. He has long, seductive eyelashes. His eyes are cerulean.

"There is order in all things," he tells me. "Even in the kingdom of birds of prey. There is always a king vulture, the strongest, the fleetest, the most merciless. The others await his signal. You will see him first, leading the circle of birds above you, the spiral becoming smaller, closer, until suddenly he will dive. I have watched this in Bombay in the heart of the city at the Tower of the Dead. He will dive straight down at you, and without landing or touching you with his talons, he will pluck out your right eye. It is astonishing how the king vulture is able to do this on the swoop. He will then climb back to the others. None of them will yet dare to approach you. Now he will dive again. This time he will pluck out your left eye. And when he flies off, the second strongest bird will dive upon you and rip at your belly button. Once these opening ceremonies are complete, the rest of the flock will fight over you. For clawing space and for the meat. They are not as interested in your skin and muscle as they are in your entrails. Here they reveal their natural brutishness. They are a most ill-tempered creature. I have seen two of them tugging at either end of a man's intestine, neither willing to release it to the other. I regret you won't be able to watch it, since the king vulture will have deprived you of your sight. But you can imagine the rest—and of course feel it. I would ask you for a few last words, John, but your tongue cannot move, so I will simply bid you adieu—and I will think of you from time to time when I am running my tongue over Dasima's body."

As farewell addresses go, I put it right up there with the best. Genghis Khan couldn't have done it better. Chien Hsiu doesn't even wish me good-bye. Not even a word.

I hear their feet on the stairs. Then I hear only the vultures. It is not music I would compare to the *gamelan* or even the Boston Pops. I do not hear the chopper taking off, so I assume that Chartwell, not to be denied his amusement, is off somewhere across the field, possibly at the top of a tree, with his field glasses trained on me. Why should he miss the flying circus?

The vultures must be especially hungry this afternoon.

They circle like Comanches around a wagon train.

I try to spot the king. They all look like kings to me—big, ugly, and voracious.

What was that exchange Guntur and I had had—life is a stage with only one entrance but many exits? I would never have anticipated being carried off by pterodactyls. A land mine, yes. A burst of automatic gunfire. A blade across my throat. The garroting wire. But not like this.

Where is my fear? Have they paralyzed that, too? Or have I numbed that part of me all by myself, long before I met Chartwell? Why have I no fear of the vultures looping closer each minute?

Could it be that all the fear was chased out of me by anger, my anger in knowing, in believing, right to this last instant of existence, that I fought a war in Vietnam for nothing, that all our sacrifices went for nothing and my young friends and comrades who gave their lives or arms or lost their mobility or their sense of reason did it for absolutely nothing at all? Is this anger all that has driven me across the Pacific, searching from island to island, for what? To stop feeling the anger so I can feel the fear again?

And what of the son I shall never hold?

What of my memories of Doan Thi that will vanish with me? Doan Thi, forgive me. I must let you die at last.

And Dasima?

In time I could have come to love you.

I see the king. He is no different from the others. He has no banded neck. He has no ID tag on his wings. Yet clearly he is the king.

He hangs in the air for a trembling moment, the breeze ruffling his feathers.

Then he pitches toward me.

What happens, I wonder, if he overshoots and gets the left eye first instead of the right? Does he get a refund?

Here he comes. What a miserable-looking bastard! God, if I could only lift the Browning and splatter him on the clouds!

I hear gunfire. Had I drawn my gun but not felt it? Not possible. My hands are immobile along my thighs.

But the king vulture disintegrates in a videoburst of blood and feathers less than twenty feet above me. He showers down over me like chili con carne.

I hear other shots now, echoing from a circle everywhere around me in the field below the tower. An explosion bathes me with sound and heat. Smoke puffs from nearby. Something tells me Chartwell's transportation has gone to shit.

Boots pound on the stairs of my sacrificial platform.

Suddenly Guntur's face is over mine.

I shall dream forever of that cookie-jar grin.

"You'll sleep *any*where, won't you?" he asks.

I regard it as one of his better remarks.

"Captain Hamzah saved your life!" he says. "I want you to know you shouldn't distrust a man simply because he uses too much wax on his mustache. He spotted you being taken away from Pac-Pet in Denpasar but couldn't catch the van in the traffic. He radioed in to me at Tabanan. We tracked the Pac-Pet chopper on radar and got here just a few minutes after Chartwell lugged you up here."

Sergeant Maru lifts me off the grill. In this sitting position I can now see the burning Pac-Pet chopper and Guntur's Red Berets everywhere, fanning out, searching.

"We have Chartwell," Guntur says. "But the Chinese slipped through our lines. We'll deal with him later."

Two Red Berets bring Chartwell in. I watch them holding him as Guntur empties a vial of liquid into his throat and makes him swallow it.

"Turnabout, old chap," Guntur says to him. "You will simply stretch out where Mr. Locke has kindly warmed up the cold grill and take his place. The drug I've given you is not a poison. It is simply an inducer of immediate paralysis."

As Guntur talks, I can see Chartwell is losing motor control.

The Red Berets lift him toward me. Maru picks me up in his arms as the paras stretch Chartwell out, his eyes darting from me to Guntur.

Now I see fear. Maybe he's been the host for all my fears. At least I know now where they went. Chartwell's the ultimate inheritor.

"I was going to strike some kind of bargain with you," Guntur says. "Your telling me where the bell is in return for your life. Of course I would have killed you afterward, anyway, but there's nothing you can tell me I don't already know. Captain Hamzah has all the details about your plan to deliver the bell to an insane priest in the mountains of Burma. You and this Sellamathu would have made quite a combination, I have to admit."

Guntur turns to me. "Only an hour ago we got the first hands-on report from our people in Burma. Sellamathu, a holy man in Shan territory, has been whipping his followers into such a lather of zealotry that bands of terrorists with bells tattooed on their heels have been attacking everyone, including women and children. But this is one atavistic lurch that is going nowhere!"

He concentrates again on the stiff figure of Chartwell lying where I was lying only minutes before.

"May you be reborn as fecal slime," Guntur says to Chartwell. "May you be shat upon by sea gulls throughout eternity."

Disdaining help from the other Red Berets, Maru carries me down the stairs and onto the field, where the Pac-Pet chopper is little more than a pile of ashes.

Guntur's choppers are parked a click away, in a clearing to the east of the fringing forest, and Maru bears me all the way.

When we fly off, back toward Tabanan, I hear Guntur telling the pilot to stay well clear of the platform for the dead. He does not wish to alarm the vultures circling over the ceremonial ground.

But when I look the vultures are no longer circling.

They are diving and ripping and tugging at all that remains of Walton Chartwell.

=CHAPTER=

29

I t starts as an afternoon of tying up loose ends. It progresses with my regaining my mobility. I see myself as a six-foot hourglass leaking sand. After a while, it becomes sheer delight to pinch my thigh and be able to feel corresponding pain.

Guntur's pilot lands the command chopper on the grounds of Juliana Chartwell's estate. The other choppers settle in beyond each corner of Guntur's flagship.

We discover soon enough that Chartwell has locked Juliana into one room upstairs, her daughter and nanny in another.

Juliana is outraged. She demands to know where her husband is. She intends to call the board of directors of Pac-Pet in London and have him fired at once. It's back to cheating at poker on a leaky liner working out of Colombo for that ungrateful sonofabitch.

"We're looking for him right now," I lie. "As soon as we have any word, we'll let you know. Meanwhile, if you see your Chinese bodyguard, shoot him on sight!"

"A pleasure!" she says.

"I mean it, Juliana. He's dangerous!"

"Can't either of you tell me what it is Walton and he are involved in? Is it dope?"

"We are not authorized to disclose anything at this time," Guntur says. "But later I will tell you what I can. Meantime, I have ordered some of my men to remain here in the event Chien Hsiu tries to return."

"What shall I do now about San Francisco?" she asks me. "I missed our flight for today."

"We'll switch you over to another flight," I tell her. "I'll meet you at the terminal."

"What has Walton done?" she asks. "Please tell me that, at least!"

"He reached too far, Juliana."

Outside, Guntur orders the paras from one chopper to spread out and deny entry to anyone. Any Chinese male who attempts to enter is to be shot on sight. Shoot first, check his ID later.

Another chopper is ordered off to set down at Pac-Pet and augment the men with Captain Hamzah who are even now arresting certain Pac-Pet personnel, especially the English secretary, and confiscating all Pac-Pet files.

Guntur's chopper—with Guntur and me, Maru and another Red Beret—lifts off, followed by the other two.

Five minutes later we are overflying the bay at Benoa.

Below, I see *Steel Tiger* but there is no evidence of the LST. In search of the missing ship we fly an expanding pattern all the way out to the point at Nusa Dua, then west to Uluwatu, then north to Kuta and once more east to Benoa.

The LST has vanished.

Guntur cries out with sudden insight. "The bell is aboard her!"

"In a sense, it has been—all this time," I say.

He stares at me.

"But how can that be?" he asks. "I personally searched the vessel! It consists of nothing except its huge tank well and its upper deck—like a gigantic floating scoop. You can stand at the bow in the tank deck and look straight back, virtually to the other end of the ship. The bell was *not* aboard!"

"It was *under* the ship. On the bottom of the sea. In a simple thirty-six feet of water fifteen hundred meters off the end of the channel at Benoa—with the LST anchored above it to prevent any screening equipment on the surface from making a contact."

"How do you know?"

"I don't."

"Inductive reasoning?"

"What else?"

"What does your inductive reasoning tell you about the present whereabouts of this LST?"

"She's at least forty-five miles out into the Indian Ocean."

Guntur peers past me and out to sea. An afternoon haze obscures visibility beyond ten or twelve miles.

"And how do you know that?" he asks.

"I don't. It's the way I would go if I were taking the bell by LST to Burma—out into the ocean to throw off the pursuit, then due west to approximately latitude one hundred; then I'd slant northwest up the coast of Sumatra, staying a good two hundred and fifty miles offshore. In terms of their present distance off, I would expect they cut out at least three hours ago."

Guntur orders his radio operator to reach the harbor master at Benoa. I listen to some back-and-forth in Indonesian until Guntur has his answer. The LST departed its anchorage at twelve hundred hours plus fourteen minutes, three hours and ten minutes ago.

"How could you fix the hour when at that same time you were already drugged and being flown to the north?" Guntur insists on knowing.

"Because you told me what time it was when Captain Hamzah called you with the information that I'd been taken away. He called not to save me but to divert you—and to get a head start. Once he called, he knew you would be fully occupied for most of the day with me and Chartwell and Pac-Pet—and he used that time slot to make his getaway."

"*Hamzah* making his getaway? Why?"

"I'm certain he was to be Chartwell's right-hand military adviser, the military liaison with the Burmese holy man. Someone had to take responsibility to whip the mountain guerrillas into fighting shape. Who better than an ambitious Indonesian Red Beret captain trained by the British at Sandhurst and by the Americans at Fort Benning? Think of the rewards. Not only the power but the incalculable riches from his share of the drug running. More in a week than he could earn in a lifetime as your adjutant."

Guntur takes personal charge of the radio controls, feeds through a call to Pac-Pet, and asks for Captain Hamzah.

"Captain Hamzah is not here, sir."

"Did he say where he was going?"

"No, sir."

"When did he leave?"

"He has not been here, sir. Lieutenant Malik is in command of the detail. Would you care to speak to him, sir?"

"No. Carry on."

"Yes, sir."

Guntur changes channels and puts himself through to Jakarta. He requests an immediate scramble of interceptors and search planes to comb the Indian Ocean as far west as Yogyakarta on Java and as far offshore as two hundred miles. No action other than tracking the target LST and continuing reconnaissance once it has been spotted is to be taken until further orders.

We return to headquarters at Tabanan.

I'm famished, but Guntur will not permit me to eat. He is familiar with the aftereffects of *upas* poisoning. He makes me drink lime juice. Lime juice alone is used as an antidote for the wounds some of his men have suffered when attacked by indigs using blow tubes, their darts tipped with the sap of the *upas* tree. The lime juice has an almost magical effect, he insists, and indeed I do feel better with each successive quarter hour, except for a massive stupor from lack of sleep.

Guntur suggests that I sleep while the aircraft are out searching for the fugitive LST. Once it's been pinpointed, time then to bring all our faculties to bear.

It is dark when I awaken.

I am in Guntur's bed in his quarters, one leg over a long hard pillow, the Dutch wife he says he cannot sleep without, my sleep so precipitate I cannot remember Guntur's leaving. But now when I open my eyes he is still there. Or has he gone out and returned?

As I open my eyes, he turns on a lamp.

I look at my wristwatch. Almost midnight. "Why'd you let me sleep so long?"

"I've been thinking—remembering—trying to make a decision . . . I was remembering the night, almost twenty years ago, when the Communists killed my father. He'd been sleeping—like you. A squad of soldiers who had joined the PKI under the command of a lieutenant suddenly appeared in our home. They awakened my father, who had no way of knowing they were traitors, and told him the president urgently needed to see him, that he was to come with them immediately. I heard the noise and woke up. heard my father tell them to wait outside, that he would put on his uniform and be right with them. The lieutenant said there woul be no time, the president was waiting, my father must come as he was. My father was enraged by such effrontery from a junior officer. He ordered the man to take his squad outside. Then he left the room, closing the door behind him. At the officer's order the soldiers fired their automatic weapons through the door. I ran to the door to see if my father was still alive. The soldiers turned their guns on me, but the lieutenant ordered them not to shoot. I pulled the door open. My father lay sprawled on his face, his back torn away. I dropped to my knees by his body. One of the soldiers struck me with the butt of his gun and knocked me aside. They dragged my father's body across the floor and out to a waiting truck. I crawled after them along the trail of his blood, but I passed out just as I reached the door.

"I must have lost consciousness for only a moment, because when I opened my eyes again, the truck was just then driving away and my younger brother, who had seen it all from another room, was standing over me and sobbing. Since our mother had died several years earlier, he and I were the only witnesses. All the servants, probably also PKI sympathizers, had been warned and had fled.

"Of course, the Communist coup failed, and we settled Indonesia's Communist problem once and for all by killing both innocent and guilty on island after island. But those terrible days still stay in our minds. The memory of them dictates most of the things we do, even today. I swore to myself that when I became an officer I would die before I would let that kind of bloodlust sweep over my country again. Well, here we are, tonight, on the eve of another uprising. I do not see how, without our getting back the bell, we can keep the knowledge of what happened at Besakih away from the people of Bali. We almost prevented it, John. Now I no longer see how we can."

"Go get the bell off the LST; that's all you have to do! The rest will follow. Damn it, Guntur, why are you sitting there like a fucking sponge? Just take the bell back!"

"It may not be possible."

"You have a navy, an air force, a marine corps, paratroopers! My God, man, one little LST commanded by that asshole Hamzah! I could take the damn thing myself!"

"Don't be so confident. I have spoken to Captain Hamzah by radio. He is holding all the aces. He has planted explosive charges on the bell. If we attack him, he will destroy the bell. And then he has promised to broadcast the whole story about Pura Besakih, the killing of the eighteen, the government cover-up, the destruction of the bell—everything—to the media. Not only to our media but to the world press and television. You see the dilemma, John? If I let him escape with the bell to Burma, I will still have rioting here, because the families of the missing will give us no more time. But if I try to take the bell from him, the result could be even more catastrophic."

"You have a third option."

"If so, it has escaped me all these hours I have sat here in darkness."

"Attack! But in a way that he doesn't perceive he's being attacked—until too late."

"How?"

"What does he expect? What is he looking for if you were to attack?"

"The only logical method would be to send surface vessels and to board him. Dropping paras would be too costly."

"Even if you could drop a few men aboard, he'd still have time to blow up the bell. That's my point, Guntur; he may think you have no other way—and that might have made him a little overconfident. Also, bear in mind that by now he's been through a number of hours of stress. Both he and his men—watching their radar, scanning the sky, looking off at the horizon for pursuing boats. On top of that, probably at least half of his men are seasick. So we're dealing here with a minimal efficiency factor among the defending forces, right?"

"Yes."

"So we hit them just before dawn, when their alertness is at its lowest. We get aboard before he knows we're there—and we get to the bell before he can blow it—and we take out his radio capability at the same time."

"How do we do that, John? He has radar. He'll pick up anything approaching."

"Not a submarine!"

"Torpedo him? He's in water so deep we could never recover the bell. Even if he didn't succeed in blowing it up while he was sinking."

"No. The submarine takes a small boarding force underwater—and out of contact with his radar—to a selected site well ahead of his course. The sub surfaces and puts the landing force into the water in Zodiac rubber boats with forty-horsepower outboard engines. The Zodiacs disperse across a waiting line until the LST approaches. His radar will not pick up anything that small and that dispersed along the surface, especially since we're mostly just air and rubber. Even if his bleary-eyed radarman should pick up almost imperceptible blips, he won't make the mental connection in time, believe me. We move in and board him, and using silenced guns and knives, eliminate anyone between us and the bell, between us and the radio room. Then we tidy up around the decks until we take control of the ship."

He leaps up, a reactivated man.

"It can be done! How many boats? How many men?"

"Pick your best men. Pick fifty—then, with your help, I'll cut them down to eighteen."

"Why so few? Hamzah could have a whole company of Burmese terrorists and who knows what else aboard."

"We don't dare risk putting more than four Zodiacs out there on the sea—too big a target for his scanners. Five men to each Zodiac—that's twenty. Eighteen of your best. You and I."

"I'll have them ready in ten minutes."

"Aside from their commando and jump training, each man must have additional qualifications."

"Which do you need?"

"They have to be able to swim—and I don't mean a few sample laps in a pool. I mean a couple of miles in dark, rough water. I want men with strong arms, men who can climb up ropes. They also have to be able to resist motion sickness and nausea at sea. It's going to be bumpy as hell in those rubber dinghies while we wait out there. And we want only men who are skilled in hand-to-hand combat and who don't get squeamish when warm blood from their opponent's opened veins splashes on their faces. Give us men, Guntur, who have killed in combat, some of those jungle lads of yours you've used in New Guinea."

"Ten minutes!" he says.

I clock Guntur, knowing he'll beat the deadline.

Seven minutes later he returns. In the interval I have borrowed his razor, shaved, and splashed my face with his cologne. I'm ready to go dancing.

"I have *sixty* men I'd go to hell with," he says. "They're waiting in the courtyard. How will you be able to pick eighteen from this gathering of young eagles I don't know. I couldn't."

STIRLING SILLIPHANT

"Going to use the Holmes-Rahe Scale," I tell him.

"What is the Holmes-Rahe Scale?"

"A psychological measuring technique for estimating stress. It's even been used in the States to predict which pro football players are likely to be injured during a season."

"How can anyone predict that?"

"By tallying up the stress in an individual's current life-change events. Take the recent death of a spouse. That's near the top of the list—one hundred points of stress factor. Even holidays take their toll. In my country, Christmas slams you with twelve points of stress. What we're talking about here, Guntur, is the fact that combat produces the highest stress response of any life event. It raises the levels of adrenaline, norepinephrine, and beta-endorphin to the max, causing profound changes within the body's biochemistry. I don't want the eighteen men who will be backing us up not to have perfect coping behavior. Take one of the men you've got waiting out there and assume you believe he's the single most qualified cat in the bunch. But suppose last month he lost his mother or his son or his wife. Then he's out, you understand? I saw the findings of an Australian study of bereavement. Eight weeks after the death of their spouses, all the widows and widowers showed a diminished immune response, leaving them wide open to infection and cancer."

"I'm most impressed, John. Did you apply this in Vietnam?"

"Whenever I could. What's important, too, is not so much the stress itself as how you perceive it. What we're looking for here, Guntur, is cool cats, men with quiet centers and superior relaxation response. So when you bring each man in, one at a time, I want you to ask them to answer a list of questions. Have them reply verbally while I watch and evaluate. You'll find me keeping score for each answer. At the end, we'll add up the stress points each man has earned. Then I'll compare the totals to our personal evaluations, and we'll make the final decision. All this may chew up an hour of the little time we have remaining, but it could spell the difference between success and failure—and our own personal survival."

I hand Guntur the list of questions I've made up while we've been talking. He scans the basic Holmes-Rahe scale I've jotted down. Ten years ago, to have even considered giving such a Western-oriented psychological test to a Southeast Asian would have been ludicrous. Back in days not too long past, type A behavior would have been hard to find among the common people of Indonesia. Not anymore. They are producing their own strain of superachiever along with most of the rest of the world's societies, hundreds of millions of people all jolting fat into their bloodstreams and undergoing constant hormonal changes with the impact of each successive stressful day.

I follow Guntur out of his quarters and down the steps to the courtyard where half a hundred and more young Indonesian Red Berets wait for us to decide which eighteen of them are going to be honored and given a chance to die with us before the night is over somewhere in the black waters southeast of Yogyakarta.

CHAPTER

30

During the silent run by submarine to the rendezvous point, I check the equipment of each of the eighteen commandos Guntur and I have selected.

Each man is equipped with a garroting wire, a fighting knife and a silenced Heckler and Koch SMG. Every man is issued twelve box-type magazines of 9mm Parabellum subsonic projectiles, each magazine stacked with twenty rounds. The HK is the MP5 model which fires with a closed bolt, giving the weapon less vibration and rise than blowback operated submachine guns. It is a truly silenced weapon, the bullets leaving the gun at a subsonic velocity of a thousand feet a second, avoiding the "crack" caused by passing through the sound barrier.

Some of the men are also equipped with M-79 elephant gun for firing grenades. These are to be used to take out the radio room.

We had decided before we flew out of Tabanan to the waiting submarine not to mount laser gunsights on the SMGs. In open area night combat they are a beautiful help to a trooper. You simply touch a remote button and a red laser dot appears on target, showing you precisely where the bullet will impact if you fire. But under the combat conditions we are about to face, close in, with wires and bulkheads and ship's equipment mucking up a clear line of sight, it is my suggestion to Guntur we should use what I used so many nights in Vietnam, belladonna drops in the eyes. The chemical widens the pupils, letting them take in more light.

Guntur has added one last tactical touch, keeping reconnaissance aircraft constantly flying within clear sight of the LST. His theory is valid. By keeping the opposition on edge, by keeping them watching for a night paratrooper drop, we help divert their attention from our surface assault.

The LST is running without lights, the aircraft advises us by radio, but holding course.

In the command Zodiac, when the sub surfaces a calculated distance ahead of our target, Guntur brings a portable radar set to pick up readings out to a range of eight miles.

We offload everything into the four Zodiacs, which we inflate from bottled air while we work on the sloshing deck of the surfaced sub. The entire operation, from the moment we climb out of the sub's hatch, inflate our boats, and move off along the black surface of the sea, then watch the sub vanish beneath us, consumes four minutes and nineteen seconds.

Our four Zodiacs spread out, forming a waiting net almost a kilometer in length, Guntur and I in the command Zodiac with the radar in the center of the line. Each boat has its own VHF hand-held radio. Radio silence is not to be broken except under certain agreed-upon emergencies and then only with one key word to be spoken as a signal indicating what the emergency is. It is unlikely that anyone auditing transmissions could get much intelligence out of a single word in the night.

We wait, dawn two hours and ten minutes into the future. If the course plotting has been correct, if the LST doesn't change heading, it should bear on us within an hour and thirty minutes, giving us an operational platform of forty minutes from the moment we spot them and close in, through the boarding procedure, then through the sorting out that will follow.

I study the faces of the three young commandos who have been chosen to accompany Guntur and me in our command boat. I sense no tight-pucker factor in any one of them. Guntur sits relaxed on the port pontoon and stares off from time to time across the darkness toward the distant, unseen shoreline of Java. His heart, I know, is harder than Chobham armor. I watch him checking out two pieces of special equipment I had not observed until now. One is a curious-looking knife. I ask him how it works.

"It's a Soviet Special Forces weapon," he tells me. "I had it as a gift from a friend in Afghanistan, who took it from a Russian officer he killed in an ambush. It has a spring-loaded blade which can be fired from the hilt. It shoots the blade straight out, point first, zeroed in all the way out to twenty meters."

The second piece of equipment is equally exotic. "*Bagh nakhs*," he calls them, developed centuries ago in India as imitations of tiger claws and used originally as weapons in ritual murders. He slips them on to show me how they fit the hand. The little finger goes into the small ring, the index finger into the larger ring, with the sharpened knives inside the fist, pointed toward the fleshy part of the palm. When the hand is closed, it appears to be wearing two rings. But when the hand is opened, the "claws" extend and are used to slash at the opponent's throat.

"What is the official decision as to prisoners?" I ask Guntur.

He looks at me almost blankly.

"No prisoners," he says. "That is a direct order from my general in Jakarta."

"And Captain Hamzah?"

"Of course, I can't ask you or any of the other men on this mission to spare him if he's firing at you. Obviously, you would have to kill him. But if he were to come through this so that I personally could deal with him, it would be a favor I would never forget."

One of the men appears to be getting sleepy. The surface is almost flat, and the gentle rocking of the Zodiac is lulling him to sleep.

I order him to kneel instead of sitting. This position will keep anybody awake.

Each man maintains his own silence until Guntur picks up the first blip on his radar screen. The LST lies eight miles off. She should be dead abeam within thirty minutes. I hold up a white paddle to signal the other boats that we are now in contact.

Faintly, we begin to hear the sound of aircraft engines from above. Soon we can see the wing-tip lights of the reconnaissance plane flying over the LST.

Moments later the opaque bulk of the oncoming LST appears as a growing image on our retinas. We can virtually see its flat whalelike bow.

BRONZE BELL

We make a last-minute check of our equipment, then start our motors, taking care to keep them revved down to a sound level lower than the engine noise of the approaching LST.

We slant in, two boats to port of target, two to starboard, angling in amidships. During the underwater trip by submarine, all of us had spent time looking over the schematics of the deck layout on the LST. We had concluded that the bell must unquestionably be in the lower deck, the tank deck, for easy loading and unloading. We had memorized all the access points. Twelve of us are assigned to the bell, the others to the radio compartment.

The LST appears more and more gigantic the closer we slide toward it. We run in, avoiding the high bow waves, and ease alongside the steel rise of the freeboard. I have ruled out noisy grappling hooks. Instead, we carry long, rigid snare wires to project our boarding ropes aloft. They are wrapped to deaden contact sound.

I stand on the pontoon of the Zodiac alongside the LST, Guntur clasping me at the knees to steady me, and I snake my wire up toward a deck stanchion, loop the rope over it, then test its tension. Secure. I climb the rope, Guntur after me. At deck level I slide aboard on my stomach and look around. Nobody on deck. I feel myself part of the darkness, for all of us are wearing night stalkers, black combat fatigues, our hair bundled into black caps, our faces, ears, necks, teeth, hands, and wrists all daubed black.

Now Guntur is beside me. Within seconds the other commandos in our two boats are with us on the port side. Across the deck to starboard I count the rest of our force.

I feel exhilaration pumping through me. These lads are magnificent. We're aboard—all twenty of us—without a shot yet fired.

Everyone fans out without being told what to do.

Guntur arrives at the ladder down into the tank deck before I do. I follow him down. Halfway, he freezes. A cluster of Burmese troopers are squatting below him, drinking tea and trying to stay awake. Guntur fires at them with his silenced SMG. He withers all but one. This one starts to raise his weapon toward Guntur, busy reloading. But our B-team is already swarming onto the tank deck. One of them thrusts his knife into the Burmese's subclavian artery. The man dies instantly, incapable of getting off even a single round at Guntur.

We're down the ladder.

The Great Bronze Bell of Agung looms ahead of us, in dead center of the tank deck, so awesome looking, we let five or six seconds tick by before we realize we're being fired at. One of the young men directly in front of Guntur pitches forward with his head obscenely out of shape.

I roll off to one side and fire at four men kneeling near the bell. I lay the full clip into the four of them, taking care to give each man at least three rounds all his own before I slop over to the next in line. One or more of my rounds must have missed or passed through someone's body, for the bell cries out its mystic complaint, "*Hsieu . . . hsieu . . .*"

But we are not to be lulled this time. We move in, as planned, and form a defensive line of fire around the bell. Guntur stands, crouched, personally defending one of the three demolition experts we've brought along.

The trooper begins to disconnect the charges Hamzah has placed all over the bell.

From above deck I hear gunfire—the automatic shots, and the thwumping of M-79s, then the responding explosions of grenades.

The Red Beret tells Guntur the bell is now disarmed.

We leave six troopers to guard it. The rest of us commence a sweep of the tank deck to make sure that the lower half of the ship is secured once and for all.

We flush out four young Burmese, who throw down their weapons and surrender. Guntur orders them to take off their combat boots. Each bears the telltale tattoo. Guntur kills them one by one with a sweep of the tiger claws across their throats. I have to turn away. None of these young men could have been more than twenty years old.

I climb to the main deck.

Off at the bow I witness a terrible silhouette, six prisoner being executed. There is no sound from the silenced SMGs. The shadows fall as silently as the gunfire that has killed them. The Red Berets begin to pitch the bodies into the sea.

I keep the bulkhead of the superstructure to my back as I slid toward the hatch opening into the bridge.

Inside, two Red Berets are already in command, sparing th Indonesian helmsman, first mate, navigator, and captain, all o whom had been taken hostage by Hamzah and his Burmese.

The radio room is clotted with human flesh and blood. Th

two Burmese operators have been devastated by a rain of grenades. The radio equipment is equally destroyed.

"Where is Captain Hamzah?" I ask one of the surviving commandos from our boat.

"With the colonel, sir. In the stern deck."

I run out, along the deck to the stern.

Katrini is back there with Hamzah.

Hamzah is bleeding from three separate torso wounds. But he remains standing proudly, almost at parade-ground attention before Guntur.

Strangely enough, Guntur is weeping.

Guntur stares at the young man through his tears.

"You have been to me like my son," he says.

"I am ashamed to have disappointed you, sir," Hamzah whispers.

"I truly wish I could show you mercy. I have no desire to take your life."

"You have no choice, sir. In your place, I would not hesitate."

"I have never hesitated before. Why should I now?"

"Stand aside," I tell Guntur.

He turns agonized eyes toward me.

But he doesn't move. I have to step around him.

I lay a burst from the H & K across Hamzah's heart.

He falls at our feet. Even falling, he manages to do it gracefully.

"You never did like him," Guntur says after a while.

"I know," I say. "That's why what I did for you was even more difficult."

I leave Guntur alone with the dead man.

CHAPTER

31

At the deadlock hour between night and day, when human consciousness hovers low as ground fog, we proceed in convoy to Besakih, the Great Bronze Bell of Agung centered in our military caravan and draped with field tents stitched hastily together to conceal it, looking like a gigantic canary cage covered for the night. It is dawn of the day after the attack on the LST.

Guntur has stationed Red Berets in a bristling rectangle about the Temple of the Triple Lotus to prevent any hapless insomniac from observing the return of the bell to the *meru* from which it has been missing.

Despite the mechanics involved in sweating the bell back up the steep pitch of the mountainside on which Pura Besakih steps to the sky, necessary religious ceremonies and symbolic rites must proceed in harmony with the physical movement of five hundred thousand inert pounds of bronze back into its appointed place.

At the moment of the bell's hanging, Dewata and other high priests begin to perform the *nedunang* ritual, in which they entreat the deities to descend and take up residence in statues or other sacred objects within the temple. Then, accompanied by the offering of what Guntur tells me is called *titi mamah*—a buffalo head, hide, and hooves, the most honored of all gifts to the gods—

two large rectangular objects wrapped in white cloth, each carried by two lower priests, are borne into the temple. These objects are the *pratima*, the resident deities of Besakih. They greet the eleven visiting gods at the foot of the main steps outside the temple, the gods of Mount Semeru, Mount Rinjani, and Pura Ula Watu having arrived last. When Dewata concludes his ritual of welcome and the buffalo and other offerings have been properly sprinkled with holy water, the gods are carried one by one across the buffalo on the ground and up to the main courtyard of the Temple of the Triple Lotus.

The gods of Besakih are seated in their meeting pavilion behind the Triple Lotus shrine. The visiting gods are enshrined on the tall *sangga tawang* shrine, the diety of Mount Agung in the exalted position at the center, shaded by an umbrella.

I stand at military ease next to Guntur and watch the ritual, Guntur is whispering to himself.

"What am I missing?"

"Nothing."

"I thought you were speaking to me."

"No, John. I was cursing Chartwell and Hamzah, asking these powerful gods around us to let the lightning strike them from a clear sky."

"They're dead, Guntur!"

"Don't be so forgiving! I pray that they are already in one of the twenty-one hells, the particular hell in which they must swim continuously in a pool filled with urine of dogs and the mucus from the nostrils of lepers. But even this punishment is not enough. Let them also be gored on the horns of water buffalo. Let them be reborn as maggots, as snails, as worms!"

"Remind me never to get you pissed off at me!" I say.

Later, well past dawn, the Red Berets dismissed, Pura Besakih threaded by worshippers bearing offerings, the Temple of the Triple Lotus no longer closed, the Balinese flocking in with their baskets, I tell Guntur I wish to say good-bye to Dewata.

I return to the parking area and from the Ferret where Sergeant Maru has been tending it, I pick up the cooler I've brought with a dozen orange Popsicles packed in dry ice. I lug it on my shoulder up the precipitous steps, the Balinese smiling at me, amused that my offering reads COCA-COLA on its plastic sides, scarcely a thing of beauty compared to their stratified baskets of flowers and fruits.

find myself in line behind a file of ascending Balinese women, each with her laden basket on her head, balanced there magnificently, and the entire column swaying their hips, their firm buttocks Ping-Ponging gracefully as they climb up ahead of me. It is an amusing vignette of erotica.

Dewata waits for me in an upper courtyard. Surely he knows I would not leave Bali without bringing him my offering. I set the cooler at his feet and settle on the ground beside it, since I know he will sit before the white man and I need to look directly into his abiding eyes.

"I brought a dozen of the orange," I tell him.

He selects a Popsicle from the ice pack, then carefully reseals the cooler.

"I shall have one each day," he says, "until you return."

"I won't be back that soon."

He begins to lick the Popsicle.

"Can you tell me if I will? Come back? Do you know?"

"I know only that death is the penalty for birth."

"You're saying I won't come back? That I'll die in Vietnam?"

"You will not die before your time has come, even though you are pierced with a thousand bullets. You will not live after your time is out, even though you are only touched by the point of a blade of *kusa* grass. But remember what I said to you when we were last together, that no weapon can hurt the self of a man, no fire can burn that self, no waters can moisten it, no wind can dry it up. It is not to be hurt, not to be burnt, not to be moistened, not to be dried up. It is imperishable, perpetual, unchanging, without beginning, without ending. So no matter where you go there is nothing to fear."

"I am not afraid. This makes me even more alone."

"Punishment is not eternal. The law of the deed—this is the highest law of all. No deed, great or small, good or bad, can be without some effect. This is your karma. Karma makes you the creator of your own destiny. I say to you, John Locke, that it is your karma to return to Bali if you wish to return to Bali. I see you as a man of many good deeds. Your part in bringing back to Besakih our Great Bronze Bell has earned you favor with the gods. They will protect you. I would not be surprised if they were to tell you so themselves."

"How?"

"Through the bell of Mount Agung."

"That would be some miracle, wouldn't it?"

"Simply your karma. In spite of the fact we live in the Fourth Age, the Kali-yuga, the Age of Misery, I shall see you again, John Locke, in this lifetime. I still as Ida Bagus Dewata, you still as John Locke."

"I would like that."

We smile at each other. I watch his old teeth nibbling on the bottom of the orange ice.

"How much longer is this Age of Misery supposed to last?" I ask him.

"More than four hundred thousand years."

"Then we'd better make the best of it, hadn't we?"

"I truly believe so. For all we know, the Fifth Age could be infinitely worse. When you return, John Locke, if you care to, you may bring more than twelve of these oranges on a stick at one time. Twenty-one is a more mystic number than twelve. Please try to remember that when you look for me again."

I find my palms touching each other, without my willing them to, my head inclining, my forehead and fingers a solemn bridge.

When I look up again, Dewata is gone.

I descend to where Guntur waits.

"With the bell in place," he tells me, "we may now proceed to discover the bodies of the missing eighteen."

"How do you proceed to do that?"

"A priest will discover them at a propitious time."

"Hopefully within the next day or so, before the travel agents fly in?"

"In fact, the bodies will be discovered at sixteen hundred hours this afternoon, so that by the time the travel agents have arrived, unpacked, and begun their tours, the most spectacular mass cremation ceremonies in recent years will be in progress. Hundreds of photographs will be taken, full media coverage will be invited."

"Most adroit. What's the official version on how these eighteen people all happened to vanish simultaneously, then reappear so conveniently?"

"This afternoon a priest, selected by Dewata himself, will discover them on his way to the temple. He will observe a human hand extending from beneath an embankment that has caved in near Pura Besakih. When he digs into the earth, he will discover that eighteen men, women, and children, a priest among them, have all been crushed beneath the weight of rocks and earth that, unknown to the rest of us until this moment, had fallen upon them from a collapsing bank the morning of *Nyepi*. Our government is so distressed by this tragic event that they will donate a special fund to ensure that the families of the deceased are able to afford funeral services on a scale beyond the reach of their meager savings. All eighteen will be given rich and complete cremations to provide suitable memories. I hope you are not planning to leave before this joyous event can be staged."

"The last time I was here," I reply, "I watched a cremation. The family was celebrating the passing of their nine-year-old boy, and about the time I saw his burning hand separate from his arm and drop into the ashes, I checked out. I couldn't afford to let myself get too carried away by joy."

"The boy's soul would have laughed at your discomfiture, for he was moving on to the next stage of existence. You must stay, John, and see how narrow your view of dying is. Our corpses are anointed with spices. Pieces of mirror are placed on the eyelids, jasmine in the nostrils, gold rings in the mouths. These are the *banten suci*, placed so that in rebirth the soul will enter a body with higher senses, brighter eyes, and a fragrant breath. I would hate to think you will miss seeing these processions, everyone wearing their finery, their jewelry, and the men bearing *krises*. I will ask Dasima to lead a hundred dancers followed by forty orchestras. The cremation towers will be erected in many different villages and town cemeteries, since these eighteen come from many parts of the island. The coffins will be shaped according to the caste of the deceased. The coffins of the Sudras—and all but one of these dead were Sudras—will be shaped to represent *ga jamina*, a mythical animal, half elephant, half fish. The priest, a Brahmana, will be cremated in a coffin shaped like a bull, carved of wood, covered with fabrics, and ornamented with gilding. After a final blessing, the presiding priests will set fire to the coffins while the orchestras play so loudly you will not be able to hear for a day. When the flames have cleansed the bodies, the ashes will be blessed and placed in yellow coconuts. Then, at sunset the ashes of all the dead will be escorted to the sea by laughing funeral parties and strewn over the water. And finally all the happy participants will bathe before returning to their homes. It is something you must see!"

"I'm leaving tomorrow," I announce.

"So soon?"

"First I'm putting Juliana Chartwell on the plane to San Fran cisco. Then I want to stop by and say good-bye to Tip. And tonight be alone with Dasima."

"What time tomorrow?" he asks.

"I've checked the tide table and the weather reports. I'd like to get off no later than ten hundred hours. That'll put me into Bali Strait by daylight the morning after."

"I beg you to reconsider. What is another week? Even two?"

"I'm sorry, Guntur. Anchor up tomorrow at ten hundred. Let's just keep it at that, okay?"

"May I speak honestly, without deceit or self-service?"

I smile. "*May* you, Guntur, or *can* you?"

"I have observed a change in you since you have come to Bali. Was it a small rite of passage—or was it something much more significant? Possibly it is too early to tell. But even as you assisted Madame Chartwell to cleanse her body of drugs, so you yourself have been cleansed on this island, turning from yourself to others, from madness to sanity, from death to life, to a state of new awakening."

Can he be right?

I don't know if I believe him.

"It's not a matter of how long I still have to live, Guntur. But what I do with what life I have left."

"Precisely," he agrees. "It is those remaining seconds, minutes, hours, days, weeks, or years I ask you to consider. Is asking you to give us another week asking too much?"

"Not if I didn't know about that little boy in Hanoi. But I do."

═══CHAPTER═══

32

I meet Juliana Chartwell at the airport in Tuban.

She and her daughter, a child with a delft face and golden hair scissored straight across her forehead just above blazing blue eyes, wait for me outside the doors to the waterclosets. *Wanita* for girls, I note in passing, *Pria* for boys.

The little girl holds the hand of an elderly Dutch woman with stubby ankles and sturdy walking shoes, clearly the nanny.

Juliana is traveling in basic black: black sunglasses, black silk jumpsuit with a jeweled zipper, black ankle boots of sea crocodile with the croc's teeth flaring out at the tops.

She speaks in Dutch to the nanny, sending her off with the child.

Almost awkwardly, Juliana turns to me. We are hemmed together by the streams of tourists passing on all sides of us with their creaky baggage carts, black front wheels wobbling ineffi-ciently.

Juliana slips off her dark glasses. She is without makeup, not even lipstick. Already she has lost some of her look of exhausted decadence. Her hair lanks down around her pale face. For the first time I see how magnificent the contour of her cheekbones truly is, how large and brilliant her eyes, how perfect the shape of her lips.

"What do you think?" she asks.

"Looking good," I say.

"Buy me a pineapple yogurt?"

"You got it."

We settle in at one of those dirty, sticky little uneven tables every airport in the world goes out of its way to provide for you to make air travel hazardous to your health, and I order two pineapple yogurts from the first surly Balinese I have encountered so far on the island.

"We don't have much time," Juliana says, "but I don't remember ever having more to say to somebody than I have to say to you. I'd like to try to keep this one of those subdued good-byes, but whenever I'm around you, John Locke, the landscape becomes very emotional. May we start with a simple question like—is my husband dead or alive?"

"Dead."

"Did you kill him?"

"Unfortunately not."

"Who did?"

"A special unit of the Indonesian Army."

"They didn't—or wouldn't—give me any details."

"Better they didn't."

"This colonel called on me, however, and explained that my husband and Chien Hsiu kidnapped you with the intent of murdering you. Is that true?"

"True. They almost pulled it off. Chien Hsiu got away. Your husband didn't."

"Did they shoot him?"

"What difference? Dead is dead."

"I wouldn't like to think he suffered."

"Then don't think so."

"Did he?"

"No more in dying than he did in living."

"In other words, shut up, Juliana!"

"You're a widow, Mrs. Chartwell. That's all that matters."

"And not a tear! You'd think I could muster up at least one tear for poor Walton. He gave me that beautiful little girl you saw. I owe him something. Happily, I never exposed her to him, so no problem there. But why wouldn't the colonel let me claim Walton's body? If I had cared for him, I'd have raised hell about this. But I'm simply curious. Nothing more."

"His death and his funeral service occurred almost simultaneously," I say. She sees I'm not going to say any more. She drops her hand on mine.

"John, I really believe I can get better at this place you're sending me."

"So do I. What did you do with your pistol?"

"Threw it into the Indian Ocean."

"Congratulations!"

"I only kept it around so I could blow my brains out if I got any worse. But now that I've decided to get my head together rather than scattering it into some rice field, who needs a gun?"

"You've got a lucky face now, Juliana."

"At least it's not numb anymore. I can actually touch it, and *feel* something. My whole body seems to be coming back together, you know? Like you're looking at a double image and you can see it snap back into a single image? I'm becoming just one person. I was so bored having to take care of that other body, the one that always demanded I dose it up. You know what my new slogan is? *Fuck chemicals!* I'm not even going to take an aspirin anymore. I'd rather have the goddamn headache!"

She watches me smiling.

"You have a nice smile, John. You should smile more often. Do I make you smile?"

"You're going to shellac 'em out in San Francisco, Juliana. That makes me feel good. And sometimes when I feel good, I even smile."

"I want to thank you for not laying a sexual 'cure' trip on me the other night. I've never known another man who wouldn't have taken advantage of the situation—for his own benefit. You put *me* first, not yourself. If you ever need anything, John, just let me know. You can always reach me through the main office of my company in Jakarta. I mean anything. Money, friendship. If you want it, you can even have my body. It's yours if you ever want it, for whatever that's worth."

"Just stay away from toga parties in Mill Valley," I tell her.

Guntur has cleared me through Immigration, so I'm able to go with Juliana and her daughter and the nanny to the boarding ramp to the waiting Garuda jetliner.

Juliana sends the child and the woman up the stairs ahead of her and turns back to me.

"Tell me what you think of my breath now," she says. Her lips press to mine.

"Sweetest mouth in town," I say. "Double your pleasure, Doublemint gum."

She hasn't cried for Walton—but she cries now—trying to keep it a subdued good-bye, almost making it but failing at the last minute as the immensity of the task confronting her strikes her consciousness.

"Oh, God, if only you were coming with me!" she cries. "I know then I could make it."

"You'll make it, Juliana. Just stand back and give yourself some running room."

"I'll see you again, John Locke," she says. "I'll find you, wherever you are. You'll be proud of me."

She goes up the steps, looking back at me all the way. I know a winner when I see one, and this one is on a learning curve, a rising graph.

Maru waits for me in his jeep in front of the airport terminal.

To reach him I have to thread my way through a minefield of luggage plastered with group labels.

The first contingent of SPACTTA is arriving.

I remember Guntur's tarbrushing of tourists. He calls them the carriers of discontent, their easy spending an infectious example to the young of Bali more virulent than the malaria-bearing mosquito, a pestilence encouraged by the central government in Jakarta for the sake of hard currency and the growth of a new nation. Must American junk food, franchises, blue jeans, six-packs, and street jive come hand in hand with American dollars? he asked me.

I told him I have no data on the matter.

Maru drives me toward Batubulan.

I smell skewered beef being simmered.

It occurs to me I haven't eaten much in the past seventy-two hours.

I tell Maru to stop at the roadside food stall from which the telltale smoke pinpoints the source of the good smell of the simmering beef. I invite him to join me, but he asks if I will grant him permission to disappear for thirty minutes while I'm having lunch. One of his sisters and her new son live with her husband's family only a kilometer away. I wish him godspeed and settle onto a stool outside the stall. The owner is an elderly woman with a naked child attached to each hand as though each is a permanent appendage. I tell her the scent of her beef is definitely prime and that I would like at least two orders as my opening course. While she disappears in the darkness of the stall to prepare my lunch, I sit at peace for a measured three minutes and watch a Honda truck across the road being unloaded of hundreds of batik shirts into a shop that is not about to be caught short during this convention of travel agents.

The owner of the food stall appears without the children and sets the still-smoking beef sticks in front of me.

"Drink?" she asks.

"Beer, please."

But the beer in no way mollifies the burning sensation of the blazing Sumatran *sambal* sauce. Lime juice and salt do manage to dilute some of the spiciness.

I nibble on the beef and watch a *saté* vendor pattering by with two canisters bobbing from the end of the bamboo pole he carries. From somewhere close by I hear a Culture Club tape being played at maximum decibel level.

In that split second the missing Chien Hsiu materializes from nowhere and glides toward me like a big-time *sifu*, keeper of all the ancient Chinese killing techniques—fingers crooking, black slippers, draw pants, and all—looking as though he has no other purpose in life than turning me into pulp.

The trick in these matters is to forget about your lunch, forget about telling yourself the whole thing is preposterous. There you sit, preoccupied with the chili sauce and wondering why there's no *gamelan* music to be heard from the village only yards away, why somebody with a cassette machine is playing Boy George's "Karma Chameleon" instead. What you have to do is bypass your cortex if you're lucky enough to have trained with yoga masters and get to the business at hand without asking, "Why me?" Response time is critical when you have to deal impactively with raven-haired maniacs looming up out of nowhere.

As I rise, shifting my own Ch'i into gear, I topple the table toward Chien's knees. He leaps over it easily, as I've intended he should, so I can heave my stool at his chest, assuming he'll have no center while he's airborne and that the stool will discomfit his ribcage.

But Chien is no candy ass. Awesomely, in midair, he swivels his upper torso, the stool hurtling past him. He lands within hand-to-hand range, and for an eye flick of time I downgrade my personal rating to slow meat in comparison to my eaglelike opponent. Mistakenly, his ego overcomes his advantage for an equal eye flick of time. He lets himself savor my inner tension rather than attacking it, and the tiny sliver of time this gives me allows me to open the gap between us and regain my self-control. I even have time to unholster the Browning, if I choose to, and wrap his heart around his spine with three button-pattern rounds, but some dominant stupidity compels me to fight him empty-handed, on his elected terms. I suppose I am still trying to recover from the degradation of his having been a major participant in laying me out for lunch. He is a person in ardent need of killing, but not by firearms. It is too impersonal an execution.

"Now that you've ruined my meal as you almost ruined my whole afternoon the other day, I think you and I have to settle once and for all who's tiger on the hill."

"This time I will not fail," he whispers. Then he kicks the other table out of the way to clear space for the dance routine he's doing, a widening circle of sinuous glides. I can't decide whether his technique is Chinese White Crane or Indonesian *pentjak-silait*, which combines looping moves with quick spider-jumps, but whatever he has in mind is clearly high on the Cook and Medley hostility scale.

As he circles, I circle, using an updated *pa kua* form of my own, a technique designed to keep you on the periphery of your opponent's vision.

"Since my time may be limited," I say, sliding around him, "would you please enlighten me? Call it the last request of a doomed man. What were you going to be in the Burma scheme of things?"

"I would have taken Chartwell's place once we had the power."

"Kill him?"

"With these!" He crooks his long fingers at me.

"And Juliana?"

The simple mention of her name enrages him. I have cost him his Burmese empire, his millions in the heroin trade, but more than anything, I have sent the woman he hungered for out of his reach. He forces himself back into the deadly calm he knows he needs to defeat me.

Now I catch the glimmer of something in his movements, a hardening of purpose. All this sinewy stuff is meant to distract me from what he intends will be his main attack. I observe, behind the screen of what he hopes is the hypnotic distraction of his ever-weaving left hand and writhing fingers, the rigid single finger of his right stiffening for a death thrust. Could he possibly know the secrets of *Tien Hsueh*?"

"For daring to touch Juliana!" he screams, leaping toward me, his body turned slightly away to assist him both in concealment and in controlling his area of impact.

I detect the blurred spearing of his right hand, middle finger extended and braced with his index and fourth fingers, firing toward me—a hand form called *chen chih*, one of many *Tsien Hsueh* attacks, the Chinese death touch, *dim muk* to Cantonese assassins, *atemi* to the Japanese—the combat application of acupressure, taught centuries ago by Shaolin Temple's fighting priests, with three hundred and sixty-five attack points over the human body, some to be grasped, some struck, some merely touched, the chief delivery system the one-finger attack.

He's timed his thrust precisely as I exhaled and filled my arteries with blood. For certain now I know he's using the Needle Finger, striking at the Hour of the Dragon, between eleven hundred and thirteen hours, when the blood is usually busy assisting digestion, the blow intended to flatten my left coronary artery, so damaging the arterial valves that my left ventricle will be blocked and bring on cardiac arrest.

These anatomical niceties are fine in theory, but they assume that one's opponent is going to stay rooted like some martini-numbed businessman in an express elevator after lunch.

One glimpse of Chien's rigid finger coming my way trips me intuitively into a counterdefense that should both disorient him and shield my center line. I drop to the ground directly under and to one side of his thrusting finger, kneeling down on one leg, as though paying him homage, the ball of my foot tucked under me, my guard high to keep him from reaching the vulnerable neck, and I whirl, one leg slicing out like a sickle.

Chien is not to be so easily swept off his feet. He dances back, and I rise from the ground with a spinning hook kick, not so much to connect as to keep him moving. I dip back again into the kneeling gesture and crab toward him, whipping out a succession of leg sweeps, my spinning advance closing the distance even while I keep him backing in circles. Without warning, I roll forward, breaking up the established rhythm of leg sweeps, somersault across the circle, ending up again in kneeling posture as he dances precisely into the envelope I've planned for him, and I rise behind a surprise front kick that shocks his groin. As he struggles to surmount the pain, I twist my upper body with all the torque I can summon and nail him in the substernal notch with an open palm strike. I can feel the impact thundering up under the rib cage and into his chest cavity, jamming his heart and lungs into fatal overdrive.

His eyes fix on me, then cipher out like meteors vanishing over Montana.

He is dead before his knees touch the ground.

Boy George's voice still echoes from the cassette player in the village.

I had lost it for a few seconds. Now I can hear it again.

I become aware of the food stall's owner. She stands in the doorway, the naked children back to holding each of her hands. She looks from me to the marbled figure of Chien, then to the overturned tables and scattered stools. She sees what I see on the earth—ants already bearing away the remnants of my skewered beef.

"Phone?" I ask.

She shoos the children inside and points toward the batik shop across the road.

Of course she has no phone!

She comes out and impassively begins to reposition the stools.

I press a fistful of rupiahs into her arthritic palm.

I run toward the shop in time to catch the last chorus of the Boy George singing "Do You Really Want to Hurt Me."

I manage to figure out how the pay phone works. I dial through to COIN-OPS and ask for Colonel Katrini. When Guntur comes on the line, I suggest he send a van to tidy up the environment and to bear away the last of the unholy pantheon who nearly brought ruin upon Bali.

Chartwell, the Brahma of the trinity, the creator of Operation Chan, has died by vengeance from the sky.

Hamzah, the Vishnu, the Preserver, has perished at sea.

One is now part of the clouds, the other part of the tides.

Only Chien Hsiu, the Shiva, the Destroyer, remains to be committed to the earth.

And the circle will be closed, harmony restored.

Watch it, Locke, you're beginning to talk like a Balinese.

CHAPTER

33

Tip and Sarna serve my last dinner in Bali in a garden outside the main house. Dasima is with me.

It is one of those evenings you know you will remember until somebody scrambles your brain cells.

Both Sarna and Dasima have the sensitivity to know that Tip and I need a little elbow room for our good-byes. Toward the end of things, the two manage to leave us alone, tapping the rims of brandy snifters together like two empire builders out of a Maugham novel.

"Wish I could come along," Tip says, "help get your son out of 'Nam, but you need tigers covering your ass, not pussycats."

"You'll never be a pussycat, Tip. Best grenadier I ever knew. Your talent's still there, but I'm not going to be the one to bring you back to war. You've got everything right here—the woman you love, a son..."

"You can have everything, too! Go get that little boy out and bring him back here! Dasima will wait. Sarna's been talking to her. The girl's in love with you, man!"

"Remember when Kesling lost his leg on that mine? When we were operating in Thua Thien?"

"I remember."

285

"Remember we visited him at the hospital before they flew him home?"

"So?"

"Remember he kept complaining about the agonizing sensations he 'felt' in the missing leg?"

"We told him what that was. The doctors call it 'phantom limb pain.' Just muscle spasms in the stump; that's all it is."

"'That's all it is.' That how you feel about it?"

"Yeh, big deal! All you have to do is learn how to relax the affected muscles. Just work on your biofeedback until the sensations disappear. John, what's your point?"

"When Doan Thi amputated herself from me, she left me with phantom limb pains—inside and out, from head to toe. I haven't been able to make them disappear. I can't lay that on Dasima or on any other woman who's crazy enough to want to commit to me. Can't you for Chrissake understand that?"

"How do you know?"

"How do I know what?"

"That Dasima can't handle it."

"It's not the kind of thing you ask about. And I care for her too much to ask her to take in an amputee."

"Two things, Shit Hook. The first is, that's just pure fucking overdose self-pity to call yourself an amputee. If you're an amputee, then the rest of us are drawn and quartered. The second thing is you're underestimating this particular lady. I'm telling you, she can handle it! You're going to travel the whole goddamned world and never—baby, I'm saying *never*—find women like these women here in Bali. You're still in love with a memory. You're still attributing epic qualities to every Vietnamese woman because you loved Doan Thi. Well, she was pretty fucking exceptional. But there were also a lot of cunts and whores and damaged broads in Vietnam, even some that would have sold their mothers to the butcher shop. These Balinese girls are raised from birth with life order. You hear me, John? Not a life-*style*, a life *order*! They live only to preserve personal harmony with their family, the community, their ancestors, their gods and demons, and they haven't yet been screwed up by the outside world. They honestly and truly believe that if they can achieve this harmony, they will be reincarnated into the next life, not as a snake or a monster but as a happier and nobler human being. Dasima is the living epitome that kind of morality. God knows why, but she's decided she loves *you*. And you're just going to piss on paradise, just going to hop aboard your little sailboat and lay into the wind and go scooting off to nofuckingwhere, and leave her and all this behind?"

"I'm going to go get my son!"

"I'm talking *after* that, goddam it! Where are you going *after* you get him? Where are you taking him?"

"First things first!"

"Dasima won't wait more than a year, if that. I don't give a shit how much she adores you, she *can't*! She has to be true to herself, to her *Balinese* self, and that means she needs a man, that she must unite with that man and bear him their child. In Bali not having a child is just about the worst possible scenario a woman can fall victim to. Childless women are doomed in the underworld to suckling a huge worm!"

"You've made your point, Tip, okay?"

"So what does *that* mean? That I should shut up or that you're going to talk to her about your future, not just wave from the stern as we bid fond adieu to fabled Bali?"

"I'll talk to her. Tonight."

"So what are we arguing about?"

He grins at me.

I reach out and clasp his forearm. He grips mine in return.

"One last thing, John. The other day I said nobody had shot at me till you showed up. I've been thinking about that. I said it not to hurt you but simply as a cold fact. Later on I remembered the look in your eyes after I said it—and I figured it was a real kick in the balls."

"It was. But I had it coming. Anyway, thanks for the addendum."

"Well, Shit Hook, I guess this is it for now."

"For this trip, anyway."

"What's that you're supposed to say to sailors as they cast off—fair winds and a following sea?"

"I'll settle for either one."

"I won't say peace on your way. Not where you're going. But come back. For *your* sake."

Dasima and I return to her family compound in Batubulan. I suggest something livelier, maybe cocktails at one of the new hotels, but since she doesn't drink and keeps reaching for my crotch as I drive, there is no way to avoid going straight home and face the few remaining hours together.

I have never been an ardent lover on last nights.

There are those, I know, who revel in the theatrics of farewell, who find comfort, even lust, in one last tearful toss in the hay, but I am not among this one-for-the-road crowd. When I'm due over the horizon and done is done, lingering in the pretense of a final covenant is much too painful. And pain, as Schweitzer so neatly hit it on the head, is a more terrible lord of mankind than death itself.

If I could have my wish now that Dasima comes with me to my *bale* this final night, smelling of champac blossoms, her expectant eyes more lustrous than when she dances, it would be that the night was over and that we could go instead back to Kuta, have a beer and a steaming jaffle, then walk onto the beach, holding hands, and watch the old women moving mystically through the lagoon, water to their waists, their long sticks with their sifting cloths fluttering in the breeze, sun hats flopping as they dredge along, smoke ghosting up from the cigarettes between their wizened lips. Without too many words we would then drive down to the anchorage where *Steel Tiger* waits for me in the shallows off the wharf at Benoa; that somehow I could instantly be aboard, leaving Dasima on the dock, and that I'd hoist my mainsail and the wind would come from the right direction, filling it, and I could wave good-bye and see Dasima waving back, her face too distant for me to see her tears, if there were tears, too distant for her to see mine, should there be any.

But it remains my last night in Bali, not my last morning, and Dasima is here. Somewhere close by, a *gamelan* spins an intricate web of metallic sound. I suspect Guntur may have set the players up near the gateway to give me one last going away infusion to remind me of what I'm leaving behind.

Dasima, sensing the quiet in my body, makes no effort to arouse me by any overt movement. Instead, she cuddles up to me like kitten, expecting nothing except the right of nearness.

"Has your uncle told you everything about my going?" I ask her after a long silence in the darkened room.

"For once he has said very little."

"What has he told you?"

"Simply that you are leaving. In the morning."

"Did he say where I was going?"

BRONZE BELL

"He said you were sailing to a port in Thailand."

"Did he say why?"

"He said you were going there to prepare to enter Vietnam."

"Did he tell you what I have to do in Vietnam?"

"Look for a son, he said."

"Did he tell you how it is that I have a son—and how until a few nights ago I never knew that I did?"

"He told me that, yes. And I know his mother is dead. I wept for you when I heard, for I know you loved her very much."

"I still do, Dasima. That's our problem."

"It is not a problem, Tanah. For she is dead. And I am alive. Until not too far back in time, a husband in Bali could take a second wife when his first wife became too old and weary. Your dead love would be almost forty if she were here now. I am not yet eighteen. I can happily accept the idea of being your second wife. Doan Thi may come and live with us if she wishes, and we will both honor her spirit, and she will bless our happiness as though it were her own."

For a second or two I almost dare imagine that Doan Thi has appeared in a flash of radiance above the mosquito net and is even now reaching down with spectral hands to clasp Dasima's hand and mine to join them and to bestow her blessing upon us. I even pretend I can hear her soft poetic voice confirming Dasima's words.

"What would your family, your friends, other Balinese, think—if that were to come about? You and I?"

"Your friend Tip has lived in Bali for eight years. Married to Sarna. With a beautiful son. Would you wish to ask him if he believes there would be a problem for you and me?"

"I've already asked him."

"And what did he say?"

I kiss her on her forehead. "You know damn well what he said. Nobody's getting *him* off this island!"

"It would be no different for us. To my own people I am still and always will be Balinese, and I cannot be cast out as long as I don't leave my land. Nor can I be cast out as long as I do not commit a grave offense."

"What do your people consider a grave offense?"

"Profaning a temple, committing an act of incest, or converting an alien religion such as Christianity or Islam. You would not expect me to adopt your faith, would you, Tanah?"

"I wouldn't ask anybody to believe what I believe," I tell her.

"Nor would you make me leave Bali?"

"Never."

"Then so long as I follow the legacy of my forefathers, what we call *adat*, I shall remain Balinese."

"*Adat?*"

"This *adat* ordains everything, our rules of marriage, birth, death, the times and methods of sowing rice, building a house, praying for rain—so many things. It makes living very simple for us, for once the ancestors had laid down the *adat*, it never cracks with the heat or rots with the rain. It is there always to guide us. Those who follow it are happy. Those who do not are no longer Balinese."

We don't talk for a while, just lie there holding to each other, our breathing the breathing of one person.

"I don't know what's going to happen in Vietnam," I say. "I don't know if I can survive it."

"Then we shall have to wait until our next lives to find each other. But if you do survive it, if you do find your son, I will be both mother and sister to him, if you wish me to."

"It could take six months or more to plan it, get in, and get him out."

"If you tell me to, I will wait."

"Then wait, Dasima. Please wait!"

At the sound of my words, at the immensity of the unexpected commitment, I almost expect to behold rays of light bursting from the wooden eyes of Vishnu, the Preserver, on my ceiling.

But I see nothing other than Dasima's eyes smiling gratefully into mine as she slips one of her legs between my thighs and begins to convert me into the most fervent of lovers, despite my distaste for emotional farewells.

CHAPTER

34

We are on the wharf at Benoa.

Guntur waits aboard a launch with two sailors.

Beyond, in the anchorage, *Steel Tiger* chafes at her anchor rode against the rising wind.

Dasima and I stand face to face, her eyes raised to mine.

I have always felt our English word for parting—"good-bye"—is an emotionless stub, lacking the dynamics of farewell captured by other languages.

"*Selamat tinggal*," I say, good-bye in Indonesian, from the Arabic *selamat*, meaning, "May your action be blessed."

Dasima slips a blossom behind my ear.

"Before I plucked this flower, I asked permission of the spirit that lives within it. We call this spirit *tonya*. This *tonya* will sail with you across the dwelling place of the forces of evil, the repository of the ashes of the dead."

For a final moment, I hold her strong young body against mine.

"May all devils, djinns, lions, and every enemy stay far away from my love," she murmurs.

And lets me go.

I step into the launch. The boatswain revs his engine. We glide into the channel.

I look back at Dasima standing in the wind, her hair buffeted around her lambent face. Her hands are clasped palms together at her breast, but her eyes are not downcast, not my love's. She smiles out at me, certain I will return.

As the launch bears me to *Steel Tiger*, Dasima's smile of sureness remains in my mind. I know she will stay on that dock, even after her uncle has rejoined her. She will stay, I know, until my sails have been tucked under the horizon, stay there against the wind and count the first hour of my absence as one already passed.

I climb aboard *Steel Tiger*. Guntur scampers up after me. The launch hovers alongside as I prepare to go to sea.

"You will find the Koenig parachute below," he says. "And all your guns and gear, including the new shotgun. And here"—he hands me the gift-wrapped box he's been carrying ever since we left Batubulan—"is the *Conus gloriamaris*. It arrived yesterday from the museum in Jakarta."

"Thank you, Guntur. I'll open it later, if you don't mind."

"I have a personal gift for you," he says.

From nowhere he draws a kris. I had not noticed he was carrying the weapon.

"Are you familiar with our forging techniques for the kris?"

"No," I say.

"We call the process *pamor*. This is a secret process by which we forge a plate of steel mixed with stone from meteors. We polish the blade with citron juice, turning the steel of the earth dark and the stone from the stars to silver. This alternate coloration gives the blade its rippling effect. When you thrust with this, it appears that the blade is a striking serpent."

He flips the kris around, extends it to me, hilt first.

"I don't know how to thank you, Guntur." The dagger appears to have a life of its own. "But where's the scabbard?"

"The heart of your enemy is the only true scabbard for this weapon. I shall not tell you to go in peace, John. But I ask that if you succeed, you return in peace. We shall be waiting."

I pull him into my arms.

"Good-bye, John," he says.

He slips over the safety lines and back into the launch.

Like Dasima's, his eyes stay on me as the launch carries him back to the wharf.

There are three possible courses from Benoa's sheltered sandy bay to the Gulf of Thailand. The most direct is along the south end of Bali, then north through the narrow Bali Strait, where an ancient Hindu god is said to have once touched his finger on the land to separate Java and Bali. The air through Bali Strait is usually light and fluky, but this afternoon a brisk soldier's wind drives *Steel Tiger* swiftly from its anchorage, along the channel past the green markers, through the reef, and out around the skaw of Nusa Dua.

I try not to think of Guntur and Dasima behind me on the dock, but concentrate on slipping in between the many *lambo*s with their Mandar crews bringing turtles to shore. From the helm I watch fishermen collecting sea cucumber from the bottom and the roe of flying fish from floating baskets where they have deceived the fish into performing their courtship ritual and into laying their eggs in the basket.

The wind shifts. It smells now of open sea, of distant India. A candescence lies upon the water.

Only now, secure again that I'm centered on my chosen planet, the shifting ocean, do I dare look back at Bali.

Serangan and Benoa have fallen from sight.

So have Guntur and Dasima.

I feel more alone than ever.

Would I have sailed had I no son in Hanoi?

I lift my eyes to Mount Agung. In my mind I see Dewata at Pura Besakih, his fingers flicking petals to every point of the compass.

And suddenly I imagine I am hearing what he promised me I might hear, the thundering of the Great Bronze Bell. It washes over me with gentle yet stunning impact. Its vibrations radiate within me, the voices of the gods warming my veins. Sound dances on my finger-tips and strums my eyelids. I reverberate in every cell of my body.

Even the depths ripple underneath *Steel Tiger*'s hull. Ahead the way lies sparkling, not empty distance, not gray solitude, but with promise on the swells and in the undulating heartbeat of the sea.

I know I am no longer alone.

About the Author

STIRLING SILLIPHANT was born in Detroit. He began his motion picture work with Walt Disney Studio. His many successful television series and screenplays include *Naked City*, *Route 66*, *Alfred Hitchcock Presents*, *The Poseidon Adventure*, *The Towering Inferno*, *Charly*, the Oscar-winning *In the Heat of the Night*, and, more recently, a thirteen hour adaptation of James Michener's *Space*, and a seven-hour mini-series, *Mussolini: The Untold Story*. He lives with his wife and two children in Mill Valley, California. His novels include *Maracaibo* and *Steel Tiger* (the first of the John Locke books), both published by Ballantine Books.

Attention Mystery and Suspense Fans

Do you want to complete your collection of mystery and suspense stories by some of your favorite authors? Raymond Chandler, Erle Stanley Gardner, Ed McBain, Cornell Woolrich, among many others, and included in Ballantine's new Mystery Brochure.

For your FREE Mystery Brochure, fill in the coupon below and mail it to:

KEEPING YOU ON THE EDGE OF YOUR SEAT... Spellbinding suspense from Ballantine Books